WHEN HEROES FALL

~~ANTI-HEROES~~ ANTI-HEROES

in love duet

USA TODAY & WSJ BESTSELLING AUTHOR

giana darling

giana darling

WHEN HEROES FALL

To the strong women who have earned their armor by battling their entire lives for respect, admiration, and a love worthy of their greatness.

giana darling

WHEN HEROES FALL

And to Annette who makes me feel loved and supported every single day. Thank you for bringing so much light to my life. I will never be able to express how much I love you.

giana darling

WHEN HEROES FALL

Nothing can be loved or hated unless it is first understood."
Leonardo di Vinci

giana darling

FOREWARD

While I consulted with a legal expert for this book, I have taken certain creative liberties with the story to make it flow the way I wanted it to. Any and all inaccuracies are my own and I hope you enjoy the story for what it is, a work of fantastical fiction.

The mafia is a very real entity today. Though their prolific presence has diminished in the 21st century, that is only because they learned from their mistakes in the 80s and got smarter. Now, they do not instigate public hits and most of their schemes have gone digital. It is true that some of the top mafia crime families operate much like Fortune 500 companies with a single operation netting them as much as multi-millions. Though the mafia remains a popular trope in media, there is surprisingly little known about its modern-day operations and there are a lot of untruths perpetuated by the organizations themselves to create a kind of cult of personality around them. I have done a serious amount of research for this story in the hopes of making it as authentic as possible, but it should be noted this is a complete work of fiction.

PLAYLIST

"Glory"--Dermott Kennedy

"To Build A Home"--The Cinematic Orchestra, Patrick Watson

"the broken hearts club"--gnash

"Who Are You"--SVRCINA

"Power"--Ruben

"One Time"--Marian Hill

"Doll Parts"--Hole

"Who Are You, Really?"--Mikkey Ekko

"On An Evening In Roma"--Dean Martin

"Buona Sera"--Louis Prima

"Rolling In The Deep"--Adele

"Riva"--Ruelle

"Neurosis"--Oliver Riot

"Play With Fire"--Sam Tinnesz feat. Yacht Money

"A Little Wicked"--Valerie Broussard

"Accetto Miracoli"--Tiziano Ferro

"Phobia Orgasma"--Oliver Riot

"Love Is A Bitch"--Two Feet

"Dollhouse"--Melanie Martinez

"The Other Side"--Ruelle

"Lies In The Dark"--Tove Lo

"Hollow"--Belle Mt.

"Call Out My Name"--The Weeknd

"Ivory Black"--Oliver Riot

"Woozy"--Glass Animals, Jean Deaux

"What Other People Say"--Sam Fischer, Demi Lavato

"Love And War"--Fleurie

"Can't Help Falling In Love"--Tommee Profitt, Broke

"Not Afraid Anymore"--Halsey

"Feeling Good"--Michael Buble

"Rescue My Heart"--Liz Longley

"Deep End"--Fouchee

"We Must Be Killers"--Mikky Ekko

"Never Be Like You"--Flume, Kai

"Down"--Marian Hill

CHAPTER ONE
elena

I t started with a phone call.

"Elena," my sister and best friend Cosima breathed into the phone, her voice stuttering like a failing engine. "I need you."

I could still recall the feeling in my chest as I heard those words. The tightening in my heart like an emerging bud and the bloom as I relished the opportunity to finally pay my sister back for her years of sacrifice and support for our family, for me.

"Anything," I'd promised instantly, an oath I would have sworn to her in blood.

That was before I knew why she needed me.

Or more aptly, who she needed me *for*.

If I'd known then, I wondered if even the genuine angst in my beloved sister's voice could have swayed me into taking on this case.

I was a criminal lawyer, but I'd made a point to avoid

representing anyone involved in organized crime even though Fields, Harding & Griffith, one of the top firms in the city, was relatively infamous for its list of rather unsavory clients.

Including the New York City Camorra.

And it's capo, Dante Salvatore.

Who had just made the front page of *The New York Times* for being arrested on suspicion of three counts under the RICO Act, including, but not limited to, murder.

The metallic hum of mechanisms unlocking startled me from my misgivings, and the guard indicated for me to follow him into the small holding cell where I was about to meet my future client.

Only, I'd met him before.

Once.

I could still remember the sheer size of his heavily muscled form bent over Cosima's hospital bed, his swarthy features and olive-black eyes immediately alerting me to the presence of a southern Italian man. The look of that face, the set of the stubborn bones in his slightly dimpled square chin, and the roughly carved cheekbones taut with strain spoke to something even worse.

A mafioso.

I had no idea why such a man was at my sister's bedside, his face creased with acute misery, but I did not like it, and I did not trust it.

We'd left Naples to get away from men like that.

Even though Cosima had woken from her coma and sworn that Dante was a friend, I'd still cornered the big lug in the expensive suit outside in the hall, my hand fisted tight in his creased dress shirt.

"If I find out you had something to do with her getting shot," I'd whisper-hissed at a man who could have easily crushed me with his bare hands. "I'll shoot you myself."

And Dante?

A man who was well-known in criminal circles as the Devil of NYC?

He only had the audacity to tip his head back and roar with deeply inappropriate laughter in the hallway of the hospital intensive care unit.

And now, there I was, about to face him again.

Not as his nemesis, though I still wanted to rake him over the coals for involving Cosima in any illegal and dangerous dealings.

But as his lawyer.

I sighed deeply before squaring my shoulders and following the guardsman into the cold, poorly lit cell at the Metropolitan Correctional Facility.

Dante Salvatore sat at the metal table with his thick legs chained to the floor and his hands bound and resting on the steel surface. He seemed unusually at ease wearing the ill-fitting hunter green jumpsuit in a cell that seemed almost hilariously small compared to his considerable bulk. It was as if the uncomfortable metal chair was his throne and this dank cell, his receiving hall.

"Ah," he said in a low, muddled accent that was somehow British, American, and Italian all in one. "Elena Lombardi. I should have known she would send you."

"Really?" I raised a cool eyebrow as I glided into the room, the click of my Louboutin heels echoing against the walls. "Then I suppose I'm more surprised to see myself here than you are."

I tried not to look into his face as he flashed me a beguiling smile, afraid I'd see spots as if staring into the sun. It was no wonder this man had gotten away with murder before with a face and body as beautiful as his. I was sure he was able to charm himself out of most situations.

Well, he would find I was immune to his charm.

In fact, immune to men entirely after the last year of my heartbroken life.

I pulled my tablet from my Prada purse, then crossed my legs beneath the table, poised to take notes.

"Do you know why you're here?" I began in the coolest, most professional voice I could muster.

Not a trace of my native land remained in my tone. I'd cut, washed, and bleached the foreignness out of my voice so that anyone first meeting me would never guess I was anything but American-born. It was the way I preferred it. And with my unusual dark red hair, it wasn't as if I looked traditionally Italian either.

Dante leaned farther back in his chair and knocked his knuckles against the table twice, studying his chains with a bored consideration. "I think there was some mention of murder."

I fought the urge to snort at his insolence. "Yes, Mr. Salvatore. As I understand it, they've arrested you on suspicion of murder, racketeering, and fraud under the federal RICO Act." Then, as if speaking to an idiot because I wasn't certain he understood the gravitas of his situation, "These are very serious charges that could level you with twenty-five years to life behind bars."

Dante blinked those long-lashed, liquid black eyes at me as he lightly drummed his thick fingers against the table. He wore a ring on one finger, a thick band of silver with some ornate crest in the middle. It shouldn't have been attractive, as gaudy as it was, but it only served to draw attention to those powerful hands, the muscle dense in his palms, veins threading through the tops up into lightly furred forearms peeking out from the jumpsuit.

My mouth went dry, and irritation flared. I was not the kind of woman to find something so uncouth attractive.

Man-killing hands, I reminded myself curtly and then affixed my stare just over his right shoulder so my untamed thoughts wouldn't run free.

"If I am found guilty," he agreed mildly even though that intense gaze belayed his faux ennui. "But Cosima has told me before you are very good at your job. Are you saying you will not be able to clear me of this?"

I glared at him, the arched brow, the too-red mouth a half-moon of humor. "As you know, I won't be the lead on your case. I'm twenty-seven and a fourth-year associate."

"A *soldata,*" he murmured. "Not a capo."

"Please do not link me even metaphorically to the mafia," I asserted coldly. "I am a lawyer on the right side of the law."

His lips twitched, his insolence grating on my nerves. "Yet you have no qualms about representing a man on the wrong side of it?"

"Normally, no. Though I usually stay as far away from organized crime as I can. But when my sister asks me to do something for her, I will move heaven and earth to do it. Even if it goes against my own moral judgment."

I watched his eyes dance and wondered at his ability to find joy in teasing me when he was in such a place and position. It made me want to shake him. Did he not understand that there were consequences for his actions?

Contrary to popular belief, being good-looking and rich was not a get-out-of-jail-free card.

"And do you think law and morality are one and the same, Elena?" The way he said my name was indecent, a long, slow blurring of vowels and a flick of his tongue over the consonant.

"*Law is reason, free from passion,*" I quoted. Aristotle's words had always resonated with me. Not just in my legal profession but throughout my life. If I could understand the reason for something, I diminished its power over my emotions, therefore freeing myself from it.

If I had a philosophy, it was that.

"Is it so cut and dry?" Dante argued as if we were bantering over an espresso in some piazza, enjoying a two-hour lunch in our mother country.

I hesitated, sensing a trap, but was distracted by this buzzing irritation I felt beneath my skin. "Usually."

"The Scottsboro Boys Trial?" he countered immediately, rearing back slowly before coiling forward over the table. He was close enough I could smell him, something sharp and tangy like sun-warmed citrus. "Those boys incarcerated for years because they were black? Amanda Knox? The LA Times postulates that the rate of wrongful convictions is between two and ten percent. Yet you believe absolutely in the law?"

I spoke through the snarl of my twisted lips. "Do not be ridiculous. The law is practiced by humans who are never infallible. To hope for zero mistakes is foolish. You don't strike me as the foolish type."

Dante only quirked that thick right brow. "You see things in black and white," he surmised, disappointment evident in his tone. He sank back in his seat like a deflated balloon, and bizarrely, I felt as if I'd failed some test.

He was wrong, but something about his demeanor made me want to confirm his worst beliefs about me. I had the bad habit of living up to people's worst assumptions and cutting off my nose to spite my face, just because my feelings were hurt that they would think so little of me.

My therapist called it a "self-fulfilling prophecy."

I called it survival instinct.

So I only tipped my chin haughtily and looked down my nose. "I suppose you don't."

"Black and white and red," he said with a wink.

"Mr. Salvatore," I huffed. "You can't be so unfazed as you seem.

This is a privileged meeting, so you don't have to play the innocent with me, and honestly, I would prefer bluntness. If you can manage it."

"Oh, *Ms. Lombardi*," he drawled, making fun of my formality even though we were virtually strangers and he was my client. "I am the most honest man you'll ever meet."

"Why do I find that hard to believe?"

A slow blink as he scrubbed a hand over his stubbled jaw. "Because you do not see me in color. You see what you want to see."

"Are you telling me that you're innocent of these charges?" I pushed.

He inclined his chin. "I did not kill Giuseppe di Carlo."

"Oh? And I don't suppose you know who did?" I asked, my voice saccharine.

Suddenly, he seemed tired, his big bones heavy beneath his frame as he sagged slightly and loosed a sigh. "It has been a long day, Ms. Lombardi. Ms. Ghorbani has already informed me my arraignment is tomorrow. Why don't we get to the point of why you came all the way down here to see me like an animal at the zoo."

I bristled. "Excuse me?"

"You came down to see what kind of monster your sister had taken for her pet. Well, here I am. I hope I lived up to the nightmarish hype."

I stared at him with narrowed eyes, scanning the broad

forehead notched with frown lines and the stubborn, almost weary set of his ruddy mouth. It was easy to fall into the trap he laid, to buy into the mirage he so skillfully wove that said he was a bad man with wicked intentions and nothing more.

But I knew more about Dante Salvatore than most.

I knew that this mafioso had been born the privileged second son of the Duke of Greythorn, and therefore, he'd been educated at the best schools in England and rubbed elbows with a more sophisticated kind of criminal as a boy than he did now in the Camorra. I knew that his father had murdered his mother and wondered if such criminality could be passed through the blood at the same time that my heart panged for the young man he'd been when he'd lost both his parents in different ways to the same offense.

I knew my sister called him the brother of her heart. That she swore up and down he was one of the most loyal and loving men she had ever known. That he would die for her.

Such fierce loyalty resonated with me.

Most girls might have dreamed of white weddings and Prince Charmings, but over the years, I'd learned the futility of such cotton candy daydreams.

All I valued now, desired now, was steadfast loyalty.

And I had to credit this man with that, even if I wanted to hate him for representing every villain I'd ever faced in my childhood.

"All monsters were men once," I finally allowed, swallowing hard because maybe the same could be said of me. "It's your choice,

Mr. Salvatore, which you want to be after I help get you out of this predicament."

He settled comfortably in his chair and spread his hands wide, chains rattling. "Maybe after all this, you'll understand that you don't have to choose between one or the other. Like Dr. Jekyll and Mr. Hyde, we have the capacity to claim both sides."

"And look how that turned out for him," I retorted.

Dante's grin was lazy and wicked, one blunt-tipped finger smoothing over his lower lip, back and forth like a hypnotic pendulum. "What a game this will be."

"Game?"

"It's usually so easy to corrupt people. I think you might prove a challenge."

Anger and a hint of nausea rolled through me. I wasn't corruptible. I was many bad things, I could admit. I had a vicious temper when wronged and held a grudge until the end of time, I didn't have a talent for making friends, and I wasn't good at taking criticism or teasing.

But I knew right from wrong.

"I am not a game, Mr. Salvatore," I informed him, my words clinking to the metal table like ice cubes as I stood and gathered my things. "Nor is this case against you. I know you've spent most of your life on the top of the food chain, but nothing is a bigger predator than the United States government. They've spent multimillions investigating and prosecuting mafia cases before, and I have no doubt they will again. So why don't you stop focusing on me and begin focusing on how in the world you are going to fool a judge and jury into believing you are anything less than a villain."

He remained silent, those spilled ink eyes watchful and depthless as they mapped my progress to the doors where I summoned the guard to let me out. It was only when the whirl of metal clogs spun and released, the doors shuddering open, that his words drifted after me like arid smoke.

"You watch too many movies, Elena. In real life, the villain always wins because we are willing to do anything to succeed." He paused as I did in the doorway. "I think you know a little something about that."

A shiver worked itself down my spine like fingers on piano keys, trilling a discordant tune that sounded very much like a portentous music score in one of those movies he was talking about.

CHAPTER TWO
elena

He shouldn't have been so distinguishable in the dark, but then again, that was where monsters like him thrived, so perhaps it made sense.

Dawn was just flirting with the ink-stained night, the anemic light half-hidden by the dense cluster of buildings blocking the horizon and the artificial lights cutting shapes into the interior of the Town Car as we passed through the almost empty streets of Midtown.

Blocks of colored light spun over Dante Salvatore's face like a child's kaleidoscope, illuminating his bold features for seconds at a time, making his beautiful visage into something like a puzzle for my overanalytical brain to dissect and wonder over.

The truth was, he really was too startlingly handsome to be a Made Man.

I knew mafiosos. I'd grown up with them circling my family like carrion at the scene of horrific carnage. My father had been indentured to them for as many years as I could remember. My childhood was defined by the Italian Camorra's presence in our lives.

I knew them to be short men with Napoleonic complexes, small eyes like glossed black beads in flaccid, flabby faces made swollen with too much indulgence in every kind of excess.

They were ugly men in ugly packages easily identified and labeled as the trash they were.

But this man?

The most infamous mafioso of the 21st century in a time when most Americans believed the mafia to be a dead and fossilized creature, well, he was another beast entirely.

He was too tall, quilted heavily with muscle that should have made him slow-moving and rigid but instead lent him the grace and constantly harnessed threat of a wild cat. He was as incongruous as one stalking through the concrete jungle of New York City, bigger and badder than the rest even though he wore the most meticulous suits and the most expensive designer brands.

Who he thought he was fooling with such a sheepish guise, I hadn't a clue.

It should have been obvious to all and sundry that Dante was a *wolf*.

"You say nothing for a woman with eloquent eyes," he said then, jarring me from my introspection.

Momentarily, I was ashamed he had caught me staring, but then I remembered part of my job was to study him, so I settled comfortably back behind my professional mask.

My smile was thin. "Knowing my thoughts is a privilege I don't share with strangers."

"Ms. Lombardi," my boss, one of the partners in my law firm and co-lead on the case, Yara Ghorbani, chastised me shortly, but Dante only laughed.

The sound moved through the Town Car like the crescendo of noise at the beginning of a jazz song, each note a building block leading to something richer, brighter.

It was a disturbingly pleasant sound to emerge from a murderer.

"Excuse Ms. Lombardi, please, Mr. Salvatore. She's only a fourth-year associate, and we believed she was ready for the kind of responsibility this case would afford her," Yara said softly, in that way she had of mellifluously delivering scathing insults. "I believe you and I *both* will be disappointed if that proves untrue."

I didn't allow a single movement to betray how harshly I felt those words score down my throat. I'd learned the hard way over the years that people had no qualms about ruthlessly attacking any perceived weakness.

And I had no doubt the *capo* of the New York City Salvatore mafia Family would exploit anything he could find, even in his own legal team.

He watched me from his slight lounge across the back of the black leather seats, strong thighs parted inelegantly in his slouch, one hand rubbing at the thick stubble on his jaw.

We'd advised him to be clean-shaven.

We had also couriered over an entire outfit for him to wear to the arraignment because perception in cases like these was everything.

Of course, he wasn't wearing it.

Instead, his big form was clad entirely in black, from the tips of his Berluti loafers to the perfectly tailored blazer hugging his broad shoulders. There was a glint of silver chain at his throat that I thought might have carried a cross or a saint's pendant, but it was nowhere near enough to save his overall demeanor.

He looked criminal, filled with wicked intent and handsome enough to tempt the pope to sin.

So *not* the look we wanted on a man being accused of three counts under the RICO Act.

Racketeering.

Illegal gambling.

And murder.

Sitting there in all that black, cloaked in shadows, he looked every inch the crime boss he was being accused of being.

"A penny for your thoughts then," he offered.

His voice was strange, Italian, British, and American accents tangling in his tone to create something wholly unique and oddly appealing. I told myself it was this odd mix of personas—the Italian hedonist, the British reserved mystery, and the ballsy American arrogance—combined into one man who intrigued me and not the almost overwhelming sight of such a beautiful body sprawled contemptuously across the leather.

I narrowed my eyes at him and adjusted my portfolio on my lap, conscious of how sweaty my palms were against the stiff paper.

"Maybe you aren't ready to hear them," I countered coolly, brow raised. "Some people take criticism better when it's not from a virtual stranger."

Yara didn't chastise me this time, probably because Dante's smoky chuckle filled the interior again and took away her opportunity to do so.

But also, maybe because Dante had *not* been an easy client thus far.

He flouted our suggestions, ignored sensible ideas, and seemed almost childishly easy to distract from the gravity of his predicament.

It was as if being accused of murder was only passably amusing whenever he did succumb to its presence in his life.

If he was enjoying my company, it might mean he would be more...pliable in the future. I decided then, even if this hadn't occurred to Yara, I would suggest it to her myself after the indictment. I had no doubt I intrigued him because of my relationship with his best friend, who also happened to be my sibling, but I was a lawyer, so I'd use anything I had in my arsenal to earn an advantage.

"You're not much like your sister." It was a statement, not a question, and it made me grit my teeth to avoid the impulse to bite back at him.

He shouldn't have said that.

Of course, I'd divulged my connection to the client before I'd made my bid for placement on his legal team, so Yara was unsurprised by the comment.

That wasn't what made irritation burst into itchy, painful flames on the back of my neck.

Even though I loved her deeply, I dreaded any comparison to my youngest sister.

Cosima Lombardi, an international supermodel, was married to a gorgeous British aristocrat and she was as lovely at heart as she was on the surface.

In a comparison battle, anyone would lose to Cosi.

Still, I hated to lose.

And I'd been losing that war since she was born.

The favorite of my father, maybe silently of my mother, and certainly of my other siblings.

Cosima was the golden child, whereas I was the black sheep.

I was the firstborn but the least liked and most unsuccessful.

My ambition surged through me like adrenaline at the thought, reminding me just what was at stake in taking this case.

If we won this trial against all odds, it would make my career and catapult me to the kind of greatness a lawyer could only achieve in the Big Apple.

I wanted that.

Not for the money or even the power, though both were more arousing than most men had ever been to me.

No.

I wanted it for the *status.*

My therapist told me there was a name for what I had, that furious drive for perfection that had marked my entire life.

Kodawari, the Japanese word for the relentless pursuit of perfection.

I didn't so much want to *be* perfect--which I was aware enough to know was an impossibility--as I wanted to *seem* perfect.

I'd been close, once.

As little as a year ago, I'd had my job at one of the top five law firms in the city and a gorgeous brownstone with my fiancé, a man both beautiful and successful in his own right.

We were going to get married, adopt a baby.

Adopt, because life saw fit to deal me another tragic blow and take my fertility from me early.

Still, it would have been a picture-perfect life.

My Daniel Sinclair and I.

After the life I'd been born into and excruciatingly endured in Naples, I'd deserved it.

Somehow, now, the brownstone was considerably less lovely when I was the only one living in the rambling, big home. Somehow, the job was a lot less satisfying without my companion at my side encouraging me in my climb up the legal profession ladder.

And it was all because of one person.

Quite simply, the bane of my entire life.

My other sister, Giselle.

Fury savaged my insides, blazing along the familiar path it

always ran through my system, obliterating everything else until I was scorched earth, incapable of harboring any other emotion.

"Elena?" Dante's voice pulled me back. "My comment was merely an observation, not an insult. I apologize if I caused offense."

I brushed away the idea with a casual wave of my hand and smiled, knowing it was thin and transparent on my face despite my best efforts.

"Please, call me Ms. Lombardi. Cosima is my sister, but she's also my best friend. Any comparison to her is a compliment in my eyes," I explained breezily. "But that's beside the point right now, Mr. Salvatore. What is important right now is the fact that you are being charged on three accounts of RICO, and today, we are fighting to get you out on bail. They're going to argue you are a flight risk and that with your underground connections, you could easily find a way to leave the country. This is our one chance to keep you out of prison until and if you are eventually tried and found guilty. You really should have listened to our advice and dressed a little more saint and a little less sinner."

A smooth smile spread across his face, crinkling his eyes and alerting me to the fact he had square white teeth behind those ruddy lips.

It annoyed me that I found him so attractive.

No, it did more than that.

It felt like blasphemy after the oath I'd made to avoid beautiful men in the wake of my fiancé leaving me. Sacrilegious that I might ever find a mafia man, once the tormenters of my youth, even marginally desirable.

"As a six-foot-five, two hundred and thirty-pound Italianate-looking man, did I ever have a chance of appearing in any way less than I do now? In my experience, it is riskier to assume a person's ignorance than it is to play into their desires. The world, Ms. Lombardi, *wants* me to the be their villain. So, I will give them one they can truly sink their teeth into." He punctuated his tidy speech with a wink.

This time, it was Yara who let out a thin chuckle, much to my surprise. "Of course, I should have known you would want to play that angle."

He inclined his head with gracious solemnity, but there was mischief in his ink-dark eyes.

"You're assuming the public loves a bad boy more than a good man," I argued. It was my job to look at both sides, but also because I'd always been inclined to play the Devil's advocate. "You expect the public to cheer for a murderer?"

His eyes narrowed, jaw clenching as he studied me again for one long interminable moment. "I expect the public to fall for an anti-hero. It wouldn't be the first time, and it certainly won't be the last." He leaned forward, his body so big it seemed he took up the entirety of the roomy car. I could smell him, something bright and sharp that mellowed into sweet warmth like lemons heated by the Italian sun. "Can you tell me, Elena, that you've never been drawn in by a bad boy?"

21

I arched a brow at him.

I'd had all of two lovers in my twenty-seven years of life.

Christopher and Daniel Sinclair.

The former was more than a "bad boy." He was worse than the scum scraped off the bottom of my shoe.

And Daniel?

He had been perfect, or as close to it as you could find on this earth.

Bad boys with their cigarette-stained teeth, their lack of proper diction and abundance of curse words, their rough hands and animalistic impulses?

My only interest in them was putting them behind bars where they belonged.

So why was I in that car on the way to an indictment representing one of the most infamous criminals in New York City?

Because my sister, the same gorgeous sister I'd loved and envied all my life, had begged me to take on the case.

Cosima was one of the only people I loved to the depths of my soul. One of two people, including my mother, who had ever supported me and loved me despite my obvious flaws.

So of course, I would do this for her.

Even though, for the first time in my career, I knew I was representing someone who, without a shadow of a doubt, was guilty of this crime and probably many others.

As if on cue, there was a knock on the side window.

My head snapped to the side to see a homeless man beside the car where we waited at a red light. He was heavily draped in threadbare layers against the deep chill of late autumn in the city, but there was something in his anticipatory manner that seemed off.

I watched as he pointed at his sign––*Cold and hungry, please help*––and opened my mouth to say something to Yara, when Dante's voice snapped through the air like a whip.

"Drive!" he barked. "Now."

But Mr. Janko was driving the car, a man who drove exclusively for the firm with a sensible manner and careful politeness.

He only blinked in the rearview mirror at Dante.

And by then, it was too late.

The homeless man had dropped his handmade sign, hand delving into his layers of clothing to produce a long gun, the barrel of which he pressed to the window.

I had time only to gasp before he fired the shot.

Crack.

The bullet shattered the glass, but I felt none of those sharp edges nor the impact of that metal projectile lodging itself in my flesh.

Instead, I gasped because the air compressed from my lungs by the weight of a large, incredibly heavy Italian man caging me against the seat.

I tipped my face up, mouth open, eyes dry and prickling with shock. Dante caught my gaze, his own burning coal black and just

23

as hot.

For an instant, just one, I felt his wrath move through me like a tangible thing, something heady and drugging like the finest whiskey or the best Italian wine.

Then he was yelling, "*Cazzo,* drive, man! NOW!"

With a squeal of tires, Mr. Janko revved the engine and gunned us forward into the intersection despite the red light.

Another shot was fired from behind us, this time wedging itself with a clunk into the trunk of the car.

Dante curled even tighter around Yara and me, protecting us with his massive frame. Surrounded in the warm citrus and pepper scent, pressed tight to his unyielding chest, I almost felt safe despite the madman shooting at us.

He remained there for a few moments until we were long gone from the scene, racing through the streets like a northeasterly storm.

When he finally pulled away, he checked Yara quickly then turned his eyes to me. One large hand went for my face, and I flinched despite myself.

I'd never seen hands like that, hands that large, that rough, that undeniably cloaked in metaphorical red.

Something in his eyes flickered at my reaction, but still, he reached out to pluck a small shard of glass from my cheekbone. I didn't notice the pain until he pulled it out, making me hiss at the little burst of hurt.

"It'll heal," he assured, swiping his thumb over the droplet of blood there then, shockingly, *disgustingly,* he brought it to his lush mouth and sucked it off.

My stomach roiled, but my thighs tingled even as my mind rebelled against the unwanted intimacy of his touch.

"Stop trying to unsettle my associate," Yara ordered calmly, righting her suit jacket as if she was shot at every day, and this was just another nuisance. "Sit down and watch that you don't cut yourself on that glass."

I blinked at the gorgeous older woman beside me, but she ignored my silent inquiry. Instead, she watched Dante grin and settle in the seat on the other side of the broken window, perpendicular to us.

"Ma'am, should I take us to the nearest precinct?" Mr. Janko asked in a thin, shaky voice.

It made me feel infinitely better to know I wasn't the only one rattled by the shooting.

"No, Janko, continue to the courthouse," Yara instructed as her manicured fingers flew over the screen of her iPhone. There was a short pause while she finished her text message before she looked up at Dante, and they shared a secret, mischievous kind of grin.

"That should do it I think, *si?*" Dante asked with humor rich in his deep voice.

Yara's answering grin was smug as the cat who ate the canary. "I should think so. Judge Hartford can't very well deny you solitary confinement if they won't post bail."

I blinked heavily again, feeling, for the first time ever in my career, completely out of step with proceedings.

"Are you saying you knew that man would shoot at us?" I asked weakly.

Yara laughed lightly, but Dante threw his head back and laughed from his belly as if my innocent question was the funniest thing he had ever heard.

Embarrassment scorched through me, turning the tips of my ears red hot.

I was not used to being made a fool of—not intellectually, not at work.

And I did. Not. Like. It.

"The likelihood of Judge Hartford, who is notorious for harsh sentencing, posting bail for our client is slim, Ms. Lombardi," Yara informed me slowly, overly solicitous as if speaking to a small child. "It is our responsibility to do everything in our power to get Mr. Salvatore the best sentencing we can."

"And so you arranged someone to *attack* us on the way to the courthouse just in case Mr. Salvatore is arraigned and imprisoned?" I clarified, the words clicking like ice cubes in a glass by the glacial cast of my tone.

She slanted her dark gaze at me, her diamond-faced Bulgari Serpenti Incantati watch winking brightly even in the low light as she pushed an errant lock of hair behind her ear. I hadn't had the opportunity to work with Yara Ghorbani before in my history at the firm. She was one of the youngest female partners and specialized in criminal defense litigation. Her reputation was ruthless, sly, and slippery as a serpent in the grass, getting even her most notorious clients off with severely reduced or completely severed sentences.

Now, it seemed, I was getting a clearer picture of how she did that.

"We merely leaked the information that Mr. Salvatore was being transported at this hour to the courthouse to certain...interested and unsavory elements. You'll learn," she said softly, menace just a silver edge to her words. "That the law is particularly malleable in the right hands, Ms. Lombardi. It was my understanding you are an ambitious associate, which was why I agreed to your presence on this legal team. Must I adjust my assumptions?"

I stared into her dark eyes, just as black and slicked with sly intent as the most seasoned mafiosos in my past in Naples, and something monumental occurred to me as I did so.

In order to represent the monsters of New York, did one have to become monstrous too?

I swallowed thickly as I fought a silent war in my head.

Ambition versus morality.

Both characteristics so elemental to me, I couldn't fathom making a choice.

But in this case, ambition was coupled with a pledge I'd made to the only sibling I ever really loved to protect her beloved Dante Salvatore from a lifetime in prison.

So, I sucked in a deep, stabilizing breath and cast my gaze to the man in question. He was watching me, eyes infinite and gravitational as twin black holes pulling me into the unknown.

"What do you say, Elena?" he asked with a roguish grin, flagrantly ignoring my polite suggestion he call me by my surname. *"O mangi questa minestra o salti dalla finestra?"*

I hadn't spoken more than a word or two of Italian in the years I'd lived in New York City. It was a matter of principle or more, a matter of survival.

My mind went to dark places in my native tongue.

But I understood clear enough what Dante was saying.

Are you going to take it or leave it?

Was I going to compromise myself and step into the shadowed world of the criminal or remain pristine and untouched by the upper echelons of success and power in the light?

I pretended it was a hard decision to make, but deep inside a heart that had long ago turned to ice, the decision felt more than a little right.

The car finally pulled up to the curb in front of the courthouse just as the sun broke over the crust of the metallic cityscape and spilled like broken yolk through the streets.

We were there hours early to avoid the media, but a few eager photogs and reporters littered the bottom steps of the marble building, and they jumped to their feet as we pulled up, ready to capture their first glimpse of the people who would be representing Dante Salvatore.

With another quiet, deep breath to brace myself, I turned away from Dante's soul-sucking eyes and Yara's cool cynicism to wrap my sweat-damp palm around the door handle.

"Let's do this then, shall we?" I asked, and without waiting for a response, I alighted from the vehicle into the bright light of camera flashes.

CHAPTER THREE
elena

The courtroom.

My haven.

A place so entrenched in rules and customs, its hierarchy so pretty and plainly delineated as rice fields. I knew who I was in this place and what I needed to do.

A lawyer who would accept nothing less than victory.

Media filled to bursting in the antechambers outside. The courtroom itself was packed with people, most of them standing, including my sister Cosima and her husband, Lord Thornton, Duke of Greythorn.

My client seemed entirely unmoved as we progressed to our seats, but the moment he spotted my sister Cosima in the row behind the defendant's table, his expression melted like a candle held too close to a flame.

"*Tesoro,*" he murmured to her as he sat, already twisting to look at her.

Cosima's golden eyes glittered with the sheen of tears as she leaned forward to place her hand on the rail separating them. "*Fratello.*"

I swallowed thickly, uncomfortable with the situation. There were three rows of media allowed in the chamber, and each camera was clacking rapidly to catch the exchange. We didn't need Dante accused of flirting with his brother's wife on top of everything else, and I didn't want Cosima caught up in the drama any more than she had to be.

"We will win," his brother, Alexander, as big and broad as Dante but golden to the mafioso's swarthy good looks. "I won't let them do this to you."

Dante's red mouth twisted. "You think you can do anything. You do know the entire world does not bow down to your grace, *si?*"

When Alexander only raised a cool brow, Dante laughed that completely inappropriate, absurdly lovely laugh that rang throughout the courtroom.

"Shut up," I demanded under my breath as the rattle of camera shutters increased. "Face forward, Edward, and for once in your life, do as you're told."

We'd discussed calling him Edward in court to further emphasize his connections to England and the aristocracy and not the seedier side of his Italian life and criminal connections.

Of course, Dante flatly refused to answer to the name.

"Make me," he taunted as if we were in a child's schoolyard and not in one of the highest courts in the nation trying to convince a judge not to send him to prison while he awaited trial.

"If only the judge could see how childish you are, maybe he would agree to try you as a minor," I countered smoothly, turning away to reorganize my already immaculate pile of papers and legal pads.

"This is not a playground," Yara said without moving her lips, her gaze still locked on her files. "Exercise some decorum, please."

My skin burned with humiliation, which was only exacerbated by Dante's smooth, smoky chuckle as he readjusted to lounge comfortably in a fundamentally uncomfortable courtroom chair.

"We'll speak later," Cosima whispered to him before adding in a soft voice to me, "Thank you, Lena."

I tipped my head down in acknowledgment of her sweet words but otherwise didn't respond. She had thanked me a dozen times already, and I had no doubt she would thank me a dozen more. This wasn't the kind of case I'd ever thought to define my legal career on. I'd thought long and hard about going to work for the DA's office or even the US Attorney's office for southern New York. They did the kind of heroic work I'd idolized as a child in Italy, where the mafia was a matter of everyday life, and a behemoth entity the prosecutors and policemen were murdered frequently trying to take down.

But I wasn't ashamed to admit my greed had won over my principles, and instead, I'd taken a job at Fields, Harding & Griffith, a top-five law firm in the city, the country, and even internationally with offices in London and Hong Kong. When you grew up poor, money wasn't only a primary motivator; it was almost an obsession. I still remembered how it felt to get my first paycheck as an associate. My fellow law students complained about their lowly wages as a first year, but my yearly salary was already astronomical compared to the means we'd had in Naples. It was the first time in my life I'd earned more than minimum wage, and it symbolized what I hoped would be the first milestone in a long and storied legal career.

So, it was my greed that led me to the courtroom that day defending a man I didn't like and didn't believe for one second was innocent of the crimes he was accused of and many more besides.

Naturally, my eyes swept over the room to the right side where the US Attorney and his assistants manned the prosecution. Dennis O'Malley wasn't a large man or even a showy one. He wore a simple, well-tailored blue suit with a striped tie in a muted green that I knew only from experience was the same shade as his eyes. There was silver at the thick hair over his ears, threading through the warm brown in a way that I'd always felt was very attractive, and he carried himself the way middle-aged men tended to, with a conservative grace and arrogance that made him even more attractive.

Dennis was forty-eight and one of the most successful prosecutors in the history of southern New York. Despite his shorter stature, he was classically handsome, cultured, intelligent, and ambitious. It was rumored that he was considering a run for the Senate, and the publicity this case would bring if he won would go a long way to ensuring he was a shoo-in for the position.

As if sensing my focus, Dennis looked up from his briefing notes and looked over at the table, his eyes snagging mine. When his eyebrows cut high lines into his forehead, I knew he was surprised to see me there.

"Why is that man staring at you?" Dante murmured, elbowing me softly in the side.

I glared at him quickly before returning to my case notes. "He isn't."

"A man knows when a beautiful woman is being admired," Dante drawled in that bastardized accent. "It isn't me he wants."

Despite myself, a little snort escaped me. "Oh, don't be jealous. He wants your head on a pike if that's any consolation."

Dante hummed, his fingers thrumming lightly on the hard thigh beneath his trousers. "Now, you're just projecting."

"I don't want your head on a pike, Mr. Salvatore. I want it free and clear of these charges so that you might go about your life and we will never have to see each other again," I quipped quickly as there was a collective stir of energy in the crowd seconds before the door to the judge's chamber opened to reveal the man presiding over this arraignment.

I could still feel two pairs of hot eyes on me, Dante from the left and Dennis from the right, but nothing existed for me except Judge Hartford.

He was a tall, bullish man with a thick neck and a nest of coarse black hair gone to salt at the temple. His robustness was magnified by the high, wide judge's bench he sat behind so that he seemed like an Olympian god preceding over his courtroom.

I'd done my research on him just as any good lawyer would have. It helped immeasurably to know who you were appealing to, and in this case, we had an uphill battle trying to convince pious, old-school Martin Hartford to let Dante out on bail.

He'd only been a young buck during the roaring mafia-crazed eighties, but he'd been there and done his time in the district attorney's office. He was known to have zero tolerance for organized crime.

I was too green to speak to the judge myself, not in a case as important as this, but I could comb through every spoken word looking for loopholes and intel that might assist Yara in persuading the judge that Dante Salvatore, born as Edward Davenport, second son to one of the wealthiest peerages in England, was worthy of bail.

"The United States of America versus Dante Salvatore," Judge Hartford began in that old-school radio announcer voice that made him seem slightly jovial when he was truly anything but.

I'd once overheard him say he believed thieves should have their right hand chopped off in punishment for their crimes as they still did in Dubai. He was archaic, and he was ruthless against those he deemed lifelong criminals.

The lead lawyers on each case were asked to identify themselves, but I remained in my seat as a lowly associate. My leg bounced with excited nerves beneath the table, a habit I hadn't been able to kick since childhood.

Only when a broad, hot palm wrapped fully around the circumference of my thigh beneath the table did I freeze.

Dante didn't look at me, his eyes fixed to the judge and lawyers conferring at the judge's bench, but he gave my thigh another squeeze before removing his hand.

I was so startled by his boldness that my mouth was still hanging open when Yara returned to the table and shot me an unimpressed look.

Bill Michaels and Ernesto Burgos snickered very lightly under their breath beside me. They were my fellow associates on the case who were allowed in the courtroom, with many more enlisted behind the scenes. I liked Ernesto well enough when he wasn't with Bill, but together, they loved to ridicule me, and no issue was too far for them to take their teasing.

Including the fact that my fiancé had left me for my sister.

For the third time that day, I'd been embarrassed by my client.

Anger coiled in my belly, a serpent caught in a snare desperate to burst free and strangle the first thing in sight. I fought through the madness, my fingers clenched too hard around my Montblanc pen, dragging controlled breaths through my nose the way my therapist had taught me.

It did little to help clear the fog of red tinting my vision when I darted another glance at Dante. He was staring at me from the corner of his eyes, his lips compressed just slightly as if he fought a smile at my expense.

It was official.

I hated him.

Didn't he realize I'd taken this case on as a favor to my sister? That I normally stayed fifty yards away from Made Men, that they made me sick with painful memories and injustices.

He was supposed to love Cosima, so why the hell was he finding ways to embarrass her sister in front of her boss?

I shifted in my seat and picked at a hangnail until it bled.

It helped calm me down.

When I looked at Dante again, he was frowning slightly at me, his hand in the inside pocket of his suit jacket. A moment later, a pristine white handkerchief floated into my lap.

I glared at it, annoyed he was the kind of man to carry such a thing because I'd always found the habit gentlemanly and attractive. Spitefully, I ground my bleeding thumb into the fabric so the blood smeared across the whiteness.

Dante's lips, nearly the same color red that I'd deposited on the fabric, tightened again with a suppressed grin.

I ground my teeth and forced myself to focus on the proceedings once again.

Judge Hartford laid out the charges under the RICO Act--the Racketeer Influenced and Corrupt Organization Act--stating that Dante Salvatore was being indicted on three counts: first-degree murder, illegal gambling and racketeering, and money laundering.

The murder charge was the real focus of the case, though. Some charges just couldn't stick unless they were adhered to something weightier with more burden of proof. Murder was the anchor for the case the state had been building against Dante Salvatore in the five years since he'd moved to America and become one of the biggest crime bosses in modern history.

If we could just get him clear of that charge, the prosecution's case would fall like a poorly constructed house of cards.

I was mulling that over when the judge asked Dante how he pleaded to the charges.

It was only then that I clued into the energy emanating from the mafioso at my side. The air around him seemed to solidify like an invisible force field, and when he spoke, the only sound in the entire room was the European cadence of his voice. It was so still, it seemed everyone was holding their breath.

Even me.

Slowly, his large body unraveling almost endlessly with a grace no man who muscled should've been capable of, Dante rose to his feet. Once there, he slanted a quick glance at the closest cluster of photogs, did up his suit jacket button calmly, and then locked eyes with the judge.

One measured blink that was somehow predatory, his attention a stalking weight on Judge Hartford, and then he drawled solemnly, "Not guilty, Your Honor."

Immediately the entire room lit up with flashes and commotion. Whispers reverberated like gunshots through the cramped courtroom, and they only disappeared when Judge Hartford called for order three times, the last voiced in a commanding yell that raised the hair on the backs of my arms.

I looked up at Dante to find a small, self-satisfied grin on his too-red mouth. Without hesitation, I tugged at the back of his suit jacket to get him to sit down and stop his bizarre gloating. He settled into his chair willingly, an innocent expression affixed to his strong features.

I didn't know who he thought he was fooling with those wide eyes and slightly raised brows, but a small part of me applauded his audacity.

On trial for murder, potentially facing a lifetime behind bars, and still, Dante Salvatore managed to have fun, however inappropriate it might have been.

Arraignments were often boring, but this was shaping up to be the most sensational one I'd ever attended.

"Your Honor, the accused has clear ties to England and Italy," Dennis stood to say when the judge addressed him to state his case for not posting bail for the defendant. "His own brother, one of the wealthiest men in Britain, is here today and would have resources enough to get Mr. Salvatore out of the country—"

"Objection," I murmured under my breath at the same time Yara stood to say the very same thing. "Conjecture."

Judge Hartford slanted Yara an unamused look. "I hardly need Mr. O'Malley to state the obvious, Ms. Ghorbani. Your client has known connections in Europe and the UK, enough legitimate business to have access to significant monetary resources if he should want to flee the country, and sufficient motivation to do so. I see no reason he should not be detained until trial."

Beside me, Dante stiffened slightly, the only clue that the idea of incarceration was unappealing to him. Then again, the fastest timeframe for a trial as big as this was at least six months but more likely one to three years. New York and its residents loved a good mafia case, and it was a prime opportunity for the city, its officers, district and US Attorneys, and government to showcase their protection of the city.

"With all due respect, Your Honor," Yara said in that misleadingly lovely voice that meant she was about to kick verbal ass. "The prosecution has fairly insufficient proof to bring this to trial in the first place."

"That matter is not currently up for debate, Ms. Ghorbani," Judge Hartford interrupted coldly.

"No," she agreed easily. "But my client is an established member of New York City society. He owns multiple businesses in the city and most of his living relations are residents. This is his first criminal offense on American soil, and therefore, he cannot be considered a threat to the public if he is granted bail. Furthermore, he was unduly attacked this morning based on these accusations, and there is a real threat of bodily harm should he be kept in the general population in prison awaiting trial."

Judge Hartford stared at her flatly before his eyes flickered over to Dante and his jaw went tight.

He did not want to grant bail.

But he would.

While it wasn't guaranteed, bail was the right of any person awaiting trial unless they were a proven danger to society, like a serial killer.

Of course, it was my opinion that Dante had probably killed numerous people in his sordid life, thus earning that distinction, but I wasn't about to point that out.

"I know your reputation, Ms. Ghorbani, and I won't have any shady business conducted in this courtroom, is that understood?" He waited for a firm nod then continued. "As I see it, Mr. Salvatore is a flight risk, but he poses no immediate threat to the public. I do not pretend to care about the safety of your client, Ms. Ghorbani, but I will allow bail to be set. Mr. Salvatore, I am releasing you on ten million dollars bond and placing you on house arrest. You will only be permitted to leave your residence for church, therapy, or medical appointments and will be monitored via GPS bracelet."

There was a clamor in the room as shutters clicked, and people balked, then whispered at the decision.

House arrest.

For a man like Dante, a man who seemed like a barely leashed beast at the best of times, I imagined house arrest was akin to being locked in a cage for the next six months to three years.

Yet he sat there beside me in his bespoke black suit, sleek and powerful as a panther, looking nothing short of mildly bored and perhaps a little drowsy. I felt like shaking him until his teeth rattled, yelling at him that this was the rest of his life at stake and demanding him to tell me why he was so utterly blasé about the whole thing.

I didn't know why I cared.

It wasn't that I'd formed some lunatic instant connection to the man. In fact, I abhorred almost everything he stood for.

Perhaps, it was as simple as the fact that I wanted some of that unshakeable calm for myself. I wanted to steal the magic of his self-assuredness and bottle it like perfume to spritz on my pulse points whenever I needed validation.

"Court is dismissed," Judge Hartford said distantly, and then there was chaos as everyone rose to leave, photogs clamoring for one last shot of the impudent mafioso.

"Well," I said, unable to curb my impulse to poke at his calm, like a child shaking a bottle of pop hoping for an explosion. "I certainly hope this lends a new gravity to your understanding of the situation."

Dante didn't look at me as he unfolded to his immense height and adjusted the silver cuff links with the same crest emblazoned on his gaudy silver ring. Only when we were pressed together by Ernesto and Bill shuffling out of their seats did his gaze lock on mine with an almost audible click. I gasped slightly as a rough hand, that same one that had left an imprint on my thigh only minutes before, wrapped nearly double around my wrist, his thumb notched over my pulse. It drew my attention to the quickened thud of my heartbeat.

Adrenaline flooded my body at being so close to and held by

such a man, a mammoth predator, but there was something else there too in the hot undercurrents, something sunk deep into my blood.

Something like lust.

I fixed a glower to my face and breathed through my mouth so I could avoid that oddly intoxicating lemon and pepper scent of his.

He wasn't deterred.

If anything, his eyes danced for the first time since we entered the courtroom as his lips barely moved around the words, "You can cage the man, Elena, but not the idea. No collection of walls is strong enough to hold me or mine."

"You are very poetic about organized crime."

"Thank you," he said even though it wasn't a compliment. "Have dinner with me tonight. It's my last as a free man."

I'd missed that somehow when I'd been dazed out thinking about the irritating man shackling my wrist. Typically, he would be imprisoned pending house arrest, but I had no doubt Yara had finagled something legally or with a well-placed bribe to give the capo one last night. I tugged free of his hold and bared my teeth between my painted red lips, not caring for once how I might look to the photographers gathered.

"I wouldn't go to dinner with you if it was our last night on earth," I promised darkly before turning on my heel and following Bill and Ernesto, leaving my client with Yara.

The tendrils of his smoky chuckle somehow threaded through

the noise of the room and wound its way into my ears, a casual, beautifully toned mockery of everything I held dear.

It was official.

I hated him.

CHAPTER FOUR

elena

The mafia 'lord' laughs in the face of his crimes.

I scoffed as I read the headline in *The New York Times* above a grainy black and white photo of a laughing Dante Salvatore that still managed to capture the depth of his beauty. It made him look like a movie star playing some kinda charming criminal the audience was supposed to root for in an HBO show. The new moniker they had given him, "the mafia lord," proved to glamorize and civilize him in a way that would appeal to millions of Americans.

Exactly Dante's intention.

Though the article was a condemnation of his criminal character, there was no doubt he had succeeded in swaying public opinion at least slightly in his favor.

The reporter, a man whose work I'd read since my arrival on American shores and who I knew to be a hard-nosed, rarely forgiving journalist, even allowed that Dante Salvatore, though built like a savage beast, still retained some of the grace his rearing as a Lord's second son had born in him.

I rolled my eyes as I tossed the paper onto the chair beside me, then pinched my nose to briefly relieve the headache stirring behind my eyes.

It had been a long day with the indictment, but we'd achieved what we set out to do.

Judge Hartford agreed to post bail.

To the outstanding tune of ten million dollars.

Cash.

For a New York mafioso, such a number shouldn't be a hardship. Dante was under investigation, which meant he had to be able to prove his bail money came from a legitimate business, but Yara had informed me that Dante had more than enough cash from his lawful businesses to post bail immediately.

In addition, he was going to be housebound, shackled to his apartment by a high-tech anklet that tracked his every move.

It was impossible not to think of him as a wild animal locked in a cage, prowling madly, growing restless as each day passed, his savagery ballooning to fill every inch of that cramped space.

In all likelihood, it was a mega-mansion, but Dante was a man with endless testosterone. I had no doubt he would turn into his basest self before too long when confined as he would be between four walls.

I was *not* relishing my interactions with him.

Almost as much as I was not looking forward to my appointment with Dr. Taylor.

"Elena?" the doctor herself said kindly as she opened the door to the luxuriously appointment room where I sat in a thin cashmere hospital gown on the exam table. "How are we today?"

"Anxious," I admitted, though nothing in my straight posture or carefully clasped hands denoted the riot of nerves ricocheting in my belly. "I feel as though I've been waiting forever to know what's wrong with me."

Dr. Taylor's severe face, Slavic and big-boned, gentled into a genuine smile as she sat on her wheelie stool and opened my medical file. "That's very normal, I assure you. So let me get right to it then. I have good news. What you have is a combination of various abnormalities that have made fertility and orgasm achievement difficult for you. A decade ago, we wouldn't have even noticed these collections of issues, let alone known how to treat them. In this day and age, though, with our advanced technology and surgical practices, I believe we can fix your primary anorgasmia and greatly improve your chances of conceiving a child one day."

I blinked as my chest compressed painfully, and heat pricked the backs of my eyes. My breath wouldn't move through my body, my lips wouldn't form the words I wanted to say, probably because, in my shocked relief, I didn't even know which ones to speak.

Thank God.

I can't believe it.

Are you sure? Please, don't let this be another cruel joke.

I can be fixed?

Instead, I sat there mutely, convulsively swallowing past the lump in my throat as I stared down at my clasped hands.

It was silly, really, that I should feel so emotional over potentially gaining the ability to orgasm after a lifetime of sex without true pleasure. Lord knew, sex wasn't everything. It was hardly and probably understandably, given my affliction and history, a blip on my radar.

But it represented so much more.

Living as a woman who couldn't orgasm with significant fertility issues in part because of an ectopic pregnancy five years ago was psychologically crippling.

Even though I'd eschewed my Italian culture for years, it was still pervasive enough to leave a lingering sense of shame that I couldn't fulfill the Italian ideal of a woman: get married, give birth to an endless stream of children to satisfy the pope or the mafia, whichever religion my people subscribed to, and raise them in that faith.

Then there was the simple and crushing fact that my fiancé had left me for another woman after having a kinky, fucked-up affair with her for weeks behind my back. This was made even more excruciating by the fact that they'd recently brought a baby into the world.

A little girl.

I'd overheard Cosima talking on the phone to Giselle one morning, and apparently, little Genevieve even had Daniel's beautiful blue eyes.

Pain lanced through me every time I thought about Daniel's

new family, spearing straight into my spine so that I felt I might break clean in two.

Given all of that, I decided to allow myself the agony of relief searing through me and the wet it brought to my eyes.

Dr. Taylor wheeled forward to place a hand on my knee and smile at me tenderly. "I don't think I ever thought I'd see you so moved."

I laughed, a choked-off, ugly sound. "Great bedside manner, Monica."

She laughed too. "I do my best for my friends. Do you need a moment?"

"No, no." I rolled my shoulders back and fixed her with my cool stare. "Run me through the procedure and let me look at my calendar, let's get this booked in."

"There are risks," she warned. "You have endometriosis and significant fibroids. We're talking about two procedures done simultaneously."

A bitter coughing chuckle erupted from my lips. "Of course there are, and knowing my luck, I should know the worst-case outcome. But honestly, Monica, this is the best news I've had in so long…" I swallowed the unexpected surge of a sob rising in my throat and powered through. "It's just good to know there's a chance."

"You'd have to continue with your therapy," she reminded me. "There are mental obstacles to these kinds of issues as well, and Dr. Madsen seems to think it's helping."

I thought therapy was a waste of my valuable time, and I didn't particularly like Dr. Madsen, but I only nodded, too relieved to put up my usual fight.

Monica smiled at me, a rich expression of joy that mimicked the feeling ballooning in my belly. "At the end of this, Elena, you'll know carnal pleasure, and one day, I hope you'll know the joy of being a mother. You might need additional hormone therapy to conceive because I'm worried about your estrogen levels, but natural conception should be a very real possibility."

I swallowed the knot of tangled emotions in my throat and gave her a curt nod. I wanted to hope, but if life had taught me anything, it was that hope was a slippery thing, and just as soon as you found purchase with your hold, it slipped away again, elusive and cruel.

I'd once had everything I'd ever wanted, the job, the home, the man, but no sexual climax, no chance at fulfilling my dream of being a mother. It seemed a steep price to pay to swap one for the other, and I couldn't help but be filled with bitterness at the thought that I couldn't have it all.

I used to love my townhome. It was a Greek Revival three-story brick affair tucked away in the elite neighborhood of Gramercy Park. Daniel and I had bought it together after walking by it nearly every evening for weeks. At the time, when he was just hitting his stride with his real estate development firm, Faire Developments, and I was taking the Bar exam, it was at the upper end of our price range and entirely impractical. We were only two people, years out from starting a family, but Daniel had seen how much I loved it. He had known how I'd longed for a beautiful place to call home since I was a little girl tucked away in a rotting house the color of sunbaked urine in Naples.

He was that kind of man, the kind who would bend over backward to give his woman everything her heart desired.

To lose a man like that…well, thirteen months had passed, and I still felt the echo of his loss in my empty chest and the once-beloved, empty rooms of my townhome.

I felt the vibration of that loneliness pang through me as I opened the elegant black door to my house and stepped into the cool, neutral-toned interior. Keys went into the porcelain catch-all on the ivory side table, my carefully maintained Louboutin pumps in the closet beside it, and my cashmere coat hung above that.

Silence pulsed all around me as my stocking feet padded down the dark hardwood floors to the living room.

I'd thought, briefly, about getting a cat just to have a living creature yearn for my company, but just as quickly, I discarded the idea. I worked from seven in the morning until eight or nine every evening. The cat would resent me in the end, just as most people seemed to, and I didn't think I could stand another rejection.

The quiet weighed on me that day, heavier than normal, so I did what I always did to shatter the silence and remind myself I was alive, even if there was no one to see it.

I cut diagonally across the room to the grand piano dominating the far corner, its surface glossy as an oil slick. My heart thundered in my ears as I dragged the stool out and perched on the cushioned edge. The metallic tang of adrenaline hit the back of my tongue as a quiver set into my long fingers, the digits trembling as I lifted the guard from the keys and pushed it back.

My body yearned for this the way addicts longed for their next hit.

Perhaps masochistically, I didn't give in to the compulsion to play very often.

My siblings might have pursued creative careers against all the odds, but I was too pragmatic to indulge in my idle daydreams when we'd been poor and circled by carrion capos from the time we were born. I set my mind to better uses, but my soul--the wretched, dreamy thing--wouldn't let me stay away from music for long.

I sucked in a deep lungful of air, trying to ignore the memories that threatened to drown me as I placed my fingertips on the cool ivories and began to play.

My eyes closed instinctively as "Somewhere Else" by my countryman Dario Crisman flowed from my hands into the glossy musical beast before me. It was one of the first complicated songs the hunchbacked old lady with nimble, youthful fingers who had taught me everything I knew about piano, Signora Donati, made me learn. It had resonated with me, the idea that somewhere else was a place I might one day be allowed to visit.

Until I was an adult, the glaringly bright and stench-strewn streets of Napoli were all I knew. Once, Christopher had taken me as far south as Sorrento. I remembered the cotton candy colors of the houses, how clean the streets seemed, and how true blue the water was without the murk and muck of a commercial fishing harbor to mar its beauty. But the memories were sullied by the very fact that Christopher, eighteen years older than me, had harnessed my girlish, sixteen-year-old excitement and made it malleable in his warm, searching hands.

I'd lost my virginity that weekend and returned feeling worldly both for my travels and my carnal experience. It wasn't until later, when Christopher grew cruel, but more, when Cosima finally got us out of Napoli and away from him, that I realized what a nightmare that pretty place of Sorrento had symbolized for me.

Sorrow warped my throat into a misshapen swollen mess, air catching in the narrow channel until I felt I might choke.

I'd lost so much of myself before I'd ever truly known who I was.

It was strange to mourn for your own life, but as I sat at the piano and poured my overfull soul into the keys, the music sweet and aching in my ears, I said a little prayer that I might recover some of those precious fragments one day. That I might not go on so hollow and brittle, ready to crack into sharp pieces that might pierce anyone so brave as to pick them up.

As the final strains of the movement dissolved in the air, the staccato slap of clapping hands reverberated through the space.

"*Bellisima*, Elena," Dante Salvatore commended over the hearty sound of his applause as he stood leaning against the doorframe between my living room and hallway. "Who knew you had such beauty at your fingertips?"

I blinked at him, prying my mind out of my dreamy introspection into the present, madly wondering what the condemned mafioso was doing in my house.

He took the time to smile; a long, slow pull of his full lips into a heart-stopping grin that carved creases into his cheeks and fine lines beside his big, dark eyes. It was the smile of a born charmer. He assumed it would work on me just as I was sure it had worked on countless women before.

Instead, it doused me in cold water, awakening me to full, alert outrage.

"What are you doing in my house?" I demanded coldly as I stood and walked to my kitchen to grab the landline. I raised the handle threateningly. "Do I need to call the police because there is an intruder in my home?"

"By all means," he allowed agreeably, extending his massive hands with a shrug. Belatedly, I noticed the white plastic bag in his grip. "But I am an intruder bearing gifts, and I've never known an Italian woman to turn away a handsome man with food."

I sniffed. "I don't consider myself an Italian woman."

"Ah," he said irritatingly in the same tone my smug, know-it-all therapist used when I said something he found enlightening.

56

"Just as I do not consider myself a Brit."

"No matter what you chose to believe, you are the brother of a duke. I'd imagine that's rather hard to ignore," I quipped, determined to cut him to ribbons with my barbed tongue before tossing him out on his ear.

"You'd be surprised," he said as he moved into my kitchen as if he had dined there a thousand times before. I watched, struck mute by his audacity, as he dropped the takeout bag on the marble counter and began to open cupboards in search of glasses. Once found, he produced a bottle of Italian Chianti from the bag with a flourish and continued to speak as if picking up the thread of a conversation we had already been having. "A little birdie told me Chianti is a favorite of yours. Typically, I would pair it with a good pasta, but that same birdie informed me you avoid Italian food. So..." He smiled again, that great big grin on his great big face. "I brought Sushi Yasaka."

Pain lanced through me so intensely, I flinched then watched Dante's smirk fall on the left side like a crookedly hung painting.

It was such a little thing, but I'd found it was the collection of small reminders that combined throughout the day to leave me aching and tired.

Sushi Yasaka had been our place, Daniel's and mine.

I hadn't eaten there in months as a result, but a small part of me yearned for the tuna sashimi Dante pulled from the bag.

"Bad memories?" he questioned so softly I found myself answering before I could stop myself.

"Old memories," I allowed before shaking my head and fixing him with another glare. "Now, *Edward Davenport*, I'd like to know what you are doing in my house uninvited? It seems you have a habit of breaking in where you aren't wanted."

The first time I'd met Dante, it had been at the hospital bedside of my beloved Cosima. The sight of such a large Italian man looming over my prone sister had instilled a fresh terror in me that I hadn't felt in years.

Needless to say, it hadn't exactly been a successful first impression.

Dante, though, only chuckled in that way I'd learned he had when someone tried to make him face uncomfortable truths. "I was invited to her bedside. *You* just didn't know it. And I am here, quite simply, Elena, to determine if you are fit to be one of my legal representatives."

Instantly, I bristled, ready to don the armor I'd honed over the years of having to prove my worth in the legal profession as both a woman and an immigrant.

Dante held up one large, deeply tanned hand before I could protest, laughter dancing in his eyes. It annoyed me beyond measure that he seemed to find hilarity in every single thing I did.

"I did not mean to imply you aren't technically a fine choice," he allowed with great generosity. "Only that I need a specific *type* of person on my legal team, and even though you recovered well enough from the shock of the drive-by shooter today, I get a sense you are the type of woman who prefers the straight and narrow."

When I continued to glare at him, he cocked an eyebrow and made an innocent gesture, hands open to the ceiling. "Am I wrong in assuming this?"

I ground my teeth together. "You know what they say about assumptions."

His head tilted to the right, strong brow furrowed. "Actually, I don't."

I shrugged tensely. "They make an ass out of you and me."

He blinked, then slapped a hand on the counter and positively *roared* with laughter. The robust sound swelled and ebbed in my narrow kitchen, too big and bright to be contained.

"The lady can be coarse," he said finally, still speaking through his chuckles. "Oh, the sound of a curse on your lips is sinful, Elena. You should swear more often."

I tipped my chin slightly in the air as my only answer. I certainly would not. If anything, his remark only served to remind me that "coarse" wasn't an adjective I ever wanted to hear in conjunction with me.

I'd worked too hard to move past the roughness of my upbringing. To be the kind of woman who worked at a top-ten law firm in the city and the type of paramour a man like Daniel might take for his partner.

Dante studied me too keenly, bracing himself on his forearms to lean familiarly over the counter as if we were two close friends having a tête-à-tête. "You know, it is the contrast between two opposites that heightens them both to keener glory. You shouldn't be afraid to be coarse, just as I shouldn't be afraid to be gentle. Too much of one thing is boring, Elena."

"I've been accused of much worse," I retorted acerbically.

I'd never been good at the unflappable act. It was one of the qualities I'd admired most about Daniel, his ability to remain physically unfazed even in the face of utter chaos. There was too much Latin in my blood, no matter how I tried to curb it, to rid myself of the wild extremity of my emotions.

Dante could have very well been teasing me in the way I knew many people did to build a rapport, but however well-intentioned, I wasn't good at taking criticism.

I felt red-faced and slightly ashamed, then angry with myself for feeling that way. The complicated knot of my own raw emotions was too difficult for me to unravel. Suddenly, I was tired of myself. So exhausted by the simple act of being me.

It wasn't an unusual sensation these days, but it made me weary to the bone.

Dante seemed to sense the shift in me, his ink-dark eyes tracing the softening line of my shoulders and the swell of my chest beneath the silk blouse as I let out a deep breath and raked in a new one.

"There," he said, almost gently, averting his eyes as if to give me privacy while he collected my plates, glasses, and the food to move to my small round dining room table. "It is the end of a long day, Elena. Why don't you sit down and help me eat all this food, hmm?"

I blinked as the large Made Man folded himself almost comically into a chair at my tiny table and then spread his thick thighs until barely any space remained for me to pull out the other chair. He proceeded to dish out food from various containers onto his plate, humming a vaguely familiar song under his breath as he did.

I blinked again.

It perturbed me how easily he could throw me off even though I reminded myself this was extremely *bizarre* behavior. The man had broken into my house to invite himself to dinner he'd bought, and somehow, he made me feel unhospitable and ungracious.

"*Seduta*," Dante ordered mildly.

Instantly and without thought, I sat.

Anger spiked through me, chased by humiliation.

It had been a long time since I'd accepted any orders from any man in any language, let alone one I'd banished from my mind.

When I went to stand again, vibrating with anger, Dante lashed out and grabbed my wrist in a light but unyielding hold, making me flinch. Our eyes caught, snagged on each other for a long, disquieting moment where he looked too deep inside me.

"We will speak only English, okay?" he promised solemnly.

I stared at him, finally pinpointing what it was exactly about Dante Salvatore that put me so ill at ease.

He was utterly genuine.

In his dominance, in his charm, in his concern.

He committed himself entirely to the moment, to that which

61

was at the center of his attention. To be in his spotlight felt like being naked, razed of every defense I'd spent twenty-seven years meticulously forging.

"Fine, I'm sitting," I offered stiffly, crossing my legs. Dante's eyes immediately went to the edge of the opaque band at the top of my thigh-high stockings. I uncrossed them and tugged my black cashmere skirt down farther. "What did you break into my house to tell me?"

"We do not do business at the dinner table," he admonished even though he shot me that wicked grin.

It was an age-old rule, one that even I knew as a civilian outside of the mafia.

"I'd rather we get on with it. You're encroaching on my plans for this evening." I arched a chilly brow at him as I reached for the tuna sashimi, my stomach rumbling quietly, reminding me I'd only eaten half an apple since breakfast.

"Oh?" The word was swallowed up in a chuckle. "Hot date?"

I looked down my nose at him as I popped a piece of silken fish into my mouth and hummed lightly as I swallowed it. There was no reason he had to know the closest I'd been to a hot date since Daniel left me was a glass of wine, a box of my favorite French chocolates, and an episode of *True Blood*. "Perhaps."

Dante's hands, the palms thick with plump muscle, looked faintly ridiculous holding the slim chopsticks, but he maneuvered them like a pro as he picked through a spicy salmon roll. "Then I insist we talk about this. Cosima implied you were... not interested

62

in men."

I choked on a piece of sushi, inhaling the wasabi painfully. Calmly, eyes dancing, Dante handed me my untouched glass of Italian red.

I glared at him as I swallowed it down, breathing with relief when the burning in my throat eased.

"I'm very interested in the right kind of men," I corrected him in a throatier voice than usual, rough from my coughing fit. "Men of honor and substance. It's not my fault they're a rare breed."

"I wonder if you'd give any man the chance to prove his worth?" Dante mused.

The words weren't unkind, but they hurt all the same. Late at night lying in the big bed I'd once shared with him, I'd wondered if I hadn't given Daniel a proper chance to be himself with me, to prove that whatever more he was could be beautiful to me.

I'd shut him down because I'd been afraid.

I could admit it now, after months of reluctant therapy.

His sexual proclivities had broken open old scar tissue from Christopher's abuse in my youth, and like a coward, I'd let my fear rule me and ruin my relationship with the best man I'd ever known.

I didn't say any of that to the mafioso sitting across from me as if we were at his house instead of mine. Something about his easy manner seemed to exacerbate every single one of my flaws. I felt naked and raw under that olive-black gaze, and I didn't like it at all.

So, I tipped my chin and slanted him a cool look. "Nothing worth having is ever easy."

An abrupt laugh erupted from his broad chest. "Oh yes, Elena, with this, I can agree."

I plucked up a piece of silken sashimi and let it melt on my tongue before I set my chopsticks down and fixed him with a cool, professional look. "As long as you're here, we should run through tomorrow's proceedings. The probation officer will be at your address at ten in the morning to fit you with your ankle monitor and set up the system. Unless you have approval from their office to attend doctor's appointments, church, therapy, or something equally pragmatic and important to your health, you will be restricted to your home."

He shrugged one thick shoulder and took a long sip of his wine. I watched his throat contract as he swallowed, wondering at the density of muscles in his neck deepening over his shoulders. I was an avid runner who never missed a workout, so I knew he must have worked every day to maintain such an outrageously fit physique.

"It is okay to admire me." His voice bumped into my thoughts, upending a flush that spilled like the wine in his glass all the way from my cheeks to my breasts. "You are a Lombardi woman, and as such, I'm certain you have a deep appreciation for beauty."

"This is why I dislike Italian men. You're so arrogant."

"Is it arrogance if it is based in fact? Why fake humility? Would you rather I deceive you than speak the truth?" he countered calmly.

I felt as if I was being cross-examined at court, his eyes searching for cracks in my façade, his mind carefully calculating every word out of my mouth. It infuriated me that he thought he had the right to interrogate me. That he thought he had a right to know me.

No one did.

I was an island, and I liked it that way.

"First of all, *Edward*, I was not admiring your so-called beauty. You may make a certain type of woman swoon, but I prefer my men un-Made and considerably more sophisticated."

"You have such hatred for the Camorra, yet your sisters both seem unaffected by this," he mused, prodding at me in that way I was learning he had, trying to get into every nook and cranny of my being.

His words triggered my first horrific memory of the Camorra and their presence in our lives.

My siblings were too young to remember the depravity of our childhood with any kind of true clarity. Our trip to Puglia when the twins were only babes and Giselle a dreamy toddler was remembered only for the turbulent private plane we took to get there.

They didn't remember, as I did, three years older than them, the horror that had led us to flee our home in Naples for the sun-beaten shores of the south.

I could still remember the taste of steel in my mouth, the feel of the gun heavy and cold on my tongue like some macabre phallus. How tears had burned the backs of my eyes like a lighter held to my optic nerves and how I'd refused to let them fall, holding my breath and clenching my fists until I was more stone than flesh.

I was six years old when Seamus and Mama returned home one day to find a *soldato* in the local Camorra holding me against his body with his gun lodged in my mouth.

It wasn't the first time Seamus had owed money, but it was the first time they'd threatened his children. Giselle was only four, the twins nearly three years old. For the first time in my memory, Mama had usurped Seamus's will, and the next day, after cleaning out our savings to pay his debts, we'd moved to Puglia to stay with Mama's cousins.

It didn't last, of course, but our time spent on the island was one of the only happy eras of my childhood.

"You might be poetic about crime, but I've lived it enough to see the horrors," I finally said, dragging my gaze back into the present and pinning him with my judgmental gaze. "You might have no problem beating a man or threatening his family if he goes against you, but I've been the daughter of that man, and I've been that child who was threatened. How you can see anything worth admiring in that, I have no clue."

"You are substituting a part for the whole. The actions of one bad man do not extend to every other man in his community," he argued.

I finished my wine, surprised by how quickly I'd downed the

lovely vintage.

"Are you suggesting you aren't a bad man, *capo?*" I asked sweetly.

He flipped over one of those big paws on the table, showing me the strength in his hand by flexing and releasing a fist. "*Si*, these hands have seen violence and retribution, Elena, but does that mean they cannot also comfort a child, bring pleasure to a lover, or protect an innocent?"

I scoffed. "Excuse me if I can't see you protecting an innocent."

Instantly, Dante's open features shuttered close, and a scowl knotted between his thick brows. "You act very high and mighty for a woman who judges me without knowing me, especially when I am trying to get to know her."

"You don't need to know me for me to work my ass off for you on this case," I rebutted, hovering off my chair as I glared over the table at him.

"Well, you need to know *me* if you want to stay on this team and get that success you're so desperate for," he countered as he pushed back from his chair and leaned across the little table, his hand wrapped around my throat in a shockingly firm grip. My pulse hammered against his fingers, but I didn't move, immobilized not by his grip on my neck but by the ferocity in his eyes.

"*Ascoltami,*" he seethed in Italian, ordering me to listen to him. "I have made sacrifices for innocents and loved ones that your neat black and white world could never compute. When have *you* made

Nausea flooded me as a memory spun like a fractured kaleidoscope through my mind's eye. A mafioso hitting me because I'd hid pretty Giselle from him and then Christopher, begging him not to harm her.

I didn't say that, though.

Instead, I looked into the burning dark of his gaze and slid my response like a blade between his ribs. "I have. I'm sacrificing my integrity by helping *you* because I made Cosima a promise."

He stared at me unblinkingly for a long moment, that hand still banded around my throat, so hot it scorched my skin. The air around us throbbed in time with my pulse. There was a flush in my cheeks I could feel and a heaviness in my gut I told myself was anger instead of something more carnal.

I watched as the darkness in Dante's eyes warmed with something other than anger. I sucked a sharp breath into my mouth, tasting his peppery cologne accidentally as he brought my face closer to his in order to rasp his stubbled cheek against my own and whisper in my ear, "Who knows, *lottatrice*, maybe you'll find more pleasure being in bed with the devil than you would have imagined."

CHAPTER FIVE
DANTE

What happens after the fall of a dynasty?

The big bang and flash of fireworks exploding in a decades-long show of glitz and glamour, dissolving into wisps and embers and then... into nothing.

It leaves a huge ink-black sky ripe for the filling.

A black hole just waiting for someone to step up and control the void.

The mafia of old died in the 80s after the trial of Arturo Accardi hit the final nail in the coffins of the Old Guard. The public hits, Made Men caricatures wrapped up in tailor-made Prada suits with gold chains and pockets bulging with rolls of fat hundreds, were gone.

But the mafia itself could not be killed.

Not then, certainly not now, and if I had to hedge a bet, not ever.

The mafia was founded on the idea of brotherhood and greed,

both so essential to the human existence it could never be snuffed out.

So, we iterated, reiterated, again and again. We were an amorphous shape, constantly changing with the times and adapting better than any other institution or organization because we didn't have to worry about pesky things like the law or morality.

The mafia originated in Sicily because, after decades of constant invasions and shifts in power, the natives developed a finely honed sense of loyalty to their neighbors over their loyalty to the government. As a result, they were able to maintain a culture based on their unique community and not that of their oppressors.

The mafia was founded as a result of a greater power trying to cut Italians down, so Italians created their own organization to fight back and police their own.

This was why even after the massive governmental and police attacks on the American mafia in the 80s, families of organized crime not only still existed… They fucking thrived. Not even cancel culture could cancel the mafia. Some institutions existed outside of time and place. *La Famiglia* was one such institution.

Where did I fit into any of that?

Well, in this life, my third in thirty-five years, I was Dante Salvatore, *capo* of the Salvatore *borgata*.

Charmingly mad, bad, and entirely too dangerous to know.

Or so they said.

Few people knew the real me, but perhaps the one who loved me most currently sat scowling beside me, drinking an expensive glass of Chianti as if it was cheap American beer.

"It is not for them to doubt us," Amadeo Salvatore muttered darkly into the wide bowl of his glass, dark brow knitted together into one long, furry line. "They are to listen and obey. You have to earn respect to get respect. Is this a concept youth today cannot grasp?"

I grinned at my pseudo-father, noting that even at eleven at night after a full day of work, his Brioni suit was still immaculately pressed. Tore prized control over almost any other quality. He was intractable with his rules, rigid in his regard for conformity within the Outfit.

Yet, he'd taken a reckless runaway British lad under his belt and groomed him like a son, even knowing the wildness in his blood would never cool.

We were a good contrast, he and I. He was cold and calculated. I was instinct and hot-blooded brutality.

Together, we ran one of the most successful outfits in a country we hadn't even called our own until five years prior.

Sitting on the patio of my two-story penthouse in one of New York City's most storied and expensive apartment buildings overlooking Central Park, the lights of the city beyond shining like jewels spilled at our feet, it was impossible not to feel the power and prestige of our urban empire.

"It might have something to do with the fact that their *capo* is currently embroiled in a years-long trial with no end in sight," I drawled dryly before sipping the full-bodied wine.

Tore grunted at that, as displeased with my arrest as picnickers were by flies at a summer spread. Arrests, police surveillance, and blackmail were all frequent and natural consequences of our illegal enterprises. Tore had been inducted into the mafia as a young man and spent his entire life living in the shadows of the Camorra's powerful embrace. He believed absolutely in its power to crush any opponent, even one so grand as the US government. After all, it had been done before. Many, many times.

I was yet unconvinced.

We were powerful men, the head of the snake of an extensive criminal empire with a widespread network of connections to grease our way out of tight corners.

But this was different.

That fuckface USA was determined to be the next Guiliani and bring down the New York City mob. No one gave a shit about the mafia in a time of national and global acts of terrorism, but Dennis O'Malley was convinced he could cut the line straight to the top of success by taking down the glamourous Camorra.

Even that was nothing, white fucking noise, compared to the real problem.

I hadn't killed Giuseppe di Carlo in that shithole deli in the Bronx.

I wished I had.

But no.

It wasn't me who planted a bullet between the motherfucker's eyes.

It seemed the di Carlo Family was cleverer than their inbred ugliness lent them credit for. They'd set up one of the only people I'd ever loved.

And I'd go to jail, the grave, whatever afterlife there was for sinner men like me a thousand times over if it meant keeping Cosima safe.

So, there we were.

It was a helluva predicament.

"We got the Irish bastards sniffing around our garbage looking for spoils," Tore muttered into his wine. "Jacopo caught a few of them lingering by the Hudson, scouting warehouses. I tell you, I should've killed Seamus Moore when I had the chance."

It was a complicated story, the one between Cosima and Elena's mother, Caprice, and her ex-husband Seamus. Caprice and Tore had fallen in love once, long ago, and had a torrid affair that led to the birth of Cosima and her twin brother, Sebastian. Caprice had cut Tore out of their lives because of his mob dealings and raised the twins as Seamus's offspring until the Irish bastard sold Cosima into sexual slavery and disappeared for years.

He'd cropped up in New York City, *our* city, last year working for Thomas "Gunner" Kelly and his group of Irish thugs. He'd abducted Cosima for reasons known only to him, and since then, he and the gang had been sniffing around our outfit.

It was hard not to agree with Tore. Some men deserved more than death, and Seamus Moore was one such person.

"Soft heart," I reminded him. "A powerful man's downfall."

His thick brow arched, cutting thick creases into his broad forehead. "And you, *figlio mio*, are a hardened criminal with no soul, *si?*"

I didn't bother to shoot the old coot a look. We both knew well enough that I had one weakness, and it was exactly that. The precious few chinks in my armor were made by the love I held for him, for my brother, and his wife, my best friend, Cosima.

I'd do anything for them. *Had* done anything for them.

Without question, without qualm.

This was what family meant to Italians.

Mafia or civilian, we protected our own at all costs.

Which was why I was on trial for murder when I had nothing to do with the murder of di Carlo and his thug.

"Yara won't let you down," Tore mused.

It was unusual for Italians to fraternize with outsiders, even taking their bigotry as far as sticking to one region of the country, but Tore was different. I was different. Thus, our *borgata* was different. The Salvatore's dealt with all manner of nationalities and genders. So while the other arseholes in the Commission might ridicule me for having a non-Italian female lawyer, I didn't give a fuck. In my experience, diversity was modern and just good business sense. Criminality and brotherhood didn't just run through Latin blood. It was color blind and sexless.

"She's not got the blood, but Persians understand family perhaps just as well," Tore continued before finishing off his wine with a pleased hum.

74

"They do," I agreed, sudden agitation coursing through me like lactic acid after a hard workout.

I stood abruptly and went to the stone balustrade, leaning against the cold barrier with my wineglass clasped loosely between my hands over the ledge. The light from the street shone up through the Chianti, illuminating it to a rich, carmine glow that brought the image of Elena Lombardi unbidden into my mind's eye.

She was...unexpected.

Nothing like *mia sorella di scelta*, Cosima. She had none of her boldness or unstudied sensuality. She was not a natural flirt or a warm, radiant energy in a room.

She was, in essence, an ice queen.

Not only because she was coldly analytical, almost brittle with latent hostility, with a cutting wit that slashed her opponent like the dangerous edge of an icicle.

It was because she seemed encased in ice, fossilized like some ancient creature at the time of their death. Only Elena's death was an emotional one.

I knew all about Daniel Sinclair's affair with Giselle because Cosima spoke openly with me about everything. I knew about Elena's shame and despair, and I could even understand it to a point.

Once, I'd fancied myself in love with Cosima. Truthfully, any red-blooded man would fancy themselves in love with her at some point, maybe even from just looking at her exquisite face across a room.

It wasn't her looks that did it for me.

Beauty was easy. I was a handsome man, a powerful one with money to boot. I could have fourteen gorgeous women in my apartment within the hour if I so desired.

Beauty was boring.

What interested me about women, about Cosima back in the day, was the intricacy of the structure beneath the façade. She was made of steel rods and titanium beams with a mind like a three-dimensional chess set.

A lifetime of deceit, duplicity, and tragedy coupled with a degree from Cambridge in psychology had given me finely honed X-ray vision. It was easy enough to see beneath the skin of a person to the bones of what made them unique.

Elena was not such an easy study.

She was elegant from the column of her swan-like neck to the tips of her high-heeled shoes, but there was also an odd nervousness in her manner, an alertness to those around her that spoke of her desire to adapt and conform, to please everyone at any cost.

In my experience, insecurity like that was corrosive, and given what I knew from Cosima about Elena's past actions and mistakes, it didn't surprise me she was known as a bitch.

I didn't mind working with a bitch.

In my humble opinion, they were underrated.

Cutthroat, whip smart, and ruthless were all characteristics anyone in the underworld needed not only to thrive but also to survive.

And I had no doubt after all the stories from Cosima, but more, after seeing that haunted look in her eye when I'd asked her about sacrifice only hours earlier that Elena Lombardi was a survivor.

"You have that look on your face," Tore noted as he joined me at the ledge.

"Mmm?"

"The look of a man figuring out a puzzle," he surmised. "More specifically, the look of a man trying to figure out a Lombardi woman."

My lips twisted wryly. "You'd know all about that."

"I am an expert," he agreed easily with that quintessential Italian gesture, a shrug so small it was almost a tic. "I hope this time it is not my daughter who has caught your eye."

"Contrary to popular belief," I drawled, "I do not have a death wish. If Alexander believed my love for his wife was anything but platonic, I'd be dead already."

Tore's laugh was full of praise for a man who'd once campaigned to murder him. If he could understand anything, it was possessiveness, and Alexander's totalitarian ownership of Cosima pleased him because it meant she would always be safe in his company.

As a man with many enemies, this was reason enough to approve of a son-in-law.

"So, Elena," Tore said, turning his back to the stone wall to rest his elbows on it, his dark gaze fixed to my face. "She intrigues you."

"The way one villain might intrigue another," I allowed.

"Cosima thought she was doing me a favor in making Elena swear to take on my case, but I have this portentous impression she will do more harm than good."

"Cosima says she is a very good lawyer, no?"

I inclined my head. "A good lawyer in general is not good enough for me. I don't need a prudish, judgmental woman caught up in Family affairs."

"No," Tore agreed. "Get Frankie to dig up what he can on her."

I was already shaking my head. "She'll be as clean as a fucking whistle. No, she will be a consummate professional, I'm sure, hardworking and loyal."

"Then I do not see the problem."

"No," I agreed uneasily, staring down at the illuminated wine; the very same glossy shade of deep red echoed in Elena's unusual hair. "But you see, I am *not* a professional, and there is something about all that studied perfection that makes me eager to break her."

Tore's grin was a slicing movement across his broad face. He clapped a hand on my shoulder and chuckled darkly. "You are facing prison, Dante. I say, have fun with the girl. Hell, make her cry, get her to quit, whatever you want. Just don't let it get back to Cosima, or she'll castrate you herself."

I smiled mirthlessly at the truth of his words, but I couldn't quell the feeling like shaken soda overflowing inside my chest cavity. The feeling that was all itch and acid and not at all pleasant that had something to do with Elena Lombardi.

My fucking lawyer.

Tore had been right before. It was the way I felt when normally faced with a seemingly impossible situation and problem. The urge to break apart the pieces and glue them back together in a way that worked for me was nearly impossible to resist.

And at my heart, I was a hedonist.

So, I admit, I didn't try that hard to resist.

"*Bene,*" I agreed suddenly, clapping my hands before I rubbed them together in anticipation. "I have little time left as a free man, so I better make good use of it. Are you coming?"

Tore's mouth twisted wryly. "I thought the time when you needed hand holding to seduce a woman had passed."

I snorted. "I was talking about going to the hanger to visit the first of our problems, *vecchio.* I just came from her house, Tore. I'm not some eager young *stronzo.* I don't want to fuck her. She doesn't look like she could even take my cock, let alone enjoy it. I just want to fuck with her. I have a feeling she'll be a challenge, and I haven't had one of those in a while."

"Not since Cosima," Tore noted with faux nonchalance, but he was a cunning old man, and there was a glimmer of intrigue in the golden eyes he'd passed on to his daughter.

I didn't respond because I wasn't thinking about golden eyes.

I was thinking about a pair of steel ones as hard as armor and wondering just what kind of instrument I'd need to break that metal barrier in two.

CHAPTER SIX
DANTE

Mason Matlock was strung up with rope from the ceiling of the airplane hangar we kept out near Newark Liberty Airport in New Jersey. He'd been there for a very long time, left to hang like a butchered cow being drained of blood. Mason too was being bled out, slowly and carefully by a thousand cuts from the blade of my right-hand man, Frankie.

I stepped through the cool pool of congealing blood as I crossed the asphalt to stop before Mason's slumped head. His clothes hung off him in ribbons, some fabric saturated in warm blood, other pieces dried to his skin from past injuries. He was a beautiful tapestry of what could happen to a man if he fucked with the Camorra.

If he fucked with me or mine.

My leather-gloved hand snapped out to smash against Mason's

cheek, slapping him so hard he woke from his semi-comatose state. His head jerked back as a groan exploded from his pale lips.

"Wakey, wakey, *brutto figlio di puttana bastardo*," I said with a sinister smile as he fixed those bloodshot eyes on me, his pupils dilated with pure terror. "You ready to talk to me yet?"

I'd learned early on that the two most powerful motivators in this life were fear and love. I'd grown especially talented at manipulating both in my enemies, even using one to heighten the other if necessary. Mason Matlock was a spineless *stronzo* who had nearly gotten Cosima killed because of his capitulation to his uncle Giuseppe di Carlo's desires, but he had no fear of bodily harm. This wasn't unusual. Most men who grew up in the mafia were inured to violence.

I wasn't deterred.

If physical pain didn't break him, perhaps emotional brutality would.

So, when Mason muttered something in the negative, I was ready.

When I snapped my fingers, Jacopo stepped forward to hand me a phone with a video already presented on the screen. I grabbed Mason by the chin and forced him to look at it.

"This is your sweet sister, Violetta, isn't it?" I purred as I forced him to watch the footage of his younger sister gagged and tied to a chair, struggling to avoid the hands of my man, Adriano, as he ran a knife gently down her cheek. She jerked, and the metal cut into her flesh, blood beading like a string of ruby across her jaw.

"You motherfucker," Mason barked, finding the energy to spit at me. I wiped it off my cheek with a flick of my fingers. "You fucking motherfucker! She has nothing to do with this."

"She does, actually," I argued. "She's the niece of Giuseppe di Carlo, the same man who tried to fuck with Cosima and therefore, who tried to fuck with me. You di Carlos have been so far up my arse lately trying to fuck up my deal with the Basante cartel that I figured I should return the favor." I paused and studied the video with him. "Violetta does have a fine arse."

Mason thrashed against the coarse ropes even though they dug into his shoulders and back. The movement opened old wounds, causing his skin to weep red tears.

I studied him without emotion. A psychologist might have called it dissociative behavior. They might have blamed it on one of three popular schools of criminal theory like the Chicago School or strain theory that postulated my tendencies were rooted in poverty, lack of education, or cultural pressures. But I was a Cambridge graduate in psychology, the son of one of the wealthiest peerages in the United Kingdom.

They might have explained it away by using subculture theory—that I was a privileged white boy acting out against societal mores.

They would all be wrong.

It was simple.

I was the son of an evil man.

There was a difference between a bad man and an evil one.

A bad man was corrupted by the influence of his upbringing or surroundings, by the people he associated with, and perhaps by the choices of other people in a position of power over him.

An evil man, a man like my father, Noel, was born a different kind of being than most others. A man whose natural expression was violence and whose moral compass wasn't so much broken as never formed at all. A man who thought and felt only of himself and his need to sin.

Noel Davenport might have been a duke of the fucking realm, but he was a criminal, a murdering sociopath of the highest order.

As his son, was it any wonder I'd drifted into crime myself?

Of course, it was Noel who drove me out of the British moors I'd grown up in, from the well-heeled society of my fellow Oxbridge graduates and peers to the dark, shifting dens of immorality in Italy's southern mafia stronghold.

But it was easy for any man to blame his choices on someone else.

Yes, Noel drove me from England and my birthright as a wealthy, ennui-laced aristocrat. But I made the choice to hitch my cart to my "uncle" Amadeo Salvatore's criminal enterprise.

Honestly, I loved life. I love the pleasures to be had in it. The sex, the food, the bloody good wines, and all those highs were only amplified by the edge of danger and fear that my existence in the underworld lent to my life. I lived every day like it was my fucking last, and I'd learned that from my mother.

Chiara Davenport, the Italian beauty who'd been seduced by Noel into moving from Italy to the cold, wet lands of England where he neglected her, abused her, and then, ultimately, murdered her. There.

My entire history summarized neatly. I was a thirty-five-year-old man with a degree in psychology and a job that relied wholly on my ability to perceive others. I knew who I was, what I wanted, and how I was going to get it.

But as I stared at Mason struggling, as if that would free his sister, I had a flash of misgiving as the high, smooth contralto voice of a certain ice queen lawyer infiltrated my thoughts.

You might have no problem beating a man or threatening his family if he goes against you, but I've been the daughter of that man, and I've been that child who was threatened.

I growled at that voice and banished it to the farthest reaches of my mind. I didn't need Elena Lombardi's judgmental voice in my head urging me to fuck up this situation even further. It was my last night of freedom before being tethered to my fucking apartment, and I needed Mason Matlock to break like cheap plastic.

"Feel like telling me what I want to know?" I asked Mason in a hard rumble. "Or should I tell Adriano to use that knife on the softest places a woman has?"

Mason swore savagely at me in English, so far removed from his ancestry that he didn't realize Italian curses were far superior. "You wouldn't dare."

I raised a brow at him, then coiled quickly to land an exact punch to his left kidney. His breath exploded from his lips, bloody spittle flying over my black shirt.

"There isn't much I wouldn't dare to do," I told him somberly as he coughed and fought to breathe through the pain. "And, Mason, any man of honor would do all that was in his power to save the life of an innocent loved one, *si?*"

"Yes," he hissed, glaring at me from under his sweaty hair.

I nodded. "Yes, which is why I must do this to you and yours. Cosima was in a coma because of your actions. And actions have consequences. This is yours, and if you don't tell me what the *fuck* the di Carlos have planned for me, this will be sweet Violetta's too."

Mason slumped against the ropes and loosed a thready sigh. "I don't know much."

"*Boh*, why don't you let me be the judge of that?" I suggested mildly. Walking over to where Frankie and Jaco sat, I dragged one of the extra metal chairs across the concrete with an ear-splitting screech so I could sit in front of Mason. I pulled my gun from its holster under my arm and held it loosely between my knees as I braced my forearms on my thighs to smile up at Mason's bloody face. "Let's start with the names of the men who shot out Ottavio's, hmm?"

He balked, his eyes trained on the heavy gun in my hand. "I only know the name of one."

I inclined my head magnanimously. "That will do, for now."

"Carter Andretti," he confessed on a breath. "I went to school with him."

"How quaint," I mocked as I flicked a finger at Jaco, who nodded immediately and stalked off, already dialing a number on his phone.

I didn't need to tell him to find Carter and kill him horribly, but only after he confessed who his other associates in the car had been.

The men who shot at Cosima would die in the most creative ways I knew how to dole out death.

I leaned forward and bared my teeth at the man who would, no doubt, die soon. It wouldn't be by my hands, if I could help it. As Elena had said, I was poetic about crime, and it was considerably more elegiac if Mason was murdered by his own blood.

"Now," I coaxed as if he had a choice. "Tell me how your scum family knew where we were meeting the Basante crew."

The Basante deal would mean an influx of untold millions into the Family coffers. They were one of the leading Colombian cartels with access to some of the highest-grade cocaine in the world. Our *borgata* had a diverse scope of interests, mostly illegal gambling, real estate schemes, and money laundering through the oil and gas trade. Drugs were messy and violent, but they paid out massive dividends. I'd been arguing with Tore and Frankie for years about staying out of it, but when Juan Basante himself approached me to cut a deal for distribution, I wasn't foolish enough to say no.

Only, the motherfucking di Carlos, the city's Costa Nostra outfit who were the biggest cocaine distributors in Europe and closing in on that distinction in North America, had taken umbrage with our move. They'd ambushed our first meeting thirteen months ago, and I'd gotten shot in the side as a souvenir.

Mason was the nephew of Giuseppe, the man who'd lured Cosima into his web, and the only witness to the drive-by shooting at Ottavio's deli that left her in a coma. He had also been very poorly guarded by his so-called family, just a single bodyguard who'd followed him about his life on Wall Street like a suited shadow. It had been all too easy to abduct him before the police could remand him into protective custody.

Mason winced. "Seriously, man, I don't know who told them about it."

"But you know someone did," I surmised.

He hesitated, absently licking up a dribble of blood leaking from the corner of his mouth. "Maybe."

I sighed heavily and called for Jaco. "Call Adriano and tell him to have at the girl."

"No!" Mason yelled, then whimpered at the pain it caused in his potentially broken ribs. "Fuck."

I narrowed my gaze at him as I gestured with my matte black Glock G19. "You claimed to love Cosima, yet you put her in danger. Now you claim to love your sister, yet you will allow me to have Adriano hurt her?"

"They'll kill me," he whispered brokenly. "It's all fine and fucking dandy when you're talking in hypotheticals, but actually knowingly exchanging your life for someone else's is another story."

"This is true," I agreed, knowing perhaps better than anyone what it was like to give up your life and everything you'd known. I'd done it in my early twenties, exchanged polo sticks for handguns and clean money for dirty. Tore had done it nearly five years ago when he'd pretended to be dead and changed his name to help Cosima and to lure out the villain who had killed my mother.

Death was nothing.

Sacrifice, that was the real killer.

And it seemed Mason was unwilling to die like that.

"You worry about the di Carlos killing you? When they have been in shambles since Giuseppe's death? When I have you here in front of me and the sight of your *cazzo di merda* face makes me want to drill a bullet through your skull? I think you have more pressing concerns," I said as I stood and trained my gun at his head. "You have five seconds to tell me what I want to hear, or I'll kill you."

It wasn't a threat.

A threat implied probability, a chance either way.

No, my words were a promise.

It was early in the morning, dawn a pale thought starting on the horizon. I was about to be chained to my house because of a murder I didn't commit, and I was fucking tired of this shit. I was tired of feeling like the di Carlos had something on my Family, something important that when pulled, would explode my operation like a hand grenade to the belly.

Mason's lips quivered as he stared at the ground, and seconds later, wet seeped through his tattered pants, the sharp scent of urine perfuming the air.

Oh, good, he knew I was serious.

I grinned at him in a way that was more of a grimace and cocked my gun.

He sucked in a deep breath and shuddered before whispering, "They...They have a mole in your outfit. Apparently, he's been working for them for a little over a year."

A shot rang out, echoing in the cavernous hangar. Mason screamed, but the bullet only skimmed past his right ear, barely nicking the flesh.

The vibration of the shot rang through my head, loud and buzzing.

A mole.

A fucking goddamn traitor.

Traditore. Piagnone.

Rage scoured through me, ripping up the inside of my chest like talons.

A *borgata* was a hierarchical organization, in most ways and in most families more like a company than an organic community. But it was also family.

Especially for me.

The pathetic little lost boy whose mother had been killed by his own father, whose own brother didn't believe him when he'd cried wolf, who'd been stranded in a country that wasn't his own.

Italy had embraced me the way darkness consumed sight, swallowing me up intractably in her shadows. Tore became my father, his *Soldati* my brothers and cousins and uncles.

To find out now that one of them had gone against a bond that was meant to mean more than blood set my soul on fucking fire.

I'd end them.

Not just because they were a threat to my business, to my freedom, and my family, because a man who turned against those who had protected him, hand-fed him success, wealth, and love, deserved to be run through with the cold blade of my fury.

In the mafia, sometimes the only honor to be found was in revenge.

And I was going to make sure whoever the damn mole was would pay with every drop of his blood.

CHAPTER SEVEN

elena

When I was little, my mother told me something that unexpectedly etched itself in my soul and became both a burden and an instinct I bore for the rest of my life.

She said to me, "Elena, *lottatrice mia*, you are just a girl in a very large world that owes you nothing. Not one thing in your life will come easy. This is the way of girlhood in Napoli. I wish it was not so. I wish I could have given you a better start, but understand, every woman must be a fighter, Elena, because history has tricked men into thinking women are less." Caprice gripped my face in her hands so tightly, I remember thinking she might pop my head like a crushed watermelon. "This is what you must understand, Elena. They are *wrong*. Women bear the trials of their men, the delivery of their babies, the weight of their families. Women are extraordinarily strong. So, you must trick the men into giving you power. Do not tell them you are strong, and do not fight them with words because words can be undone. Fight the injustice with action, *lottatrice mia*, because action can be understood in any language, by any man."

A young girl in Italy was not typically encouraged to pursue "male" careers like lawyers, doctors, or policemen. A woman I grew up with became a mafia prosecutor, one of the most dangerous professions in the country, and when she was killed by a car bomb on the way to work one morning, the community said it was sad but avoidable... if she had stayed home and had children like the rest of them, she would have been safe.

I didn't want to be safe. I wanted to be brave and bold in the only arena I'd ever felt capable in—my job.

So even though I was only a fourth-year associate at Fields, Harding & Griffith, I already had a reputation in the office as a ruthless fighter. I went to bat for my clients with a single-minded ferocity that shocked most people because outside of the courtroom, I was polished, prim, and ultra-feminine. I was only given relatively low-profile and pro bono cases the more senior associates and partners didn't want, but no cases were too little to give my all to.

Perhaps because I hadn't known much kindness or luck in my life, I appreciated all too much how poignant small acts of service and valor could be.

Sometimes, unfortunately, the silk blouses, high heels, and red-painted lips and fingertips confused my male co-workers into thinking they could condescend to me.

"So, Lombardi, you got saddled with the Salvatore case," Ethan

Topp said as he leaned against the glass wall of the conference room where I was working.

I didn't look up from my research on historical mafia trials in the southern New York District to spare him a glance as I said, "Saddled with the same case you practically begged Yara to work on?"

There was a brief silence then, from my periphery, I saw as Ethan pushed off the wall and leaned over the glossy black table, attempting to use his size and masculinity to cow me.

"You know, you can be a real bitch," he sneered.

I swallowed the weary sigh that swelled in my throat. This wasn't the first time Ethan had come at me. He was the son of a well-established lawyer at the firm who didn't understand why nepotism couldn't make up for his lazy work ethic.

"I'm wearing heels bigger than your dick, so if this is a pissing contest, I think it's safe to say I win," I said lightly, finally looking up to deliver Ethan a mega-watt smile I'd learned from Cosima.

"You fucking--"

"Ms. Lombardi," Yara's silken tones sounded from the door, and Ethan swiveled almost comically to face her. "I take it you're well briefed now on the specifics of the case?"

Ethan gaped as I nodded. "Yes, I've already filed for a speedy trial as you asked, and I have some ideas of how we can approach pre-trial motions."

"Excellent." The elegant older woman nodded at me, which was as good as a hug coming from her before she turned to finally lift an eyebrow at Ethan. "Mr. Topp, while Elena has accomplished all of this, have you only succeeded in trying to distract her, or have you completed any of your own work?"

Ethan flushed as bright as his copper-toned hair, muttered something about being busy under his breath, then excused himself, practically running out of the room past Yara.

When he was gone, Yara smiled slightly at me. "It takes a certain woman to wear shoes like that, Ms. Lombardi." She shifted her weight to one heel to showcase her own towering high heels, velvet black Jimmy Choo Anouk pumps.

A startled laugh worked itself out of my throat, falling past my lips.

I couldn't help but beam at her as I sat back in my chair. "I agree."

It was no small thing to discover an ally, especially a powerful one in a top NYC law firm. Associates were treated as lowly factory workers by most of the partners who strutted through the halls like capricious dictators, and lawyers were often encouraged to pit themselves against each other. It was like high school on steroids with bullying, comparisons, and associates crying in the bathroom stalls a daily occurrence.

It was nothing compared to my upbringing in Naples, so it didn't faze me, but I could recognize that Yara had just extended her protection. By the end of the workday, every other associate on our floor would know about the subtle put-down she'd handed to Ethan and the validation she'd gifted me.

I felt high on the moment, which was why I didn't notice the saccharine set of Yara's smile. It was only when she closed the door to the conference room and stepped forward to curl her hands over the back of the chair across from me that a little thrill of premonition worked up my spine.

"I understand you have a working relationship with USA O'Malley," she said casually, even though the moment she spoke the words, I knew there was nothing casual about where she was leading me.

I blinked at her. "I wouldn't go that far, but we have a passing acquaintance."

Which was an understatement.

Yes, I'd first met Dennis in the hall at the Pearl Street Courthouse two years ago, but the USA had known about me my entire life.

This was because, against all odds, he was my criminal father's best friend growing up on the streets of Brooklyn.

I could still recall the look of utter shock on his face as he'd automatically reached out to steady me when we bumped shoulders in the crowded hall and the way his mouth had formed around my name, more breath than sound.

Elena Moore.

That wasn't my name, and it hadn't been in years. Not since Seamus disappeared shortly after Cosima left to work in Milan at the age of eighteen. Every one of us—except for Giselle, for reasons unknown to me—had decided to take our mother's name because our mother had always been our only real parent.

But it was chilling that he had known my birth name. He'd seemed even more surprised when I'd jerked out of his hold and turned the other way to walk down the hall without confirming my identity. In the two years since, he'd reached out through the office, explaining that he was "old friends" with Seamus and would love to connect with me.

I never called him back.

It didn't do much to deter him, though. He was a lawyer and a winning one at that; my refusal only heightened his excitement and turned the chase into some kind of game for him.

But my only recourse was to ignore him, so I did.

"Well, when we spoke earlier about discovery, he gave me the impression you were acquainted." Yara's gaze was assessing as her eyes swept over my carefully curled shoulder-length hair, the high collar of my intricate lace blouse, and the precisely filled-in color of my blood-red pout. "You recently broke up with your partner, if I'm not mistaken?"

Of course, she wasn't mistaken. Yara knew everything that happened in the firm, and Daniel leaving me for my sister had been water cooler gossip for weeks.

Still, I inclined my head as I smiled thinly in response.

She paused, seemingly thinking through something I knew she had already decided. "Well, as Mr. O'Malley seems to have a… curiosity around you, I think it would be appropriate if you were the one to deliver our motion to suppress personally."

I blinked at her then dared to speak my mind. "In the hopes my feminine wiles might soften him?"

Yara's mouth tightened with something like a smile. "I believe a personal touch is always best. Leave after lunch and then swing by Mr. Salvatore's apartment to make sure his tracking bracelet has been properly set up."

It was menial work, something one of the paralegals could have handled, but I had a feeling Dante Salvatore was a high-maintenance client, so I didn't complain. My involvement in such a high-profile case could mean the difference in reducing the finish line at partnership in the firm from ten years to three years. I'd have the edge against my peers for in-house competition for cases, and it would make the name Elena Lombardi well-known in the criminal law circuits.

So, I nodded at Yara and began to collect my papers to stow at my desk in the associate bullpen without another word.

The office building of the US Attorney for the Southern District of New York was an old concrete building, weathered and outdated compared to the towering chrome and glass skyscraper that housed three floors of Fields, Harding & Griffith. The lawyers within typically didn't wear three-thousand-dollar shoes and bespoke suits like my fellow associates, but they weren't driven by monetary success the way us sinners uptown were. They were the heroes of the legal profession, taking little gains while making moves against big bads who needed taking down.

A little corner of my heart yearned to be included in their echelons, to be the good guy and the hero bringing down the tyrants and bullies.

Instead, I'd sided with the wicked and the unlawful by defending behemoth companies and individuals using their wealth and prestige to mask their own villainy.

Prestige and power.

In some ways, I was no better than Dante Salvatore and his lot.

I told myself my pro bono work helped to balance the scale. That I volunteered at the Bronx YMCA every month and donated ten percent of my monthly paycheck to a childhood domestic abuse charity.

But in my heart, I knew the truth.

I was the child of a sinner, and sin was in my blood.

I was too proud to go unnoticed in my profession, too greedy to accept pennies, too envious to be content with what I had at any given time, and too aroused by power to let it slide through my fingers.

The romantic idealist and the calculated ice queen, the two sides of my personality that often flipped like a coin whenever I was faced with a new path in life. It seemed the latter won much more than the former.

I wanted to be the kind of a woman who was called a hero, but I'd spent most of my life being called a villain.

If enough people treat you like a villain, you become one.

So when I was ushered into USA O'Malley's office by his harried assistant, I set my face into its icy mask and prepared to protect the rights of my criminal client even though it unsettled my heart to do so.

"Ms. Lombardi for you."

I stepped out from behind the secretary as I was announced and stopped in the middle of the large antiquated room with the peeling plaster, my hands clasped at my front over the handles of my Prada purse.

"Good afternoon, Mr. O'Malley," I greeted coolly.

He barely spared me a glance before addressing his assistant, "Thank you, Mrs. Nanquil. That will be all for now."

I tried not to bristle at his negligence as she closed the door behind her, and Dennis went back to his task on the computer. Indignation soured the back of my tongue, but I refused to beg for attention so I only stood there demurely as he finished his work.

Once done, he leaned back in his chair with a sigh, tossed off his thick black-rimmed glasses, and folded his arms over his chest. He was a good-looking older man, one who, under other circumstances, I probably would have found attractive. As it was, I found his posturing incredibly annoying.

His eyes fell down my body once before locking on my own. "Elena."

"Ms. Lombardi, if you please," I corrected as I finally moved forward to collect the papers from my bag and lay them on his desk. "Ms. Ghorbani asked me to deliver these personally. As you may know by now, we have filed for a speedy trial, and we are moving for a pre-trial notion to exclude the testimony of Mason Matlock given after the shooting. As you know, he is related to the deceased Giuseppe di Carlo and had reason to lie for the Family. His statement was taken without a lawyer present at the scene of a violent crime where trauma could have clouded his thinking. As he is now nowhere to be found, we cannot corroborate his words or cross-examine them."

His thin mouth flattened. "Not one for pleasantries? You certainly don't get that from your father."

"Hopefully, I didn't get anything from him," I agreed easily even though my belly clenched against a surge of acid.

Any comparison to Seamus Moore was an insult.

Dennis studied me with narrowed eyes, ignoring the documents I'd laid out. "You look exactly like him. Though, I must say, a far sight easier on the eyes."

I pursed my lips around the sour lemon taste of his words. "Well, if that's all, USA, I'll leave you to the rest of your business."

When I turned on my heel to leave, he chuckled lightly. "Sit down, Elena. I promise to behave professionally. Can you blame a man for being intrigued when he sees a ghost from his childhood?"

I ignored him, continuing on toward the door. It wouldn't jeopardize the case, and I was tired of men and their games. I felt as if I'd been a pawn in them all my life, first with Seamus then with Daniel and now Dante. I had enough to deal with. I didn't need Dennis assuming control of any aspect of my life, even if it was only for a ten-minute meeting.

"Please, forgive me," he called out as I wrapped my hand around the doorknob. "I would like to know Ms. Lombardi, the lawyer. Only a fourth-year associate, but it seems you've already made quite the name for yourself in criminal court."

I hesitated. His thread hooked through the eyelet of my pride stuck into the pincushion of my heart.

"Assistant US Attorney Jerome Hansen almost refused to take the Arnold Becker case when he found out you were representing him," he continued, laying into the flattery.

Unfortunately, it worked.

I spun on my red-heeled shoe and arched a brow at him. "I have time to take a seat if you want to continue praising me."

Dennis laughed, his features even more pleasing crinkled in amusement. "Then sit, please. Tell me how you found out WDH had unfairly terminated him. Our private investigator wasn't able to figure that one out."

I leveled him with a coy glance. "That is between our company PI, Ricardo Stavos, and me."

He sighed, and even though I hadn't dated anyone but Daniel in years, I recognized the hint of flirtation there. "A woman with secrets."

"A woman with integrity," I corrected.

"Good to know the apple fell far from the tree." I pursed my lips at another comment about my father, but Dennis held his hands up in mock surrender. "You're really not curious to hear childhood misadventures about your father?"

"No. Nothing you say can humanize a man I know to be a monster."

He seemed shocked by my bluntness. "He was always a bit of a rascal... but I didn't know he'd gone down such a dark path."

"Don't be surprised if you're making a case against him one day if he ever ends up back Stateside." I'd had nightmares about such a thing happening and thanked my lucky stars I'd had the presence to take Mama's name years ago so that I wouldn't be linked to him. "And for the record, I would prefer people not know I was related to him."

"Of course." Dennis gave me a calculating look. "Look, I'll get straight to the point so we can move on to better topics of conversation. If your client is willing to turn on any of the other families, we can offer a tempting plea deal. Reduced sentence time in a mid-level penitentiary."

Without my permission, a little laugh escaped me. The idea of a man like Dante Salvatore, so assured of his own magnificence and the sanctity of his criminal brotherhood, would no sooner turn on his own mother than on another capo.

I didn't have to voice that for Dennis to read my refusal.

"You're obligated to take it to your client," he reminded me somewhat insultingly. "It could mean the difference in dying behind bars and getting out before he's an old man."

"This isn't the first time you've offered," I said. Even though I wasn't certain, I had no doubt he'd relayed the same thing to Yara before the indictment. "It probably won't be the last. You don't care about one man. You want the entire operation."

He smiled charmingly. "What man wouldn't?"

"Careers are made on these cases," I agreed, but there was an edge to my voice.

It could have been competition, my desire to beat anyone in court because I was possessive of that arena. But a tiny voice told me it could have been a misplaced sense of loyalty too. Even though Dante was a criminal, a man who deserved to go to prison, I suddenly found myself incapable of wishing him inside a cage for the rest of his life, even if I wasn't on this case.

He was too...vital to contain. For the same reason I avoided going to the zoo, I wanted to avoid the sight of Dante trapped in a steel box.

"Or broken," Dennis added, and I knew he'd read my tone correctly.

One of us would win, and one of us would lose.

Dennis needed the win to fill the sails of his political campaign.

I needed the win so I could get out from under the shadow of my family, their accomplishments and pitfalls, and stand strong in the limelight as my own person.

It would come down to who was the more desperate of the two, I knew, because it always did. I'd grown up in Naples where children fought with their fists in the sandbox because they'd seen their own parents do it in the streets, so I knew all about winning at any cost.

But I didn't underestimate Dennis O'Malley just because he lived a life of privilege now. If he was anything like my father, whom he grew up with, he'd started poor and hungry.

It took more than a couple of decades to satisfy the insatiable appetite such an upbringing instilled in you.

"May the best person win," I offered with a tight smile as I stood and offered my hand in farewell.

Dennis stood to take it, his hand smooth and callous free around my own, his eyes an inch below mine where I stood in my towering heels. He was not cowed.

"To the winner, the spoils," he agreed as his thumb stroked over my palm. "To the winner, the spoils."

CHAPTER EIGHT

elena

ante lived on Central Park East in a penthouse suite that covered two floors overlooking the greenery of the multi-block park. It was an older stone building with gargoyles carved into the layered balconies of the top floors. I was surprised by its elegance and old-school charm. Dante struck me as a glass and chrome, modern kind of macho man in his design sense. Still, I recognized the cost of a space like that in the city and was awed again by the fact that mafia families operated like Fortune 500 companies, accruing so much untold wealth that reporters could only speculate at the dividends of their schemes.

There was a private elevator to his floor, and the man who let me up was as Italian as they came, thick neck, broad shoulders, short in the way of southerners with wiry black hair.

"*Ciao*," he'd greeted me with a robust yell that startled me. "You are here to see Mr. Dante, *si*?"

"Mr. Salvatore, yes," I allowed, offering a polite approximation of a smile as I followed him into the elevator, clutching my bag to my front as if it could shield me from his Italianisms.

As if such things were contagious and I was in danger of catching it.

He grinned a gap-toothed smile at me. "Shoulda known Mr. Dante'd have a good-looking *ragazza* to represent him."

I didn't know how to respond to that, so I just rolled my lips between my teeth and kept my feminist retort on the back of my tongue.

"Busy day?" he continued in the same friendly vein as if we were good buddies. "Got all three floors moving out and in today."

"Excuse me?" I asked, my interest piqued as the elevator began its smooth glide up the tower.

"Mr. Dante bought out the two floors beneath his," he said, frowning at me like I was stupid. "Man's gotta have his family close to him if he's stuck here. Loneliness does terrible things to the human spirit."

I raised my brows at him incredulously. So, within the space of forty-eight hours, Dante had bought out the top three floors of a luxury apartment building in order to have his associates nearby.

Oh, but in its own way, it was a genius move.

He wasn't allowed to leave the apartment building, but within the structure, he had free rein to use the amenities and no one would flag him for visiting other apartments. It was a clever way to slip past the requirement that no known criminal associates could visit him while on house arrest. If they already lived in the building, it made it that much easier to meet and collude.

Oh, yes, Dante was clever.

And powerful, evidently, if he could bribe or coerce people to leave their homes on such short notice.

The lobby man, who was beginning to remind me of some kind of Italian leprechaun with his jaunty grin, short, stocky body, and oddly jovial wisdom, flashed me another smile as he touched the side of his nose.

"Name's Bruno," he introduced, sticking out a plump, hairy-backed hand to shake mine. "I know all the goings-on in this building. Mr. Dante's eyes and ears, if you will."

"You could be deposed by the prosecution," I warned him. "I hope you're not so free with information with them as you have been with me."

Instantly his small eyes folded into heavy creases cast by his frown. "I'd die before I turned traitor."

"Because he's your boss," I surmised, testing him because I was curious about how Dante's soldati related to him. Was he a tyrant, an angry heathen like I wanted to believe?

"'Cause he's the kinda man'd take the shirt off his own back for anyone," he asserted in a voice that was nearly a shout. He thumped his fist over his heart and glared at me. "Even for the likes of me."

I didn't have a response to that, but luckily, the elevator pinged, and the doors slid open to reveal the reception area of Dante's apartment. Forgetting about Bruno, I stepped into the room, transfixed by the moody ambiance of his space.

Everything was black, gray, or glass.

The round walls of the foyer were a charcoal plaster, Italianate and modern at the same time. A huge circular skylight cut into the ceiling spilled pale autumnal light onto the towering olive tree at the center of the small room. It perfumed the air with its green, rich aroma even though there was no fruit on its boughs. The fragrance instantly took me back to Naples, the trees in our neighbor Francesca Moretti's yard, and the feel of the fruit bursting beneath my bare feet as I chased my siblings through the trees during the summer.

I blinked away the memories and the accompanying ache in my chest as I noticed the music swelling through the apartment through surround speakers.

Dean Martin was crooning about an evening in Roma, but that wasn't what had me creeping forward to peer into what I assumed was the living room.

It was the swelling, robust sound of a vaguely familiar voice singing along to the music.

When I turned the corner, the open living and kitchen space sprawled before me, everything the same black, gray, and glass theme of the foyer, starkly masculine yet also comfortable. Dante himself was in the huge kitchen at the black marble island singing as he rolled gnocchi by hand.

I blinked.

Others in the room had paused what they were doing when

they took notice of me, but my eyes were trained on the singing mafioso making delicate pasta with his man murdering hands.

I blinked again, at a loss for words.

Someone must have alerted him to my presence because Dante looked up from his work to lock eyes with me and a slow, liquid smile spilled across his face.

Something in my belly fluttered.

I cleared my throat, squared my shoulders, and moved through the living room toward the kitchen. "Well, if you're trying to be a cliché, you're certainly succeeding."

Dante laughed, the sound just as musical as his prior singing. "Ah, Elena, I'm beginning to enjoy your wit."

"Don't get used to it," I cautioned dryly as I placed my bag on one of the stools at the island and rounded it to check out his anklet. "Ah, I see they set you up."

He presented his left leg, lifting the fabric of the worn jeans molded to his thick thigh to show me the device. "Pinched the hell out of my leg hair, the *bastardo*, but he got it done in ten minutes. I was surprised."

"It doesn't take long," I agreed. "If you could just show me the system, I'll be on my way."

"You should stay for the party," Dante decided, wiping his flour-coated hands on a dish towel before he crossed his arms, the muscles bulging dangerously beneath his tight black tee. He leaned a hip against the island and considered me. "You could use the fun, I think."

"You don't know me well enough to know what I could use," I countered idly as I moved to the monitoring system I noticed set up on a sleek desk in one corner of the kitchen. "And honestly, it's the first day of your house arrest. The probation office is probably surveilling the building. There is no way they will let you host a party."

The smile he flashed me was all handsome arrogance. "It's already taken care of."

"You paid someone off," I surmised with pursed lips, channeling my lack of approval through my narrowed eyes.

It only seemed to amuse him further, the creases beside his dancing eyes deepening. "Sometimes, Elena, charm is enough."

I rolled my eyes at him before turning my back once more to actually check out the system they'd installed. It was a standard setup. The probation office would have a man set to monitor Dante's movements through the GPS device in the living room. If he strayed too far from the tracking beacon at the apartment, an alarm would alert the office and the police to his violation.

Violating the terms of his bond could mean as many as fifteen years in prison regardless of whether he was found guilty of his original crime.

"You are Italian, a Neapolitan, certainly you realize what day it is," he said, watching me as I looked over the system. "September nineteenth, the day of Saint Gennaro."

I rolled my eyes. "I don't celebrate the saint days."

He frowned at my flippancy. "You judge those who do? All of

Little Italy and the Italians who revere such things?"

"I didn't say I judged them," I argued, crossing my arms over my chest as I turned to face him, settling in for the argument I could feel coming.

"The eye roll says differently," he countered. "Now, I must demand you attend. When was the last time you conferred with your fellow Italians? America is a lonely place for an immigrant without community."

"I have a community," I said even though I wondered if my single close friendship with Beau counted toward that.

Dante just cocked an arrogant brow.

I bristled, trying not to let him tempt me into acting like my worse self. I'd been going to therapy once a week for the past year, and usually, I found myself capable of harnessing the dark heart of my temper and pride, but something about Dante lured my worst self out from hiding.

"Besides, you may be my client, but you aren't the boss of me," I informed him. "In fact, any relationship or interactions we might have outside of our professional relationship are incredibly inappropriate."

"The best things often are," he agreed solemnly, only his glittering obsidian eyes giving away his humor.

"I could lose my license."

He pursed his lips then waved a hand dismissively. "Only if someone reported you."

"A transgression is still that even if there is no one there to witness it," I snapped, my mind immediately fixating on Giselle and Daniel.

No one knew about their affair at first, but that didn't mean what they had done was anything short of abominable.

Dante's voice softened, his eyes too observant. "It is those in power who decide the rules, Elena. I don't feel I have to remind you of this, but I will. In this case, I am the one with the power..." He pushed off the counter and strode toward me on a strong, rippling gait that made my throat dry.

I backed up slightly only to bump into the desk, suddenly trapped by his large body as he bore down on me. My heart raced, leaping and bounding over the hurdles of fear, anxiety, and something like desire that cropped up in my chest.

When he raised his hand to collar my throat again, I flinched, baring my teeth at him, and flung off his grip.

His eyes went dark, all black, no definition between his pupil and iris, just twin black holes trying to suck me up. With deliberate slowness, he raised that meaty palm and gripped my neck again, squeezing tight for just long enough to feel my pulse flare against his thumb.

He leaned close, his voice a whispered hiss. "I am the one with the power here, Elena, not you. And I say, you will come to the party tonight."

"*Perché?*" I croaked to my horror, my voice tight and rough. In my panic at his proximity, my thoughts turned Italian, reverting to the identity I'd tried so long to stifle. One I associated with fear

114

and weakness.

"Because," he said, his tone rife with dark humor as he bent down to say the words an inch from my open, panting mouth. For a moment, I thought I could taste them, olive bright on my tongue. "I said so, and what the *capo* says goes."

"This isn't some psychopathic game of *Simone dice*," I seethed, leaning into his grip so I could sneer into his face. "I'm not one of your pliant Italian women who will do whatever a man wishes."

"No," he agreed, abruptly releasing his grip on my neck so that I stumbled forward on my high heels and fell into the hard expanse of his chest. Once there, he pinned me briefly with a hand on the small of my back, fingers spanning nearly from hip to hip. "But you will obey me, nonetheless. Not because you respect my authority, but because you won't do anything to risk your position. One call to Yara and she'd order you to do anything I asked."

No. He was right.

But why was he treating me like this?

I felt like taffy in his strong hands, constantly pulled and stretched as he tried to reform me into something I was not, something I would never be because it was something I abhorred.

"If it makes you feel any better, Yara will be here," Dante mentioned, turning away to walk back to the kitchen where he continued to prepare his gnocchi. "You might even recognize a few politicians and celebrities in attendance. You could use it as an excuse to rub elbows with some of the more powerful figures in the city."

When I only glared at him, wishing I had the power to kill someone with a single gaze, he sighed gustily as though I was some unruly child who wouldn't eat her dinner. "Despite what you may think, Elena, I truly want you to come to the party to have some fun. I know life has not been so easy for you. In my experience, we must make the most of opportunities we have to enjoy ourselves between the drama and the chaos."

It vexed me that he sounded exactly like my therapist, so I only pursed my lips and stalked forward to grab my purse. It occurred to me as I turned my back on Dante to leave that Dante's sunken living room had five people in it. The men all stared at me with varying degrees of amusement on their faces at having witnessed my altercation with their Don.

I kicked my chin into the air and glided past them with my eyes trained on the entry hall, refusing to be cowed by their humor or ashamed of Dante's bossy disregard.

It was only when I was pushing the button to call the elevator that Dante called out, "Oh, Elena? I ordered some of your mama's famous tiramisu. Bring it with you when you come back tonight. Eight o'clock sharp."

Giving in to a childish impulse I hadn't indulged in since I was a girl, I leaned around the wall hiding the entryway from sight of the kitchen and flashed Dante my middle finger.

Laughter erupted in the main room, and I stepped into the elevator with a smug, grim smile.

Little Italy transformed for eleven days every September from an urban mecca with faintly Italian leanings, some of Chinatown's ever-expanding influence popping up here and there, to something straight out of the Old World. Red, white, and green everywhere, from streamers to awnings and elaborate arches of balloons. Saint Gennaro himself stared at the tourists and locals gathered to celebrate him from posters, banners, and arches set up over the teeming streets. Over the course of eleven blocks for eleven days, there would be parades, floats, concerts, and so much food there was no possibility it would all be consumed.

Typically, I avoided Little Italy at that time of year even more staunchly than I usually did. It was impossible to skirt entirely because Mama's restaurant, *Osteria Lombardi,* was situated on the edge of Little Italy and SoHo, and for years, the family had congregated there for Sunday lunches. In the past year, Giselle and Daniel had given me those lunches, not daring to show their faces around me. Instead, they hosted the family at their mega-mansion apartment in Brooklyn every Sunday evening for drinks or dinner.

They'd invited me a few times, but I'd rather skin my own flesh than attend, and that was before they'd had baby Genevieve. Now, I never wanted to witness my sister living the exact dream I'd once wished for myself.

It wasn't surprising that Mama, like many other Italian cooks and delicatessens, had a stall on Mulberry Street where she served cannoli stuffed full with fresh ricotta and cones brimming with her famous tiramisu.

I watched from a distance, jostled by the festival-goers as my mama interacted with her customers. She was a gorgeous older woman, though still fairly young because she had basically still been a girl when she'd given birth to me. A few older neighborhood men flirted with her shamelessly as they bartered for food and maybe a kiss, but Caprice only ever offered them a soft, secret smile that said more than words could that she would never be interested, but she wasn't offended by their attention.

It was the babies, though, that she loved the most.

I watched as a young Italian-American mama with baby fat still in her cheeks and a toddler on her hip approached Mama. The baby was fussing, and Mama didn't hesitate to pluck the girl off her mother's hip and plunk her down on her own side. Though I couldn't hear the words she spoke, I knew she was cooing in Italian as she bounced her and swayed back and forth.

The baby girl laughed and hit Mama in the chest excitedly as they danced together beneath the red, white, and green streamers rippling in the warm Indian summer breeze.

Sorrow wrapped around my heart and constricted like a serpent, squeezing so hard tears popped into my eyes.

I wanted so badly to give her a grandchild, to watch as she cooed to my daughter and taught her all she knew about cooking, about motherhood, about the secrets of being a strong woman in a culture that valued subservient women.

An arrow of agony pierced through my chest as I thought of

Giselle and Daniel's Genevieve. I realized inevitably, one day, I'd have to bear witness to Mama, not only my parent but my closest confidant, loving and cooing over the baby they'd conceived while they had been cheating on me together.

Someone elbowed me in the side so painfully I gasped, jerking me out of my self-pity. When I turned sharply to bark at the offender, I was face-to-face with a slight auburn-haired man with close-set eyes and a soft, full smile. There was a bad scar at the corner of his jaw, puckered and still pink with healing.

"*Scusi,*" he begged of me in a poor Italian accent as he patted my arm and readjusted my purse on my shoulder for me. "*Scusi, bella raggaza.*"

Before I could forgive him, he was off in the crowd, powering upstream away from the festivities. I frowned after him for a long moment before I shook my head and finally made my way to Mama's booth.

"*Lottatrice mia,*" she cried loudly, spreading her arms wide the instant she saw me, uncaring that one thudded into the young woman who was working beside her. "What a lovely surprise this is!"

My troubled mood, my worries about work and Dante, and Giselle and Daniel all faded away under the beaming light of her love. I could feel myself open and expanded like a flower soaking up her rays and I let myself relax my shields as I hurried forward through the thicket of people to duck beneath the stall awning and let my mama take me in her semolina-scented arms.

119

She hushed and clucked her tongue at me nonsensically as she gathered me to her and stroked my hair.

A sob rose in my throat and lodged somewhere behind my voice box, robbing me of the ability to speak. There was nowhere I felt safer than in the arms of my mother. Nowhere I felt more loved and accepted than against her plush side, face buried under her thick black hair. She was the only person who was never disappointed in me, the only one who believed in my goodness and rooted for me no matter what.

She was the only one who stayed resolutely by my side when Daniel left me for my own sister.

I knew that over a year after the affair had come to light, with a newborn first grandchild, Mama saw Giselle frequently again, but I didn't care. Mama had shown me, like no one else had, that she had my back first.

That I was a priority for her.

It meant more to me than I could ever express that she would do that for me, so whenever I saw her, I battled the overwhelming urge to cry like a baby with gratitude and love.

Only with her did I ever let myself succumb to such tender, weak emotion.

She wasn't perfect, I knew, not even close. She'd stayed with Seamus far too long because she clung to her Catholicism and she'd been oblivious to Christopher's evil ways, but it was hard to blame her too much for either. She'd grown up in Naples where getting married and staying married was a cultural prerogative and the only thing she'd ever known.

As for Christopher, he was a sociopath through and through. No one saw the monster if he wanted them to see the man. I knew that better than anyone because I'd fallen in love with one as a girl and ended up with the other.

At the end of the day, Mama had done her best for us and I'd always love her for the simple fact that she'd always loved me.

"There she is," Mama murmured as she pulled away with her hands on my shoulders to study my face. "Such a beauty."

I smiled at her and smoothed my hand over the raw silk of my belted black button-up dress. "It's new, thank you."

"Not the dress, Lena," she said, clucking her tongue at me and wagging a finger. "You. My beautiful daughter. I love to see you smile. So rare like a jewel."

I laughed, leaning forward to press a warm kiss to her soft cheek. "You are biased, Mama."

"*Si*," she agreed gravely, eyes sparkling as she reached out to snag the arm of the teenage boy who was replenishing her bamboo cutlery stack. "Gino, is my daughter not very beautiful?"

The poor boy stammered and blinked as a blush stained his cheeks, but he nodded before he ducked his head and went back to work.

"Mama," I scolded in a whisper. "You shouldn't embarrass him."

"*Boh*," she countered with that typical Neapolitan word that meant I don't know or meh. "It is good for children to learn

121

humility."

I laughed again, letting Mama pull me farther into the stall so she could hand me a scooper. Following her silent order, I began to spoon tiramisu into paper cones and slot them into the holders on the table. Mama silently worked beside me, leaving the orders to her assistant.

"I didn't come to help you," I teased her. "Dante actually...*asked* me to come. He said he's ordered some food from you for his party tonight."

"Ah, *si*." She nodded casually, then shot me a sidelong look. "You are becoming close with Dante, to be getting his dessert?"

I scoffed. "Apparently, in his world, being his lawyer also means being his slave."

Mama only hummed.

"What?" I sighed, pausing in my duties to fist my hands on my hips. "Oh God, Mama, do not tell me you like him."

"Do not take the Lord's name in vain, Elena," she reprimanded. "But yes, I do like this man. He is very...*sicuro di sé.*"

"Self-confident," I translated for her. "And he's like that because he's a capo, Mama. He's used to getting his own way or killing the men who disobey him."

"Mmm," Mama hummed again. "I do not think such a man needs to kill for his orders to be obeyed."

I thought of Dante, all six-foot-five inches of muscle, the intimidation of his glower, but also his acute charisma.

"Maybe," I allowed grumpily.

Mama laughed under her breath. "Ah, *figlia*, sometimes I wonder if I should have kept so many secret things from my children. Maybe if I had shared my history, your own would not be so disappointing."

"No one blames you for Seamus," I said instantly, horrified that she would even think so. "He was responsible for his own actions, and he was the one who put us all in impossible situations."

"*Si*, Elena, but you see, in the beginning, your father was not a bad man. He was a *professore*, very, very smart and very different from the men I knew who I thought were boring as dead fish." She sighed wistfully, her eyes trained on the crowd, though her mind focused on memories. "He was very good at pretending to be what he was not, you understand?"

Oh, I did.

In a way, Daniel had done the same with me. Maybe I'd encouraged him to hide the extent of his sexual proclivities from me, but he hadn't been honest about so many things. He told me he didn't want marriage, then married my sister after knowing her for a few months. He said he wanted to adopt a baby with me, then months later, he decided he did not, only to get that same sister pregnant immediately. He told me he loved me, and I assumed that meant something.

But it was just another lie.

So, I understood Mama.

"This is what I like very much about Dante," Mama continued. "He is like his brother, Cosima's husband, yes? They are who they are. No lies, no masks. Dante Salvatore is exactly who he made himself to be."

I am the most honest man you'll ever meet.

Dante's words unwound from my memory and laid out before me beside Mama's, and I had to admit they both had a point.

There was no pretense. Even when Yara and I had encouraged him to act the gentleman, to dress like the saint he would never be, Dante remained true to himself.

In fact, it was admirable and enviable in equal terms.

I'd often wished I felt comfortable being myself, when the truth was, I wasn't even sure who that true self was.

"This, I like," Mama reiterated, bumping me softly with her hip as she blew a lock of hair from her face. "This, I think, you will like, too."

"Mama," I warned with a groan. "I hope you aren't trying to matchmake. Dante is, well, all fire and impulse. I'm ice and control. He is a *criminal,* and I'm..." I failed to find the word to describe myself.

I wasn't a hero, and I wasn't a villain.

I was just a woman trying to navigate life.

A twenty-seven-year-old who felt newborn after the dissolution of my life with Daniel. For the first time ever, I wasn't sure what I wanted anymore or how to get it.

Mama shrugged one shoulder. "You do as you like; you always have. I just wanted to say I like him. He is very different from your *papa.* From Christopher, too." She hesitated when I stiffened at the mention of his name. "I will never live well with myself, *lottatrice mia*, that I did not shield you from the man who was really a snake. But it is a mother's wish to see her daughter happy in love, and this I still wish for you."

Acid ate at my heart, a corroded battery. I pressed my hand over it as if that would help.

"I hope so, too," I whispered quietly as if I might spook the dream if I spoke too loudly. "But there is no happily-ever-after with a man like Dante, Mama. I know you know this. *La mafia* is a living nightmare."

Mama hummed again noncommittedly. We worked silently for a bit, the scent of cocoa powder and the Amaretto-soaked ladyfingers perfuming the air around us. I wanted to open my heart up to my mother and have her sort out the broken fragments that remained of my soul, but I was afraid of what she might find there.

Because the truth was, I was intrigued by Dante in a way I'd never been with another soul. He was such a contradiction in terms, a puzzle that my lawyer's mind couldn't help but want to piece together.

Thoughts of him haunted me as I finished helping Mama and collected the trays of tiramisu, schlepping them back to my apartment to put in the fridge while I finished some work from home.

Silence echoed all around me as I worked, and even though it made me feel morose, I didn't play music to comfort myself.

Instead, I worked until seven thirty in the evening, only stopping because of a knock on the door. The house was dark. I'd forgotten to turn the lights on as I worked into the night.

I sighed as I checked the peephole on the door, then let out a little squeal when I saw Beau standing outside holding a huge box and a plastic bag I knew would be filled with Japanese food. I opened the door and immediately stepped forward to take him in my arms, box and bag of food and all.

Beau Bailey laughed as he tried to hug me back with his hands full. "My darling, I missed you too."

I pulled back to smile at my handsome friend, noting the wrinkles in his otherwise gorgeous Armani suit. Pushing a lock of errant brown hair back over his forehead, I smiled at him genuinely. "Did you come straight from the airport?"

"I dropped my luggage at home, but basically," he agreed, gently bustling me back into my foyer then kicking the door shut before he handed me the bag of Japanese food. "I missed you, and I needed to decompress with my favorite girl before I went home to my empty apartment."

"I know the feeling." I gave his hand a squeeze as we walked together into my kitchen and set about our ritual of getting out wine and plates for dinner. It reminded me briefly of Dante storming my house to bring me Japanese food just days before. How ridiculously at home he'd made himself in my space.

"What's that, then?" Beau asked as he uncorked a bottle of red from my collection.

"What?"

"That look," he insisted with a jerk of his chin. "That almost smile."

I waved my hand, dismissing him with a gesture that I'd tried for years to curb. It was the one Italian idiosyncrasy I couldn't seem to kick. I always spoke with my hands more than I meant to.

"Nothing."

"Oh!" he exclaimed, setting down the bottle before pouring the wine in order to waggle his brows at me. "It's definitely something."

This was one of the reasons I loved Beau. He wasn't perturbed by my coldness or my reserve. He respected them just as much as he strove to abolish them. He loved to tease me, to make me laugh.

He reminded me that sometimes, life didn't have to be such a competitive sport.

Still, I changed the subject. "I'll have to eat and run, handsome. One of my clients has practically ordered me to show up at a party he's throwing."

"Should you be eating?" he asked, hesitating as he pulled my favorite, tuna tataki, from the bag.

"You know I don't eat Italian food if I can help it," I said as I snatched the tuna from him with a feral look.

He laughed at me, and God, it felt good to have him home, to have him laugh with me and love me. I hadn't realized how lonely I was without him for the past month while he'd been in England shooting with St. Aubyn fashion house.

"Do you have to go? I thought we could watch *Vampire Diaries*," he suggested seductively. "Damon is totally getting to Elena."

"He is," I agreed. The teenage vampire show was one in a long line of television shows Beau and I had binge-watched together. We were both busy professionals with tragic personal lives, so we spent a lot of time drinking wine, bitching together, and living our romantic fantasies vicariously through fictional characters. "But if I don't show up, I have no doubt he'll send someone for me."

Beau's expressive brows rose nearly into his hairline. "Wow."

"Yeah," I agreed.

"This being Don Salvatore?" he surmised. "Infamous mafia capo and one of the sexiest men ever to breathe air?"

I shook my head at him, but my lips twitched despite myself. "He's okay."

"Okay?" Beau turned me to face him with both hands on my shoulders, his face extremely serious. "Lena, honey, do you need to get your eyes checked?"

I burst out laughing and pushed him away. "You are so dramatic."

"Only about important matters," he sniffed, resuming his duty of pouring our wine and taking the glasses over to my travertine table. "And handsome men are non-trivial."

"He's an asshole," I promised him, then winced slightly because I wasn't really sure if that was true.

He was bossy.

Arrogant.

Annoying as hell.

But he wasn't exactly an asshole.

"Language, Lena," Beau said on a laugh, teasing me for swearing. "Well, he definitely provokes a response in you. Even that is something. I was beginning to think you'd never thaw."

A twinge of hurt accompanied his words, and before I could mask it, Beau was reaching out to squeeze my hand. "Not a bad thing, darling. You've been through a lot."

I squeezed his hand back and smiled, hoping it wasn't shaky. "Trust me, I'd love to spend the night with you instead."

"Oh!" Beau gestured with his chopsticks at the large box he left on the counter. "There was a package on your front step."

I frowned, popping some tuna into my mouth before I got up to investigate. The red box was embossed with the gold logo for Valentino. I looked up at Beau with wide eyes, one hand automatically covering my mouth as it dropped open in shock. Returning my eyes to the box, I carefully lifted the lid and pulled back the voluminous layers of tissue paper.

Beneath it lay a pool of deep red silk.

I loved fashion.

And no matter my attempts to contradict it, I was an Italian.

Valentino was one of the country's most covetous brands and inside this luxurious box lay something I knew in my bones was tailored exactly to me.

My fingers trembled slightly as I lifted the heavy, cool silk up and out of the box to hold against my body. It was the same color as my fingernails, as my favorite lipstick, just a few beautiful shades brighter than my own deep red hair.

"My God," Beau breathed, knowing exactly how exquisite the dress was because he was a fashion photographer. "Elena, that's *vintage* Valentino."

I didn't have the words to respond. Instead, in a fit of uncharacteristic immodesty, I gently settled the dress on top of the box and undressed. Beau didn't bat an eyelash until I was lifting the sumptuous fabric up to my body and then, he only gasped slightly before getting up to help me fasten it closed.

I couldn't stop petting the silk that skimmed perfectly over my hips as I stepped away from Beau then turned to face him.

"Well?" I breathed, completely seduced by the garment.

"You look sensational," he promised. "If I wasn't a gay man, I would get to my knees right now."

My laugh was slightly breathless as I lifted the excess fabric off the ground and tiptoed to the full-length mirror by my hall closet.

Oh.

I'd worked hard on my self-image over the years even though it often seemed like a fruitless, uphill battle. When you had a sister who was a supermodel, a brother who was an actor, and another sister who had stolen the only two men you'd ever dated, it was difficult to appreciate your own beauty. Dr. Marsden taught me self-affirmations, meditation, and acts of kindness that helped, marginally, but I'd never felt the way I did standing in my hallway in that dress.

I felt transformed.

Like Cinderella in her ball gown, it seemed to me I was a totally different person, the woman I'd always aspired to me.

The bold red wasn't a color I would have ever picked myself, but it made my pale olive skin pop beautifully and contrasted wonderfully with my cool gray eyes. My hair seemed darker, a red as deep as fine Italian wine. The fabric skimmed my long, lean planes and nipped in at my waist and breasts, plumping the slight mass of the latter until I had natural cleavage.

I looked dangerous, dramatic, and powerful.

Confident.

Only the right kind of man would dare to approach a woman wearing such a dress, and I found the idea of that wonderfully appealing.

"Lena, there are shoes," Beau called, drawing my gaze to see him pull towering black spike heels from the nest of tissue. "And a card."

With one last look at the stranger in the mirror, I went over to pluck the envelope from his fingers. I dug my red nail under the edge and ripped it open.

Wear it tonight.
Capo

A noise somewhere between a laugh and groan emerged from my mouth as I read the short card three times in quick succession.

"Dante?" Beau asked, leaning over my shoulder to peer at the spiky script.

"Mmm," I agreed, staring at the card as if it would reveal the secrets of the man who wrote it.

"He likes you," Beau decided.

I let out a little scoff, but I couldn't deny it confused me. "At the most, I would say I intrigue him. The way one predator intrigues another."

Beau considered me for a second. "It sounds as though you might have met your match."

I fought the urge to snort because it wasn't ladylike, but as Beau ushered me into my bathroom to freshen up my makeup, I wondered with a tangled sense of dread and wonder if perhaps he was right.

CHAPTER NINE

DANTE

The party was in full swing by the time Elena Lombardi deigned to show up. I was leading a toast for the Feast of San Gennaro when the air in the room seemed to shift, the particles rearranging themselves to make room for a bold new presence.

I continued my toast, but I could feel her eyes on my skin like an electric prod.

"*Aiz' aiz' aiz', acal', acal', acal', accost', accost', accost', a salut' vost',*" I cried as I led the group around me to lift their glasses up, down, together, and then to their mouths for a robust sip.

It was over the rim of my wineglass that I finally swept my eyes across the packed room and narrowed in on Ele

na.

I sucked in a breath, nearly choking on my wine as my gaze widened at the sight of her.

Ah, to think I'd thought she had lacked the inherent sensuality of her sister Cosima.

I was more than happy to be proved so spectacularly wrong.

Ammazza, she was glorious.

Even in the seductive dress, she was still a vision of elegance, hair held off her neck in some kind of hairstyle that had the odd thick curl brushing the creamy skin of her neck and cheeks, only a simple gold chain at the column of that long throat. I'd only ever seen her in feminine but extremely conservative suits and blouses for work and once in a tuxedo dress when *Osteria Lombardi* had been bombed by Noel in an attempt to kill Alexander, Cosima, and myself.

Never like this.

Apparently unaware of the gaze of dozens of lusty men and envious women pinned to her, she handed off the boxes of tiramisu to a server and began to wind through the bodies on her way to the kitchen. She looked like some heathen goddess of sex and war, conquering the room with her allure with every step she took toward me.

Toward *me*.

Something primal in my gut tightened and went white-hot. With any other woman, I would have given in to instinct and surged forward to claim that red hair with my fist and that red mouth with my own. I would have steered her toward the nearest room with a door and fucked her against it, rending that red dress in two so it stained the floor like spilled blood, leaving her naked for my ravishing.

Fuck.

My cock jumped and hardened in my suit pants.

It was irrational and ridiculously stupid to become attracted to one of my lawyers, my best friend's sister, a woman I was certain wouldn't know sexual passion if it slapped her in the arse.

So, instead of offering one of the dozen compliments that lingered on my tongue like the taste of my Chianti, I pinned her with a haughty look and drawled, "*Bene*. You wore the dress."

Instantly, her carefully controlled expression dissolved in the vinegar of my words. "I wasn't aware I had a choice."

"There is always a choice," I said with a *tsk*, condescending to her just to see the way a flush would spill down her cheeks to pool at the top of her exposed chest. "You made the right one."

"You flatter yourself if you think it had anything to do with pleasing you," she countered easily, so quick and cold, her words landed like flurries on my skin. She idly smoothed a hand down her flat stomach to the slight flare of one hip. "The dress pleased *me*. It was too exquisite not to wear."

"Of course," I agreed, secretly pleased because I'd chosen it myself from a selection Bambi had shown me earlier that afternoon.

We were speaking loudly to be heard over the ambient noise of the party around us, and I used it as an excuse to lash forward and grab her hand before she could protest, tugging her closer so she stumbled in those high heels and right against my body.

It was a move I was coming to deeply enjoy.

She scowled up at me, trying to push off my chest with little success as I kept her pinned close with my hands on her silk-covered hips.

"Take your heathen hands off me," she snapped. "People are watching."

"I bought the dress," I argued calmly, my fingers splaying over her slight hips and loving the feel of her long, delicate bones. "It's only right I should enjoy it."

"I'll take it off immediately if you're so obsessed with it." Her eyes, a dark gray mottled with bright silver patches and black striations, were frozen with disdain.

It shouldn't have turned me on. Her vitriol, her constant battle against my will.

I was a man used to getting his own way, and I preferred it that way.

But there was something hypnotic about her, a cold pull like the magnetism of the arctic poles.

Despite myself, I wanted to see if the infamous ice queen would melt under my tongue.

"Do it," I dared her, bending down to sneer softly in her face. "Give us all a show."

"I'd rather be naked in front of everyone than have your hands on me for a second longer than necessary," she practically spat.

"Be my guest," I purred, already imagining her long, thin body stripped of the luxurious cloth, even more beautiful bared to my eyes. "In fact…" I moved one hand off her hip, banded the other

136

over her low back to keep her immobile, and tucked my raised forefinger under the thin strap of her gown, drawing it slowly down her shoulder.

It was small.

Barely a movement so much as a vibration.

But I felt her shiver against me a moment before she jerked away, stamping her heel on my foot. I released her with a growl that dissolved into loud laughter as I stared at her panting and glaring at me in that dress the color of sin.

"It's not funny, Dante," she hissed as those around us turned to watch me laugh at her. A stain of embarrassment marred her cheeks. "Stop it."

I held a hand up to stall her as my laughter rolled into chuckles and then softened into a broad smile I felt tight in my cheeks. "It's not a crime to have a bit of fun, Elena."

She pursed those perfectly formed bow-shaped lips at me like a school marm in a sexy dress. "I could lose my license for having the type of 'fun' you consider appropriate."

My amusement fled, and I took a hard step toward her, glad she didn't flinch the way she usually did when I approached her like that. It was a small victory, but I'd take what I could in the battle against Elena's hatred of me and everything I represented. "You and I may have different ideas of morality, but I'm sure I do not have to tell you about the concept of *omertà*. Silence between brothers is a holy thing."

"And I'm your brother?" she asked dryly, hands going to her

hips to strike a pose full of sass and fire.

It was a heady thing to know I could make the ice queen *burn.*

I grinned rakishly as I slid my gaze down her exquisite form. "Not in that dress. Comrades, though. Allies. Whether you like the association or not, Elena, you are now a lawyer for the Camorra. It seems you are only aware of the downsides to the arrangement, but there can be many boons, too."

Unable to resist, I reached out to run a thumb over the silken skin of her shoulder.

She jerked away, but not before I saw goose bumps erupt over her flesh.

"I don't need boons from the likes of you," she said haughtily, adjusting that simple necklace in an oddly provocative way she was completely unaware of. "I want to be professional, nothing else."

"Ah, *lottatrice,*" I sighed dramatically and snagged a wineglass from the collection on the kitchen island, offering it to her. "You don't seem to understand you work for me now. And I make the rules. It is my game for you to play."

"I could leave your legal team," she suggested.

She was glaring at me, those storm cloud eyes dark and raging beneath her delicate red brows. It should have been an ugly expression, full of hate, but I saw only the beauty of her face beneath it and the fire of her fight shining through.

I was beginning to understand the intricacies of her character, despite her best efforts to remain aloof. At first, it was difficult to like Elena Lombardi. She was constructed like a work of modern art, all sharp angles, rigid lines, and dominant sensibilities; beautiful and intriguing but difficult to understand. It was only upon further reflection and intense study that the impact of her beauty moved through you, as complicated a feeling as she was a woman.

I was looking forward to furthering my studies.

"You wouldn't. Success means too much to you," I noted, leaning back against the island and crossing my arms over my chest. Her eyes dipped to the swell of muscles beneath the fabric before she could curb the impulse.

"You're one to talk."

I inclined my head. "The drive for success motivates me, *si*. Not more so than the drive for happiness."

"They are one and the same," she concluded with a shrug that was the physical expression of the word "duh."

"They are not. Success is defined by society. Happiness is defined by our hearts and minds. I think, *lottatrice*, you would be much happier if you learned to value the latter."

"Don't call me that and don't preach to me, *capo*. You're in no position to offer me advice."

"Am I not?" I opened my hands wide to gesture to the party surging around us. "I am a successful businessman with powerful friends who support me even when I am on trial for murder."

"Success," she countered, lifting her hand to show me her red fingertips as she counted them off. "A fancy apartment, probably a few ridiculous sports cars, enough money to bribe these powerful 'friends' to look the other way from your misdeeds." She raised an eyebrow. "Would you like me to call you a hypocrite yet?"

I laughed, finally having fun at my own party, and it was at the hands of the most unlikely woman I'd ever met.

"Who is making my son laugh?" Tore said as he stepped up beside me and clapped a hand on my shoulder.

I watched, fascinated, as Elena's entire demeanor changed. Her bristling, hostile energy cooled, her features relaxed into an expression of polite interest and even her stance shifted, weight distributed evenly, and shoulders rolled stiffly back.

She smiled slightly at the only man I considered my father and offered her hand. "It's a pleasure to meet you officially, Mr. Salvatore. I am Elena Lombardi, one of Edward's lawyers."

I rolled my eyes at her deliberate use of my old name, but Tore only laughed and accepted her slim hand between both of his, turning on his mega-watt charm.

The same charm that had seduced Elena's mama into an affair. Based on Elena's placid greeting, it was safe to assume she had no idea she was talking to the father of her two youngest siblings.

"You are many more things than Dante's lawyer," Tore was saying as he patted her hand in his. "One might say we are old family friends. Please, call me Tore."

Something dark flickered in her eyes, but her lips were plastic molded around the shape of a stock smile. "If you'd like. Of course, I heard of you in my childhood."

There was an underlying sentence that seemed to echo as boldly as if it had been spoken.

You were the orchestrator of the nightmares in my youth.

Of course, she didn't know that when Tore had arrived in Napoli years after his affair with Caprice, he was as shocked as anyone to discover the twin children with his golden eyes in her home. He'd done everything in his power short of losing that power to shield the Lombardis from Seamus's dangerous dealings with the Camorra.

But he didn't say anything about it.

Instead, he took the silent hit she doled out like he deserved it.

Anger sparked in my blood.

It was one thing for her to judge me but quite another for her to skewer Tore with her misplaced hatred.

"He did more for your family than you know," I cut in, glowering down at her from my advanced height. "Do not cast stones when you are blind to your surroundings."

Elena ignored me, those gray eyes thunderous as they stared at Tore. "You might not remember this, but I was there the day you dragged Cosima from my mother's house in Naples."

I remembered that day too. Alexander had sent Cosima back home to Italy in order to get information on Tore and me, information about our mother's death. It was that evening that Cosima learned the truth about what happened to Chiara and the truth about her paternity.

Elena didn't know anything about it, about Tore and Cosima's father-daughter relationship or that Cosima had been sold to Alexander at the tender age of eighteen as his sex slave to satisfy his role in an ancient secret society, the Order of Dionysus.

Truly, she didn't know a thing about her own sister.

Either of them, probably.

And even though that wasn't exactly her fault, I wouldn't have her berating the only man who had taught me what it meant to be loved.

"You should ask your sister about that day," I suggested, my mouth a cruel sneer as I glared at her. "For a woman who values knowledge, you do not ask questions when you should."

"Dante." Tore tried to soothe the tension with a chuckle. "Please excuse him, Elena, as he is fiercely protective. *Figlio*, have some of Caprice's tiramisu to sweeten your disposition, si?"

I shook my head at him, but I did take one of the bowls filled with sweet cream and cake from the counter. Elena's eyes tracked me as I brought the spoon to my mouth, as I hummed a little louder than necessary at the explosion of the flavors on my tongue.

"Perfetto," I praised, then offered a spoonful to Elena with a brow raised in a silent dare. "You could use some sweetening too."

"Boss," Frankie interrupted, his face pinched with concern as he stopped in front of him. "Gotta talk to you."

I opened my mouth to reply, but Tore got there first.

"Enough talk," he decided, a wicked gleam in his eyes as he took Elena's hand and pressed it into my own. "This is the feast of San Gennaro! We must be dancing."

He shot me a hard look before I could argue with him, and I knew he wanted me to get her away from whatever grim news Frankie was carrying before her curiosity got the better of her. So I tucked Elena's stiff arm through mine and tugged her into the living room, where a number of people were dancing between it and the terrace.

When I pulled her close, she went as stiff as a board in my arms.

"Dancing typically requires coordination," I drawled. "Are you capable of that?"

She blinked at me blandly and rolled her shoulders back as she adjusted her hands on my shoulders. "I was concerned about you. It can't be easy to move all that weight around."

I tipped my head back to laugh at the ceiling as I hauled her even closer, flush against my chest. Through the thin silk of her dress and the crisp linen of my shirt, I imagined I could feel the hard points of her nipples.

"What are you doing?" she demanded, struggling slightly to pull away.

I clamped my hand over her hip and engulfed her hand on the opposite in my own before I ducked down to whisper over her lips. "I am dancing with you."

"Indecently," she hissed, her eyes scanning the crowd for any judgmental eyes. "Yara is watching."

"Yara doesn't care," I countered as I moved us fluidly to the music, grinning at my man Davide as he spun his wife out beside us. "If you know the steps to the Saltarello, we could dance that

143

instead."

She rolled those pretty eyes at me, but her body was relaxing in increments against mine. I was reminded of her piano playing and made a note to play music around her more often. It was evident she was moved spiritually by it, even if the words were in her dreaded native tongue.

"Only old people dance the Saltarello," she said. "Then again, you're basically an old man, aren't you?"

I scowled at her, the hand on her hip moving to the small of her back so I could press her fully to the quilted muscles beneath my suit. "I assure you, I'm still incredibly virile."

"For an old man, maybe."

"I'm thirty-five, Elena. I'm hardly ancient."

She shrugged flippantly, but I caught a hint of a smile at the edge of her mouth.

We danced then for the length of one song, and when she would have pulled away, I spun her back into my arms for another. I liked the way she fit there against me, tall enough I didn't have to break my back to look down into her romantic face, slim enough I got an aroused kick out of knowing I could bend her easily beneath my hands.

Her eyes caught mine as I moved us in a bastardized version of the salsa. Our bodies moved together with a synchronicity that surprised us both. I stepped; she followed. I indicated an upcoming spin with a twist of my wrist, and she was already swirling out in a flare of red silk. We moved faster, tighter against each other. Her breath fanned against the open skin at my collar as she panted with her efforts, her chest cresting again and again pressed to mine, her nipples hard as diamonds abrading my skin beneath the fabric.

A fire built in my gut, a slow burn that built deeper and deeper than the ache in an overused muscle. Sweat beaded on my brow, but it had more to do with the effort to restrain myself from savagely taking her mouth with mine than from the dance.

"This is inappropriate," Elena panted at one point, but even her eyes were dancing beautifully in time with me.

"*Si, indecente,*" I agreed.

Indecent.

And she was. Indecently tantalizing warmed with amusement and the heat of excursion. I wanted to trail the flush from her neck down her chest, discover if her nipples were pink or brown, sweet or salty with sweat.

I pressed her intractably to the swell of my cock trapped in my trousers, and she faltered, losing time and tripping over her heels to end up straddling my thigh. Her eyes were all black, the steel gray a fine frame for her blown pupils as she stared at me, afraid and alert to the presence of a predator.

I grinned wolfishly as I lowered her down the hard length of my leg, enjoying the way she shuddered against me. I opened my mouth to tease her, to enjoy the contrast between her sharp-tongued wit and her pliant body against mine when suddenly, I couldn't breathe.

Elena frowned as I hesitated against her. "Dante? You look

pale."

I wanted to tell her I was fine, but the air seemed to have been vacuumed out of my chest. A bead of sweat dripped into my eye, blurring my vision as I angled my head to see the buttons of my shirt and shakily undo even more. My fingers fumbled on the buttons as my head swam.

"Dante," Elena repeated, alarm in her tone as she wrapped her hands around my body, alerting me to the fact that I was swaying. "*Tore*!" she yelled over the music.

Her hand went to my neck, sharp tipped fingers digging into my pulse as she struggled to hold me up. "Tore, his pulse is really slow."

The father of my heart was there, taking my other side to prop me up and lead me to the couch.

"Is Dr. Augustus Crown here?" he demanded of someone I couldn't make out over his shoulder.

I blinked because my eyes were dry, but when I tried to open them again, the lids seemed weighted by cement. The last thing I heard before I succumbed to the blackness was Jacopo's loud voice growling, "You, bitch. You did this!"

CHAPTER TEN

elena

"You, bitch. You did this!"

I blinked at the short, slight man who was suddenly in my face yelling at me.

"Jaco," Tore snapped, wrenching him away from me and lightly slapping his face. "Do not accuse anyone without foundation. We do not know what happened."

"He was clearly fucking poisoned," Jaco cried, pointing at Dante's pale, sweaty form passed out on the couch. "She was the one dancing with him."

"Oh? And you think I poisoned him with a kiss?" I asked venomously. "Don't be an idiot."

"Both of you, quiet," Tore demanded in a voice that brooked no argument as a large man with a dimpled chin, thick gold hair, and blue eyes pushed through the gathered crowd. "Dr. Crown, I thought you were here somewhere."

"You're lucky I bring my bag with me everywhere," was his grim reply as he knelt beside the couch and removed a stethoscope and blood pressure cuff from his leather bag.

"Party is over, people," the man I knew was named Frankie called out as he stepped up on a marble side table to address the crowd. "Get out."

"Is he going to be okay, *dottore?*" a beautiful woman in her mid-to-late thirties appeared over the couch, bending to sweep a sweaty lock of black hair out of Dante's face.

Dr. Crown knocked her hand out of the way without looking at her. Instead, he addressed Tore. "Get everyone the fuck outta here."

Instantly, Tore transformed from the suave and debonair Italian host to the mafia boss I'd heard rumors about since my youth in Naples.

Unbending, vicious, and controlled.

"You have five minutes to get out!" he ordered, his voice carrying without him having to yell the way Frankie did.

I remained where I stood as everyone quickly gathered their things and left, ushered out by a group of men who were no doubt Camorra soldiers. No one told me to go, and Yara hovered by my side, so I stayed where I was.

The sight of Dante's massive body pale and slick with sweat was oddly impactful even though I told myself I didn't particularly like the man. He was just so potent, so vivacious and full of passion that to see him depleted felt absolutely wrong.

I was shaken as much by his sudden illness as I was by my lapse of judgment in dancing with him. My only defense was flimsy at best, but true enough, I had to admit it to myself. I'd never known a man who exuded such raw, palpable sexual energy. Being around him, with the full glory of his attention pinned only to me in a room full of nearly a hundred affluent and beautiful guests, was heady. The walls I'd erected between myself and the male species felt battered and war-torn against the force of his charm, and before I'd known it, I was dancing with him.

Dancing like I hadn't in years.

Dancing like sixteen-year-old Elena in a piazza in Sorrento with a man I'd thought was my soul mate.

I hadn't even danced like that with Daniel because somehow, I'd forgotten how much I loved it.

A shiver rippled down my spine, threatening to spill my emotions all over the floor for any of these people to rifle through. I sucked in a deep breath and cleared my mind, focusing on Dante, who still lay pale and seemingly passed out on the long leather couch.

Dr. Augustus fitted a portable oxygen mask to his face, then pricked his finger with some handheld blood monitoring device.

"You think it is poison," Tore surmised grimly from where he stood at the head of the couch hovering over Dante like he could protect him from invisible enemies.

The doctor grunted. "Most likely cyanide. Easy to get your hands on and fairly difficult to detect."

"Treatable?" the same beautiful Italianate woman who'd worried about him before asked.

I peered at her, something ugly churning in my gut at the sight of her sitting on the back of the couch to be closer to the capo.

They looked ill-suited, I decided. The woman was too blond, northern Italian for sure, with the olive skin and flaxen hair of the border regions near Switzerland and Germany.

Dante wouldn't look good with a blonde.

The doctor, too, didn't seem to like the woman because he ignored her again as he pulled a jar of black tablets from his endless Mary Poppins-like bag and then a full IV bag. He glanced over his shoulder, catching eyes with me.

Wordlessly, I extended my hand to hold up the IV bag for him. He nodded curtly as he handed it off then efficiently inserted the needle into one of the thick veins on the back of Dante's hand before taping it down.

"He will be fine," Dr. Crown asserted as if he had a direct line to Death.

I knew about cyanide poisoning because one of my first cases as an associate at Fields, Harding & Griffith had been defending a woman who poisoned her abusive husband over the course of a few months until he died. We'd plead guilty for a reduced sentence of five years with the possibility for parole at three.

I knew cyanide was deadly, especially in large doses.

My mouth was dry, and my palms were sweating. I swiped them on the silken dress Dante had bought me. A dress worth thousands of dollars. A dress I'd only ever found in my dreams.

Acid rushed up to eat at the walls of my chest.

I was shocked by it, but I truly didn't want this man to die.

"He'll be fine," I asserted, an echo of Dr. Crown.

Dante's associates, the only ones left in the messy and shockingly empty apartment, turned their black eyes to me. There were varying levels of curiosity and concern in those gazes, but I ignored them, tilting my chin up stubbornly to reaffirm my words.

"*Si, Dante va bene,*" Tore said with a tight smile aimed my way. "Now, what did Dante eat or drink that no one else did?"

I knew.

Of course, I did.

I'd known before that jerk, Jacopo, had yelled it in my face.

"The tiramisu," I whispered, my tongue rasping against the dry roof of my mouth. "I brought it from my mama's stall on Mulberry Street. But you have to know, she would never do anything to harm Dante. She was just telling me how much she liked him."

Instantly, one of their men, surprisingly not an Italian but someone who appeared to be Japanese, moved toward the door. I had a cold flash of memory, a mafioso shaking Mama so hard as he interrogated her about Seamus's whereabouts that she broke a tooth.

"Please, don't hurt her," I said, stepping forward then stopping helplessly.

"No one is hurting Caprice," Tore promised darkly, casting a look at the Asian man who hesitated then nodded and returned to his vigil around Dante on the couch. "This is too simple, yes? Of course, the feast of San Gennaro in Little Italy is visited by thousands. Even vigilant, there is a possibility her stall was compromised, and we have many enemies."

His mouth was a grim flatline as he considered, eyes pinned on something in the distance. I noticed with shock that Amadeo Salvatore had the same peculiar and striking shade of gold in his eyes as my twin siblings.

"Did you see anyone when you visited?" he asked me suddenly, stepping forward to grasp and squeeze my biceps. "Think, *cervellona.*"

I pursed my lips as I ran my mind back over the afternoon and remembered the thin limbs of the man who had bumped into me near the stall.

"A man bumped into me in the street." I shrugged a little helplessly. "He wasn't doing anything strange, though."

"What did he look like?"

"He had auburn hair, close-cropped, and he wasn't very tall, maybe an inch or two shorter than my five foot ten," I described, uncomfortable with all the eyes on me. "He had a scar at the corner of his jaw, just here."

The air in the room went flat, then flickered with energy and erupted as the men burst into motion.

"We're hitting them now," Frankie growled, his dark hair disheveled from his agitated hands. "Kelly and his crew hang out most evenings at that sports bar in Marine Park, Father Patrick's. They'll be done by the end of the night."

"Frankie, *chiudi la bocca,*" Tore barked, ordering him to shut up.

"We do not discuss these things outside the family."

I looked at Yara, wondering how she was dealing with the crisis and the potential knowledge that Dante's associates were determined to kill a group of men in the Bronx.

She turned her large dark eyes toward me, expression entirely imperturbable, and blinked slowly.

It occurred to me for the first time in a very real way that Yara Ghorbani was not the woman I thought she was. I'd wrongly assumed that because she wasn't Italian, the mafia wouldn't include her in the mechanisms of their schemes.

But I should have cottoned on the day we were shot on the way to court.

I should have known when Yara was so easy with Dante's familiar treatment of me.

She was not just representing Dante in this RICO case.

She was their *consigliere*.

Not "other."

She was Family.

In that room of shadowed eyes, I was the only one outside the Family.

Something curdled in my stomach, a reaction that surprised me as much as it ashamed me. Once again, I was left out of the group dynamic. At work, my fellow associates saw me as a threat. They called me the ice queen or the bitch because I was driven and didn't know how to make anything beyond polite small talk when I could feel their disdain every time we spoke. Growing up, I'd been the red-headed girl playing with the true-blooded Italians who could be incredibly discriminatory. Even in my own family, I was different, set apart. I wasn't vivacious and bold like my siblings. I wasn't easy and comfortable with talk of love and sex and the ribbing that I knew logically was par for the course between sisters and brothers. Then Giselle and Daniel happened, and the entire family seemed to have known about it before I did.

Alone.

God, I was so fucking tired of being alone.

"I can leave," I offered as if I didn't want to be there anyway while inside my chest, I burned.

Tore slanted me an assessing look. "We will go to the office. You and Yara stay with Dante and Augustus."

Dr. Crown grunted. "Good, you're distracting me. If you stay, don't hover."

I nodded, relieved I could stay to see if Dante would be okay. *Cosima would want a report*, I told myself, and it was my sisterly duty to stay so I could give her the full story.

The men filed out of the room, the one named Jacopo glaring at me before he rounded the corner and out of sight.

"Ignore Mr. Salvatore," Yara suggested mildly, but her eyes were sharp on my face, peeling back my skin with scalpel-like precision to read things beneath it I wasn't willing to share. "They call him Grouch."

A wan smile tipped my lips. "Good to know it's not just me. Is he Dante's...cousin?"

Yara nodded as she finally took a seat with a sigh, rearranging her long limbs under her stunning black dress. "He is the son of Tore's cousin, the same cousin who helped them establish their... business when they first moved here from Italy."

"What happened to him?" I knew better than to ask questions about mafia dealings, but I was also a lawyer. My mind formed questions and hunted down answers the way a Rhodesian ridgeback stalked down lions.

Yara waved a hand, watching as Dr. Crown continued to administer care to Dante. "He was killed."

I fought the urge to roll my eyes because I'd obviously already arrived at that conclusion. I wanted to know the how, which was frequently much more interesting than the why of a thing.

"And this Kelly person?" I asked, shifting my weight on my heels as they bit into the soles of my feet. I was tempted to sit down, but I figured I should stay immobile, holding the bag of saline for Dante.

"You haven't heard his name?" she asked, faintly surprised. "Thomas 'Gunner' Kelly is the leader of the Irish mob."

"I was under the impression such a thing didn't exist anymore." I thought back to articles I had read about the demise of Irish gangs in America, about the diluted sense of Irish identity after so many years of integration and an influx of more powerful foreign criminal outfits like the Triad and the Mexican cartels.

"In my experience, criminal gangs are like cockroaches," she said with a wry smile. "You stomp one out only to look over your shoulder and discover another."

"And if you can't beat them..." I dared to imply that this was why Yara had joined forces with a known criminal entity.

Yara stared at me for so long, my skin itched, and I fought the urge to squirm like a girl under her mama's scolding gaze. "If all people were pure, Elena, there would be no laws. When we become lawyers, we are disbanding our perception of right and wrong in order to do our job to the fullest extent of our capabilities. Anyone who gets into law to defend the weak and innocent will inevitably become heartbroken and disillusioned." She paused for dramatic effect. "Do not tell me you, the woman they call a gladiator in the courtroom, became a lawyer for such a nonsensical reason."

I didn't tell her, though she wasn't far off the mark. In truth, I wasn't sure how to express the complicated tangle of contradictions that clogged my throat and made it hard to breathe.

I could have told her I wanted to fight injustice because my entire childhood had been rife with it. With people who were so poor they had no choice but to appeal to *la mafia* for loans and jobs and unrepayable favors. I understood why so many Italian revered the mafia as much as they feared it. It was a necessary component of their lives.

But a horrific one for some.

When I was growing up, I wanted to be a lawyer so I could stop the mafia's exploitation of the poor.

But then we moved to America, and I lost the threads of my dream and only saw the broader tapestry.

Become a lawyer.

My idealism was replaced with realism and capitalism.

Yara let me marinate in my conflict for a long moment before she dealt her deathly blow. "Some people argue that lawyers are more criminal than their clients, Elena. Perhaps it would make you feel better to know that there are more villains in this profession than heroes. It might ease your adjustment period."

People had always led me to believe I was cold, but looking into Yara's morally bankrupt gaze, I reevaluated myself.

"I would rather work with good people," I said somewhat lamely, feeling lopsided and upside down.

Anxiety spiked in my blood as I realized that spending time with Yara and Dante was already taking a toll on my perception of good and evil.

Yara shrugged easily. "I do too. I suppose it depends on your definition. Mr. Salvatore, for example, is a man I consider to be one of the best. He is a fair boss, a loyal friend and family member, and he does his part for the community."

"For a tax break, I'm sure," I muttered truculently.

"Just because someone loves and values different things than you do does not mean they are heartless, Ms. Lombardi. Dante would and *has* risked his life and livelihood for his loved ones and those he feels need championing. If you can't understand that, perhaps you aren't the woman I thought you were. Why don't you head home? If there is any update on Dante, I'm sure tomorrow morning will be early enough for you to receive it."

I blinked at her, properly chastised but still conflicted. Having dismissed me, Yara retrieved her phone from her clutch and began to work. I looked at Dr. Crown who was staring at me with pursed lips, judging me just as readily as I'd judged Dante and his crew.

"He'll be okay?" I asked quietly, my voice stripped raw so that it throbbed with vulnerable sincerity.

Whatever my feeling about his criminal enterprise, I didn't think Dante deserved to die.

In fact, the thought made me sway on my feet.

Dr. Crown fixed that pale blue gaze on me, and despite his classic all-American good looks, a distinct apathy in his gaze spoke to a cold heart. I recognized the look because I often saw it staring back at me in the mirror.

"It's not the first time someone has tried to kill him, and it won't be the last," was his stoic answer.

A shiver rolled through me like morning fog off the harbor, and it felt an awful lot like a premonition of things to come.

It was only later, when I was between the silky sheets of a bed that was much too large without Daniel in it, that I mulled over Yara's words. Unbidden, I recalled a quote I'd read in law school from the ever-lauded Thoreau.

"It is not desirable to cultivate a respect for the law, so much as a respect for right."

I lay in the dark shadows of my echoing empty home, wondering if I'd become so entrenched in society's perception of right and wrong that I'd forgotten to form an opinion of my own.

CHAPTER ELEVEN

DANTE

Death hadn't scared me for a very long time.

Growing up at Pearl Hall in the moors of northern England where gold and pearls were inlaid in the furniture and my baby rattle was made of solid silver, very few people would have suspected I'd know the darkness of pain and death.

But very few people knew my father was a madman.

I'd suspected as much from an early age when I heard moaning from the basement, the inverse of some Jane Eyre novel where the ghostly calls in the night were real nightmares caged within the walls of our home. My older brother, the golden child, was blind to the dangers of Noel, the cruelty of his treatment to our mother, the servants, and the occasional pale apparition of a woman emerging from the basement at dawn some mornings with bruises on her throat like jewels.

And then my mother was killed.

Chiara and I were visiting her childhood friend, Amadeo Salvatore at his villa outside of Naples when she decided we weren't going home to England. She was tired in a way I didn't think, even if she had lived, she would have recovered from. Her black hair was brittle, cracking off in pieces under my hands when I hugged her bony frame, and there were troughs of inky blue beneath her eyes that I couldn't remember not being there. She was still beautiful, but in the way of a broken thing, a doll played with too hard, then tossed to rot in the corner of a grown child's room.

She was smiling that trip, though. I had just graduated from Cambridge with honors, and she was proud of me, almost ridiculously so because she always tried to make up for Noel's lack of regard for me. I was the spare, not the heir, and from the beginning, I'd been too much like my mother and her people.

There wasn't a subordinate bone in my body, and Noel knew it, so he pretended I didn't exist or, if I got in his way, forcibly put me in my place.

We were eating dinner one night, a few days after she had begun to make plans to move permanently to Italy, when her cell phone rang. I knew instantly it was my father by the shadow that passed over her face dark as an eclipse.

"Don't answer it," I'd said, standing up from my chair at the dining room table to reach for the phone so that I could crush it the way I wanted to crush my father's heart in my hands. "He can go fuck himself."

"Edward Dante," she scolded, but her eyes were distracted, her lips a bloodless line in her face. She watched the phone in her hand ring the way I imagined a soldier watched a bomb countdown to detonation. There was almost a macabre resolve in her face I only recognized in retrospect. "There are some demons you cannot run from. Your father is one of them."

I looked at Tore, but his face was a grim mask. He knew better than to argue with Chiara and think he could sway her when her mind was made up.

I'd gotten my stubbornness from her too.

We both stared at her silently as she stood from the chair and palmed the phone, ignoring the call even though, seconds later, it began to ring again.

"I think I'll retire now," she murmured in that mixed British/Italian accent I was coming to share with her. "*Buona notte, figlio mio.*"

I accepted her kiss on my cheek, closing my eyes as I carefully pulled her closer to my body. She was so slight compared to me. I felt I might accidentally break her ribs if I wasn't gentle.

Guilt surged through me as she kissed Tore on the cheek, then slowly walked up the back stairs to her room. I'd been gone for four years at uni, throwing myself into my studies of the human mind and my freedom out from under Noel's thumb. My criminal tendencies were already showing. I'd started a sports gambling ring with some of the posh students that had netted me over a million quid by the time I graduated with my master's, and I was looking forward to moving to Rome to see what trouble I could get up to with Latin girls.

I hadn't realized until this trip that in my absence, Noel had been beating Chiara much more than he had when I was a boy.

I should have known, but I was a stupid, selfish twentysomething kid with too much swagger and not enough sense. Whenever I spoke with her on the phone or she visited on the weekends, she was always all smiles and positivity, promising everything at home was fine.

But she only did that for us, for Alexander and me, so that we could get free of that pearly cage and free of Noel without obligation to her dragging us home.

"I didn't know, either," Tore admitted that night, looking older than he ever had before, his broad sloping forehead creased and rumpled like a used napkin. "I've let you both down."

"No," I argued, loving him so fiercely at that moment for being the kind of man who cared about his childhood friend and her family enough to risk Noel's fury. "I should have watched her more closely."

He sighed, swirling his glass of red wine so that it caught the candlelight and brightened to a blood red. "She's safe here. We won't let her go back to England."

"No," I agreed. "I'll move with her. She needs--I don't know-- love and attention after living with that monster for so long."

Tore had agreed. We spent the next hour drinking wine and discussing what I might do in Italy. If maybe I was interested in working with Tore and his crew.

I wasn't seriously considering it. I was a man with a wild, untameable heart, but I didn't like the idea of becoming a criminal like my father.

And then we heard it.

The scream.

The hairs rose on the back of my neck as adrenaline poured like a bucket of ice water over my head.

I was up out of my chair and running before my mind had a chance to compute the noise into thought.

Tore was right behind me, one of his men trailing after that with his gun raised.

My legs took me to my mother's room. The door was locked, but I didn't think twice before I kicked in the old wood with one brutal thrust of my right foot.

The room was empty, the sheer linen curtains billowing into the room from the slightly open balcony doors.

And I knew.

Elementally, spiritually, I knew that what I found outside those doors would change my life forever.

My heartbeat thrummed in my ears like a ceremonial drum, my steps stomping heavily in tandem as I moved to the door and pushed it open with one finger.

The small balcony was empty, the climbing ivy over the stone walls rustling in the olive scented breeze.

"Edward," Tore protested, reaching forward to grab my arm

when I tried to go to the balustrade to look over the edge. "Don't."

I shrugged him off ruthlessly, not taking my eyes off the ground I could see from my angle. When I reached the edge, I held my breath as I curled my fingers over the stone and looked down.

But she wasn't there.

In fact, over the next few days and months and years, Chiara Davenport was nowhere to be found. Local authorities ruled it a runaway, but we knew better.

It was Noel.

He'd killed my mother, and to make matters worse, he'd convinced my brother, Alexander, that Tore was to blame and that I had deserted them to take over his mafia outfit.

In one way, he was right.

From the day Chiara disappeared, I started to work for Amadeo Salvatore and reinvented myself as Dante Salvatore.

Because I had realized something vital, a life lesson that could only have been imparted to me by Death itself.

If I wanted to defeat my demons, I had to become the ultimate monster.

So many years later, I was still ruled by the essential lessons I'd learned from her death.

Trust no one, attack first, and, above all, protect those who cannot protect themselves.

I was kicking myself a few days after my attempted murder because I had failed to follow the first two mandates.

"The Irish scum," Adriano said before spitting over the edge of the balcony as if the taste of the word in his mouth was venom. "Tore should have let us end them."

"No," I disagreed from where I stood at the balustrade, remembering a decade ago when I'd looked over one very much like it to see if my mother lay broken below me. "We have to be smarter than them, Adriano."

"They're fucking cowards to try to poison you," Marco sneered as he cleaned his gun at the table. "No *Italiano* would lower himself to that."

I cocked an eyebrow but secretly wondered if an Italian hadn't been behind the Irish attack. The truth was, my trial made the entire Commission nervous as hell. I was an outsider, a *sconosciuto*. I could speak Italian like a native, adhere to every antiquated custom and cultural norm, but the truth was, Italians were decidedly purist, even Italian-Americans, and they did not like that I'd been born and raised a Brit.

Until me, there had never been a boss whose father wasn't Italian, and even though my mother was Italian, it wasn't the same thing for the Old World bosses in NYC.

They'd never liked me, preferring instead to do business with Tore, and the fact that I was being investigated and tried under the RICO Act might have been as good an opportunity for them to rid themselves of me before I had the chance to roll over on them.

I was no rat, but I had to admit, I was glad the head of the di Carlo family was dead and I'd fucking love the opportunity to make the Dons of the other four families——Lupi, Belcante, Accardi, and

Maglione--follow him to an early grave.

Not one of them was younger than seventy, and while I didn't consider myself ageist, there was no denying the old mafia Dons had fossilized at the table.

In my opinion, new blood was needed, and I'd been pushing for change for years only to be rejected at every turn.

"You think one of the other Families is behind this?" Adriano asked, cracking his scarred knuckles. Even taller and broader than me, with arms like bags of rocks and shoulders so thick with muscle they made his neck look freakishly short, Addie was the biggest man in our immediate circle.

I shrugged one shoulder, but I wasn't ready to talk about my theory. My men were loyal, but they stayed loyal because I was careful not to point out a problem until I had a solution.

"The Irish are small potatoes," Marco joked with a snigger. "Wouldn't put it past them to be working with someone else to get cut in on something. What do they got for their own anyway?"

"Shylocking," Chen piped up, always ready with information. The man was like a human encyclopedia. He got a lot of shit from capos outside the family for being Japanese, but he'd saved my life three times, and the moment I'd met him in a back-alley gambling den counting cards like a fucking pro, I'd known he needed to be on my team. "Some low-level drug muling. Nothing much."

"First the Basante deal and now this," I mused, scrubbing a hand over my stubbled jaw. I hadn't shaved since the day of San Gennaro, and my beard was coming in thick. "Tore was right to hold you back from a massacre when I'm already in the fucking hot seat with the feds, but we do have to strike back."

Marco, Chen, Adriano, Jaco, and Frankie were quiet as I thought on it, used to giving me my head. None of them, save Jaco and Frankie, had the knack or lust for leadership. Jaco was too hotheaded to be boss, and Frankie hated people too much to deal with them regularly. They were happy to defer to my leadership.

But I took a second to scan their faces, aware as ever that Mason Matlock, still hanging like dried meat in my airplane hangar, had told me there was a mole in my operation.

As much as I didn't want to think it was one of the men I considered brothers, I knew better than to trust blindly.

"Addie, you feel like having a friendly talk with one of the bartenders at Father Patrick's? See if we can't get a beat on what's going on down there."

His grin was all big, jagged teeth, his brutish face utterly intimidating. It almost made me smile to think about his fierce love for his massive black mutt, Toro, and his obsession with cannoli, the cream somehow always finding its way onto his shirts.

This was the contrast of all my men, of Tore, and of me.

We were sinners of the highest order, driven to make money, end our rivals, and succeed at almost any cost.

But we were also men.

Men driven by lust and love and loyalty. By our dogs and cannoli and comradery.

This was what a woman like Elena Lombardi was incapable

of understanding. That two opposites could coexist in one whole. That you didn't have to be all or nothing, black or white, good or bad.

Such narrow-minded thinking should have repelled me, but I found myself thinking more and more about how I might change her mind. The idea of corrupting her was heady, as arousing mentally as it was physically.

What might she be like warmed with passion, alight with vengeful anger, so ruthless in her ambition she didn't give a single fuck about the obstacles in her way.

For the first time since I'd been poisoned, my dick twitched with arousal.

"You're distracted," Frankie noted because he knew me better than the rest of my men, and he wasn't afraid to speak up.

He was originally from Sicily and the very same Cosa Nostra we were currently feuding with, but I had no doubt he wasn't the traitor. His family had made him seduce and defile a woman in order to bring down a rival family, and he'd ended up falling for her. Now, they lived together in the city and were safeguarded from their past by *my* protection.

"Thinking about the redhead with the legs?" Marco asked with a waggle of his thick brows. "Damn, but I couldn't look at her the other night without getting a hard-on."

I was up out of my seat baring my teeth at one of my best soldati before I could curb the impulse. *"Stai zitto."* I told him to shut up. "Do not talk about her this way."

He frowned, eyes darting around the small group of my six most trusted men. "Am I missing something?"

"He wants to fuck her," Frankie surmised with a slow grin. "I fucking knew it! Lombardi women are your kryptonite, D."

"I don't want to fuck her," I said calmly, tossing my hand as if the idea was garbage I was throwing in the bin. "She wouldn't know the first thing about taking my cock."

It was true, in a sense.

They didn't need to know that I was more than mildly intrigued about teaching her how to please me and herself.

"Leave it to you to have two hot lawyers," Jaco muttered around his cigarette. "I hope they're more useful than just being pretty to look at."

"They are. Yara's never let us down, and even if Elena wasn't driven like a fucking race car by the idea of success, she would do anything for her family, and Cosima asked her to take this on..." I trailed off as my mind snagged on the teeth of my words.

And there it was.

That simple.

An idea.

A way to be smarter than those Irish scum and bring them to heel without starting a full-fledged war with them or the pieces of shit di Carlos they seemed to be in bed with.

It stemmed from one basic principle.

Most people would do anything to protect the ones they loved.

I would have gladly taken Chiara's place buried in the maze

behind Pearl Hall.

Elena would gladly have taken Cosima's when she lay comatose in the hospital last year.

Now, it just remained to be seen if the Irish mob had enough decency to look out for their own in the same way.

I pulled out my cell phone without discussing the plan with anyone and dialed Yara's number.

"I've got a plan," I told her. "But you're not gonna like it."

CHAPTER TWELVE

elena

I didn't see Dante for six days.

That wasn't unusual for many reasons.

A federal trial like his could take years to go to court, and even though we had filed for an expedited trial, the legal clogs still took months to churn.

We were busy, though.

Our pre-trial motion to suppress Mason Matlock's testimony was going to court that morning, and it was absolutely vital that we won. Giuseppe di Carlo's nephew had testified to police following the shooting at Ottavio's that it was Dante who had driven by in an unmarked black SUV with a few of his "thugs" to shoot out the deli.

The problem was, Dante didn't have an alibi we could use because he was protecting someone.

After studying the particulars of the case, I had to wonder if he wasn't protecting my sister.

Cosima had been shot three times that day, but arguably, she could have killed Giuseppe di Carlo before the drive-by shooters arrived.

It was one of the many theories circulating through my mind as I worked long hours on the case each day, not only his case but also the man himself a dominant feature in my thoughts.

It wasn't easy to admit I was intrigued by him.

So, I didn't credit my theory about Cosima and his protection too much. It almost seemed like wistful thinking on my part, trying to make a rogue into a gentleman through any means possible.

But I couldn't kick the suspicion as I walked to work that morning, and before I could curb the impulse, my fingers were tapping out Cosima's phone number.

"Hallo, my Lena," she answered in a jaunty British manner, her voice filled with radiant happiness. She always sounded like that now, high on her life, grateful for every moment. "How is my favorite lawyer?"

The smile that pulled my lips over my teeth was inexorable. As if it was Cosima's beautiful face, I cupped the phone tight to my cheek. "Hello, my beautiful Cosi. I'm fine. Just getting coffee before a long day of court and research. How are you?"

There was a deep voice in the background and then my sister's breathy giggle. "Xan, stop it. I'm talking to Elena."

"Tell her you're busy," he ordered, loud enough for me to hear. "Very busy."

Cosima's warm laughter spilled like honey through the line.

"Sorry, Lena, you know Alexander. He can be so *bossy*."

There was a throaty chuckle and then a shuffle as Cosima moved. "Let me just leave the room, or he won't stop bothering me."

"I'll remember that next time you're begging for me to make you come," he yelled deliberately so I could hear.

A blush warmed my cheeks, and I groaned as I pushed open the doors of my favorite coffee shop and stood in line. "Oh my God, Cosi, I'll just call you back."

"No," she demanded. "He's gone now. I apologize. I know these kinds of things make you uncomfortable."

I hesitated, picking at the side of a hangnail as I considered being honest with her. "I'm working on that, you know."

Her voice was velvet, a soft place for my confessions to land. "Oh? With your therapist?"

"Yes, and Monica, she told me there is hope for me... I have surgery scheduled in two weeks. Apparently, post-op, I'll be able to orgasm, and maybe..." I sucked in a shaky breath, almost afraid to say the words out loud as if they might dissipate forever like smoke in the air. "Maybe I'll be able to conceive naturally one day too."

"*Dio mio*, Elena," my sister breathed, tears instantly thick in her voice. "My love, I cannot tell you how happy I am to hear that. You must be over the moon."

"I am," I agreed before quickly ordering my coffee from the barista with my hand over the phone. Then I moved away and said to Cosima, "It's just...strange. I feel like my life is empty still. A year ago, I would have been thrilled. I can't help wondering what would have happened if Daniel and I got this news together before he met Giselle."

"Oh, my love, please don't let your mind go there. Aren't you the one who has always told me the past cannot be altered and to focus on the future?"

"Yes," I agreed on a sigh, the knot in my chest slowly loosening under the careful tending of her calm attention. "I know I should be over it, but it's easier said than done. It's not just Daniel who lied to me and broke my heart. Somehow, Giselle's disloyalty is even worse. Betrayal from someone who is supposed to understand your pain and should stand by you no matter what feels impossible to move on from."

"You and Giselle haven't been tight in so long...I know what she did is not forgivable, but the fractures in your sisterhood gave room for her relationship with Sin to grow. By the time she knew you were the girlfriend, she was too in love to change the outcome. I know it hurts, but they're really happy together. Happier than *you* were with him, my Lena. Don't waste any more time on a man who isn't spending time thinking about you."

I swallowed convulsively past the lump in my throat, struggling to digest her words. Not because I disagreed with them, but because I didn't.

The way Daniel had acted after he returned from their affair in Mexico... it was as if he was a different man, one I didn't know very well at all despite being with him for four years.

I hadn't made him happy, not like her.

And God, that burned like frostbite emanating from my arctic heart.

"One day," Cosima said so softly, so quietly, as if she was afraid to spook me. "I know you'll find a man who makes you forget every fear you've ever had, who soothes all the ragged wounds you've had to endure in your life, who makes you feel more alive than you ever have before."

"Like Alexander and you," I said with a tight smile, happy at least she had found that.

No one deserved that kind of love more than the most loving woman I knew.

"Like Alexander and me," she agreed. "Don't be afraid of a rough start, either. Sometimes, you are too quick to judge. Give things time to develop. Lord knows I hated Xan before I fell for him."

A hiccough moved through my chest as I remembered the real reason for my call.

A man I'd thought was hateful who I was beginning to question might not be so awful after all.

"Cosima, you know I'm happy to finally repay even one iota of what you've done for our family," I began, acknowledging the fact that she and Sebastian had provided for our family since they were teenagers, that they had been the ones to move us to America and get us out of that Neapolitan stink hole. "But I need to know, what is your relationship with Tore and Dante?"

The pause that followed was filled with words in a language I didn't understand. I was thrown back to childhood when Seamus had relentlessly taught all of us English, my siblings catching on quickly, but my own mind lagging behind.

I was tired of the language of secrets.

"I need to know," I pushed. "I'm representing him, Cosi. I need to know the facts."

"You want to know," she argued, but she wasn't angry, just weary. "You've always wondered, but now, you finally want to know the truth. Even if it's horrible."

"Yes," I whispered, my eyes unseeing as I stood in the middle of the bustling coffee shop imagining what horrors my sister had endured for our family. "Tell me."

"I won't tell you the whole story over the phone, Lena, but I'll come to visit. It's been a while, and this is something I should tell you in person. But as far as Tore and Dante are concerned... they're my family. I know you have bad memories of the Camorra and you hate everything they represent, but those two men are two of the best I've ever known, and they've proved that to me too many times to count. I trust them with my life and my heart, and I'd trust them with *yours*."

"What really happened that day at Ottavio's?" I demanded, leaning forward as if I was in front of her, bearing down on her to squeeze more of the truth from a woman who was as porous as a stone. "Is Dante trying to protect you by not giving his alibi?"

A brief hesitation so quick it shot past like a shooting star.

Then, so solemnly it felt like a vow spoken by a monk at prayer. "Dante is always trying to protect me."

Does he love you? I suddenly wanted to ask, the question burning up my chest like gasoline-lit tinder.

Does he love you? Does he love you? Does he love you? my inner voice screamed.

But I didn't say anything.

I wasn't sure why, but it might have had something to do with the fact that I couldn't deal with the knowledge of another man showing me some level of attention only to find one of my sisters far superior.

Not that Dante liked me.

I was just a game as he'd told me from the very beginning. A game of corruption.

But my chest, it burned and burned.

"Be careful, *amore,* you are a lawyer for one of the most powerful criminal families in the country. I hate to put you in danger, but I know you are strong enough to endure. It brings me peace to know the smartest woman I know is protecting the bravest man and vice versa. Don't do anything foolish and watch your back."

A shiver sank pointed teeth into the back of my neck and dragged down my spine, leaving me flayed with fear. Suspiciously, I looked around the coffee shop as I picked up my coffee from the station.

It was only because I was looking that I saw the flash of red.

Red like a flag tossed before a bull.

Instantly my back went up, and my fight or flight impulse surged through my limbs.

"Cosima, I have to go," I said before hanging up the phone and dropping it into my purse.

My eyes were still trained on that red.

A deep red that was almost black.

The same color as my own.

Seamus Moore continued to stare at me through the floor-to-ceiling windows of the coffee shop with the faintly interested expression of someone considering a work of art.

My own expression, I'm sure, was filled with horror.

Seamus Moore.

The father I hadn't seen in nearly six years.

I wasn't surprised when fight won out for flight. There was a reason my mother called me her *lottatrice*, her fighter.

Mouth pursed against the force of the fury building on my tongue, I stalked through the café, burst through the doors, and turned to face my father.

Only to find him backing away with his hands in his pockets farther down the street, a sly smile on his face I recognized too well. When he ducked into an alley, I allowed impulse to rule me, and I followed.

He was leaning against the wall deep in the shadows of the narrow brick corridor. I took a single moment to stare at him, noting with disdain that he was still as handsome as ever despite living hard for much of his life. He was classically beautiful; his coloring striking and features finely honed. His hair was longer than he'd worn it when I'd known him, brushing the upturned collar of his black peacoat, and there was a thick, deliberately groomed beard over his jaw, but the sight of those gray eyes sucking up the shadows were the very same ones that had haunted me for years, even after he'd gone.

He watched me silently as I unfroze and stalked toward him, but I knew he wasn't prepared for what I did next.

I punched him.

As hard as I possibly could, remembering my years of self-defense classes in the torque of my hips and the angle of the blow to the underside of his left cheekbone.

Pain exploded in my hand at the same time air burst from his mouth at the impact.

When I recoiled to do it again, fury blazing over every inch of my scream, he grabbed my wrist in an iron vise and yanked me closer so that I didn't have the space to strike him again.

"My little fighter." He had the audacity to chuckle in my face. "I should have known you'd hit me."

"Not hard enough," I hissed as I jammed the hard spike of my six-inch heels into his tender instep.

He cursed viciously in Italian and shoved me off. I staggered, then caught myself on my back heel, fishing in my bag for the pepper spray I carried with me religiously.

When I aimed it at Seamus, he blinked in total shock then slowly lifted his hands.

"*Dai,* Elena, it's me. What the fuck are you doing?"

It was my turn to blink incredulously. "I'm protecting myself from a man who is a stranger now and a monster from my past. What the fuck do you think I'm doing?"

"I'm your father, Elena, put that shit down," he demanded in that patriarchal way he had of ordering his children around.

It never worked, not then and certainly not now after years of negligence followed by years of abandonment.

It disgusted me how obsessed he was with being Italian, how he still punctuated his speech with it. He was an actor typecasting himself in a role he'd never fit.

"I'll put it down when you tell me what you're doing here."

He barely resisted the temptation to roll his eyes. "Here in New York or here *attempting* to have a conversation with my firstborn?"

"Both," I bit out behind my bared teeth.

It hurt to look at him, to see the resemblance on the surface and to know that his tainted blood was also inside me. He was everything I reviled in this life, and I truly thought I'd never see him again. When he disappeared after Cosima moved away to model at eighteen, I'd just assumed he would end up in some ditch somewhere, killed by the Camorra or some other wastrel he'd gotten too involved with.

Our reunion only served to emphasize that I'd actually hoped he was dead all these years. Even living and breathing in front of me, looking at me from the same stormy gray eyes as my own, he was still dead to me.

He dropped his hands in exasperation, treating me like an unruly child. I was reminded that he'd never favored me, not like he did Cosima for her beauty and Sebastian for his maleness, not even like Giselle who had appealed to him for the longest, holding out hope he might one day change. Seamus had never liked me because from the time I could cogitate, I was smart enough not to like *him*.

"I moved to New York shortly after you did, *figlia mia.* I wanted to keep an eye on you and your mother." He ignored my uncharacteristic snort of disdain. "Before you hit me with that poison, you should know. Cosima made me swear not to contact any of you again."

Every atom of my body stilled then burst into a flurry of movement as thoughts fell like dominos in my path of understanding.

"Why would she do that?" I spoke slowly through numb lips because I was almost there.

Almost at a conclusion my mind had been trying to draw for years, only I hadn't allowed it because the truth was too eviscerating to acknowledge.

He pursed his lips, another characteristic I'd inherited. "Cosi, well, she offered herself to the Camorra in order to repay my debts. It was all her idea, you understand. I only found out about it after the fact and tried to stop her, but it was too late."

His words had an echo, my head empty of everything but what his speech confirmed.

Madonna Santa.

Cosima had sold her body to repay our father's gambling debts.

Bile surged over the back of my tongue, and before I could control it, I leaned to the side and vomited all over the back wall of the alley. The poison of the truth worked through my system, pulling everything from me in a toxic rush I spewed onto the dirty asphalt. Tears sluiced down my cheeks as I retched painfully, but I held myself up with one hand on the wall and closed my lids to hold on until it passed.

Done, I wiped my mouth with the back of my hand and leaned against the wall a few feet from the crime scene. My hand trembled as I brushed clammy sweat off my brow.

It was so atrocious. So unspeakable.

My poor Cosima, the most beautiful human I'd never known. I couldn't fathom what she'd had to do in order to get us out of our Italian nightmare and into our American dream.

"Do you know who bought her?" I whispered, staring at Seamus through lowered lids, unable to bear the sight of him.

I didn't believe for one fucking second that he hadn't been behind the exchange. Narcissus himself had nothing on Seamus goddamn Moore. He would have no remorse exchanging anything for a chance at his own freedom and betterment.

He hesitated, licking his lips nervously. "Her husband, Alexander Davenport."

Physically rocked by his words, I let the wall at my back anchor me. "You're kidding."

"Would I kid about something like this?" he countered with a raised brow. "Listen, it's all turned out for the best. Your sister is wildly in love with the bastard."

"She probably has Stockholm Syndrome," I yelled.

He shrugged. "They were apart for years, so I don't think so." Watching me struggle, he sighed gustily and dragged a hand over his beard. "This isn't why I wanted to talk to you, Lena."

"Don't call me that," I snapped, settling my hand over my oceanic stomach to steady myself. I pushed off the wall to face him as I wanted to, strong, shoulders back, chin hiked high so I could look down the length of my nose at him.

"Elena," he tried to cajole, hands widespread in surrender to my mood even as he took a little step forward and affixed that crooked smile to his face that was a facsimile of Sebastian's. "I'm here because I don't want you to get hurt."

The laugh that erupted from my throat was all fire and smile, burning up my lungs and scorching my mouth. I laughed bitterly, a little manically at the thought.

"How can you take yourself seriously?" I asked, genuinely interested. "You haven't cared about any of us in years."

"I care," he countered, his features flickering like a bad TV connection between placid tenderness and curdled anger. "I wouldn't be here if I didn't."

"Say what you have to say, then." I waved my limp hand at him as I was hit by a wave of exhaustion.

Was this it?

Was this to be the pattern of my life forever?

Men fucking up my happiness?

No, not even that. I'd never been truly happy. They'd kept me from even obtaining it for longer than a fleeting moment.

And it all started with Seamus.

For the first time in my life, I understood cold-blooded violence, the desire to murder someone who felt like nothing more than a trivial decision akin to taking out the garbage.

Seamus was trash, and he deserved to be taken out.

If I'd had a gun, instead of a canister of mace, I might have.

He read the violence in my eyes, but instead of taking it to heart, he seemed challenged by it. His eyes went dark as steel bullet casings.

"I heard you were working for the Salvatore *borgata*," he drawled, too casual, a fox lying still in wait.

I barked a hollow laugh that hurt my throat. "Did you?"

He cast me a sidelong look. "The entire underworld knows now that you're the Camorra capo's lawyer. It puts a target on your back, Elena. How could you be so reckless?"

My mouth gaped in furious wonder. "How you can ask me that with a straight face is beyond me." Wrath ate at my incredulity, fueling me to stalk toward my dad once more, each step punctuating my hard-bitten words. "You sold my sister to repay *your* debts to the Camorra. I am representing a capo because *you* involved us in the mafia before we were old enough to speak. You do *not* get to tell me I'm reckless when all I've ever tried to do is get out from

184

under the mistakes you've made that nearly ruined our family."

Anxiety had plagued my entire childhood, wondering when the men with black eyes would come calling and I'd have to hide my siblings from their vicious intent. Hours spent cramped in the hiding space beneath the kitchen sink. Holding Giselle as she cried once when huddled in our shared room while someone beat Seamus in the living room for taking money he'd never be able to repay.

"You didn't have to work for the *bastardo*. I had nothing to do with that," he argued even as I reached for him and shoved a hand hard into his sternum, pushing him into the wall. He hissed at the impact, then leaned forward into my face to snarl, "Everything I do, I do for my family."

"You don't know the meaning," I snapped. "Spare me the fatherly bullshit. I can fight my own battles."

"Clearly, you cannot," he countered, a smile twitching his upper lip. It wasn't an expression of joy but one of calculated satisfaction. "How would you like to know that it's your dad keeping the Irish off your back, Elena?"

"Let them come for me, then, dear old Da," I mocked, my red lips pulled back over my teeth. "I'd sooner trust Dante Salvatore to protect me than you."

Hurt flared through his features before he carefully stowed the expression behind his mask. His hands went to my shoulders, fingers curling into the trench coat and the flesh beneath it with a painful bite.

"You want to die, huh?" he demanded coldly. "Because there are worse monsters than the Italian mob in New York City, and all of them have their eyes on Don Salvatore and his crew. And you. They'll take you and crack you open like a fucking piggy bank to find whatever treasured intel they can get on the Camorra."

"I don't know anything. I just represent him in court," I said, but it lacked conviction because it honestly hadn't ever occurred to me I could be risking my life for a man I hardly knew just by doing my job.

Seamus knew my face well enough to read the fear at the pinched corners of my mouth. "You should be afraid, *cara.* You're in my world now, and the people who inhabit it are fucking cannibals."

I wrenched from his hold and took a massive step away from him. I'd heard enough. Seamus was every bad part of me, the pride, the explosive temper, the inability to forgive, and the tendencies toward superiority. He lived in me more than enough. I didn't need his presence in my life for him to take a toll on me, and I was done giving him the benefit of the doubt.

He would never love me.

I might not have understood adoration all that well, but I knew whatever Seamus claimed to feel for us was the antithesis.

"Don't contact me again," I told him in a deep voice that emerged from somewhere dark and low in my gut. "You do, Seamus, and I swear to God, I'll kill you if that's the only way to get rid of you."

He laughed. Actually laughed at my threat, tucking his hands in his pockets and rocking back on his heels as if we were just having a lovely father-daughter chat.

"Little fighter," he said again, affection in his tone. "If I don't protect you, however ungrateful you may be, you'll die."

"A part of me died the day you introduced Christopher into our lives." The words were wrenched from the fabric of my soul, and I found suddenly that there was wet in my eyes and a harsh tickle in my sinuses. "When you let him seduce a little girl who didn't know better and again when you *knew* he hurt me, but you didn't step in." A shadow passed over his face, but I was too far gone to feel anything but rage. "Another part died when you took Cosima from us, when you disappeared even though we were better off without you. You killed my ability to love, Seamus, and you almost killed my ability to even *live*. Most of what plagues me is because of you, and that is the only legacy you've ever given me. If you care at *all* about me, you'll leave me with the scars you've already inflicted and never bother me again."

I turned to stalk down the alley only to flip my hair over my shoulder and snarl one last threat, a warning that wasn't mine to make, yet I felt fully assured of its validity. I knew I wouldn't tell Dante I'd seen my father, that he'd told me the truth about Cosima and Alexander, but I knew even if I never did and I had to cash in my warning, Dante would do it without question.

"And if you think to fuck with me again, the Devil of New York City himself will come for you, and I won't stop him when he does."

CHAPTER THIRTEEN

elena

The pre-trial hearing was successful.

In fact, it was almost ridiculous how easy it was to suppress Mason Matlock's testimony. Judge Hartford wore a furious scowl on his thick brow during the entire proceeding, but there was no denying that Mason Matlock was an unreliable witness, and without him present to cross-examine, it was impossible to validate his testimony the night of the shooting.

It was brilliant to watch Yara Ghourbani at work. The legal profession was all about puzzles. Researching and cross-examining until you found the right piece to fit with the overall picture of what you were trying to present. It was finding the right words and the right tone, about knowing how different laws interacted with each other and how you might use one to cancel out the other. Yara, clearly, was a master dissectologist.

She parried everything US Attorney O'Malley said with calm clarity, used his own need to posture against him, and never for a moment forgot who her audience of one was and what he stood for.

"Your Honor," she'd finished, hands folded before her, eyes locked on Judge Hartford's even though her expression was deferential. "Without Mason Matlock present as a witness, it is impossible to determine where his loyalty to his uncle Giuseppe di Carlo ends and the truth begins. As we have presented to the court, Mason accepted an apartment on the Upper West Side from his uncle only a few years prior and used his connection to Mr. Stewart Sidney on Wall Street to get his first job in the market. If he was so willing to accept his uncle's favors, it stands to reason that he would have no qualms about lying for his uncle and their family to the police and this court. Without his presence in your courtroom and your judgment on his testimony and cross-examination, his statement should be suppressed."

I smiled slightly at her subtle manipulative flattery. Even though I'd compiled all the research for the trial, it was like seeing it for the first time through the lens of such a powerful female lawyer.

Dennis sat at the opposite table with his lips pinched and hands crossed, unable to say anything because everything had already been said.

Judge Hartford too, seemed irritated by his lack of options. He shot USA O'Malley a quick look, then sighed. "I have read and listened to the motion to suppress objections, and the defense does have an...extensive argument for striking Mr. Matlock's statement from evidence. Mr. Matlock is a problematic and prejudice witness due to his familial association with the deceased Giuseppe di Carlo. As Matlock has failed to appear, I have no choice but to rule in favor of the defense."

The truth was, we had been sure going into the pre-trial hearing that we would secure a victory, but that wasn't the only reason we had pushed to disallow Matlock's statement. Going to court before trial allowed us to gain insight into how the prosecution was structuring their case and, potentially, what it hinged upon.

Even something as little as Dennis's flatlined mouth gave away too much. It was obvious he was unhappy about the outcome, but he wasn't fighting as hard as he could have to keep it. Which meant, probably, that he had something different up his sleeve to pin on Dante.

Yara thought it was another important witness.

I didn't know why she was so certain, only that she'd emerged from a phone call with Dante in the office a few days ago and appeared in the doorway of the conference room I usually worked in to tell me so.

I didn't pry. I was learning that the Camorra had their own ways of gathering evidence.

Which was why I wasn't immediately on guard when Yara and I were leaving the courthouse, and Yara stopped me from getting into a cab back to the office.

"Have a coffee with me," she suggested mildly as if we did such things all the time.

We did not.

And as far as I could tell, Yara didn't have a friendly coffee with anyone at the firm ever. She was a lone pillar of strength. It was one of the reasons I was so drawn to her.

Even though suspicion spiked through me, I agreed because I would have been foolish not to. We walked together a few blocks from the courthouse to a little Italian place that served espresso through a window at the front of the small storefront. Yara ordered without asking me what I wanted, paid for our two double espressos, and then left me to carry the small white cups and saucers to the table she picked on the sidewalk farthest away from the door.

With every second she was silent, my pulse raced harder. She and Dante both had a similar predatory quality, their gazes too watchful, too hungry and calculating.

She took a small sip of the thick crema on the coffee and hummed her pleasure.

I followed suit, but the coffee, good and strong, tasted like mud on my tongue.

"So much more patient than I would have given you credit for, Ms. Lombardi," Yara said with only a trace of a smile. "I know you must be bursting to question why I brought you here."

"I have a feeling it wasn't for the coffee, as good as it is," I demurred.

Her lips twitched. "Astute. No, I brought you here for two

reasons. The first is to tell you a story." She paused, studying me so intently I could track the way her gaze mapped my features, drawing a line down my straight nose, over the arch of my brows, tunneling into my eyes. "When I was a girl, I fell in love with an Italian while I was on a summer abroad in Rome."

My eyebrows hiked into my hairline. That was not how I thought the conversation would start.

"I was so young, barely nineteen, but I knew the moment I saw him that he should be mine. He had that Italian hair, you know? Thick and silken, so lush and curling I could already imagine my hands carding through it as we kissed." She laughed, and it was an easy sound, a strange one coming from so calculated a woman. "He noticed me a moment later, and I knew when we locked eyes that he wanted me. So, when he approached, I went with him easily. He was funny, and I liked the way he was always using his hands to tell me things in ways his mouth could not. There was such confidence in him it made me feel important to be next to him."

She paused to take a sip of espresso, and I was struck by an overlay of her as that young girl, a beautiful Persian intrigued by the different culture and beauty of the Italian boy.

"My family hated him, of course, when they found out we were going together. I only told them because I fully intended to marry him. I was in law school, but I wanted to drop out and move permanently to Italy. I wanted to drink wine with him in Piazza Navona every night for the rest of my life and have his babies. My parents told me if I didn't at least finish my degree, they would never talk to me again. I figured, what is one more year in the grand scheme of life and our love? So, I returned to America at the end of the summer, and we wrote letters to each other every day for the next six months."

Her smile was sad, but then, I'd already known it would be a tragic story.

"I was graduating in three weeks when I got a phone call from Donni. His father needed money. Their butcher shop was struggling, and the bank wouldn't give him a loan. So, he'd gone to the local capo of the Camorra and asked him. Not only did they give Signore Carozza the loan, they also offered Donni a job."

My chest tightened with dread as I realized where this was going, that I was hearing yet another story about how the mafia had destroyed a life.

"Like any American girl, I'd watched movies about the mafia, but I didn't really understand the intricacies of the institution. I didn't know enough to ask Donni not to work for them. He started to make good money, saving to buy a house for us when I moved back." She sighed, pain stale in those beautiful dark eyes, lip lax with remembered sorrow. "He'd only been working with them for a month when he was in a car accident."

I frowned, my mouth opening as if I could correct her because I had been sure that wasn't where the story was going to go.

Yara's mouth tightened in recognition of my shock. "He was just twenty-three, and he was hit straight on by a drunk driver. There was massive damage, including trauma to his brain. When I flew out to Rome after getting the call, it was to visit Donni in the hospital, and he was hooked up to life support. He was in a coma, and the doctors didn't have much hope he would recover."

Tears glistened in her eyes, but her voice was strong, her eyes almost wild with mad intensity as she leaned across the table and grabbed my hand tightly in her own. "The Camorra paid for his hospital fees, to keep him alive for as long as Signore Carozza and I needed to say our goodbyes. Their women brought flowers every single day until Donni's room was like a garden. The capo himself visited while I was there, a handsome, strong man with more power in his little finger than I'd ever seen in another man's entire body. He took my hand and he promised me he would take care of Signore Carozza and his family until the day he died. He told me that even though he'd only known Donni for a short time, he knew in his bones he'd been a good man and would have made me a good husband. Apparently, my Donni talked about me all the time."

Yara's nail dug into my skin painfully, and when I winced slightly, she smoothed the pad of her thumb over the hurt. "They held a beautiful funeral for him. The capo gave me a traditional black lace veil one of the wives had made herself, and I saw my Donni off the way he would have wanted to go, with his family surrounding him and the man who'd saved them from destitution beside us. Do you know who that man was, Elena?"

I knew.

My lips spoke the words before my mind could even compute

195

them. "Amadeo Salvatore."

"Yes," she almost hissed, and I finally recognized where that manic intensity vibrating from her entire body stemmed from. Loyalty. "Amadeo Salvatore did right by a man he barely knew. He took care of an entire family just because a young boy who worked for him died. When Signore Carozza died, Tore paid for his funeral. When Donni's sister wanted to go to school, he sent her to the Universita di Bologna." She paused to smile, all teeth. "When I needed a job after returning heartbroken to America, Tore found me one, and when he moved here five years ago, I was finally in a place to return his loyalty."

My mouth was dry, my tongue coated with the bitterness of coffee. I had difficulty swallowing, maybe because I didn't want to ingest Yara's tale. I didn't want to hear stories about the mafia being the good guys.

I'd already had to rethink so many fundamental beliefs since Daniel left me. I wasn't ready to empathize with the villains who'd haunted me and mine my entire life.

Yara seemed to sense my recalcitrance, her mouth twisting tight over the carbonate anger I could see bubbling inside her. "A poor lawyer follows the law to the exact letter; the best lawyer makes the law work for them. Law and morality can't always coexist, Elena, and sometimes, the difference between the two is loyalty."

"What are you asking of me?" I demanded, tugging my hand free from her damp grip to reclaim my cold coffee. "I'm already on the case."

"Are you?" she asked, one brow arched high like a question mark. "I was of the impression Elena Lombardi didn't half-ass anything."

"I don't," I countered immediately, unthinkingly.

"Good," she said, her smile smug as the cat who ate the canary. "Then you'll be willing to do anything to win this case."

I glared at her truculently, unwilling to answer.

"I know you don't want your sister's best friend to come to any harm." Her voice was warm again, cajoling. "You saw what this trial is doing to Dante. That won't be the first attempt on his life if he can't shake a conviction. His other...associates don't trust a man on trial anymore. Rats are too common in the sewers of the underworld since Tomasso Bruschetta and Reno Maglione turned in the 80s."

"I don't want him to die," I agreed because I'd found it was true. The sight of that massive body sprawled and lax on the black leather couch, broad face sheened with clammy sweat, all vitality lost, still made my stomach ache.

Yara leaned back in her seat, crossed her legs, and folded her hands in her lap. I recognized the pose because I'd often adapted that false coolness when I was about to go in for the kill.

My blood hummed beneath my skin in a way that felt like a pulled alarm, alerting me to leave at once.

I didn't.

I should have.

But I sat there frozen in the amber of my curiosity and almost morbid desire to be included.

And Yara delivered her blow.

"In such an important case, where information is swift-moving, and I don't have the time to communicate with Mr. Salvatore as regularly as he requires, we've come up with a solution."

No.

I knew what she would say, heard it as if spoken by the devil in a voice of smoke and brimstone as she said the words I echoed in my mind.

"We need you as point person on this, Ms. Lombardi. We need you to move into Mr. Salvatore's apartment."

I'd always had a bad temper.

Irish and Italian blood didn't exactly lend itself to serenity, and at my heart, I was deeply emotional, too sensitive for my own good. So, I often lashed out violently at anyone who wounded me, the instinct to inflict hurt on those who injured me almost animalistic.

I'd hurt Daniel, ridiculing him about his sexual deviancies because I was so ashamed I couldn't get past my own sexual issues to even attempt to understand his kinky inclinations.

I'd hurt Giselle when I found out she was pregnant, wanting to eviscerate her with my words if I couldn't with my hands. Wanting to destroy her as surely as she'd destroyed my dreams.

I'd hurt Christopher when he'd tried to assault Giselle at her gallery opening, not only for hurting me so long ago so irrevocably but also for hurting my sister. In a perverse way, only I was allowed to do that, and only then because I felt I'd earned the right.

I tried to hurt Yara after she struck me with those career-killing blows.

I'd honed the edge of my blade-like tongue, slashing at her with comments about corruption and betrayal, blackmail, and abuse of power.

Because it was all true.

She didn't have to tell me, though she did at some point in my tirade, that I would be fired, and if she had any say in the matter, blacklisted in New York if I refused her demand. She didn't have to imply that anyone who refused the Camorra was often found soon after beaten within an inch of their life or dead in some gutter.

I fought with her until my voice was hoarse, my throat cut up by the barbs I tried to throw at her, and then worn weak by the pleas I'd followed up with when nothing else seemed to work.

Yara was unmoved.

She stared at me with that frozen expression I'd once admired so much, watching as the flame of anger and injustice erupted within me and melted me from the inside out.

I felt so young, so weak and naïve to have ever believed she might be my mentor, might take me under her wing and nourish me with love and guidance. Hadn't I learned better yet? Why did I allow myself to hope for kindness when I saw a hand extended my way when I knew I'd more than likely receive a slap to the face instead of a handshake?

I was at the point in my life where I didn't even dream of happiness. I just yearned for a life without further pain.

But it seemed God or fate or whatever forces of nature had cursed me since birth had decided to fuck with me again by threatening the only thing I'd ever derived confidence from, the only dream I had left.

If anyone found out I was living with the capo of the New York City Camorra, I'd lose my licence to practice law.

The degree I'd spent four years studying for in Italy and another year computing into American law at NYU, then the last four years of my life practicing with a rabid kind of ferocity.

It could all disappear in a puff of smoke.

I was fucked if I agreed, fucked if I didn't.

When I left Yara at the café, too furious to say goodbye, it was nearly impossible not to drown in the ocean of self-pity and sorrow rising tidal strong from my gut up into my throat, choking my airways, leaking from my ducts.

I hadn't cried in over a year, not since I found out Giselle was pregnant with the baby I'd yearned so hard to have with Daniel.

But I cried then, and I discovered just how many types of tears there were.

Angry tears, so salty they burned my hot cheeks.

Wallowing tears, the kind that seeped into my mouth and made me nauseous as if I'd swallowed too much sea water.

Lonely tears as I realized how few people I had in my corner, how few loved ones I could call my own. As I realized much of that solitariness was my fault because I'd pushed so many people away out of fear of being hurt. Only, didn't this situation prove exactly why I'd done that?

I'd admired Yara, respected her and yearned for her validation.

I'd even...come to appreciate Dante the way one might appreciate a worthy adversary. After all, what was a hero without her villain?

But it seemed even that was crumbling to dust.

Dante has promised a game of corruption, and this was his trump card.

How could I remain unmoved by his heady charisma and the toxic fumes of his criminality if I was forced into such proximity with him for the next six months to three years? Would I have to stay that long if the trial was postponed as such cases often were?

What about my apartment?

Suddenly, the echoing loneliness of my space felt like an Eden, and through sheer coercion, Dante had force-fed me the forbidden fruit and damned me to his hell.

I walked the streets aimlessly, letting the idiosyncrasies of each neighborhood I passed through lend me their solace. From the moment I'd gotten off the plane and cabbed to our new home in New York, I'd fallen in love with the ever-changing nature of the city. It reminded me, in some ways, of myself. I wanted to be like the city herself, all things to all people depending on where you looked.

But as I walked, I realized I'd lost that somewhere in the last few years. Instead of being multifaceted like a prism, refracting light and beauty, I'd compressed in on myself and stagnated like coal where I would have been diamante.

I felt so lost in the maze of my own mind, I stopped seeing my surroundings and the hundreds of people who passed me. One of the things I loved most about the city was the anonymity you could experience in the teeming streets, the fact that I was a crying mess and no one stopped to stare or inquire about me.

It reinforced what I already knew.

I was an island, and I was okay that way.

I didn't need anyone to look out for me. I didn't need to be coddled or protected the way the entire family had done to Giselle for her whole life.

I didn't need *anyone* for anything.

By the time I reached my brownstone, my shoulders were pinned back, my chin high, my lips compressed around my righteous anger.

I didn't have to cave in to this bullshit.

Yara was only acting on Dante's behalf, and he was only acting like the capo he'd been for years.

But I wasn't his soldier, and I didn't have to go down without a fight.

There was a kernel of smug satisfaction in my heart as I walked up the stairs and unlocked my front door.

"I'll wait here for you to collect your things," a voice said as darkness separated from itself on the corner of my landing, and a man solidified from the shadows.

My heart slammed against my ribs, desperate to flee from the threat, but a small part of me recognized the voice.

"Frankie," I greeted coldly. "Do you make it a habit of scaring women half to death?"

His smile was a flash of white in the darkness. "You'd be surprised."

"I doubt that."

Ignoring him, I pushed into my house and closed the door.

He could wait there all night.

I wasn't going anywhere.

Twenty minutes later, I was drinking a glass of wine in the kitchen eating leftover noodles from the Thai place around the corner when the phone rang.

I answered by saying, "You might want to get Frankie's address changed. If he insists on waiting for me to go with him, he'll be living on my porch for the foreseeable future."

And then I hung up.

When the phone rang again minutes later, I found my hunger had fled and tipped the rest of my dinner in the garbage before topping off my wine and moving into the living room to watch the latest episode of *The Bachelor*.

I almost didn't hear the sound when it started up ten minutes after that, a faint whirring like a dentist's drill, and then it took me too long to process why that sound would be emanating from my front stoop.

Moments later, there was a slight thud and then the sound of hard-heeled shoes against the wood floors in my hallway.

Frankie appeared in the doorway flanked by two men I recognized from the night of the San Gennaro party, a short, bearded man and a mammoth man with a face like a poorly chiseled block of granite. The tiny one held a drill in one hand, and Frankie tossed a small metallic object I recognized as a screw in his.

The bastards had taken my goddamn door off its hinges.

I gaped at them furiously, then exploded to my feet and stalked toward them with a finger pointed at them like a loaded gun. "Are you *kidding* me? You better put that door back exactly where you found it, and if there is *any* damage, your *stronzo* capo is paying for it, do you understand me?"

Frankie nodded solemnly, but there was a wicked gleam in his dark eyes that had me stopping in my tracks a few feet from him. "Whatever you say, *Donna Elena.*"

The big thug took a step toward me. Panic sizzled through me, an electric shock that faintly excited me even as it terrified me. I held my hands up and backed away, but he continued forward with zero expression on his craggy face.

"Do not touch me," I ordered him imperiously.

He didn't stop advancing.

I looked over his shoulder at Frankie, who had lost the battle with his smile and was grinning madly at me.

"If he puts one hand on me, I swear to God, I'll cut it off," I promised them both.

The short wise guy laughed, then covered it with a cough.

"This is kidnapping!" I snapped as the big guy reached for me, and I realized I was running out of living room and was almost up against the kitchen counter.

Frankie shrugged one shoulder. "I gave you a choice. You just made the wrong decision."

"You don't want me anywhere near your precious capo," I swore darkly. "I'll kill him for putting my career at risk. I'm serious."

"I have no doubt you are," he agreed easily, almost jauntily, enjoying the entire situation way too much. "I'd actually love to see you try."

Clearly, there was no reasoning with these mindless savages.

So, when the man with the face of a mobster from a classic Hollywood film reached for my wrist, I resorted to the only thing I had left.

My self-defense training.

I brought my captured wrist up as if I was holding a mirror in my palm, which twisted the man's arm upside down. Then I grabbed his wrist with my opposite hand and wrenched it hard until a bone popped beneath the skin, and his grip loosened as he grunted in pain.

Before he could recover, I leaned back to grab a knife from the block on my kitchen counter and held it up between us.

I was panting hard, the blade shaking in my hand, but somehow my voice was sturdy when I said, "Touch me again, and I will cut you. Now, I'll go with you but only to give Dante a piece of my mind. Excuse me while I grab my purse. You can get a head start of putting my door back exactly the way you found it."

The three men all shared a quick look before Frankie tamed his feral grin enough to say, "You got five minutes."

"I'll take ten," I bartered without waiting for him to answer as I dropped the knife and stalked from the room toward my bedroom.

"You don't want Adriano's dirty hand on your panties, you best pack a bag," Frankie called after me.

I shuddered at the thought of those thugs going through my things, so I resolved to pack an extra pair of underwear in my purse just in case, but nothing more.

There was no way I was moving into Dante's den of iniquity.

"*Madonna Santa*, that woman's got balls," one of the men I didn't know hooted loudly enough for me to hear in the hallway.

"Wouldn't want to be the boss," the other one muttered.

"Oh, I don't know." Frankie laughed as the sound of their heavy footfalls sounded behind me, going back down the hall to fix my damn door. "I'm looking forward to the fireworks."

CHAPTER FOURTEEN

DANTE

She rolled in like a northeasterly winter storm, the air crackling with static, the wind through the open patio doors kicking up a gust as she powered out of the elevator and stalked on the harsh clip of her heels into the living room where I sat waiting for the thunder and lightning to fall.

It was obvious she had cried at some point by the slight smudge of makeup under those glimmering gray eyes, but I couldn't picture how she might have looked vulnerable with tears when she presented such a force standing before me now with her hands fisted on her hips and her flaming hair tangled in the breeze tunneling in from outside.

"You've got some nerve demanding I move in with you just because you want constant status updates," she began, each word punctuated with fury, dripping with disdain. "Poor little capo can't take the consequences of his actions? Then he shouldn't commit felonies. You reap what you sow."

I tilted my head as I crossed a foot over my opposite knee, settling deeper into my couch as I studied her. "How fitting because you have sowed this."

Indignation turned her delicate, overtly feminine beauty into something hard and deadly. It shouldn't have turned me on to see such rage in a woman. It never had before, but something was deliciously wild about her energy like this, a static restless hunger I felt echoed in my own blood.

She was fucking magnificent.

"I've worked my ass off on this case already," she countered, pointing her finger at me as if it was a loaded weapon. "We just succeeded in getting Mason Matlock's statement suppressed, and we have dozens of people working on finding out who the other witnesses might be and what else the prosecution might have on you. How the hell you think I deserve this treatment is beyond me."

"Cursing, Elena," I said, clicking my tongue as I shook my head. "I thought such coarseness was beneath you."

I watched as her skin warmed with a blush I wanted to taste with my tongue. It was so much fun to rile her up. I sincerely thought I could sit here and argue with her for the entire night.

"I should have known blackmail wasn't beneath you," she hissed, storming forward so that she could loom over me from where I reclined against the cushions of my couch. She was a tall woman made taller by those sexy as fuck high heels she was always wearing, but I found the position more arousing than intimidating.

After all, I probably had a hundred pounds on her, and the idea of clutching her wrist to send her tumbling down on top of me was practically impossible to resist.

The only reason I did was because Frankie, Adriano, and Marco were in the doorway to the entryway enjoying the show, and I didn't want to embarrass Elena further by disrespecting her personal space in front of my men.

"You do make me out to be quite the villain," I told her, adjusting my cuff as if the entire conversation bored me just to feel the way the air around her went molten because of my provocation. "Maybe I'm just trying to be the hero, here, Elena?"

She snorted, inelegant, more real than I'd ever seen her. "By forcing me to live with you? Forgive me for sounding dramatic, but I can't see much worse a fate than that."

I brushed my fingertips over my lips, watching the way her furious gaze dropped to my mouth and lingered before snapping back to my eyes. "Have you ever considered it may be dangerous for a woman living alone in a house with a security system? A woman who has become a known associate of a very dangerous man with enemies who will stop at nothing to hurt him."

"Don't pretend you made this move because you have a bleeding heart," she scoffed. "You did this just because you could."

"There may have been that as well," I agreed easily with a wide, slow grin that dominated my entire face.

She blinked at the sight dispassionately. "I am your lawyer, Mr. Salvatore, not your slave and not your soldier."

Oh, if only she knew the truth about my family and its history of taking female slaves. If only she knew that Cosima had paid that price in servitude to my brother before they'd actually fallen in love.

I wondered how the cool Elena would react, knowing the extent of the sacrifice her sister had made for her? If she'd be broken by the weight of it, knowing there was no hope to repay her. She seemed like the type of woman who could not abide a debt remaining unpaid.

I stood then, unraveling from the low couch to my full height. She was discomforted by my proximity, only a thin wedge of vibrating space between our two bodies, but she didn't stand down. Instead, she cocked her chin high in order to look me dead in the eye, her brows arched with haughty disdain, her lush red mouth a contrast to the tightness in her jaw.

There was such a thin line between love and hate, just as there was between heroism and villainy. It all depended on the circumstance and perspective.

At that moment, I wanted to crush her to my body and ravish that prim mouth, dishevel that perfectly curled hair, tear open the silk bow on her blouse with my teeth, then rip apart the bra barely visible beneath that so I could suck on her breasts. I wanted to make her shake for me, quake for me, fucking *break* for me.

Because I knew no one had ever broken Elena Lombardi.

That fucker Daniel Sinclair hadn't even come close.

I'd grown up around horses in England, learned to ride about the same time I learned to walk, and I knew all about the wild, willful beasts. Elena reminded me of an Arabian, she had all the raw power and majesty of the stead, but someone had mistreated her, taught her to bite and shy away from the rider.

I knew with the right training and a patient master, she would be glorious.

It was the worst idea I'd ever had, and I'd had my fair share, but suddenly, irrevocably, I wanted to be the one who earned that hard-won trust. The man who would be rewarded with the glory of those spoils.

Eyes locked on her, jaw clenched against the lust surging inside me, I lifted my hand and cupped her long throat easily in my palm, curling my fingers around the side over the mad thrum of her pulse.

"No," I agreed in a low purr. "You aren't a soldier or a slave. You are a fighter, my fighter until you've won this war with me. But I am the general, Elena, and the sooner you get used to taking orders from me, the better."

"I don't take orders from any man," she snapped, teeth clicking together with the force of her delivery.

Ah, I'd hit a nerve.

"Ah, but I am not just a man," I promised her, gentling her the way I would a nervous mare, my thumb stroking down her throat. "I am *capo dei capi* of the New York City Camorra. If you do not know how to obey, I will teach you."

She seemed to have forgotten I was holding her so intimately, but my movement made her swallow hard against my hand. I was close enough to see the way her pupils expanded, shadows eating up the silvered gray.

For one uninhabited second, I thought she might let me kiss that mouth.

And for one vivid breath, I wondered if that might become one of the biggest accomplishments in my already storied life.

And then Marco coughed.

It echoed like a bomb in the silent room and tore Elena from my grip. She stepped back immediately, and then, before I could blink, she struck out with her right hand and slapped me right across the cheek.

Heat blasted over the side of my face, a spike of pain on the side of my cheekbone where one long, red fingernail tore my skin.

We stared at each other for a long interminable moment, her breath a harsh rattle, her eyes wide and pewter, brushed with fear for the first time that night.

Good, the beast inside me growled, loving the sight of vulnerability in her gaze.

Fear me.

I moved closer on one heavy step, and she flinched but otherwise didn't move even when I leaned close enough to taste her breath on my lips so I could snarl softly, "Next time you hit me, *lottatrice*, I will hit you back. Only it will be on that sweet little arse I've glimpsed behind your tight skirts, *capisci?*"

"You wouldn't fucking dare," she said, but her voice was all breath, her pulse a visible beat in her pale neck.

"*Boh,*" I said as I ducked my head to speak hotly against her ear just to feel her slight shiver. "Try me."

The air crackled around us, and our hearts thundered. I'd known she would bring the storm when she heard her marching orders this afternoon from Yara, but this was more than I'd hoped for. This woman who was barely alive made me feel like a live wire, a lit fuse raw with power.

I hadn't even kissed her, and I felt like roaring, like beating my chest and crowing with glory.

All because the ice queen didn't realize it yet, but the thaw had started and soon, so fucking soon I could almost taste her—something warm and plummy like wine—on my tongue.

Soon, she'd be mine.

For one kiss, one hour, one night, I didn't fucking care.

I'd moved her into my home for pragmatic reasons, but in the end, I couldn't fool myself.

Elena Lombardi was an acquired taste, something to be appreciated by only the most refined palette, the most exquisite mind. As deep and brilliantly complex as expensive Italian wine, the more I learned about her, the more I wanted to drink her down like a glutton and force her to be mine.

CHAPTER FIFTEEN

elena

I spent the rest of the night in my room and hated that I felt petulant and childish for doing so. I'd had an idea of who I should be and what I should want all my life, and this mafioso with obsidian eyes and absurdly long lashes, with man-killing hands and an arrogant authoritative manner, made me feel...undone. As if the years of work I'd spent carving my public persona, my refined mannerisms, and thoroughly educated speech were transparent before the eyes of the Don. He seemed to see through my shields, tearing them in his mighty hands as easily as tissue paper. It was more than disconcerting; it was harrowing.

I didn't want to be seen by anyone, let alone a man like *him.*

But his presence had left irreparable cracks in my foundation, just enough space for doubts to grow like weeds.

My sister said she trusted him with her life.

With mine.

I'd tried to call her again to talk about what I'd learned, but she had only texted me back assuring me to keep calm and that she would explain everything next month when she visited. It was poor consolation, but even knowing she was happy now, it made me sick to think of what she had truly gone through for us.

For me.

It only proved to heighten the feeling of obligation that had led me into taking Dante's case and knowing she loved him at the end of that ordeal, that maybe he had...*helped* her cemented my loyalty to his cause if not his person.

To top it all off, Seamus had all but threatened me if I didn't offer good intel on the capo. At least, if I was living here, I'd be safe from him and his.

I knew Dante's enemies were circling in the waters, scenting his blood after his RICO indictment, and that potentially, they could use me as some kind of pawn in their game of domination.

So, I was safe from external forces in Dante's two-story Upper East Side fortress.

The problem was, I had the distinct feeling the greatest threat to my safety was inside that same apartment prowling the halls like a caged beast.

The room he'd given me was lovely, which annoyed me too. The walls were gray plaster, the same dark shade as my eyes, but everything else was either a pearly white, silver, or accented black. It was like living inside a cloud with its ever-changing moods, light to dark, everything soft and opulent.

216

He had good taste, a quality I felt was underestimated in a man.

I fisted the satin sheets in my hands and wrenched at them.

I hated to be maneuvered, and I hated to lose.

And there was no doubt that I had.

Restlessness coursed through me, and though it was only four in the morning, a full hour and a half before I normally got up, I pushed out of bed and padded over to the black dresser to investigate.

Clothing lay neatly folded in the drawers.

I puffed a breath through my lips as I fingered a cashmere cardigan.

Of course, the bastard had bought me clothes, knowing I wouldn't pack my own.

Anger fueled me better than coffee ever could as I wrenched open drawers until I found a pair of black leggings and a sports bra. I knew there was a gym somewhere in the massive apartment, and I decided I'd lift weights in bare feet because I didn't have appropriate shoes.

Tying my hair in a messy bun, I quickly applied some mascara and lip tint before leaving the room.

I wasn't the kind of woman who went anywhere without looking her best.

I found the gym almost immediately down the same corridor as my bedroom on the second level, at the end of the hall where it opened into a massive space lined with mirrors on one side and floor-to-ceiling windows on the other. My eyes immediately sought out the view of the nightscape through the glass, transfixed by the glitter of lights like sequins woven into the velvet night. I walked to the window and touched my hand to the cool glass as if I could feel the texture of the night beneath my fingertips.

"New York City is the most beautiful at night."

I closed my eyes against the sound of his voice, furious with myself because a small part of me, something wild and unbridled in my chest, had hoped I might run into him.

"Then again, most things are," Dante continued as he appeared in my periphery, a monumental shadow next to me.

I didn't turn to look at him. "I'm a terrible sleeper, so I've come to enjoy the night. It's peaceful. Sometimes it feels like you're the only one awake in the entire world."

"Mmm, that seems rather lonely," he murmured. "Night should be spent on passion."

I rolled my eyes, ignoring his light chuckle. "Fucking indiscriminately, you mean?"

"Oh, Elena, be careful cursing around me," he purred darkly, moving just a little closer. "I like the sound of something dirty in that red mouth."

I told myself the tingle I felt at the base of my back was from a cold draft in the room.

"If I'm going to stay here, there must be rules," I decided primly, finally turning to face him.

My God.

I turned back to the window immediately, seeking solace in the

New York night.

Because Dante was half naked beside me.

The broad expanse of his chest was quilted with deeply defined muscle, his abs a boxed chain in his abdomen, his pectorals round and hard topped by dark nipples covered in light, crisp black hair. An ornate silver cross hung at the end of a thick chain around his neck, the tip of the cross resting in the crease between his chest and tight belly, sexy in a way that was blasphemous. But it was the corded length of his arms, the ripple of muscle in biceps the size of my thighs that had my legs clenching together against a vague ache at my core.

He was astoundingly magnetic, a perfectly formed monster of a man.

The sheer size and strength of him should have made me tensed, frightened. Christopher was a quarter the size of Dante, and I knew from experience what a man that slight could do to a woman if he tried.

Yet the barely harnessed power kind of...aroused me.

I was a woman who appreciated control. Therefore, I appreciated the care Dante must have taken to build that body and take care with it around others. I'd seen him hold Cosima's face tenderly, hug Yara gently, kiss Tore robustly on both cheeks, clap hands with some of his soldiers. I'd witnessed the rolling grace of that densely muscled body unfold and prowl across a room, so much control lashed around his sheer power that it made my mouth water.

That he was so robust was attractive, but it was his mastery over that power that made my knees soften like butter.

"Elena?" His voice cut into my thoughts, amusement in his tone as it always seemed to be when he spoke to me.

"Mmm?"

"I asked what kind of rules you were attempting to install in my home."

"Ah." Yes, rules. We needed lots and lots of rules. I cleared my throat and forced myself to face him so he would think I was unmoved by his naked torso and the thick thighs stretching his black athletic shorts. "Rule number one, no touching."

"No," he said simply, shaking his head in a way that made me notice he didn't have product in his hair yet, the thick, silken strands flopping slightly onto his forehead. "I am Italian. My people are Italian. We touch."

"Not me," I countered.

"You ask a tiger to change its stripes just because a friendly kiss on the cheek from a countryman makes you uncomfortable?" he argued calmly, once again making me feel selfish and slightly foolish. "No one will touch you without your consent, Elena. You have my word that you are safe in this home. But, in return, I ask that you be kind to the people who live here and visit me."

"I'm always polite," I said, but he'd hit an old bruise.

I could be mean. It was in me to give, and sometimes I was so cruel, there was no coming back from it.

Sometimes, I didn't want to, like with Giselle and Daniel.

But even then, a little voice buried alive in the ground of my mind where I'd left it long ago whispered that maybe I didn't want them to hate me either.

"I think you mean to be," he agreed, his voice soft. I could feel his gaze on me, the quality of it warm, almost gentling against my cheek. "But the women in my family are very friendly. They might view your reserved nature as rude."

I rolled my lips under my teeth, feeling wounded somehow.

Dante sighed and stepped even closer, the heat of his body buffeting mine. "Elena, I do not mean to imply you are mean, only that I wish for you to get along with the people in this house. Do you understand me?"

I shrugged a shoulder as I looked out the window again. The night hours always made me feel melancholier, the dark thoughts in my mind drawn to its shadows. "I'm not here to make friends, but I understand. I don't like reminders of Italy, but I will try to be...warmer."

I could see the bright flash of Dante's smile from the corner of my eyes and couldn't resist the impulse to face it full on as if it was the sun itself and I wanted to bask in his rays.

"I appreciate that," he said genuinely. "I know you do not want to be here, and you can hate me for it, but this is best. This is necessary."

I didn't agree with that, but I'd already battled with Yara and Dante both, and in the velvet quiet of the night, for once, I didn't feel like arguing again.

"Rule number two, I don't want it widely known I'm living here. If anyone found out, I could lose my license to practice law, and…" I fought to find the words to express what such a tragedy would mean to me and finally settled on an Italianate shrug. "It would not be possible for me to recover from that."

"Done," Dante agreed, reaching forward to take my hand as if for a shake, but instead, he just held it loosely in both of his own. I could feel the thick callous along the ridge of his palms. "In fact, Adriano will drive you to work in the morning in my Town Car. The windows are tinted, and you will leave from the garage, which is accessed directly from the suite. No one should have reason to see you leaving the building."

Of course, the criminal had thought of everything in order not to get caught.

"Rule three," I continued with a glare. "My privacy is paramount. No snooping in my room and invasive questions."

I was laying the groundwork for the next week when I was scheduled to have my surgery with Monica.

"I have a procedure next week and will be out of work for a few days. I would like to be able to convalesce at my own home," I requested with what I hoped was a pleasing smile.

From Dante's scowl, it wasn't. He crossed his arms over his chest, muscles bulging beneath the bronze skin like coiled rope. "Is it serious?"

"No," I said instantly, hoping to offer as few details as possible.

"Then no, you will stay here," he decided, nodding like a king bestowing his grace on a subject. "Bambi can see to you if you need anything while you rest, and no one will disturb you otherwise."

"Bambi?" I asked, unable to leave the name alone.

"The woman who cooks and cleans for me," he explained, eyes dancing again as he read my reaction. "Her name is Georgina, but she has the big eyes and the softness of Bambi. She hasn't been called anything else since she was six when her mother died."

I shook my head at Italians and their nicknames, but I was not happy about staying with Dante after my surgery. There was no extensive aftercare except rest because they were doing the surgery laparoscopically, but it was too vulnerable to stay with a virtual stranger after having something so intimate performed.

"Please, Dante," I started to explain, but an expression overcame him that arrested me mid-speech. "What?"

"The sound of 'please' from your lips sounds even better than a curse," he murmured, stepping closer to raise a thumb to the edge of my mouth.

I sucked in a little breath I hoped he didn't hear and stepped back. "I would rather stay at my house."

"I would rather you didn't," he countered easily as if my opinion didn't matter one jot.

"Uh," I growled in frustration. "Are you always so pigheaded?"

"Not always." His grin was large and boyish, slightly crooked between his cheeks, the faint dimple in his chin deepening. "Are you done with your rules now?"

I hesitated, worried I was forgetting something. Dante's chest kept distracting me. I'd just noticed the thicket of black hair below his naval and the deeper shadow of raised muscles angling in from his hips to his groin.

"For now," I settled on after struggling not to swallow my tongue. "If we have an agreement?"

I was too aesthetic not to appreciate beauty in its many forms, even heathen ones like Dante.

"You can call it what you want. A game. A deal. But don't forget who it is you're dealing with, hmm? I'm nothing but the devil, and I'll take you for all you're worth. When I'm done with you, your precious rules will be in tatters just like your clothes around your feet." He stepped forward smoothly, diminishing the remaining space between us to a single pulsing inch of air between our torsos. The scent of him, bright like citrus and pepper, invaded my nose as I was forced to tip my head back to look up into his coal-dark gaze. I didn't flinch, but I wanted to when his hand caught mine and lifted it to his mouth. His words were hot breath against my skin. "I can see the fear in your eyes. I feel it in the pulse just here. What are you afraid of, Elena? That my wickedness might contaminate your thoughts... or your body? Are you so certain entering into this agreement with me is so wise?"

No.

No, in fact, I was fairly certain it was a terrible idea. But he was making it sound as if I had a choice when I did *not*. At least, not one my pride could live with. My life had been razed to the ground when Daniel left me, and only one dream still lived in the ashes of that fire, pulsing madly.

I wanted to be a nationally renowned lawyer.

This case, written about in the papers and splashed on the news, was already gaining me notice in the right circles. If we could actually win against all the odds, I'd be one of the most highly sought-after attorneys in the city, in the entire goddamn country.

My father's sinner's blood ran through my veins, and I couldn't pretend for one second longer that I was above my avarice and egotism.

I wanted success, money, fame.

I wanted to be seen and known and heard.

I wanted it all.

And Dante Salvatore was the only man who could satisfy those base desires.

So, I blinked slowly, disdainfully at the disgraced mafia capo and pressed my hand in his even closer to his lips like a queen offering her servant the opportunity to kiss her ring.

"It's you who should be afraid. You just don't know it yet," I promised as I resolved to keep him at bay with every single one of my resources while I used his case to make my career.

His eyes were dark as freshly tilled soil, fertile with wickedness as they locked on mine, and with a slight brush of his lips against my fingers, he agreed to my terms.

Just like that, I made a deal with the Devil of NYC.

"Excellent, now for *my* rules," he countered brightly, tugging me by my captured hand away from the window and the exercise machines toward black mats laid out near the back of the room. "One, you must obey me, Elena. I will not ask much of you, but if I make an order, you must heed it." When I opened my mouth to argue, he placed his entire palm over my lower face to stop me. "No. This is nonnegotiable. You are in the belly of the beast now, and while it's safer for you here, it is also still dangerous. If I tell you to do something, it is mostly for your own safety."

Caving into my childish impulse, I lashed my tongue out against his palm. He pulled away, staring at his moistened hand incredulously. "Did you just *lick* me?"

I shrugged, the urge to giggle bubbling in my throat. "You wouldn't let me speak."

He blinked at me once, then threw his head back to laugh so hard he held on to his belly as if to contain his humor. I watched him, enjoying the sight of all those muscles contracting with mirth that I'd caused.

It felt good to make someone laugh.

To make *him* laugh.

It was a pleasant sound, that was all, and it wasn't often I relaxed enough to make anyone laugh like that.

When he recovered, he tipped his head down to look at me with a soft smile pleating his ruddy mouth. It was somehow an intimate expression that made my belly ache.

"What an interesting woman you are, Elena Lombardi," he said in that same vein, quiet and steady like he was imparting wisdom.

A blush threatened to overtake my cheeks, so I moved away

onto the mats as if to test their cushion.

"I've decided I like you," Dante told me as if I'd asked or cared about his opinion.

"You don't know me," I countered, starting to stretch for my workout, eager to exert myself physically to rid my body of this... excess energy fizzing through my blood like soda pop.

"Oh, I wouldn't say that. I'm beginning to, and it's a journey I've found I am enjoying," Dante said as he moved toward the wall and flicked on the overhead lights.

I was glad when he moved out of my view so I could duck my head and take a few steadying breaths.

Why was that somehow the nicest thing anyone had said to me in years?

"Now, for my second rule," Dante began as he crossed back over the mats on that rolling, athletic gait that made my mouth go dry.

He stopped a few paces from me and crossed his arms as he assessed me. I tried not to squirm under the intense perusal. I worked out five times a week, so my long, lean body was tight with muscle, my curves slight and distinctly lacking unlike my mother and two sisters.

"I heard from Marco--when he finally stopped laughing-- that you disabled Adriano and held a knife to his throat. Is this true?"

I studied my nail beds. "Maybe."

He chuckled, a dark note that pulsed between us like a plucked bass. "*Molto bene*. I like to hear this, Elena. A woman should know how to defend herself. I'd like to see what you can do."

"Why?" I asked suspiciously, suddenly seeing his thickly formed limbs in a new light. I did *not* want to fight him. Even my instructor at the dojo wasn't as big as Dante.

His lips flickered with the urge to suppress his humor. "Humor me. I need to see the moves of the woman who caught the most able man I know off-guard."

I wanted to protest because I definitely did not want to fight him. Not because I was truly afraid—despite everything, I didn't think he would hurt me—but more because I didn't want him to touch me.

It was an irrational fear, something like a superstition that each time Dante put his hands on me, something elemental changed in my physiology. I didn't like his hand on my throat or my hand in his, so why had I let him do that to me? Why had I leaned into that strong collar just to feel my heart beat faster?

It hinted of darker, deviant things I wasn't ready to think about, let alone confess any kind of liking for.

But I couldn't voice any of that because suddenly, two hundred and thirty pounds of hard-muscled British-Italian man was barreling down on me.

Instinct kicked in, thrumming through me like music, prompting my body to step into fighting the way most people did into dancing, the moves programmed into my muscles by memory.

He grabbed for me, meaty hands going for my shoulders. I

ducked slightly to the right, leaning down into his body as if going for his groin. Instinctively, he lowered one of his hands to protect his family jewels. I took advantage of his distraction to pop up on that right side and jab a short, strong punch to his low belly.

He laughed.

A warm, rich chuckle that increased in volume as we continued to tussle.

He grabbed me from behind when I spun away from his questing hands, his arms banding around my torso nearly twice over. I kicked back with my left foot, connecting with his shin, then quickly dug my right heel into the tender arch of his other foot. His hold loosened just enough for me to pull my arms from the bear hug. I reached up to slap them over his ears, hoping to disorient him. I must have gauged the angle wrong because he only chuckled menacingly, his entire body hot and hard with exertion pressed front to back against mine. Thinking quickly, I wrapped my leg around his and tipped my weight, trying to take him off balance. The big lug was just too heavy, and instead of falling to the mat on his back, he tossed me to the ground on mine before kneeling over my prone body.

I was panting hard, the metallic burn of adrenaline on the back of my tongue as I glared up at his smug mug. He wasn't breathing hard at all, nor was there a single bead of sweat on his smooth skin.

"*Non male*," he praised.

Not bad.

I huffed, blowing an errant curl out of my face as I struggled to break free of his hands pinning mine to the mat by my head. "I haven't had to fight someone so fat before. It's a lot of weight to offset."

His laughter scored through me like a shot of grappa. He leaned back, releasing my hands to pat his tight, boxed stomach. "I like your mama's pasta."

"I can tell," I sniffed, but inside, my blood was bubbling and popping, warm inside my veins.

For one second, I wondered, was this comradery?

I was close with Beau. We saw each other all the time, snuggled and chatted, shopped and dined. But we had been friends for five years. It made me realize I hadn't made a new friend in a very long time and maybe, I was out of practice.

But that was kind of what it felt like lying there with the urge to laugh in my belly while a big mafioso crushed my torso where he straddled me after his fake attack.

Like maybe we could be friends.

"*Che palle,*" someone exclaimed from the door. "Is this the way we train now, Boss?"

I raised into a crunch so I could see the door only to wish I hadn't.

The short man from yesterday who I now surmised was Marco, and the big one, Adriano, along with Frankie, the Grouch, Jacopo, and the Japanese man I hadn't met yet all stood in the doorway watching us.

I flopped back to the mat and wished briefly for a return to my senses.

"Only when I'm training her," Dante said flippantly over his shoulders before he rolled to standing with utter ease and offered me his hand to help me up. "*Amici,* let me formally introduce Elena Lombardi, my lawyer and unwilling roommate."

Marco winced. "He does snore."

"Thankfully, I have a separate room," I said dryly, pulling my hand from Dante's lingering grip after I stood to offer it to the short man with the strong Brooklyn accent. "It's a pleasure to meet you, Marco."

His thick brows arched comically wavy lines into his forehead like a cartoon character. "You're a real classy woman."

A little laugh escaped me at his reverence as he kissed the back of my hand. "Thank you, I think."

"For sure," he said like it was no problem. "This here is Frankie, he's the brains. Adriano is the brawn, but he also cooks like a fucking dream. Chen is our secret weapon, and Jaco here is... hey, Jaco? Why do we keep you around again?"

Jacopo scowled at him while the others laughed.

"Are you...?" I wasn't exactly sure how these things worked. "Capos too?"

They laughed again, but it was Dante who stepped in line with me to say, "Rule number three, don't ask questions."

"Because you won't give me the answers," I bandied back.

I'd grown up in Naples, so I knew all about the antiquated constructs of our culture around women. We weren't allowed in on "the business" because we weren't to be trusted.

"Because you won't like the answers," he surprised me by offering.

"You skipped rule number two," I reminded him.

His grin was feral, lips so red they seemed stained with wine pulled back over big, white teeth. "Rule number two, you learn how to fight."

"I just showed you," I argued, side-eyeing the assembled men, all visibly strong and *scarred*, even the short guy, Marco. "I can defend myself."

"Not from me," Dante countered.

"Not from us," Marco agreed a second later.

The others nodded, though Adriano hesitated to do so.

My pride, the wicked thing, surged through me, and before I could appeal to my rational side, I was assuming a fighter's stance and facing off with the group of *soldati*.

"Try me," I dared, a sharp smile on my face.

It didn't occur to me until later, lying on the mat covered in sweat, hair matted with it, clothes soaked through with it, that I hadn't stopped smiling the entire hour I sparred with Dante and his crew.

CHAPTER SIXTEEN

elena

Adriano dropped me off that morning at my favorite coffee shop, The Mug Shot, a block down from my office. He wasn't a chatty guy, but I noticed a photo of a pretty dog as his phone screen saver and had to hide my smile behind my hand when he'd caught my eye in the review mirror.

It was busy as it always was with local businesspeople on their way to work needing their first, second, or third cup of joe, so I settled into line to wait while I replied to emails on my phone. I was midway through the line when I felt awareness trickle like cold water down my spine.

Looking up from my phone through my eyelashes, I immediately caught a pair of brilliant green eyes only a few feet away at one of the small tables in the shop.

They belonged to a man I'd never seen before but still had the vague sense I knew, like an actor or a famous model. He had the looks of one, the hard-carved face with a strong jaw and a hawkish nose that somehow looked perfect on his tan face. The verdant green of his eyes was almost startling, especially against that golden skin and the short, styled waves of his inky hair. He was broad through the shoulders, his suit tailored to his tapered torso, and something about his demeanor was as compelling as a shout from across the room, his energy palpable, almost overtly forceful.

I blinked at him, more intrigued by why he watched me than by his stark, almost bluntly masculine looks.

I'd seen handsome.

I'd dated Daniel for four years, and he *had* been a model for a short time.

And currently, I was being forced to cohabitate with a man who quite simply would take any woman's breath away.

So, this man only intrigued me the way I would have been by a gorgeous painting or a new set of Louboutin pumps. Which was why I was confused when he slowly folded the newspaper he was reading and pressed it under his shoulder before he stood to walk, quite clearly, to my side.

"Good morning," he said with a slight smile, the expression all mouth and no eyes.

I returned a polite smile. "Hello."

We stood there for a moment, not speaking just cataloging each other. He was younger than I'd previously thought, his skin silken and mostly unlined but for two creases between his slashing brows.

234

I realized what it was he emanated, what had my teeth slightly on edge as if I'd been struck like a tuning fork by the power of his dynamism. It was dominance.

Dante exuded the same tangible tension, this invisible aura that made you instinctively want to obey him, but where he had charisma to soften the delivery, this man just stared at me with determination in those bright jade eyes. He looked as if he didn't intend to take no for an answer.

So I waited for him to ask the question.

When we seemed to be in some kind of holding pattern as the line moved up and I was fourth from the top, a slight, almost begrudging smile overtook his firm mouth.

"I'd like your number," he said, finally.

"Oh?" I asked, flattered despite myself but enjoying our little stand-off too much to act anything but cool. "That's interesting. What would you presume to do with it?"

He seemed to actually consider it, his hand stroking the facial hair that was a little longer than stubble but not quite a beard. "After waiting an appropriate amount of time, I would call you."

"For what purpose?"

"To tell you where I'm going to take you on our date," he quipped easily, narrowing his eyes as he looked me up and down. It wasn't a salacious gaze, but a calculating one. "Somewhere you can wear those heels with a tasteful suggestive dress."

Immediately, I thought of the dress Dante had bought me, the gorgeous vintage Valentino that had fit me like a dream. Unbidden,

I considered what Dante might do if he knew I was being asked out by a handsome stranger.

Irritated by my line of thinking, I acted uncharacteristically impulsively and smiled the way I'd learned from Cosima, my lips wide and parted to reveal my blessedly straight smile.

"My name is Elena," I offered with my hand extended. "And as long as it isn't Italian food, I just might answer your call."

His expression was smug without being a smile, satisfaction softening his hard-green eyes as he took my hand. "Excellent."

And when I gave him my number, I wasn't thinking about the black-eyed gaze of a certain mafioso I knew in my bones would probably strangle this man for asking me on a date.

I definitely didn't experience a flash of spine-tingling arousal at the idea of a man like him being possessive of me.

And if I did, I consoled myself with the truth. It had been a long time since someone had been possessive of me, and it was only natural to be intrigued.

Still, I swore an oath as I left the coffee shop for my office that I wouldn't breathe a word of it to Dante.

That evening, I was barely through the elevator doors with Bruno, the man who attended the lobby reception having personally taken me up so he could talk my ear off about his wife and children, when I heard a sound I'd never thought to hear in

Dante's palatial apartment.

A child's laughter.

It was high, melodic, and utterly lovely.

Something in my chest where my heart used to be flipped over like a half-done pancake. My hand went to my upper breast unconsciously, rubbing at the sensation as I moved into the living room and stared over the long room into the kitchen where the sound had emerged from.

A small girl with long, curling chestnut brown hair was seated on the long matte black kitchen island. Her white and pink dress pooled over the dark granite as she carefully rolled orecchiette pasta in her hands. Her tongue poked between her teeth in concentration as she studied her pasta dough, then darted a look over at Dante, who occupied the same task beside her.

I couldn't move as I watched them, overcome with something that hurt.

It rolled through me hotly, molten like lead poured into my veins. I felt poisoned by the sensation, unable to breathe the way Dante had when he'd ingested cyanide.

"You okay, *Donna Elena?*" Bruno asked from the elevator where he still had a clear sight of me, stalled at the mouth of the living room.

His voice tuned Dante in to my presence, his face forming a smile before he even lifted his head to look at me.

Dio mio.

I rubbed the heel of my hand so hard into my chest I felt certain it would bruise.

"*Buona sera,*" he greeted me, already abandoning his dinner project to wipe his floured hands on a towel. "I was hoping you would be back in time to meet the love of my life."

The girl laughed, throwing her little folded piece of pasta at Dante so it left a mark on his black button-up shirt. He growled at her, causing her to shriek with joy and throw more pasta grenades at him. When he lunged for her, she lifted her arms for him to pick her up even though she screamed as if she was frightened. By the time he planted her on his hip, she was over their little game and happily settled in his arms.

"Hello," she called to me as Dante approached. "My name is the Love of Dante's Life."

The smile that warmed my face felt alien and vulnerable. I touched my other hand to my lips, then immediately lowered it when Dante frowned at me.

"Hello, beautiful," I greeted as they trekked through the living room to my side. "Dante speaks of nothing but you."

"I know," she said confidently with a sage nod of her head that made me want to burst into laughter. "Boys are always falling in love with me, you know?"

"Are they?" I asked, then clucked my tongue. "You know, I'm not surprised. You're very pretty, and more, I bet you're smart."

"One time, someone called me a genius," she told me solemnly.

"That was your mum, *gioia*," he pointed out. "Mothers always tell us we are better than we are because they love us. That is why

238

you have uncles, to tell you the hard truths."

She frowned at him. "*Zio*, am I a genius?"

"Absolutely," he agreed immediately to her avid delight.

I couldn't help the laugh that emerged fragile as a blown bubble from my lips. They were absolutely adorable together, and I just couldn't understand what was happening.

I'd thought Dante's only sibling was Alexander.

He read the confusion in my look and grinned as he set the girl down and offered his hand for her to do a twirl. "Elena, this is Aurora."

"Don't call me Sleeping Beauty," she warned me before I could say anything, fisting her hands on her hips. "I don't like princesses."

"Alright," I agreed. "I don't really like them either."

She eyed me suspiciously. "Not even Cinderella."

I wrinkled my nose. "Especially not her."

"How come?" she pushed.

I thought about it because she deserved a good answer. "Princesses always need saving, and I've always wanted to be the type of woman that saved herself. Maybe even the one who saved her handsome prince in the end instead."

Aurora's big brown eyes went wide before she nodded soberly. "Yeah, that's why I don't like them either. They're *sciocco*."

"There are different types of women in the world, *gioia*. There are soft ones who need saving, but maybe they have good, tender hearts that need protecting. And you know what?" Dante asked, stroking a big hand down her head as he shot me a sidelong glance.

"Even the strong ones need saving sometimes."

"Not me," she crowed, turning to jump up on the marble coffee table, dislodging a vase that tumbled harmlessly to the carpet. She struck a sword-fighting pose. "I'm going to be the saver."

"The savior," I corrected.

"Okay," she said easily. "That's why I think my name's stupido."

I considered her for a second, then grabbed the long vase from the floor and used it to dub her like a knight. "Then, I think we should call you Rora, warrior princess."

Her eyes bugged out at me. "Like the lion's roar."

"Exactly like that," I agreed, beaming back at her.

"Okay," she said again in that adorably confident way like nothing in life fazed her. "You and me can be friends, okay?"

"*Bene*," I agreed, offering my hand to shake.

She took it in her little one, and we smiled at each other so big it hurt.

"I knew you two would get along," Dante interjected as he winked at me before heading back into the kitchen. "Elena is a fighter too."

I passed the wink on to Rora as we both followed him into the kitchen. The place was a disaster zone, double zero flour and eggshells everywhere along with little folded ears of the orecchiette pasta.

"Your mama is not going to be happy about the mess," Dante admitted as they returned to their stations at the island, Rora using my hand to help herself up onto the stool and then the counter.

"No, but you're lucky. You're old enough you don't get time-outs," she pouted before looking over at me. "You want to make ears with us?"

I was wearing a five-hundred-dollar white silk blouse and Chanel wide-legged pants that I usually meticulously kept clean, even going so far as to sit on napkins if I had to take a seat in public. I could feel Dante's eyes on me as I nodded.

"Sure, Rora."

She rewarded me with a smile and then launched into a monologue about her day at school and her best friend, Maria Antonia.

While she babbled happily, Dante appeared from the pantry with an apron and approached me. Instead of handing it over, he stood behind me, close enough I could feel his heat, and reached around my body to tie the fabric around my waist. Once secured, he lifted my hair with one hand to tie the other strings beneath it.

But he didn't.

Instead, his hot breath fanned over the back of my neck, followed closely by the warm press of his nose skimming along the side of my throat.

"Mmm," he hummed, the vibration tickling thin skin. "You smell *intossicante*."

A shudder wrenched between my shoulders, impossible to hide from the predator at my back. When I spoke, I made sure my voice wasn't as weak as my knees felt. "It's just Chanel number 5."

"The body's natural chemistry reacts with a scent," he

murmured as he slowly slid the apron strings against my sensitized flesh, the rough fabric somehow deliciously sensual. "No one scent ever smells the same on different people. And this? It suits you. Elegant and sultry like a midnight assignation in a garden."

"Can I smell?" Rora asked, interrupting the electric tension between Dante and me.

Silently, because my voice was somewhere at my toes, I offered her my wrist. She pressed her entire nose to it and sniffed deeply before smiling at me. Her happy, easy energy was contagious.

"Smells like warm flowers," she decided. "Maybe I should wear some too?"

Dante chuckled, moving out from behind me having secured the apron. He tweaked her nose. "Little girls do not need to wear perfume."

She frowned at him. "What do you know about it?"

I laughed.

God, but I laughed. It burst out of me indecorously, seizing my belly and warming my chest. When I recovered, eyes wet with mirth, Rora had gone back to shaping pasta in her little fingers, but Dante was watching me with something written in black ink in those long-lashed eyes.

"*Bellissima,*" he mouthed.

A blush worked itself under my skin, but I ducked my head to focus on the pasta, letting a curtain of dark curls fall between my cheek and his gaze. It was disconcerting how much interest Dante seemed to have in me. I wasn't used to being...watched.

I could be an emotional terrorist, my broken pieces weaponized like shards of broken glass. I was used to being the bitch, the warrior, something strong and impenetrable, more a worthy adversary than a worthy friend.

But Dante looked at me as if I was some priceless, mysterious work of art, and he wanted to know the story behind my almost smile.

I wanted to be furious with him for forcing me into a situation where I could not only be called off the case that could make my career but one where I could lose that career entirely. And in a way, I still was. The wariness and the bitter tang of anger lingered on the back of my tongue. But emotions had a funny way of boiling together in the same cauldron of the gut, and right then, in his messy kitchen with an adorable little girl who adored him, it was impossible not to feel something completely contrary to rage.

"Ciao raggazzi," a woman called from the entryway, drawing my notice.

A moment later, the beautiful and blond Italian woman I now knew to be Bambi walked into the living room in a form-fitting dress. Rora scrambled from the table, jumping awkwardly to the floor, falling to one knee, then taking off at a run to hug the woman.

Bambi smiled as she accepted the girl into her arms even though they were laden with grocery bags. *"Bambina."*

The word made me grit my teeth. It was the nickname Sebastian and Cosima had called Giselle since they were young even though she was older than them both. It was perfectly emblematic of their

243

relationship with her too. They coddled her, protected her, lavished her with affection and praise.

Dante's hand was suddenly lightly pressed to the middle of my shoulder blades. He was looking at Bambi, but something about his touch told me he'd sensed my tension and was trying to offer relief.

Like an idiot, I was moved by the gesture.

"Bambi, this is Elena Lombardi," he introduced as they came into the kitchen. I noticed he didn't mention I was his lawyer, but I figured she already knew.

I offered a small smile. "It's a pleasure to meet you."

Really, I couldn't get past the question of their relationship. Was she his girlfriend?

Bambi eyed Dante's somewhat protective stance beside me, a small smile fluttering over her lips. "Likewise. I see you've met my daughter, Aurora."

"Rora," the little girl shouted, then proceeded to make a fierce little growl. "Because I roar like a lion."

Bambi blinked at her, then looked up at Dante questioningly.

"I'm sorry, that was me," I admitted. "She was expressing some dislike of her name because of the connection to Sleeping Beauty." I shrugged, a little embarrassed.

"Rora," she tested, then cupped her daughter's plump cheek. "Beautiful and strong like my girl."

My heart warmed even as it pulsed with hurt witnessing the genuine love and admiration between the mother and daughter. I yearned for such a connection so badly, even my teeth ached with it.

Dante's thumb stroked over the bumps in my spine. I sucked in a small, shaky deep breath.

"I see you wanted to help *zio* Dante with dinner," Bambi noted, eyes sweeping over the mess on the island.

Dante grinned, completely unabashed. "Every Italian should know how to make pasta."

"This is why I don't like you in my kitchen," she grumbled good-naturedly as he took some of the grocery bags for her and cleared a spot on the counter for them. "I ran into Adriano in the entry. He said he wanted to speak to you in the office."

Dante shot me a look, but Bambi shooed him and practically pushed him out of the kitchen. "Leave the cooking to the women. We do it so much better than you."

He left with one last look at me, leaving me with a woman I wasn't sure I could like.

Jealousy was a bitch, and I'd struggled with her my whole life.

"Honestly, I'm happy to have a moment alone with you," Bambi surprised me by admitting as she began to put the groceries away. I moved to help her by route, remembering the years in Naples when I'd been Mama's co-parent doing such things for the entire family.

"Oh?"

She nodded, eyeing Aurora who had rifled through her mum's purse to find an iPad she was now playing some game on. "I wanted the chance to ask you for some…legal advice."

I frowned at her. "I practice criminal law, but I'm sure I could offer some insight, whatever it is. Is everything okay?"

Bambi's eyes really were the widest and bluest I'd ever seen, so perfectly round and opaque they seemed like marbles. "Everything will be, if you can help me. I think I need a lawyer."

"Okay," I said slowly, studying her agitated movements as she spun around the kitchen putting things in their place to fix a sauce for the pasta. "Why don't you start with the why of it all?"

She bit her lip, eyeing me from the fridge for a second before moving over to where I leaned against the counter. I was shocked when she took my hands in her own, only Dante's voice asking me to be kind to the women in his family keeping me from snatching them from her grip.

"Can I trust you?" she asked, desperation laced through her words. She squeezed my hands so hard the bones ground together beneath my skin. "I know Dante does, and usually that's enough for me, but I need to know if *I* can trust you."

"Yes," I confirmed instantly, reading the panic in her eyes. The edge of her desperation reminded me of Mama in those moments when Seamus put our family in jeopardy, and she felt filled with impotency and fear. "As long as it doesn't usurp my privilege with Dante, I can help you."

She chewed her lip so hard the flesh broke, a bead of garnet blood leaking onto her chin. "I…I don't know if it usurps that. It's about Aurora's father."

"Does it have something to do with his case?" I pressed.

Those massive eyes blinked rapidly. "I-I don't really know for sure. But I'm worried."

Technically, I couldn't take her into my confidence if it meant she might have information on the case. It might put me in the position to have to testify at court, which would mean I'd have to recuse myself from the legal team.

"Are you safe?" I asked because I still wasn't sure where her fear was coming from.

She nodded on a heavy sigh. "For now."

"Elena," Adriano's heavily accented voice carried from the mouth of the hallway. "Dante needs to see you in the office."

"Can it wait a moment?" I asked, tugging Bambi even closer to me by our joined hands. "Bambi needs me."

"No," Adriano said flatly, crossing his hulk arms over his chest.

I rolled my eyes at him, then gave Bambi's hands a squeeze. "I'm going to give you my card, okay? If you need to speak to me, you can call me at work or at home. If you can say for sure whether it involves Dante or not, I can help or get one of the other associates to."

Bambi beamed at me, the same wide, gorgeous smile as her daughter, before pulling me into a quick, tight hug. "*Grazie*, Elena."

I nodded awkwardly as she pulled away and then turned to follow Adriano down the hall to Dante's office. I hadn't had a chance to explore the entire apartment before, but it struck me just how large it was when we passed several closed doors on the way to the room Dante used as his office at the very end.

"*Buona fortuna*," Adriano grumbled as he opened the paneled black door for me to walk through.

I frowned over my shoulder at him as I passed through, but he was already closing the door in my face.

When I turned around, I noted vaguely that the entire room was once again done in rich blacks, the only color popping from the spines on the books lined on the floor-to-ceiling shelves on two of the walls. But I didn't have time to catalog more because Dante was leaning against the front of his palatial desk with his arms crossed over his broad chest, his features set into a dark scowl.

"You must really like black," I quipped lamely because the buzzing tension around Dante seemed to increase with each breath I took as we stared at each other across the large room.

"*Vieni qui*," he ordered brusquely.

Come here.

My lips flattened. "Don't order me around. I'm not one of your *soldati*."

"No," he agreed on a low purr that was more threat than seduction. "*Vieni qui, lottatrice mia*."

Come here, my fighter.

I hesitated, my mind battling with the impulse to obey. My teeth clenched so tightly my jaw panged, but finally, I moved closer, stopping an arm span away from the tense mafioso.

"What?" I demanded mulishly, feeling like a child called to the principal's office to atone for her misdeeds.

Dante studied me with those liquid black eyes, his entire body clenched with the force of holding back the anger that toiled beneath his surface.

"I heard you met a man today," he said finally.

Instantly, I went to take a step away from him, but Dante was already moving, knowing me well enough to stymie my flight. His hot hand curled around my wrist, engulfing it in his meaty palm. He didn't say another word, but he watched me with those predatory eyes, those hungry animal eyes that said he wanted to eat me up for his next meal.

The adrenaline sluicing through my limbs pooled warmly in my gut and seeped lower, heating the place between my thighs I hadn't felt the urge to touch in months.

"Who told you?" I made the mistake of asking.

Dante bared his teeth. "You should have told me. Do not be angry with Adriano for doing what I asked."

"For spying on me?" I snapped, leaning closer to the angry Made Man even though I knew it was dangerous. Fear and excitement tangled in my chest, dancing together in a way they never had before. I felt alive with sizzling energy, restless with the need to poke at the growling bear before me until he snapped.

The perverse side of me wanted to see what would happen when he did.

"For watching out for you," he ground out, pushing off the edge of his desk so that our bodies collided, my slight curves yielding to his iron edges.

My nipples beaded so tight they pulsed as they brushed against his upper stomach.

"I can take care of myself, Dante. I don't need to be watched like some child," I argued, raising up to my toes in my high heels to get even closer to his sneering mouth.

"Like a child? No. A child has more sense than you sometimes," he countered cruelly. "*Ma dai!* Do you know the man you gave your number to, Elena?"

"Does it matter? Unlike you, he was a gentleman." I never raised my voice, but I found I was nearly yelling at him, the slim space between our snarling mouths filled with our comingled breath hot as dragon fire.

"*Gentiluomo?* That man was Gideone di Carlo," he growled, cupping my shoulders in his hands to give me a little shake. "The same man whose brother is trying to assume leadership of the fucking Cosa Nostra. The same man whose family nearly murdered your sister. The same family who tried to kill me at my own party."

I blinked, shocked by the revelation.

Dante continued, battering into my defenses ruthlessly. "I told you my enemies would want to use you against me, Elena, and I told you to be careful. Instead, you give a man who wants me dead your fucking phone number."

Anger leaked from the puncture wound in my pride. I sagged slightly in his hold and pinned my eyes over his shoulder to avoid his censorious gaze. "I didn't know."

He sighed harshly, his warm, wine-scented breath against my face as he surprised me by hauling me tight against him in a sudden hug. His arms nearly crushed me, fury still palpable even in the tender expression. "For a smart woman, you can be very blind."

I struggled out of his arms, face flaming, skin pricking with shame. "Excuse me for thinking for one moment that a man could have taken a genuine interest in me."

I winced slightly as I realized the vulnerability of my words.

Some of the antagonism vibrating through Dante quieted as his expression morphed into somber consideration. When he shook me again by the shoulder, it was almost gentle.

"Elena," he said, clearly exasperated. "You are the most complicated woman I've ever known. So tough and strong, a born fighter because life taught you the need to survive, and that's a beautiful thing."

I pulled away from him, stepping back because suddenly I couldn't breathe well. He let me go, but his eyes were hooked through mine, forcing me to witness the sincerity there, to hear the words I knew would eviscerate me.

"Yet, you're so afraid," he said in a low voice, his words creeping across the space toward me like the slow roll of thick, ominous fog. "You're so goddamn afraid of being soft and tender because all that silk beneath your armor would rip so easily in the wrong hands. This insecurity blinds you to the truth. It corrodes the goodness in you. If you saw what I saw when I looked at you, you would never doubt yourself again. You wouldn't be tricked by the easy flattery of some *stronzo* like di Carlo into thinking he was good enough for you."

"Oh," I lashed out, hand slicing through the air as if my words were a knife I could wield. "And I suppose you are?"

His gaze was unnerving, unblinking on mine, so dark I lost my way in the black maze of those eyes. Finally, he shrugged that eloquent Italian shrug and put his hands in his pockets as if to contain them. "*Forse.*"

Maybe.

I shook my head, back and forth, back and forth, unable to stop because I didn't for one second want to forget my denial. "Don't be absurd."

"I prefer romantic," he offered, making light of me as he always did.

Only this time, it wasn't funny.

It was dangerous and potentially lethal.

I backed up another step. "I'm your lawyer, Dante. Nothing more."

"You were more than that from the moment I met you," he countered, stepping forward, stalking me across the room step for step. "You were my best friend's sister, the woman she admired most in the world. How could I not be intrigued? And then you saw me in the hospital room, and I thought you would fight me there and then to protect her. But it wasn't until you pushed me up against the wall with your little fist in my shirt and threatened me with death if I ever hurt Cosima that I knew you were something special. A true *lottatrice,* a female gladiator."

We were both across the room now, beyond the entrance at the back wall of books. I took one more step back, and my spine hit the shelves. Dante was on me in the next breath, his body a careful inch away from mine, but his hand, as it seemed to do, found the column of my throat and cupped it, his thumb stroking my pulse almost soothingly.

He leaned closer until his eyes were my entire world. "How could a man like me resist a woman like that?"

"Try harder," I suggested, but the impact of my cold words was lessened by the heaviness of my breath and the mad beat of my pulse against the pad of his thumb.

"For once in your life, be brave," he demanded. "And maybe I'll give you what you're too terrified to ask me for."

"I want to leave."

"No," he purred darkly. "No, you want me to fuck you senseless without asking for your permission. If I don't ask, you don't have to pretend to be a lady and say *no.*"

My core clenched at the darkly provocative thought, my mind spinning the fantasy faster than I could quell it. His hands turning me around, pushing me into the books so he could undo the pearl buttons down the length of my blouse. His teeth on my neck, pinning me in place as he loosened my trousers and sent them pooling to the floor at my heels, then the sharp bite of satin at my hips as he wrenched off my underwear and used his fingers to spread me apart for his cock. He'd take me there, without preparation, working himself into me with short, powerful thrusts until I opened up around him, until I screamed as he seated himself to the hilt.

The air was thin in my lungs as I tried to regulate my breath, turning my head to the side so Dante wouldn't see the desire I knew blazed from my eyes like neon lights. The hand on my neck moved up to grasp my chin, tilting my face back and up so he could look down into it.

His own features were coated in shadow, his beauty stark and forceful in the low light. It took my breath away, the contrast between the ferocity of the body poised just over mine and the gentle way he cupped my chin. His night dark eyes swallowed me up as he looked into me, through me, behind every shield I'd painstakingly constructed.

"*Coraggio, lottatrice mia*," he coaxed softly.

Courage, my fighter.

"Let me show you all the ways a man can appreciate a woman," he continued, running his nose along my cheek to my ear, where he took the lobe quickly between his teeth in a sharp nip that made me gasp. "Let me teach you all the ways you can appreciate me."

Helplessly, I tipped my head back against the books to give him better access to my neck, my fingers trembling uselessly at my sides.

Dio mio, I wanted him with an acuteness I hadn't felt in years.

No, that was a lie I couldn't begin to swallow.

I'd never felt like this. This hammering, all-encompassing

fervor that struck through me with each beat of my heart like a lightning strike. I wanted to prostrate myself for this beast of a man and witness all the ways he could bring my body back to life.

He kissed the hollow of my throat, just a flutter of silken lips against warm skin, yet it made me want to cry. When was the last time someone had touched me with such reverence?

Never?

But it was more than sexual. That simple kiss laid roots through my flesh and bones, deep into the very center of my chest, where they wrapped intractably around my fragile heart.

The kiss was *kind*.

That was it. That simple and that profound for me.

Dante was showing me kindness, the depths of which I hadn't experienced much of in my life.

It was a blow to the already fractured walls protecting my heart, body, and mind from intruders, and it was the last one I could stand to take. With a sound that was half growl, half shriek, I pushed Dante away with both hands on his steel chest.

He moved away more as a result of my intent than my strength. I noticed he was breathing hard, that there was a sizable tent at the groin of his black pants I didn't allow myself to focus on for more than a nanosecond.

"Elena," he said, just the one word, just my name, but in it a wealth of promises, an invitation in.

Come to the underworld with me, it seemed to say. *Come and play with me in the shadows where you belong.*

But I didn't belong there.

I didn't belong anywhere, really, but certainly not on the dark side of life with a man on trial for murder, a man with blood on his hands and sin stained through his soul.

My head was shaking again, back and forth almost manically as I beat a hasty, backward retreat to the office door.

"I won't go out with Gideone di Carlo if he calls," I promised weakly.

"I forbid it," he barked, face darkening immediately, body tensing to move toward me again.

I held my hands up between us as I moved to flee. "I won't. But this can't happen. This... this just cannot happen. Don't push me on this, Dante. I'll leave. I'll ask to be off your case."

"Elena," he protested, and I hated the way he said it with the lyrical Italian accent as if it was exotic and beautiful. As if I was.

"No," I said, locking down my battered defenses as I wrapped my hand around the door handle and opened it behind me. "I mean it. Forget this ever happened."

"What if I cannot?" he defied, crossing his arms and bracing his feet apart like a general preparing for battle.

Good Lord, let him give up on me before it came to that. I was strong, and I was resilient, but I was not prepared to go to war with a man like him when the prize could mean more than my body.

"*Per favore,*" I asked softly, remembering the way he had reacted to the word in my mouth once before. "Please, Dante."

And then before he could respond, I spun on my heel, and I

ran like the devil was at my back. I didn't stop until I was in the bedroom he'd given me, but even that didn't seem safe enough, so I locked myself in the en suite and braced myself on the sink, breathing hard as I stared at my haunted eyes in the mirror.

My pale olive gold skin was flushed, my pupils dilated, my hair tousled as if from a lover's hands. I looked well fucked, and he'd only kissed me on the neck, nipped my earlobe in those strong teeth.

What would he do to me if given the chance?

His demeanor held an unmistakable dominance, but from the first time since Christopher, I felt curious about it, almost entranced by it. Dante was dangerous, violence dressed in a thousand-dollar suit, but beneath it all, he was also the kind of man who wept at a friend's hospital bedside and made pasta with a girl who called him uncle.

He was a contradiction, a bigger mess of contrarian values than anyone I'd ever known outside myself.

He was tall, dark, and sinfully handsome, a masterfully created man.

My heart raced, and the primal urge to flee spiked hot again through my veins because even though walls separated us, I knew instinctively he was not done hunting me.

And I thought, for the first time in my life, that I might have just met my match.

CHAPTER SEVENTEEN

elena

My life settled into an odd kind of routine over the next week. I woke up early every morning to use Dante's state-of-the-art gym. Sometimes, I ran on the treadmill the way I had at my own gym, reading *The New York Times* while I warmed up, then doing intervals for forty-five minutes. Most of the time, I worked out with Dante and some assortment of his crew.

As I said, it was odd.

They were all criminals, rough wiseguys who cursed freely, flouted everything I stood for, and made money hand over fist through ill-begotten means.

I shouldn't have liked them.

But I found I kind of did.

They were fun and free in a way I'd never seen people act before. They joked with each other just as easily as they delivered brutal blows when they fought on the sparring mats. There wasn't competition between them as there was between every lawyer and me at the firm, that edge of envy and wariness that curdled socialization. They were brothers in crime, bonded over battles in alleyways and on street corners, in backrooms and ballrooms. They were as capable of sophistication––I learned Chen actually had a master's degree in mathematics and Frankie was COO of the Salvatore-owned Terra Energy Solutions, a well-known energy and gas company––as they were of ruthlessness.

They were a tangle of contrasts I found myself wanting to sit cross-legged on the ground and pull apart until I held each individual thread in my hand. I was curious by nature, a puzzle solver by trade, but there was something primal in them that called to me like the howl of a fellow wolf at night.

I felt moved by them and moved by their acceptance of me when normally, I would have judged them and found them wanting without ever giving them a chance. It shamed me to acknowledge that as much as it awed me to know they were above that.

I caught Dante watching me sometimes when I sparred with Marco, who was short enough that we were more evenly matched, or when I spoke to Chen as I stretched about the recent economic downtown. He watched me with this look in his eye I couldn't quite figure out, but it looked something like pride. I didn't speak to him, avoiding any alone time with him as if it was essential to my safety, and in a way, it was. But I could admit to myself that I watched him too, and what I found continued to fascinate me.

They clearly respected Dante, deferring to him in a myriad of different little ways I cataloged with more interest than I should have. They mimicked his movements sometimes, shifted their positions throughout the room in correlation to him like planets around a singular sun, and followed his orders without blinking an eye. They teased him often, fought him hard when they sparred, and seemed relaxed in his company, but an alert attentiveness in the soldiers spoke of their willingness to do more than just his bidding, an intensity that spoke of their readiness to dive in front of a bullet for him.

It was heady to observe their dynamic.

Not just observe like a witness, like the fly on the wall I'd been most of my life, but to participate in it.

They enfolded me into their morning routine like sugar into egg whites, beating us together until, at the end of eight days, I felt like a homogenous member of their five a.m. practice sessions.

From there, I did my ablutions, grabbed a banana from the bowl in the kitchen, and had Adriano take me to work, where I focused mostly on other cases while we waited to find out when the trial date would be set for Dante. Until we knew, we didn't have access to the witness sheet, and therefore, it was difficult to know how to defend Dante against whoever they would find to replace Mason Matlock. The only evidence they seemed to have of Dante's racketeering and illegal gambling was a low-level bookie in New Jersey who'd been arrested eight months ago and rolled over on Dante to reduce his sentencing time as well as a wiretap they'd taken of Dante speaking to a known sports gambling shylock in the Bronx about betting for the 2018 World Series years ago.

It wasn't much, and it would be nothing if we could squash the murder charges.

I worked through the weekend to avoid spending time at the apartment with Dante even though he was often as busy as I was, working in his office deep into the night, always on the phone or entertaining a variety of men and some women who all had that trademark wet black mafia look in their eyes.

I was taking the Thursday and Friday off from work then working remotely for three days the next week anyway for my surgery, so I told myself it made sense to work longer hours than usual, staying at the office until ten o'clock every night when Adriano would arrive to drive me back to the apartment.

It wasn't that I was avoiding him or the feelings he seemed to stir to life beneath my frozen skin.

I was just busy with work, as always.

The Wednesday night before my surgery, I stayed even later at the office, the small silver clock on my desk in the bullpen glowing with the number 11:17.

Seventeen was an unlucky number for Italians, signaling death, and even after years of stifling my cultural history, I shivered at seeing it on the screen, instinctively reaching for the cross I'd once worn at my neck.

It was as good enough a cue as any to end the night there. I'd finished my research on a hit and run for a client who had claimed there hadn't been a stop sign at the corner where the accident had occurred. Fortunately, the company PI, Ricardo Stavos, had located the vandals in Brooklyn Heights who had stolen it, which meant when we finally went to court in two weeks, we had a solid chance of getting him off with a heavy fine and license penalty given the victim had only suffered a fractured collarbone.

I laughed resentfully as I stood from my uncomfortable chair to stretch the kinks out of my body from sitting at my desk for hours. As a girl, I'd dreamed of being a lawyer, imagining myself like a superhero in a Prada suit, then when I'd first moved to America, I'd been caught up in the idea of glamor and prestige as one of the city's top attorneys.

The truth was fair less dazzling. Very few lawyers ever made it into the papers for their work or won cases that made a serious change to the dynamics of society. Most people were in it for the power, the money, or the nepotism. We all worked endless hours, ate at our desks, and eschewed normal social conventions like dinner dates and Sundays at Central Park for work, work, and more work.

It was an endless toil.

And in a way, it perfectly mimicked my life.

I'd had my nose to the grindstone since I was ten years old and realized if I wanted a chance to get out of the stinking hole of our poverty in Naples, I had to hone my mind into my mightiest weapon, the only one in my arsenal.

It was no wonder I was always tired. It was as if I just needed a night of good, deep sleep, but I still felt exhausted even when

I woke up. It was more than physical exhaustion or mental. The brunt of it was emotional weariness, all of my hope and optimism worn smooth by the continued battering of life's antagonistic waves against the shores of my heart.

All I wanted was to go back to Dante's apartment, crawl into that huge, decadent bed, and sink into the silky sheets with a glass of wine and the latest edition of *The Economist*.

Not exactly exciting, but after a day like I'd had, a week, a year, it was all I wanted. My needs were small and simple because I never let them become blown out of proportion by dreams.

"Burning the midnight oil?" Ethan asked as he sauntered into the room in a beautiful blue suit, his voice slurred slightly with drink. "Why did I know I'd find the invulnerable Elena Lombardi still at her desk?"

I ignored him as I packed up my things. In my experience, men like him wanted any kind of attention, so if you starved him of it, he'd leave you alone.

The drink made him bolder. He sauntered forward, slammed his hip into the side of a desk, and hissed before saying, "You should relax a little. 'S not like you're next in line for the partner track."

I sighed heavily. "Maybe if you spent less time out drinking with your buddies and more time at work, you'd have a chance at it someday too."

"I have more than a chance," he countered, his flushed faced furrowing. "My father is Horace Topp. I'm just paying my dues here in this pit with the rest of you."

264

"The rest of us who actually work for our success," I countered superciliously, giving him a wide birth as I walked around him to the door.

I was tired and human, and he was irritating. I could only resist his idiocy for so long.

He lunged forward, surprisingly quick for his drunkenness, and grabbed my wrist. "You're a real bitch, you know that? You should be nice to me. I could do you a favor or two if I was properly motivated."

"If being a bitch means being smart enough to know the truth and brave enough to speak it, I'll count it as a compliment," I told him calmly, peeling his fingers off the silk of my blouse, frowning at the oily print his grip left there. "And one day, Ethan, I have no doubt you'll be needing a favor from *me* so why don't you go home to Daddy's lush apartment and have some sweet dreams while you still can."

I walked away from his gaping mouth and furious flush even though he stammered behind me and called out some choice curse words as if they'd have any effect on me. When your own family thought you were a bitch, it was difficult for anyone else's knife to inflict the same kind of wound.

It shocked me to see Frankie just outside the glass doors to the bullpen, his mouth twisted up with rage, his eyes over my shoulder on the idiot that was no doubt still staring after me.

"He was giving you trouble," he said, tone flat with fury.

I was momentarily surprised by that. Why should Frankie care if one of the associates was haranguing me? It happened literally every day, and I'd had much, much worse confrontations in my life. This was a blip, a nothing.

"It doesn't matter," I assured. "I'm used to his nonsense."

Francesco Amato, Dante's right-hand man, a sharp-minded, quick-fingered hacker, pinned me then with a gaze that reminded me all too much of the wet black eyes of the mafiosos in my past. For one fleeting second, I was terrified.

"You shouldn't have to deal with nonsense," he said firmly. "One thing rolls into another, and before you know it, you've let a pile of shit a mile wide accumulate at your back, and no matter how hard you run, you'll never outpace it. No." He leaned closer, conspiratorially. Naturally, I bent to meet him. "Someone gives you hell, Elena, you give it to 'em right back. You teach them that for every move against you, however slight, you're ready to battle. So many of the wealthiest, most successful men you'll ever see are bullies at heart, and there's nothing a bully hates so much as pushback."

I didn't know how to respond to that, mostly because I wasn't sure I agreed. My family had called me a bully before for my cruelty to Giselle, and Lord knew, I was met with pushback for every word I'd ever spoken against her, even if it was warranted. It still didn't stop the poison of hatred for her and self-loathing for myself seep through my bloodstream.

"Besides," Frankie continued, cuffing my chin lightly the way I'd seen fathers do to sons, as if he was imparting life wisdom.

"You're with us, now. You think the Salvatore *borgata* puts up with limp-dicked *stronzi* like this *bastardo?*"

Before I could say anything, Frankie sauntered past me into the bullpen, his gait easy, hands in his pockets, and a whistle through his lips like he was taking some kind of jaunty midnight stroll through the office.

"Hey man," he called to Ethan, who'd leaned against a desk to text. He dropped his phone; his fingers numb with drink as he startled. "You got the time?"

Ethan stared at him numbly for a beat before he jerked himself out of it and bent to look at the clock on the desk he was perched on. "Yeah, it's eleven--"

Frankie was there so quickly I barely saw him move, lunging across the space to curl his hand over the back of Ethan's neck, using it to slam his face down into the clock he peered at. There was slap, crash, and wet garbled cry as Ethan collided with it.

Frankie yanked him back up and stepped closer to smile at him, patting Ethan's bloody cheek with his free hand as he said, "There ya go. Now, next time I see you fucking with Elena Lombardi, I'm gonna put your head through a window, you get me?"

"Jesus," Ethan groaned, trying to hold his broken nose as blood slipped through his fingers. "You fucking psycho."

Frankie shrugged a shoulder modestly. "Hey, you think I'm a psycho, you should see Dante Salvatore when he's been crossed. *Cavolo,* they call him the Devil of NYC for a reason." He reached up again to squeeze Ethan's bloody cheeks in one hand then turned his head to face me lingering in the doorway. "You fuck with Elena, you should know, that's you fucking with *him*. And he'll do a lot worse than I would, *capisci?*"

When Ethan didn't immediately respond, Frankie shook his head in his cruel hand, blood flying from the broken nose over the desk.

"Yes," Ethan finally squawked. "Okay, alright, fuck! Chill."

"Chill?" Frankie asked, then looked at me as if he was affronted. "I look anything but chill to you, Lena?"

"As a cucumber," I agreed, because what else could I say?

A secret part of me deep inside thrilled at the sight of entitled, whining, asshole Ethan bleeding in Frankie's hands. He wasn't just a prick to me, but to every single associate in the office he felt was below his status, which was most of them.

Honestly, if Frankie hadn't done it, it was probably only a matter of time before someone else did.

Even though I didn't like the position it put me in, jeopardizing my job yet *again*, I also had to admit it was unlikely that Ethan would go crying to our superiors about it. His enormous ego would be too bruised to admit what happened. I had no doubt by tomorrow he would have circulated an epic tale about getting beaten up on the subway or for trying to steal some guy's girl at a bar.

I didn't care.

It was enough to know that Frankie cared enough about me to stand up for me.

It was nice to hear that he felt Dante would do the same.

As Frankie dropped Ethan's face and started toward me, reaching for a handkerchief he kept in the inside pocket of his suit jacket, I surprised myself by smiling at him.

"That was more than slightly awesome," I whispered as he met up with me and continued forward down the hall in tandem. "I won't say I fully approve of your methods but thank you."

"Hey," he said with a blasé shrug as if it was nothing. "You remind me of my wife. It was nothing to do."

"What's she like?" I asked as we took the elevator down to the street level.

He shot me a sidelong glance. "She's a real bitch."

I laughed the entire ride down.

It was dark in the apartment when I stepped from the elevator after Frankie dropped me off on his way home to his wife and children. A tiny flash of disappointment flared in my chest when I didn't see Dante in the living room or kitchen, his normal haunts late at night. There was a restless energy coursing through me I wanted to satisfy with the bite of our banter, the feel of those deadly hands lightly touching my flesh.

The truth was, I wanted to play, with our minds if not our bodies, knowing how dangerous it would be to tumble over that last hurdle and into bed with my client.

With a mafia don.

I got ready for bed feeling oddly deflated as I washed my face and applied my seven-step skin care, as I massaged lotion into my body and read my requisite thirty minutes of news before bed.

It did not surprise me that I couldn't sleep.

Not with Dante lodged in my consciousness like a splinter.

With a ragged sigh, I threw off my eye mask, tossed my earplugs to the nightstand, and slid out of bed. I decided a nightcap was the only solution for my insomnia, so I padded down the dark halls to the back staircase and down to the kitchen. There was only the faint light from the streets spilling in through the floor-to-ceiling windows to light my way in the black-on-gray-and-white spaces, but I managed it.

I was opening the fridge when I noticed the faint glow of light coming from down the hallway.

My heart tripped over the excitement that collected in my chest, and before I could think through the impulse, I walked down the back hall toward the light.

It came from the office near the end of the hall. The door was just barely ajar, but through the gap in the wood, I could hear everything I needed to.

A faint, growling moan.

My body went white-hot then ice cold as I realized what could be happening behind that door.

Was Dante *fucking* someone in there?

Agony spun through me like a tornado, ripping up the foundation of confidence I'd found I'd unwittingly built around my relationship with the capo. I blinked hard against the disbelief that he would be with another woman when it had seemed so wonderfully apparent he wanted me in his bed.

Clearly, I'd forgotten myself.

I wasn't some siren like my younger sister, Giselle, capable of enchanting men with her song, luring them to her depths even if it meant a rocky death.

I wasn't a sensational beauty like Cosima, so radiant inside and out even a blind man would want her.

I'd been with two men who had both found me a disappointment, even if, in the end, they'd been a disappointment to me too.

Why would a man like Dante Salvatore with his raw, tangible magnetism and almost animalistic energy want to bed me?

I couldn't even come.

Shame spun its path through every inch of my body until I had to brace myself or fall into my weak knees. I caught myself on the frame, but my shoulder caught the door, knocking it open a little more.

Just enough to see into the clearer shadows of the interior.

My breath caught, the cyclone inside me falling flat like the eye of a storm.

Because Dante was inside lounging totally naked in a deep suede chaise before the bookshelves in the corner of the room with the dregs of whiskey sweating in a glass on the side table and a jar of lube beside that, the cap still open.

But he was entirely alone.

271

And those strong hands threaded with veins I found myself fantasizing about far too often were wrapped around the obscene length of his cock.

He was jerking off.

I was arrested by the sight of him like that. His big body sprawled in the seat, his thickly muscled thighs spread wide to accommodate his hands, one pulling hard and slow at his shaft, the other cupping his lightly furred sac. He had his head thrown back against the pillows, neck corded with tension, wine-stained red mouth lax with pleasure. All that golden olive skin glimmered like oiled bronze in the low light of the single lamp, illuminating the scene. The hair that dusted his broad, steeply defined chest and under his naval in a dense line to his trimmed groin was ridiculously masculine, highlighting his rugged masculinity as much as it provided a delicious contrast for his beautifully carved form.

He was simply and extraordinarily exquisite.

I couldn't tear my eyes from him if I tried.

When he hissed, looking down as he pulled those thick fingers up his shaft again and a bead of precum pooled like a pearl on the head of his cock, I couldn't quite swallow my gasp.

His eyes shot to the door the next instant, his torso jacking up, hands falling from his groin.

I meant to back away, to look into his eyes at the very least.

But his new position had put his erection predominantly on display, and my eyes were pulled there inexorably.

Maddona santa, he was perfectly proportioned, his cock a thick, long length of muscle covered in dusky golden skin at the base, the head as swollen and deeply purple as an Italian plum. It jumped, spitting precum as I studied it.

My mouth actually watered.

Dazed, confused, horribly aroused, my eyes shot back up to Dante's.

I didn't know what I would find, how he would react, but somehow the awareness that burned in those coal dark eyes wasn't what I expected.

Slowly, knowingly, he leaned back in his chair and spread those lightly furred thighs wide again.

I swallowed thickly, captured in his sights like a deer before a wolf.

When he wrapped a palm around his swollen shaft again, we both moaned, mine a light breath of sound and his a resounding growl. My gaze moved along his length in time with his tight grip, watching as he squeezed the flesh tightly, almost violently each time he passed over the crown. All those tense muscles clenched and twitched as pleasure worked through him, as it escaped in a hiss through his clenched teeth.

He worked faster, unfathomably harder, fucking into his fist with long, brutal strokes.

Distantly, I was aware of my own arousal, wet seeping into the seat of my silk shorts, crawling down the inside of my right thigh. But nothing mattered at that moment, in that vibrating, softly yellow luminated space between us but Dante's pleasure.

It was impossible not to wonder what that heavy cock would feel like in my own smaller hand and finer fingers. What the liquid leaking steadily from his crown might taste like, salty or musky or sweet. If I could make him shake and groan the way he was watching me watch him fuck himself. If I could fit even half of that wide shaft inside my fairly untrained mouth.

Such dirty, salacious thoughts, the kind I never allowed myself to think, all triggered unalterably by the sight of that big, beautiful beast of a man beating his shaft in time with my panting breaths.

I didn't think anything could have pulled me from that moment, from the seismic sexual awakening beginning in my gut as I derived more pleasure from simply watching a man than I ever had from sleeping with one. Not someone walking in on my voyeurism, not the call of my phone or the blare of a fire alarm.

I was rooted to the spot by Dante's shadowed black gaze hooked through the belly of my desires and the sight of his sex glazed with oil churning through his heavy fist.

When his breath went harsh, chest pumping like billows, his back hunching into a slight curve as if everything in him contracted around his swelling cock, I actually held my breath, waiting for the inevitable conclusion to rock us both.

I sucked a sharp breath through my teeth when his neck strained, his tempo went erratic, and he called out, *"Elena!"* a second before he climaxed.

His cock thrust one last time through that tight grip, cum

shooting across his boxed abs, sliding down the gutters cut between each one, up onto his chest, splattering against that silver cross nested in the hair there. He came almost endlessly, so much of it on his chest, belly, and thighs, even dripping off his fingers as he relinquished the hold on his softening organ. The sight of all that seed was deeply erotic, literally mouth-watering. I couldn't believe my own reaction to it, thinking for the first time in my life that I could understand fetishism if there was such a one for that.

For the sight of Dante, big-boned and heavily muscled gone limp with pleasure in that chair covered in his own spend.

I swallowed thickly, light-headed and off balance. At that moment, I wasn't even sure who I was because the Elena I'd known would never have stood in the door watching the private display of a man's pleasure as if it was hers to watch and hers to own.

I startled when Dante began to right himself, breathing deeply in recovery as he used a hand towel to clean up most of the spunk. Even that invigorated me, a separate pulse beating like a ceremonial drum between my thighs.

When he stood up, I almost fled like a deer caught in the garden, but there was an order in his expression that held me in his thrall as he moved closer. Only when he reached the door, less than a foot between his naked body and my clothed one, only the angle of the open two-inch-thick door obscuring his softening cock from my sight, did he stop stalking me.

Then, eyes still puncturing straight through mine into the dark, calamitous heart of me, he brushed one hand down his chest, his thumb dipping into a cooling streak of cum he'd missed while cleaning up.

My heart beat so hard my ribs ached from the impact as he slowly raised it to my lips and smeared just the tiniest deposit on my mouth, a smudge like lip gloss. Unconsciously, my lips parted at the press, but he was already retreating his hand back through the door, pushing it slowly but firmly closed.

"*Sogni d'oro*," he murmured just before closing the door in my face with a slight, secret smile. "Have sweet dreams of me, Elena."

The moment I was alone in the dark hall, my tongue peeked out of my mouth to tap at the salt slick on my lips. The flavor of saline and musk exploded on my taste buds, more delicious for the intimacy of having some of Dante in my mouth than it was for the true taste.

I wandered back to bed on wobbly legs like a drunk, slamming into tables, tripping on the stairs back up to my room. I was high off the fumes of our encounter, off the lingering oceanic taste of him on the back of my tongue.

My skin was tight and hot. Even the gray silk camisole and short set too much for my inflamed flesh. For the first time ever, I stripped down naked and slid into bed, almost shivering with the acute yearning that burned through me.

I wanted him.

I squeezed my eyes shut as if the sight of him wasn't branded on the inside of my lids, spray-painted on the walls of my skull like crude graffiti.

I wanted him more than I'd ever wanted anything, even my own sexual release, and wasn't that a revelation in itself.

Tomorrow, I was going in for a surgery that would hopefully change my life forever, bring the kind of lustful fervor working under my skin to a gorgeous boiling point.

I had been incandescently happy about the surgery since Monica told me it was possible, but now, in the wake of the most intense and positive sexual experience of my life, I was almost breathlessly excited.

What would Dante be able to do with those exacting hands on *me*?

If anyone could take my broken and newly healed body in his hands and make it sing, it would be the mafioso I shouldn't, couldn't have. The only man I'd ever wanted with this level of physical zeal and the only man I truly could not let myself want.

CHAPTER EIGHTEEN

elena

Thursday morning dawned grim and gray with the staccato ping of rain chiming on the windows outside. I enjoyed the pathetic fallacy of the weather as I got ready for surgery. In the wake of last night's outlandishly out-of-character spectatorship, I found myself as grouchy as Jacopo and bloated with a lonely melancholy.

I hadn't told anyone in my family I was having surgery done except for Cosima, and even then, I hadn't given her the date.

It wasn't that I was embarrassed per se, but admitting I had reproductive issues, let alone anorgasmia, was vulnerable, and I didn't want to have to explain it to anyone more than I had to. I didn't even tell Mama because I hadn't told her I was temporarily living with Dante.

So, that morning I fasted and dressed to catch a cab to Monica's private clinic. A flock of anxious and excited birds flapped in my belly at the thought that I could be *fixed* in twenty-four hours.

I was almost out the door when Dante called out for me from the kitchen.

Everything in me wanted to avoid him and the embarrassment of being called out for my voyeurism the night before, but I knew we had to interact eventually, seeing as how I was his lawyer and his enforced roommate.

So, I sucked in a deep breath, told myself to stop acting like a shame-faced schoolgirl, and went into the living room.

"A late start for you today," he noted from the island where he sat on a stool drinking espresso and reading *Il Corriere*, a popular Italian newspaper.

It amazed me that he could sit there looking so cool and unaffected when I'd seen him at his most vulnerable last night, naked and splashed like a Pollock painting with his own cum. But then, wasn't that part of his appeal? Dante felt no shame, he did not hide, and he did not suffer fools. If I wanted to be embarrassed, I could, but that wouldn't affect his perception of what he undoubtedly felt was a natural activity.

That I could admire him somehow, respect him even more than I had before the incident, was as outrageous as it was somehow right.

From the beginning, Dante had caught sight of my red hair and turned to me like a bull, set on destroying whatever barricades lay between us in his quest to get to me. It still chilled me to wonder what he might want to do when and *if* he finally succeeded, but that chill was only a cool breeze compared to the firestorm of lust that swept through me lately whenever we were in the same space.

I hesitated, smoothing my hand nervously down my cashmere turtleneck. "I have that appointment I told you about."

His brow knotted, and I hated how handsome he was, how much I'd missed looking at his broad, beautiful face while I'd been avoiding him the last week. He was wearing a black turtleneck too, his thickly woven and snug over all those rippling muscles, heightening the fathomless black of his eyes and hair so that he looked nothing short of sinfully sinister sitting there.

I was thrown immediately back to watching him naked and aroused in his office. Those muscles bared to my eyes as they tensed and jumped in time with the sensations he pulled from his cock.

A shiver rippled through me.

Dante saw it and seemed to think about commenting on it before his frown descended again. Instead, he shocked me by offering, "Let me drive you."

"No," I almost snapped, moving back toward the entry room. That was the last thing I needed, this incredibly virile man knowing I couldn't even come like a normal woman. "No, I'll grab a cab. There's no need to go out of your way."

"It's surgery, no? Shouldn't someone pick you up when you're through?"

"I asked a friend to bring me back," I explained.

"He knows you're staying here?"

"I trust him." And I did. Beau would never do anything to harm me, and I could count the people I trusted on one hand, so that was saying something.

"You need me, you call me, *si*?" Dante demanded, still scowling. "I don't like this. You should tell me what it is you are having done so I can be prepared to care for you."

A hard bark of laughter erupted from me, my mortification from last night obliterated by the dark edge of my humor and prideful solitude. "I don't need looking after, and I can hardly picture you as a nursemaid. Don't worry about me, Dante. I'll be fine. I always am. Now, I have to rush, but have a nice day."

I glided out of the room before he could protest, catching his muffled, "Only she would wear heels to surgery," then a shouted, "*In boca al lupa!*" before I got in the elevator.

Good luck. Literally translated as "into the wolf's mouth."

Exactly where I currently felt myself, clasped between Dante's unshakeable teeth, unable and gradually more and more unwilling to get free.

It took me a moment to decide if I was grateful or irritated that he hadn't pushed me about watching him masturbate, but I eventually settled on grateful. I had more important things to focus on, even if my mind slipped back to those scandalous images like a hard grip on wet soap. As the cab crawled through morning traffic toward my destination, my nerves began to corrode any other thought in my head.

I was a nervous wreck by the time we pulled up to the curb, my palms sweating profusely as I paid the fare and entered Monica's building. By the time I got to her floor, my forehead was cold with anxious perspiration, and when Monica came out to greet me, she frowned.

"Nervous?" she asked gently, taking my hand to lead me to the private waiting room. "There is no reason to be, Elena. I've done these procedures hundreds of times. After all, I'm the best in the city."

I laughed weakly as she meant me to, following her into the room and sitting in the deep suede chair waiting for me. "I don't mean to doubt you. I'm not nervous about the surgery, really. Just what it means for afterward."

"Ah," she noted, nodding sagely as she collected my chart. "I understand that. Do you have an appointment to talk to Dr. Marsden following your recovery?"

I nodded even though I didn't think my therapist was equipped to help me deal with decades of sexual trauma and scarring.

"You're strong and brave, Elena. I see very good and passionate things in your future," she said with a wide smile. "I'll have the nurse come in and explain things to you. Please change into this gown and robe. I'll see you in the OR."

Brave.

The word echoed in my head, a reminder of Dante's benediction for me to be brave with him.

Coraggio.

I smiled tightly at my doctor and my friend as she left and tried to breathe deeply.

But I couldn't stop thinking about Dante and his indecent

proposition.

If this operation worked, I would be able to experience pleasure like I had never had before, not even with Daniel, who I knew logically had been a good and generous lover.

If Dante could light my icy flesh on fire with just the touch of his lips to my pulse point, how would he make me feel with those lips on other parts of my body?

I thought about it all through the check in with the nurse and then as I followed her down the hallway to the operating room.

I came to the inevitable conclusion that Dante would be a gregarious lover, throwing himself into my pleasure the way he seemed to throw himself with singular intensity into everything he did, but that didn't mitigate the risks.

The fact that I could lose my job.

Though just living with him could do that, the devil on my shoulder whispered. So shouldn't I make the risk worthwhile and get something more out of it?

No, it was the other threat, the one I hadn't been able to ignore that night in Dante's office pressed to the shelf of books by his hand on my throat and his big body at my front.

The threat to my heart.

After the tragedy of Christopher and Daniel, I didn't have anything more in me to give. I'd felt so much all my life I'd resolved to feel nothing at all. For years, I'd kept my heart black, my lips red, and my personality ice cold.

I didn't need anyone to be fulfilled, and I didn't trust anyone to try.

So, it was ridiculous to consider changing any of that for a man like Dante.

A man on trial for murder who could spend the next twenty-five years to life behind bars if I didn't do my job to the full extent of my capabilities.

I couldn't trust a mafioso with my life or my happiness.

To do so was suicide.

So why did I secretly yearn to, and why did that yearning feel like a crime I was committing against myself?

"When you wake up, Elena, you'll be a new woman," Monica promised as the anesthesiologist held the mask to my mouth and told me to breathe deeply.

I wanted to argue with her, but the gas was already pulling me under.

I wanted to tell her I was happy with the woman I was, and I was terrified of becoming anyone else.

But then I passed out, and when I woke up, my first thought was of a mafioso with eyes like the velvet black New York sky.

CHAPTER NINETEEN

DANTE

I was in a meeting with three of my captains when Marco appeared at the door to my office and tipped his chin.

Elena had returned.

The urge to go to her immediately was surprisingly powerful, but I tamped it down with the iron will I'd been born with as a Brit, then cultivated as a capo.

She would need space to get settled, and I'd already had Bambi clean her sheets, put a box of tissues, a bottle of water, and some saltine crackers by her bedside just in case. She'd be fine until I finished business.

"It worked," Gaetan was saying with a massive grin. "Heard through the grapevine that Moore and Kelly went at it over Elena staying with you. Apparently, the *figlio di puttana* has some kinda heart 'cause he straight-up refused to do anything that could hurt his precious daughter."

"You gonna hurt her, he steps outta line?" Joe asked, leaning forward somewhat eagerly.

Whoever said women were terrible gossips clearly had never met an Italian man.

Whatever plans I had for Elena were decidedly more about pleasure than pain, but Joe Lodi didn't need to know that.

Just as Elena didn't need to know I'd forced her to move in, in part, so that her arsehole of a father would back off our operation. It was a risky bet, given I'd doubted the man had a heart, even in regards to his daughters, given he'd sold Cosima into slavery to pay off his gambling debts to the Italian Camorra, but it was worth a shot.

I loved it when those paid off.

I arched a brow at Joe, watching as he deflated slightly under my cold regard. "No, Joe, I'm not going to beat a woman who is a guest in my house just because her father is a *pezzo di Merda*. I don't trust those Irish *bastardi*, so we stay vigilant, but now we've got something on them, so I'm hoping we can focus on the di Carlo problem."

"Mason Matlock's been moved to a safe place like you asked," Enzo promised. "He'll stay there under surveillance until you say so."

I nodded. "Good, though I have a feeling that broken fucker has told us all he knows. Now, we know the di Carlos have a civil war brewing over leadership between the di Carlo brothers and Giuseppe's underboss, Italo Faletti, and we can use that to our advantage."

Irrationally, I wanted Gideone di Carlo and his older brother, Agostino, to die horrible deaths just for approaching Elena, but I knew if I was going to back a horse in this race it had to be the younger di Carlos.

There was an idea lurking at the periphery of my mind when I zoned out on the myriad of problems facing me. A solution to the feud Giuseppe had started with us and the Irish problem, even the irritating fact that the other heads of the five families in the Commission still didn't accept me as one of their own.

Could I wipe them all out in one fell swoop with a singular, explosive idea?

It was still too murky to detail out loud, but if everything came together, including a certain icy redhead in her room upstairs, I could emerge from this *cazzato* trial with more power than I'd had even before it.

I grinned at my men as I decided to set the wheels in motion. There was a mole in my operation, a fact I wouldn't soon forget, but hopefully, this scheme would also draw them out.

"Enzo," I ordered, "Have Violetta Matlock brought close by and get Caelian Accardi's information for me."

"The son of the 'Ndrangheta boss?" he questioned.

Gaetan hit him on the back of his head. "Just do as the boss says, numb skull."

Enzo winced, then excused himself to make a call at the back of the room.

"What're you thinking, D?" Frankie asked from the coffee table in the middle of the room where he'd set up shop.

The smile that overtook my face was as lethal as a weapon. "I think it's time to shake things up a little. These motherfuckers think this is their world just because they were born on American soil. Let's show them what it's like to die in ours."

She was sleeping when I finally got the time to check in on her. I almost laughed at the image she made in the mammoth pale gray bed with a black silk face mask over her eyes and black foam plugs in her ears. Only Elena Lombardi would look like she was preparing for war just to take a simple nap.

But there was no denying she looked exquisite in slumber, her classic features softer in repose, her mouth pink without the usual lipstick. I found I wanted to lean down to savor it with my own, exploring the small white teeth beneath those bow-shaped lips, sliding my tongue alongside hers to taste her dreams.

I wondered with a fierce surge of possession that nearly stole my breath if she was dreaming of me. There was no doubting the powerful arousal she had felt watching me jack off in my office last night. It was there in the flush I could detect even though she was tucked in the shadows of the hallway, in the way her mouth bloomed open like a rose ready to be pollinated, her breath a harsh pant. She had been fucking captivated by me and by her reaction to me, almost scared and awed of the crackling chemistry between us.

It was heady as fuck to know I could have that effect on a woman who had clearly never harnessed the power of her sexuality. My usual ironclad control was tenuous at best now, knowing that beneath that gorgeous, cultivated class lay the heart of a wanton, desperate for a man to show her how to navigate the world of pleasure and hedonism.

I ached to wake her up just to see those wintry ocean gray eyes flare back at me, to test the edge of her tongue against mine and know whether it was as sharp as her words or soft like the tender heart she was so careful to guard.

I wanted her, and I would have her, but Elena required a contrarian mix of forcefulness and care, my seduction a tightrope walk that could fail with even the slightest provocation. And I wasn't more and more unwilling to fail.

I moved closer to her bedside in order to move a thick lock of deeply red hair out of her face, rubbing the silken strands between my fingers as I did so. I leaned over to press a slight kiss to the surprisingly small shell of her ear, unable to resist.

When I pulled away, the papers on the nightstand caught my eye.

I was a curious man.

And a criminal.

It wasn't in my nature to refuse myself much, and I found I didn't even try as I reached out for the folded pages and opened them to read. I wanted to know what Elena had been in the hospital for. As her host, I felt it was my prerogative to know so I could take the best care of her. As a capo, I felt it was my right to know anything that happened under my roof to someone in my circle.

I was not prepared for what lay in the neatly printed words.

Anorgasmia.

Cysts, fibroids, infertility.

I couldn't take my eyes from the page even though I knew I was crossing a line Elena would never have given me access to herself.

Madonna santa, it was difficult to comprehend the life this woman had lived in her short twenty-seven years.

A scumbag father constantly in debt to the mafia, the poverty that plagued so many Napolitano families, every single one of her siblings taking off to greener pastures while she remained in the hellhole of her youth.

Then the new world, a boyfriend she respected, a job she worked hard for.

Only for the boyfriend to leave her for her fucking sister. Only for some asshole mafioso to threaten her job by forcing her to move in with him because it suited his needs.

And this.

Issues with infertility and even the simple ability to orgasm.

Tore always used to tell me not to judge someone before I knew what they'd been through to get to that point. Survivors came in all shapes and sizes, and not all of them came out on the other side of their trauma shiny and bright with hope and renewed optimism.

Some of them ended up like Elena, fractured and glued back together through sheer resolve and tenacity of spirit.

Was it any wonder the world thought this woman was a bitch?

With all she'd been through, it was a miracle she ever smiled.

I thought about the night with Aurora, when Elena had transformed before my eyes. It was like watching a bear emerging from hibernation, foul-tempered and faintly aggressive with the outside world, turn to her cub and suddenly become all warmth and love.

The smile she'd given Aurora, the way she'd made her feel strong just by bestowing a playful nickname.

That was the night I discovered the true, tender underbelly of my fighter and decided, irrevocably, that I needed to have her.

Not just have her to own her, because a woman like Elena couldn't be owned and that was part of her powerful charm.

I needed to have her to understand her. To have the privilege of unwrapping layer after layer until I got to the heart of her. Once, I'd thought her soul would be frozen through, an icy vessel used only to pump blood through her body, but I was beginning to understand the truth.

Elena Lombardi had so much heart. She was overfull with emotion, and she had no idea how to hide that vulnerability from people unless it was behind a mask of icy indifference and cool disdain. It wasn't so much that she didn't trust others with that tender, swollen organ so much as she didn't trust herself to use it.

I stared down at her sleeping face feeling my own heart shift in my chest, the tectonic plates of my life fluctuating to accommodate a new presence there, one I didn't intend to let go.

At that moment, I had no thought to my *borgata*, my responsibilities, or the risks associated with having a romance with my lawyer, a woman who hated so much of what I loved.

I considered only the magnitude of the challenge I was setting for myself and the eagerness I felt setting out to conquer it.

To conquer her.

Because I resolved in much the same way I resolved to solve my mother's murder and resolved to save Cosima from the Order of Dionysus that I would show Elena Lombardi what it was like to live and love freely.

And I'd do it by loving her.

First, I just had to trick her into letting down her shields long enough to let me try.

CHAPTER TWENTY

elena

I woke up because someone was sitting at the edge of my bed with their hand on my cheek. Immediately, I thought it was Dante, but the scent was off. The hand was rough tipped and broad like a man's, but the fragrance was all spice and musk, not the bright tang of lemon and pepper I recognized as Dante's.

When I pushed back my eye mask, I was shocked to see my brother, Sebastian, seated on the bed beside me.

I hadn't seen him in a few months, but that wasn't unusual. He'd moved to Los Angeles to be closer to a film project late last year, and though he visited often, I didn't always make the time to see him, and he didn't always ask. There was no bad blood between us, as there was with Giselle and me, but there was a…wariness. We both had demons, and ours were too incompatible to play nice for long.

But seeing him there in my room, still shaky from the anesthesia and emotional from the impact the surgery would have on my life,

I felt, to my horror, tears spring to my eyes.

"*Patatino,*" I whispered through my thick throat before I carefully tried to sit up higher on the tower of pillows to prop me up at a forty-five-degree angle.

His grin was gorgeous, but then again, everything about the twins was pure beauty. I cataloged the way his golden eyes creased at the corners into charming crow's feet and how his wide, full mouth pulled apart in a perfectly symmetrical smile. His black hair was long on top and short on the sides, a trendy haircut for one of the hot young actors of our day. He looked handsome, of course, but also a little lost somewhere in the depths of those tiger yellow eyes.

"Hey, Lady."

I'd honestly forgotten that nickname. It had been so long since he called me that affectionately, Lady Elena or Signora Elena, because I was always badgering him about manners and decorum while he was growing up.

I was sore, and it was fabulously out of character, but I gave in to the impulse and gently leaned forward to wrap my arms around my little brother.

He laughed in my ear softly as he hugged me back, holding me to his strong chest as if I was a child. I could still remember when he had his growth spurt at fourteen years old. One day, he was this scrawny little kid, shorter and thinner than me, and the next moment, I was craning my neck back to look him in the eyes. The tears stubbornly refusing to leave my eyes alone swelled in my ducts and rolled slowly off the edge of my lids onto my cheeks.

"Hey, hey," he hushed, his familiar lightly accented baritone smooth and soothing. "What's this about, hmm? I don't think I've seen you cry in years."

I laughed a little weakly as I pulled away from him to dry the drops on my cheeks with my fingertips. "I want to say it's the drugs, but I've been a little...off lately. I guess it took me off guard how much I've missed you."

It hurt to see the surprise on Seb's face, but I knew I deserved it. I couldn't remember the last time I'd told him I missed him, let alone that I loved him or was proud of him.

And I was.

So proud of him.

So in love with the man he'd grown into against all the odds.

Tears burned and burned in my eyes, but I didn't let any more fall.

"I'm happy to see you too, *sorella mia*," he finally said with a genuine grin, reaching out to tug on a curl. "It's been too long."

"It has," I agreed before it occurred to me that we were in Dante's Upper East Side apartment. How the hell did Sebastian know I was even here? "How are you here?"

The humor fled from his face, replaced by an uncharacteristic scowl. "Dante answered your phone when I called earlier to see if it was cool I stayed with you at your place for the weekend. He told me you were in the hospital and just got out. Why didn't you tell me, Lena?"

I worried my lower lip, wishing I had on even a stitch of makeup for some armor between me and the acute scrutiny of those golden eyes. "It was minor."

"Lena," he warned. "Are you kidding me? Do you remember when you practically tore my ear off because I didn't tell you Leone Valeria broke my index finger?"

I pulled his right hand into my lap and pinched the misshapen middle knuckle. "It never did heal right."

"No," he said with an eloquently raised brow. "It didn't. It's been a long time since you've told me about any of your pain, Lena."

I looked down at his tanned hand in my own, tracing the lines on his palm the way I'd done when we were children. He and Cosima both had the same long emotion line bisecting their upper palm. They'd always been more emotionally intelligent than Giselle and me, always ready with the right words and the right kinds of hugs.

"I have a therapist now," I explained, still avoiding his eyes.

"You've always had a brother," he offered. "Some people say I'm wise beyond my years."

I laughed. "It doesn't count when you say it to yourself in the mirror, Seb."

"Hey, self-validation is important too," he quipped easily before sobering and enfolding my hand in his. "I used to think we were such a close family. It took me a long time to realize that we are a collection of strangers pretending to be family. We'll never know each other well enough to love each other properly if we keep secrets the way we have."

I winced slightly as his words hit the bull's-eye. "Ouch, Seb, take care, will you? The drugs aren't that strong."

"I am," he countered, not to be deterred, that famous Lombardi tenacity setting his face to stone. "If you want to share with me."

Gingerly, feeling the sharp pangs in my abdomen, I leaned back against the tower of pillows to stare at the elaborate molding on the ceiling and blew a burst of air between my lips. "How long do you have?"

In response, Seb stood up, kicked off his leather boots, and crossed to the other side of the bed so he could lever himself on top of the covers beside me. Once he arranged the pillows to his liking and propped a hand behind his head, he turned to face me with an expectant eyebrow raised.

For some reason, I was sick with nerves even though I knew rationally Sebastian wasn't going to ridicule me for the myriad of fears that kept me up at night and made sleep nearly impossible.

He was my brother.

That should mean something.

Only Giselle had taught me, and maybe I'd taught her, that it didn't mean much.

It hadn't always been like that, though.

When I was very young, I had many friends in our neighborhood, clusters of boisterous children whose mamas grouped together as they did in the open doorways of houses chattering as they hung laundry from the line and occasionally tended to various pots on the stove. This was when I was too young for true memory, so I'd often wondered how much of these hazy images I made up to soothe myself when I got older.

By the time Giselle was born, Mama and I were no longer part of that tight-knit community of Italian mothers and their babies. They knew us for what Seamus had made us.

Outsiders not to be trusted; a family whose words were no good.

In a place like Napoli, where almost everyone was poor and the Camorra ruled, your word was the only currency that really mattered.

And Seamus had robbed us of it.

So when Giselle was born, red-headed like me in a sea of dark-haired youth with little freckles on her cheeks she'd taken from our Irish father, I loved her instantly. I felt profoundly, or as profoundly as a four-year-old can, that Giselle was my gift from God. I constantly badgered Mama to hold her, feed her, brush the fragile, silken tangle of her curling flame-colored hair. I cooed to her in Italian, sweet little rhymes I made up and stories about foreign sister princesses who might one day be queens.

It was so long ago, yet even now, sitting in Dante's apartment with Sebastian at my side, a lawyer at a top-five firm with a gorgeous house of my own in Gramercy Park, almost as far removed from the past as I could possibly be, I felt the ache of those emotions like a latent echo in my chest.

I'd always wanted to love Giselle, but life had conspired against me, as it often did, to ruin whatever good there was between us.

I wondered if there was any wedge more destructive to the bond between two sisters as the love of a shared man.

No wonder the love and attention of two was our utter demise.

My mind was on her, on our family, so I started there.

"Do you remember me when we were young?" I asked him, reaching over to grab his hand because suddenly I needed comfort, and touching him was the only way I could find it. He wrapped his fingers around mine and squeezed. "Tell me about the Elena you remember."

Sebastian didn't laugh or tease the way he usually might have. Instead, he considered me. "You were like our second parent. Seamus was never around, and Mama was working in the restaurant in town, or depressed, lying in her room, or out looking for Dad. You were always bossing us around, getting us ready for school, making sure we were clean and doing our homework and in bed before nine." He shook his head. "It was annoying then, but Cosima and I have talked about it a lot since. How grateful and lucky we are to have had you keeping our noses clean."

"The Camorra wanted you," I said, thinking back on the other boys who were recruited as errand boys and messengers as early as eleven.

Seb nodded, his eyes distant as he played with my fingers. "How different my life would have been."

"It didn't happen."

"No," he agreed, pinning me with the full weight of his golden stare. "Mostly because of you. You always bore the brunt of those horrors for us. I haven't thanked you in a very long time for that."

I shrugged. "I can be annoying."

When he laughed, I couldn't help the smile that spread across my face. I was tired, and the pain was muffled by the meds, but my womb was cramping in a way that felt like being stabbed with a shard of glass.

But I didn't feel a thing when I made my brother laugh for the first time in a long time.

"You can," he agreed easily with that confidant nonchalance I'd always admired. "But you've had reason to be less than you should be."

"My therapist doesn't like me to make excuses," I muttered somewhat petulantly.

He chuckled. "Therapists typically don't."

"You've been?" I was shocked by the prospect of my infallible, affable brother needing therapy. It seemed like the kind of forced introspection only the deeply unhappy were forced to seek.

He shrugged. "Secrets, remember? There's a lot you don't know about me."

"A secret for a secret?" I suggested.

There was reluctance in the set of his stubborn mouth, but when I pointed out it was *him* who had said secrets had corroded our family dynamic, he agreed.

"You obviously know about Savannah Meyers, er, Richardson,"

he corrected, referring to the older woman he'd dated briefly a few years ago. I'd teased him often about liking older women, perhaps callously, so I only held his hand and listened with an open face now. "I met her when I was driving for a Town Car service in London when I first moved over there. She was glamorous and elegant, like nothing I'd ever seen before. I fell in love with her before I even touched her."

It was hard to listen to the throb of heartache in his voice. Sebastian was usually so full of sunshine and charm, laughter and easy affection, that seeing him haunted felt heretical.

He sucked a deep breath in through his teeth, sat up a little straighter, and pinned me with a somber stare. "It was through Savvy that I met Adam."

I blinked.

He powered on. "When he showed up at one of my shows, I thought he was going to punch me for hitting on his wife. He didn't. Instead, he propositioned me." His free hand moved through the air like an agitated bird. "He was powerful, handsome, successful, but there was just something about him that called to me."

Called to him like a wolf song in the night. The way something about Dante, about this life of his, called to me.

I squeezed his hand in understanding.

"I lived with them for a year before it went sour," he said, his eyes lost to the past. "I tried to follow Savvy to America, but you know how that turned out."

I did. The whole world did. The beautiful power couple that

was the famous actor Adam Meyers and his pretty wife, Savannah, had suffered an acrimonious divorce. Almost immediately after, Savannah had moved to America and married the media tycoon, Tate Richardson.

"Seb, I'm so sorry," I whispered. "I only lost one person I loved, and it felt like the bottom fell out of my world. I can't imagine losing two."

He didn't deny that he'd loved them both, but he shrugged tensely, clearly uncomfortable.

"You know," I said slowly, teasing him gently. "Beau has been my best friend for five years, and in his words, he's 'as gay as they come.' I would never judge you for loving a man."

"Just an older woman, then," he asked pointedly.

I shrugged. "You dig. I dig. It's how we've been for ages. I think I have you to thank for the quick wit that makes me a good lawyer."

"You're welcome," he said magnanimously. "Cosima might suspect, but Giselle and Mama don't know about Adam. No one does."

Why did it mean so much more than the money or success I'd coveted for years to know that Sebastian had trusted me with such a secret?

"I won't tell a soul," I promised, then conjured up the word we'd used growing up when we were afraid in the dark, mafiosos at the door coming for our father. *"Insieme,* Sebastian."

Insieme meant together.

The four of us together against the world.

Against the mafia and Seamus, even against the obliviousness of our poor, stressed mother.

Somewhere along the way, we'd lost that.

"*Insieme, cara mia,*" he repeated with the massive movie star grin that I'd seen on billboards and magazine covers in the past few years. "Now, your turn."

It was easy to take a scalpel to my own wounds after hearing the extent of his. "I had surgery to try to fix my fertility issues."

"Oh, Lena," he murmured, sliding closer so he could wrap an arm gently around my shoulders for a sideways hug. "That's good news, right?"

"It should be. I only have one ovary left after an ectopic pregnancy, and we were worried they'd have to take out the other because of a few large cysts, but Monica said they were able to save it. Monica, she's an old friend and one of the best women's doctors in the city, seems to think I might be able to conceive naturally or with some help with IVF when I'm ready."

"You'll be a wonderful mama," he replied instantly. "You were a great one for us, and you were only a kid."

I submerged myself in his praise like sinking into a hot bath, my flesh, blood, and bones warmed through by his words.

"Thank you," I said empathetically. "Sometimes, lately, I've wondered." I hesitated. "Have you met her?"

He knew without clarifying who I meant.

"Yes, she's beautiful," he told me, gentle but firm. "They already call her Genny. She has red hair like Gigi, just a little lighter than yours, but Sinclair's blue eyes. She can't do much of anything yet, you know, except fart and smile, eat and sleep, but she's a cute little thing."

I knew she would be cute and lovely like Giselle had been as a baby. I'd expected the words to tear through me like a windstorm, eviscerating the ramshackle walls I'd built around that pain. Instead, I felt only a profound sense of loss.

"I don't know how I'll feel when I meet her," I admitted. "It's hard to imagine hating a baby."

"You don't have to," he suggested mildly. "But I think we all understand how hard it is for you, Lena. *Per la misera*, the man you thought was the love of your life left you for your sister. It's like something out of one of Mama's soaps."

It was hard not to laugh around Seb, even talking about something so painful. "Do you understand, though? I felt like when it happened, you and Cosima were team Giselle."

Sebastian huffed. "There were no teams. You are both our sisters, and we love you. It was just…It was easier for us to see that you and Daniel weren't as well suited in reality as you seemed on paper." He hesitated before admitting in a soft voice that struck me like a hammer to the soul. "Gigi has always been so…dreamy and fragile. She has an artist's soul and all of us, you included, safeguarded her from the bad things as much as we could. I think it became a habit. It was harder to be angry with her for hurting you, especially when she was doing it because she was in love, than it was to be angry with you for being cruel to her about it.

It wasn't fair, Lena, and I'm sorry it's been one in a long line of circumstances that have made you feel unloved."

It was probably surprising how much comfort I took from his words. Not because I felt they were just, but because they validated what I'd always wondered.

"I was cruel," I could admit as I wrapped my arms around myself. "But can you imagine what it felt like to have not one but two men prefer your younger sister to you?"

"No, though Christopher was more monster than man."

A sharp laugh tore itself out of my throat and fell bloody between us. "You don't know the half of it."

"You could tell me," he suggested, his body coiled tight on the bed beside me, as if Christopher was in the room and he was about to duel him for my honor. "It eats at me all the time that I didn't know what he was doing to my sisters. I'm the brother, *il padre di famiglia*. I should have protected you."

"Seb," I soothed, reaching out to pat his handsome cheek, remembering how round it had been as a boy when I gave him the nickname *little potato*. "I was the eldest. Just because I'm a woman doesn't mean it wasn't my responsibility to protect *you* even from information that could hurt you. There's no point in rehashing it all now, though. It's in the past. He's in prison for assaulting Giselle, and he should remain there for a very long time."

"So, you never think of him?" he pressed skeptically.

Only every few days now, I thought but didn't say.

Still, Seb read my silence and grunted unhappily. "I hope one day you share it with someone you love, even if it's not me."

"I think this has been enough for one night," I joked weakly, wincing at a pang in my belly.

A loud bang at the door startled both of us a moment before it swung open to reveal Frankie and Adriano holding a large black frame in their hands.

"*Buona sera*," Frankie called out as he maneuvered through the door with what I realized was a massive television set.

"What in the world are you doing?" I asked, straightening instinctively, then gasping when it pulled at my surgical sites.

"Take it easy," Adriano ordered gruffly without looking at me as they lugged the set to the wall opposite my bed.

A moment later, Chen appeared in the doorway, barely offering me a cursory glance as he carried in a wall mount and a drill.

"What the hell are you guys doing?" I demanded again, irritated that they were piling into my room when I was bonding for the first time in years with my brother.

Annoyed that I wasn't looking my best *at all.* The minimal makeup I'd been able to wear into surgery had smudged off after hours of sleep this afternoon, and my hair was a wild mess of curls and flattened waves around my face.

I didn't even like my brother to see me like that, let alone men I hardly knew. Men I could barely admit I wanted to like me.

"You can talk while we do it," Marco offered as he sauntered into the room with his hands in the pockets of his black joggers. "Won't take a minute."

"I don't need a TV in here," I insisted as he took a seat on the end of my bed.

I thanked God I was tidy by nature, and no spare unmentionables were lying around.

"Sure, you do," he insisted. "You're sick. Binge-watching TV is the only good thing about being stuck in bed. You like HBO? My wife's addicted to that *True Blood.* You like vamps, too? Lady catnip, I'm telling ya."

"Marco," I said, snapping my fingers to get his attention. He had the bad habit of rambling on and on away from the original conversation. "I really don't need a television set, and I'm not sick."

He eyed me suspiciously. "Don't seem like the kinda lady to lie in bed all day, and that's what you've been doing. Besides, I don't follow your orders. I follow the boss's, and he said, I'm quoting him, 'Marco, get Elena a TV and set it up in her room within the hour.'" He winced. "'Course, it took me a little longer than that, but he don't have to know that."

"He already does," Dante himself drawled from the doorway where we both turned to see him leaning against the jamb with his arms crossed like he'd been there a while.

Marco shot me an "oh shit" look, then smiled crookedly at Dante before ordering Adriano, Frankie, and Chen to pick up the pace.

"I don't need a TV," I reiterated to the "boss."

It was difficult to look over at the long, broad glory of him in that tight black tee and gray sweatpants, more casual than I'd ever seen him outside of the gym, and not feel the ghost of his lips on my neck or those huge hands on my body. Not imagine the sheer power of the naked body beneath his clothes and the size of the dick that was a noticeable swell down the side of one thigh.

I shivered delicately but tried to hide it.

He stared at me steadily, unfazed by my messy appearance and my lack of gratefulness. "Beau said you liked watching it. He mentioned something about a show called *Vampire Diaries.*"

The only sign of his amusement was a twitch at the left side of his full mouth.

Marco hooted, slapping his thigh. "Didn't I just say? All women like vamps. It's a thing."

"You're a lady whisperer, Co," Frankie remarked dryly over the sound of Chen drilling the mount into the wall above the dresser.

"Damn right," Marco agreed with a cheeky grin.

I couldn't help but grin back.

"They're sexy," I admitted with a little shrug.

"It's the blood, isn't it?"

This time, I had to gasp as laughter rippled through my belly. "No, Marco, it's not the blood. It's the…I don't know. The passion, the possession, the animalistic tendencies."

"Noted," Dante drawled again from his place in the doorway.

The look on his face was pure hunger, the dark in his eyes expansive enough to drown in.

I swallowed thickly, then reconsidered what he'd said before. "When did you talk to Beau?"

Dante straightened from his lean and strolled in the room on the rolling gait that made my mouth dry, stopping only when he was at the side of my bed.

"Move over," he demanded before reaching into his pocket and tossing my cell into my lap. "You should really change the passcode on that. Your mother's birthday isn't exactly original."

"Hey," I protested, hugging my phone to my chest. "Rule number two, *no snooping.*"

"When you keep things from me, I have no choice," he said in that agreeable tone that made me see red.

"You are the most frustrating man on the planet," I muttered.

Dante sat on the edge of the bed even though I hadn't moved over and gently reached over to reposition the pillow at my back and neck so I was close to the middle of the bed and cozier than I had been before.

If I closed my eyes to breathe in his lemon and pepper scent while he leaned over my torso, he didn't notice.

"You are the most infuriating woman," he countered, but his eyes glittered like the New York City nightscape outside my windows.

"What a pair," Sebastian interjected in a long drawl.

I shot him a glare, but he only widened his eyes in faux innocence and readjusted against the pillows on my other side. "The last time I saw you two together, you were practically choking Dante out for information on Cosi."

Seb shrugged. "We're men. We shared a glass of wine and

311

talked about women one night this summer when we were both visiting Cosi in England."

"Old friends," Dante agreed.

"Men," I muttered under my breath, secretly wishing things between women could be half as easy.

"Done," Adriano announced, stepping back from the TV with a little smile on his big face.

"Took you long enough," Marco grumbled.

"You did shit all," Chen pointed out.

Marco sniffed. "I supervised."

Frankie threw the remote control at his head in response.

"Interesting company you're keeping these days," Sebastian murmured to me.

As I looked at the motley assembly of criminals in my bedroom trying to make me comfortable after an invasive, personal surgery I thought I'd recover from alone in my brownstone, I considered the fact that Seb was right.

The nightmare that had started out as Dante and Yara forcing me to move in with him to keep him abreast of the RICO case had become something surprisingly more.

For now, these interesting men had made me one of their own.

"What're we gonna watch?" Marco demanded as he settled at the foot of the bed. Chen and Addie also took seats in the armchairs by the vanity. "As long as it ain't vamps, I'm good."

"I don't know, Co," Frankie said, winking at me before he took a seat at the foot of the bed. "You might learn something valuable."

Everyone, even Sebastian, laughed.

And that was how I ended one of the most vulnerable days of my life, surrounded by laughing men, most of whom had probably killed a man or committed any other half-dozen felonies.

And for the first time in my life, snuggled between the two big warm bodies of my brother and the mafioso I was coming to like more than I should, I didn't care.

CHAPTER TWENTY-ONE

elena

Four weeks of little touches, a hand wrapped around my neck when he wanted me to focus on him, a stroke of my hair when he passed me in the kitchen, a squeeze of my hip when I stood beside him at the island making dinner, late nights spent watching movies in my room or on the couch with our shoulders pressed tight.

A few times when I'd fallen asleep on the couch following my surgery, Dante had even picked me up, all five-foot-ten inches of me, and carried me to my bedroom. I'd pretended to be asleep, too embarrassed to do otherwise when I was so close to his heart beating through the hard wall of his chest.

Four weeks of little touches while I recovered from my procedure and nothing else.

It was death by a thousand caresses, slowly shredding my ten-foot walls to ribbons.

My skin pebbled into goose bumps just being in the same room as Dante now, just catching the gravitational pull of those dark eyes across the living room.

I had to remind myself sternly that Dante was a criminal, a killer, essentially a beast in a multi-thousand-dollar suit. He wasn't fooling anyone, least of all *me*.

I knew better.

Every experience in my life had taught me to know better.

But there was this flutter, a palpitation that I wondered if I should get checked out at the doctor whenever he found an excuse to touch me. And he did. Touch me. Often.

It wasn't personal. I was learning that Dante touched everyone. He kissed Tore freely on both cheeks, hello and goodbye. He clamped a hand on the shoulder of a *soldato*, shook hands, and rubbed shoulders with his men the way a puppy might in a pen with its siblings.

He was incredibly tactile, which struck me as odd for a man in this day and age. Society had moved to a more cerebral plane, perhaps because of the influx of technology that allowed us to interact with minimal physical effort to obtain whatever we desired. Dante seemed to go out of his way to remain archaic. He had a young boy, Tony, deliver three physical copies of the paper every morning––*The New York Times, The Guardian, and Corriere della sera*. He demanded in-person meetings whenever he could manage it, even under the close watch of FBI surveillance, when there were countless platforms he could have used to conduct his business online that would have undoubtedly been less circumspect.

It wasn't just his physical closeness that was wearing me smooth like waves against rocks.

Of course, as a woman and an educated, strong-willed one at that, I took fundamental umbrage with the mafia. How could any woman romanticize a system that viewed families as a feudal system run by men and only men, with the women used as janitors, cooks, nannies, and the occasional matrimonial bargaining chip?

This, I was learning, was not the *borgata* of Dante Salvatore. Of course, there was still a hierarchy. Dante and Tore at the top, a kind of bizarre co-captaincy you didn't often see between mafiosos who were, as a rule, power-hungry and incapable of compromise. Then Frankie Amato, the tech whiz and right-hand man, who magicked whatever the Salvatores wanted seemingly out of thin air. There were the underbosses below that, manning their own mini fiefdoms, but they were not, I'd learned, exclusively male.

Frankie's wife did work for the family.

Yara was their consigliere, a woman, and a non-Italian.

It was obvious that Dante had flouted the traditional norms that had ruled the Camorra and other Italian organizations like it for decades.

And it seemed to be working, financially at least.

No one seemed to want for anything. I'd seen the matte black Ferrari 458 Spider in the garage, secretly lusting after it; the Rolex, Patek Phillipe, and Piaget watches on the wrists of Dante and his men; the sheer size and expensive furnishings of the apartment I lived in temporarily. Dante and his crew of merry criminals owned hotel chains and construction companies, an incredibly lucrative and innovative energy company, and restaurants and bars across the company. The sheer scale of their legitimate or at least legitimate-facing businesses was staggering. In combination with their illegal dealings, the loan sharking, gambling, and fraud I never caught wind of, I could only guess at the billions of dollars coming in.

It also seemed evident that this new-fangled way of doing things did not go over well with important members in other organized crime families. I eavesdropped without shame, the lawyer in me unable to resist, and Dante didn't try as hard as he could have to shield me from things.

I knew the di Carlo family was after him. The same family that had wrapped Cosima up in a drive-by shooting and put her in a coma.

When Gideone di Carlo called me, not once but twice, I didn't answer, and eventually, I blocked his number.

In short, I knew too much.

Too much about the men behind the criminal masks, Chen's quick mind, Marco's humor, Frankie's charm, Adriano's quiet kindness, and even Jacopo's bursts of good-natured ribbing. It was so much more difficult to hate them for their crimes when I knew more about their personalities than their illegal activities.

I had always found, if you could understand something, it was almost impossible to hate it because then you could empathize with it.

The same, of course, could be said for their boss.

Slowly and irrevocably spending time around Dante's heat had thawed my icy demeanor toward him. I found myself bantering with him instead of trying to cut him to pieces with the sharp edge of my tongue. After going back to work from my surgery, I spent my late working hours at the living room desk or coffee table instead of the office because I liked the company.

His company.

One month of our forced proximity, and I was dangerously close to capitulating to his game of corruption.

Giving in to the lust I felt swelling tsunami strong in my gut. A sensation I had never in my twenty-seven years felt before meeting Dante.

The thaw he'd instigated with that simple neck kiss and extraordinary show of masturbation had never made me more aware of my body and its yearnings. I felt almost sensually *alive*, aware of the taste of food on my tongue, the very air on my skin, the cashmere I pulled on my body to ward against the deepening winter chill. I found myself craving things I'd eschewed for so long, chocolate and whiskey, dance and song, but most of all, *sex*.

I wanted him so badly even my teeth ached with it.

The last few mornings, I'd even woken up with wet between my thighs from dreaming of the ways a man like Dante might touch me there.

I squeezed my thighs together beneath the table on the patio that morning as Dante and I sat drinking coffee, both of us reading our respective newspapers before I headed into work. It was an oddly domestic scene, but I didn't allow myself to linger too long on that.

"You seem...agitated this morning, Elena," Dante noted in that smooth, accented drawl he used when he was teasing me.

I glared at him, irritated with us both for the interminable dance we were locked together in. "I slept badly."

"Bad dreams?" he asked with a quirk of a black brow.

I pursed my lips and arched one of mine. "About a bad man."

"Oh." He folded his paper in his lap and leaned forward with a wolfish grin. "Do share with the class."

I snorted. "Not likely."

"*Va bene.* Then I will tell you about mine," he offered, leaning back to cross those thick arms over his chest.

I pulled my stare from the bulging muscle only to land on that square jaw still ink-stained with stubble from the day before. Unbidden, I imagined what it might feel like under my tongue.

"That's unnecessary." My starched delivery was ruined by my breathiness.

Those eyes, twin galaxies, glittered. "I think it's very necessary."

He reached into the fruit bowl set between us and selected a red pomegranate. I watched avidly as he gripped it between his two mighty hands and easily cracked it in half with his thumbs. He smoothed a finger down the inside of the fruit almost sensuously, then brought a kernel of the bright fruit to his mouth. It summoned the memory of him trailing those fingers through his own cum and painting the liquid on my lips.

He hummed as he swallowed it.

I reached for my water glass and drank heavily.

"I dreamed that I was with a beautiful woman," he began, still holding the fruit and feeding himself intermittently. There was red juice on his lips I wanted badly to lick off. "She was naked but nervous. I gentled her, stroking down all that creamy skin with just the tips of my fingers, the edge of my rough knuckles until I made her tremble."

I blinked, so absorbed in the rolling cadence of his voice that I completely forgot myself.

"She didn't want to get on her knees for me when I asked..." He pulled a few seeds of pomegranate onto his fingers and then inclined forward slowly to raise them in offering to me as he said, "So, I got on my knees for *her*. And when I put my mouth on her pussy, do you know what she tasted like, Elena?"

I didn't answer because I was too busy telling myself not to take those thick fingers into my mouth with the proffered fruit.

He read my hesitation, and his eyes went from liquid ink to intractable obsidian. A moment later, he pressed the fruit to my closed mouth, painting my lips with the tart juice. When I opened my mouth, to protest surely, he slipped the seeds onto my tongue.

"Like pomegranates and red wine," he finished, returning to a comfortable lounge in his own chair where he proceeded to suck the tips of his fingers clean.

"Are you flirting with me?" I asked, proud that my voice didn't

321

shake the way my thighs did beneath the table.

"Will you hit me if I say yes?"

His playfulness was infectious. I tamped down my urge to smile and nodded somberly. "Yes."

"Good," he said with a wink, "then hit me. I like it rough."

"You're ridiculous," I said, giving in to my laughter but sobering slightly when I caught the look he was giving me. "What? Do I still have pomegranate juice on my mouth?"

"I've never been so proud to make another person laugh," he told me seriously.

I swallowed the mass of emotion that rose in my throat. "Don't say I should do it more often."

"No, the rarity of it makes it more beautiful. I'm becoming rather possessive of the sound."

I blinked at him as more of me unraveled, rolling across the space between us as if I wanted him to take the unspooled length of me and reassemble it in his hands.

It was hard not to wonder what the Elena Dante saw could be like if I let her out of the shadows.

I cleared my throat, dabbing my lips with my napkin as I stood up to leave. "I have an appointment on Staten Island at nine."

He stood too, dropping the pomegranate to his plate and wiping his hands before he came around the stone table to corner me against the door. One hand went to my hip and the other braced on the door beside my head as he crowded me. The sheer size of him shouldn't have excited me as it did, but all the things

I had once found horribly savage now seemed to light me up like kerosene-soaked tinder.

"One day, Elena," he practically purred, the sound a rough vibration that hummed through me. "I am going to kiss you until you melt, and then I am going to lick up every inch of you."

A shiver rattled my shoulders against the glass door. I was reaching some kind of boiling point, my blood gone to magma beneath my skin, and I was desperate for something to finally rip the cap off my control and send me bursting free. I wanted him to kiss me *now* against all of my better judgment, but I wasn't ready to ask for it. He had to be the one to take it so I could blame him later when my cooler head reigned.

I canted my chin into the air and challenged, "Don't hold your breath."

The hand on my hip moved up my side, his thumb dragging over the underside of my breast beneath my lace blouse as it traveled up to my throat. I swallowed hard against his palm as he cupped my neck and squeezed just firmly enough to feel my pulse kick against his skin.

"No, *lottatrice*," he murmured as he angled his nose over the shell of my right ear. "I'll hold yours when I finally fuck you. Eat it off your tongue when I kiss you as you beg me for more."

There was a cool breeze moving over the balcony, but Dante was an inferno against me, my resistance evaporating with every second I remained caged within his heat.

"You're everything fire, and I'm solid ice," I protested because

323

nothing about us made sense, and he needed to remember that.

If I couldn't make things work with Daniel, a man seemingly perfect for me, nothing could ever amount to anything between Dante and I.

"*Si,*" he agreed gruffly. "That's why I know I'm the one who will finally make you melt."

"I'm already risking my career by just staying here." I was throwing grenades blindly, hoping one of them hit the target.

He was wholly unperturbed, his eyes so focused on mine I could almost read what he was going to say in the black screens before he spoke. "So, make the risk worth something."

"I'm not a gambler."

"No, but I am, and I rarely lose." He ran the tip of his nose down the side of my ear and feathered his lips against the sharp edge of my cheekbone. "Let me show you passion, Elena. Let me teach you how to love again."

My heart stopped in my chest as if he'd reached through the cage of my ribs and gripped it tightly in one of those powerful hands. For one breath, I was paralyzed entirely by the fear of what he was hinting at.

Love.

There was no way I could love a man like him, a mafioso, a criminal like the kind who had played the villain in my life for so long.

It was impossible.

But when my heart started to beat again, it did so with a bone-rattling bang like an engine backfiring, and then it set to racing.

I'd promised myself I would never love again.

"The contents of my heart are confidential," I told him archly as if to suggest that he might ever read about the private agonies of my heart was ludicrous.

In a way, it was, but not in the way I made it sound.

It was ludicrous because, for one moment, I thought if anyone could understand what was written there, it would be this man with the black eyes and shockingly kind heart.

"Not all love is romantic," he pointed out rationally, staring into my fearful eyes. "I don't think you've had enough of it to know that, but I'm offering the love of a friend and the love of my body. The love of a man who can see you are not hateful. You are not villainous. You are misunderstood. And Elena, you don't realize this yet, but I see you, I know you, and I'm fucking undone by the beauty of you."

"You don't know what you're saying," I insisted. "You don't know half of the bad things I've done."

"And you don't know mine," he agreed. "But we are more than our flaws and our mistakes. Who told you that you were hard to love? Give me a chance to prove them wrong."

"I don't want to be loved," I asserted, almost baring my teeth at him because I'd never felt so threatened in my entire life. Not when I'd hidden under the sink and watched mafiosos beat my father. Not when Christopher forced me to do unholy things with my body. Not when he showed up at Giselle's art show and assaulted her, and I'd stepped in to fight him myself.

None of the boogeymen in my life held a candle to the power Dante seemed to yield over me compared to the length of time I'd known him.

One month of constant contact and I was in danger of throwing away everything I knew just for one single kiss.

"Let me love you anyway," he suggested.

And then he was moving.

They say there is a thin line between love and hate. The moment Dante Salvatore twisted his hand in my hair and yanked me in for a savage kiss, I knew he had just pushed me over that invisible line into something infinitely more dangerous than hate.

But all I could do as thoughts swirled into one furious tornado of sensation in my head was curl my hands into his silky cotton shirt and hang on for dear life.

The kiss tasted like the smoke, but not because of my anger. It tasted like the ashes of my once solid self-control. Because I knew this wouldn't be the last time we kissed.

It was like nothing I'd ever experienced before.

The way his mouth sealed over mine like a stamp of possession, his tongue parting my lips as if it was his right to claim this kiss and he'd already been patient for too long. The scent of him, bright as a citrus grove with an undertow of masculine musk was in my nose, the sound of his low, throaty growl vibrating from his tongue across mine. When he brought the long, impossibly hard length of his body flush against me, I couldn't breathe from the feel of the hot erection pressed to my belly.

At that moment, every single atom in my body was owned by him.

One kiss.

For one kiss, I risked it all.

My career, my family, my freedom.

And my life.

But, *Dio mio*, I'd do it again and again if it meant feeling like this.

So alive I burned.

Only the sharp vibration of Dante's phone on the patio table cut through the smoke and reminded me of myself.

Of my rules.

I tore my lips from his, my chest heaving with the effort, and pressed myself tight to the door as if doing so made me less conspicuous to that dark and hungry gaze.

"This is on pause," he growled, his thumb stroking possessively over my thudding pulse point as if each beat spoke his name. "Now that I've had that red mouth, I'll need it again."

I just blinked at him as I tried to regulate my body, harness its wild impulses with the cool rationality of my mind. It took longer than it should have, than it ever had before, but finally, I found my voice.

"My meeting," I reminded him weakly, shoving him back with two hands to his chest, trying not to luxuriate in the feel of his steel muscles beneath the soft fabric I'd left irreparably wrinkled. "I'll be late."

He let me push him away, putting his hands in his pockets as he followed me into the living room instead of answering his cell phone. I watched as he crossed to the desk while I collected my coat and purse, narrowing my eyes as he suddenly sent something flying across the room at me.

Instinctively, my hand reared up to catch the object. When I brought it down and uncurled my fingers, a bright red key fob with a silver horse rearing on it in silhouette stared back at me.

I gaped at him. "What is this?"

"Any Italian girl worth her salt knows what that is."

"Yes," I agreed. "But why did you just give me the key to your Ferrari?"

His grin was spectacularly wicked, and I realized with some degree of awe and concern that Dante didn't have to have me pressed up against the wall to continue his seduction of me. "Addie told me you've been eyeing her. Why don't you take her for that drive to Staten Island?"

My fingers curled around the key. Even though I didn't want it to mean something that he trusted me to drive his million-dollar car, my heart panged like a plucked instrument in my chest.

"Thank you," I muttered, my focus on putting my coat on so I wouldn't have to bear the brunt of his megawatt grin.

"That sounds almost as good as please," he told me in that smoky voice that made me high. "Not quite as good as your laughter, though."

"Stop it, Dante," I said firmly, shooting him my best schoolmarm glare. "Forget this happened. It was a momentary lapse in judgment."

He nodded somberly, his lean hips against the desk, one hand playing with the chain of the ornate silver cross he'd taken out of his shirt. He looked like an invitation to sin on an altar, the worst decision a woman would ever make, but the wicked gleam in his eyes promised he would make it worth her while.

"I'll try my best to make sure your judgment lapses again," he called as I turned on my heel and started for the elevator. "*Frequently.*"

I shook my head but didn't turn around.

Only when I was safely ensconced in the elevator on the way to the garage and that gorgeous car did I hit my head back against the ornate gold scrolled metal wall and curse myself for the smile that broke free across my face.

When I touched my lips to force the expression off my face, I traced the feel of his kiss echoed there in my flesh and closed my eyes on a groan.

I was already on the legal team of and living with the most infamous mafioso of the twenty-first century. It was debatable, but I'd already started down the slippery slope of moral degeneration.

Maybe Dante was right about making the risk *worth* something.

Something more than my career and its success.

Something worth the cost of my soul.

If I was going to damn myself anyway, I might as well do it by sleeping with the Devil of New York City.

CHAPTER TWENTY-TWO

elena

"Nice ride."

I tossed my head to clear my face of my windswept hair and smiled at Ricardo Stavos as I closed the butterfly door and locked the car.

"It's a…friend's," I explained with a lopsided shrug.

He grinned roguishly. "Sure, Elena, whatever you say."

I shot him a look as I adjusted the Prada bag stuffed with papers and my iPad on my left arm. But still, I accepted his kiss on the cheek. Normally, I couldn't abide such a lack of professionalism, but Ric was impossible to resist, and the kiss was part of his Ecuadorian culture as much as it was part of my Italian youth. In his early forties with dark brown hair he wore shorn close to his scalp, a deep tan all year round, and eyes that crinkled charmingly whenever he smiled, which was often.

He was the lead investigator at Fields, Harding & Griffith, and he mostly refused to work with associates. But he'd caught me smoking a rare cigarette outside of the Pearl Street courthouse one day, and we'd bonded over growing up in cultures where smoking was as normal as drinking soda was in America.

I was glad he was with me for this. It always made me nervous going to interview witnesses. One wrong step and it would be easy for a lawyer to end up having to testify against a witness in court, which would effectively end their participation in the trial.

But it was paramount we convince Ottavio Petretti to testify.

To our knowledge, he was the only living person other than the disappeared Mason Matlock to have been in or near his self-named deli the day Giuseppe di Carlo was murdered. Up until now, he'd flatly refused to talk to a single soul, but I was hoping a good old-fashioned dose of guilt and a little elbow grease would sway him.

"Let me have the first crack at him?" I asked Ric because even though I was the lawyer and higher up the food chain at the firm, he was vastly more experienced and incredibly valuable. I almost always deferred to him when we worked together. I had no problem taking the back seat if it meant I could learn how to be like those I admired one day.

He cocked a brow but nodded before gesturing me to proceed him up the sidewalk to Ottavio's small bungalow home. "He's going to be a hard nut to crack."

I patted my purse and grinned at him. "The meatiest ones always are. Don't worry, I have my bag of tricks."

It felt good to walk up the cracked concrete stairs in my six-inch power heels and tailored gray houndstooth St. Aubyn suit. After the morning I'd had, defenseless against the inexorable pull of eyes darker than the night sky, I needed to be reminded of my own authority and independence.

Ric knocked on the door with a heavy fist, but I made sure to stand slightly in front of him so I was the first thing Ottavio might see through his foggy peephole.

A moment later, the door creaked open, and a true Roman nose poked out. "Don't speak to cops or men in suits."

"Good thing I'm a woman then, *Signore Petretti*," I practically cooed.

When he tried to close the door, I wedged the toe of my pointed Jimmy Choo into the space between it and the jamb, effectively stopping his retreat. Ric followed my cue and slapped a hand on the door to push it intractably open.

Ottavio huffed as he was forced to back up. "You aren't welcome in my house."

"Are you going to call the police?" I suggested sweetly as we moved into the cramped, dark hallway. "I'm sure your neighbors would love it if you brought the cops around."

His fleshy, pink-hued face contracted like an octopus as I called his bluff. No one in this neighborhood called the cops. There were mafiosos and their associates thick in the streets here, and if he was caught at home with two lawyers and the cops, he was as good as dead.

Screwed if he talked to us, screwed if he didn't.

I was well-versed in such situations, so I knew how to handle them.

"Why don't we sit down, Signore Petretti?" I offered graciously, indicating the sitting room with the plastic-wrapped floral couch I could see to our left.

He grumbled Italian curses under his breath as he reluctantly turned and trundled down the hall into the living room. When he took a seat in the only chair, Ric and I moved to the couch and sat down with an awful creak and groan of thick plastic.

"If you are here to talk about the murders at my deli, I'm not speaking of this," he grunted, the "th" in his words transformed by his thick Italian accent into a "d" sound.

I shrugged easily. "I actually came to talk about something else. Or, should I say, someone else." He watched me with beady brown eyes as I reached into my purse and produced an eight-by-ten glossy photo of my sister Cosima. It was a candid shot I'd taken when I visited her in England last spring, and she looked especially radiant in it. The reason for that was behind the camera, just to my right, her eyes were trained on the sight of her husband laughing with Mama. The sheer love and joy shining from her golden eyes and wide, full-lipped smile was palpable even through the photo.

Ottavio leaned forward, bracing his hairy forearms on his thighs to get a better look. I watched the magic of my sister transform his grumpy features into something softer, his eyes warming as they studied the photograph.

"Cosima," he almost whispered. A finger uncurled from his fist

334

to gently touch the print. "*È una ragazza bellissima.*"

"Yes, she is very beautiful," I agreed, smiling at him when he caught my eye to show him that I meant no harm. "Of course, I'm biased because she is my sister."

His wiry eyebrows shot up on his forehead, and if he'd still had a full head of hair, they would have disappeared into it. "You?"

I laughed lightly, not offended at all. "We don't look much alike."

He scratched his chin as he studied me, his demeanor still relaxed, Cosima's magic still working to make him forget the real reason we were there. "A little in the eyes."

"*Grazie,*" I said earnestly because it felt good, always, to be compared to her. "She is beautiful inside and out."

"*Si,*" he agreed with a vigorous nod. "She came to my shop very often, your sister, and she always ate an entire plate of my wife's tiramisu. I do not know where she put it. So skinny!"

I laughed again. "She can eat like a horse."

He nodded, his eyes closed with solemnity. "Yes, this is very good. She was a good girl, Cosima. Always told people to come to *Ottavio's*. Just seeing her in the window was good for business, drew in all the neighborhood men."

"Mmm," I hummed in agreement before I frowned and made a show of rifling through my bag before producing yet another photo that I stared at for a moment. When I finally turned it to face Ottavio and placed it on the table before him, he reeled back in his chair, his mouth open and pursed raggedly like a bullet hole blown through his skull. "You seem to have admired her. I'm surprised you let men do this to her in your own shop."

This photo depicted my sister on the yellow-tinged linoleum of his deli, her hair a curling mess like spilled ink around her head, ribbons of brilliant red blood pooling around her prone body from the three bullet holes torn through her torso and the one that had grazed her skull, splitting flesh open to the bone over one ear. There was so much blood that she seemed to be floating in it, her face almost peaceful in her comatose state.

It was a jarring, ghastly contrast to the previous photo of her smiling and whole that lay beside it.

Ottavio looked at me with his mouth still open in horror.

I nodded as if he'd spoken because I'd felt much the same way when I'd first seen the photos. "Three bullets to the torso, one to the head. Did you know she was in a coma for weeks?"

He shook his head almost imperceptibly.

"Do you know why they did this to her?" I asked, my tone hardening with every word I spoke, weaponizing them to kick the man while his defenses were down.

Another tiny shake. Sweat beaded on his thick upper lip and dripped down the side of his mouth. He licked it up unconsciously.

"Did you know they *would* do this to her?" I asked, subtly changing my question.

We weren't on trial in court before a judge. I could lead the damn witness as much as I wanted to.

And I was going to lead the horse straight to the hay.

"They don't tell men like me anything," he muttered, his eyes back on the photo of Cosima.

"You have a daughter nearly Cosima's age. Rosario, isn't it?" I knew because Ric had done the homework for me. "Does she know her father let this happen to someone else's daughter?"

"I did not want this to happen," he finally barked, breaking out of his stunned stupor. "No one wants these things to happen, *capisci*? Who am I, simple Otto, to stand between those men and what they want, huh?"

"What did they give you for your silence? A grand, two?" Ric interjected, his words like gunshots.

One by one, they found their way into Ottavio's round chest. He jerked at the impact and placed his hands over his heart as if to protect it.

"You are *estraneo*, an outsider. You know nothing," he practically spat at Ric.

"But I do," I told him, shifting into Italian, leaning forward to tap the horrible photo of Cosima. "I know the horrors of the Camorra because I lived them while I was a girl in Naples."

"Ah, *si*, then you know," he said, almost eagerly, yearning to alleviate his guilt. "You know to talk is to die."

Continuing in Italian because I didn't exactly want Ricardo to know how far I was taking things, I said, "I know that good people die every day because they don't stand up for the things they know are wrong. An innocent man is being accused of murdering Giuseppe di Carlo and his thug because no one will say a word. Is that just?"

"It's not my problem," he beseeched me, opening his hands to the sky on a shrug, more expressive with his gestures than he was with his words.

"I think it is," I argued. "I know you are afraid of the di Carlos, but they are fractured from Giuseppe's death. Do you know who is being accused of killing him?"

"I stay out of this," he reminded me angrily.

"Dante Salvatore," I said, unfazed by his returned belligerence. "Have you heard of him, Ottavio? They call him the mafia lord, the Devil of New York City."

"Don Salvatore," he whispered, moving to clutch the small gold-plated cross he wore at his throat. "Yes, I know him."

"He is a very scary man," I agreed with his unspoken fear. "Have you seen his hands?" I held my own up and fisted it. "Each one is the size of a man's head."

Ottavio scowled at me, reading exactly what I was trying to do.

Illustrate just how much he was screwed if he did and screwed if he didn't.

I smiled kindly at him, leaning forward on that creaking plastic to pat his hand comfortingly. "The way I see it, Signore Petretti, you could side with a fractured family, one that has much better things to focus on right now, or you could hitch your cart to the Salvatores. Earn their protection and admiration."

"They'll kill me," he insisted, eyes darting to Ric for support even though the investigator couldn't understand Italian.

"Maybe," I agreed with a nonchalant shrug. "I suppose it's a gamble. With whom are your odds of survival better?"

We stared at each other for a long moment, unblinking. A woman trundled down the hall to the mouth of the living room, her hair big and bouffant, her body thick and soft with curves.

"Who is this?" she asked her husband in Italian.

He waved his hand at her wearily, dismissively.

"Signore Petretti," I said, moving in for the kill as I smiled at his wife. "How would you feel about a trip to your ancestral home? Where is your family from?"

"*Pomigliano d'Arco*," he muttered.

"Well, when this is all said and done, I think you and the missus deserve a vacation. On us," I offered.

Us.

Fields, Harding & Griffith.

Yara Ghorbani.

Don Dante Salvatore.

Me.

I'd used slightly unscrupulous tactics before. To be a lawyer was to know how to twist words and actions into the results you needed for victory.

But I'd never railroaded a man so succinctly, leaned on him the way a mafioso might with threats of violence.

It should have made me sick.

Once, before all this, before I made that promise to my sister to protect the brother of her heart, it might have given me indigestion or a sleepless night.

But I only felt bone-deep satisfaction and a hint of acute relief as I pulled the papers out of my bag for Ottavio to sign in order for him to act as a witness for us in court and handed them over to him. With only a brief glance at his wife, than another longer one at the photos of Cosima, he accepted the Mont Blanc pen I handed him next and signed on the dotted line.

When I accepted the papers back, I did it with a grin like a wolf, a distant howl ringing through my blood.

CHAPTER TWENTY-THREE

elena

"That was something else, Elena," Ric said as we reached the Ferrari. "I've seen you in fighter mode before, but that shit was full-on gladiator."

I laughed, a pleased flush in the cheeks that were pinned back by the force of my smile. "It felt good."

"I love a ruthless woman. When you told him the size of Dante Salvatore's hands…" Ric held his side as he laughed from his belly and then wiped a tear from his eye. *"Bravissima, Elena."*

I blinked at Ric, then fisted my hands on my hips. "I've known you, what, four years? And you've never once let on you speak Italian."

He winked at me. "And women are the only ones who can keep secrets? A man of mystery is a thing of beauty, no?"

I laughed at him, always put at ease by his self-confidence as if some of it rubbed off on me. "You have many talents."

He shrugged with faux humility. "As do you. Yara will be pleased. Partnership, here you come."

I hesitated for just a split second, my smile faltering.

Because honestly, I hadn't been thinking of partnership in there.

There had only been one thing on my mind, and it was six foot five with thick black hair and the propensity to look at me as if I was the Mona Lisa, to be wondered at and admired.

Ric frowned at me, but I waved him off. "You'll make sure he gets somewhere safe?"

There was no way in hell we would leave Ottavio to be picked off by the di Carlos or the prosecution. His testimony could mean the difference in winning or losing. Ric would transfer him to a safe house guarded by hired security until the trial. We still didn't have a date, but the wheels were in motion, and we suspected a start time in the next few months.

The Salvatores' bribes and Fields, Harding & Griffith influence made an expedited trial a reality even though it was usually unheard of for such notorious cases to go to court in under one year.

"I will," Ric agreed, slotting his hands in the pockets of his jeans, and he rocked back on his heels. "I almost hate to mention it, but have you considered the possibility that Cosima might have been the one to kill Giuseppe."

Every atom of my body stilled.

Of course, I had considered it. It was still one of my top theories.

I liked Ric, but I wasn't sure I trusted him enough to divulge

342

something that could put my sister at risk of arrest.

So, I slanted him my best cool look of incredulity.

He shrugged good-naturedly. "Just a thought. The autopsy and witnesses say di Carlo was killed before the drive-by shooting. It's a fair assumption that someone in that deli could have murdered him. Going by the supposition that his own thug didn't shoot him before dying himself, that leaves two people we know for sure were in *Ottavio's*. Cosima and Mason Matlock, who is missing."

Presumed dead, he didn't have to say.

It was safe to assume someone, maybe even the Salvatores or Mason's own di Carlo family, had gotten to him before the cops could find him.

Of course, Ric had arrived at the same theory I had.

"My sister is a model, Ric," I said in my best condescending voice, acting as if Cosima was nothing more than a bimbo when she was anything but. "I don't think she would even know how to fire a gun if she wanted to."

He nodded affably, but his brown eyes were keen on me from under his lashes. "Of course. It was only a theory."

I nodded curtly at him, then threw up a bright smile, hoping to blind him from the truth. "It was good to do this with you."

"Always," he agreed, kissing my cheek again and grasping my elbow with a little squeeze. "You seem...easier today."

Instantly, my brow notched, and I was even more on guard than before. "Excuse me?"

He held up his hands in surrender on a laugh. "Jesus, don't go all icy on me again. I meant it as a compliment, Elena. You seem easier in yourself today. There was no hesitation in doing what needed to be done in there for our client. Before, you might have struggled with it. And..."

"And?" I almost snapped at him, panic flooding my system like water spilled over a hard drive.

I was glitching hard at the idea I might be giving something away that could link me to Dante beyond a professional capacity.

"And," he drawled. "if I didn't know better, I'd think you had gotten laid."

My chest tightened until I couldn't breathe, but I forced myself to laugh lightly and brush his words away with a casual wave of my hand. "Trust me, Ric, I'm over all that."

"Sex or love?"

I leveled him with a cool look and opened the door of the Ferrari, signaling my closure of the subject. "Men," I countered before I ducked into the low car. "Goodbye, Ric."

It was only after I started the car, the smooth rumble of the engine vibrating through me, that I took a deep, shaky breath.

I hadn't lied.

I was done with men.

Unfortunately, Dante Salvatore was so much more than a man.

He was a beast and, the truth was, he was the only one to ever make me feel like a beauty.

A sigh leaked out of my mouth like air from a puncture wound as I instructed the car's system to dial his name and pulled out from the curb to drive back to Manhattan.

"*Ciao lottatrice mia,*" Dante's deep rumble, so similar to the smooth purr of the car around me, settled some of the panic lingering like lactic acid in my tissues. Somewhere along the line, I'd stopped being annoyed when he spoke to me in my mother tongue. "How are you enjoying my beauty?"

I rubbed my hands over the buttery leather steering wheel with glee. "She's exquisite."

"Say it in Italian for me," he coaxed.

Humor and giddiness bubbled up my throat at his flirtation. It had been so long since I enjoyed such simple banter with anyone. "*Lei è squisita.*"

"*Molto bene,* Elena," he praised darkly. "Next time I kiss that gorgeous red mouth, I'm going to make you so crazy that all you know is Italian."

I tried to snort derisively, but the idea was oddly appealing. Usually, Italian was the language of my panic, my fear, its roots deeply seated in past trauma. The idea of Dante coaxing it out from the shadows into the light with something as powerful as his touch was both arousing and heartening.

"I didn't call to flirt with you," I told him archly, remembering myself. "We just interviewed Ottavio Petretti. He agreed to turn witness for our defense."

There was a long pause.

"I was under the impression he would not be turned," he said carefully, but there was a wealth of unsaid thoughts behind the words.

"He was persuaded." It was difficult to keep the smugness from my voice, and I knew when Dante chuckled that I hadn't succeeded.

"How I would have loved to be a fly on the wall for that. You'll tell me about it when you get home."

Home.

Dante's apartment was definitely that for his community. Chen, Marco, Jacopo, Frankie, and Adriano practically lived there as did Bambi, who cooked and cleaned, and her sweet little girl, Aurora, who visited often. Tore was in and out at least once a week, down from his home in the Niagara valley, and he always stayed the night at the apartment, making dinner himself elbow to elbow with his pseudo-son. They filled the space with laughter and their tangible admiration and adoration of each other.

They were ruthless mafia dons, yet the way they treated each other and everyone else was a far cry from the cruelty I'd witnessed from soldiers in Naples as a girl.

Tore and Dante relished in the games they played with Aurora, laughing with her as if she was a treasure. They played chess together after dinner over wine, exchanging trash talk in a mixture of English and Italian.

They were patriarchs not only of a criminal conglomerate, but of a family.

And that family, that home, had been opened to me without reservation.

For the first time in a very, very long time, I felt part of a happy family.

Part of a whole home.

The feelings it stirred in me left me almost nauseated as I checked my rearview to pull onto Korean War Veterans Parkway leading out of Annadale. There was a motorcycle a few yards behind me, a dull black but sleek and powerful.

It stirred a memory that was instantly forgotten as I remembered the real question I wanted to ask Dante.

"Did Cosima kill Don di Carlo?" I asked, the words exploding from my mouth without my normal tact.

I needed to know.

There were so many secrets Dante and Cosima kept from me as individuals and as friends. I was tired of being on the outside looking through foggy glass.

It was time I knew what the hell their history entailed.

I didn't push myself to admit why I was so desperate to know the particulars of their relationship, but I almost couldn't breathe for the need of knowing.

"Let's speak when you get back," Dante suggested over the sound of men arguing in the background. "I am not alone."

"Just answer the question. Yes or no. It's simple," I pressed.

"Do not push me," he warned, low and hushed. "You want my secrets, Elena? You earn them."

"I've lived with you for a month," I snapped, feeling cornered somehow, desperate to lash out because panic was creeping through my blood. "I haven't breathed a word about anything I've learned since then."

"You haven't learned anything I didn't want you to," he countered, all cold, hard mafia capo.

"So, you don't trust me," I surmised, shocked by the pain that wrung out my spine and left me slumped against the seat.

Why did I even care if he trusted me? I was his lawyer. I'd worked with clients before who lied to me constantly and were suspicious of my every word.

So what if he didn't want me to know his dirty little secrets?

I didn't really want to know them anyway.

"Elena," he murmured in that way he had of making my name an Italian song. "If I didn't trust you, would I let you inside my home? Would I tell my men to buy every season of that god-awful vampire show and send Bambi to get that expensive French chocolate you like? Would I train you with my inner circle every morning and laugh with you over good Italian wine?"

He paused, letting that sink in, knowing better than most that it could take a while for things to seep under my thick skin.

"Come home, Elena," he ordered gently. "We will talk when you return."

I was about to agree, somewhat petulantly because I was still shaken by Ric's observation of my happiness, by the revelation that Dante was probably risking his entire life and livelihood for my sister, when the roar of a motorcycle cut through the air.

My eyes darted to the rearview mirror in time to see that same sleek bike accelerate around an old Buick and settle in behind me again.

I frowned. "Hey, Dante..."

A massive black GMC SUV appeared from the lane to my right, its windows tinted inky black so I couldn't see the driver.

Apprehension skittered down my spine.

"Dante," I repeated, my breath lost to the adrenaline spiking through my system. I revved the powerful engine of the Ferrari and changed lanes without indicating.

A second later, the motorbike cut into the same lane.

A moment after that, the SUV pulled into the lane in front of me, tires screeching.

"What's going on?" Dante demanded, his voice hard and alert.

The ambient noise of conversation in the background went quiet.

"I think I'm being followed," I whispered stupidly as if the people in the other cars could hear me.

"How many?" he demanded, snapping his fingers at someone in the room with him and then muttering something in Italian I couldn't discern over the roar of blood in my ears.

"I think I recognize the motorcycle from that day we drove you to the arraignment." The body on the back was large and helmeted, almost completely anonymous, but it was hard to forget the details of a man who'd shot at you, even through a car window. "There's also a black GMC SUV."

"Adriano and Chen are coming for you," he told me over the

renewed cacophony in the background. "Where are you exactly?"

"Korean War Veterans Parkway in Arden Heights. I'm almost at Latourette Park. What should I do?" I asked in a way that was almost begging, desperate for guidance.

I was a lawyer.

The most action I'd ever experienced in my job was being doused with red paint on the way into court when I'd defended a low-level fashion company for cruelty against animals.

Car chases were outside of my purview.

"Should I try to find a police station?" I guessed, frantically beginning to type it into the GPS system.

"No," he ordered, his voice heavy as a weighted blanket over my raw nerves. "I don't trust the cops on Staten Island, too many Cosa Nostra there. Can you try to lose them?"

An exit was approaching on the right. The SUV in front of me slowed down to a near crawl while the bike behind me sped up to kiss the bumper of my car. The Ferrari jerked under my hands on the wheel. They were trying to force me into the exit.

I explained as much to Dante as I fought to keep control of the car without letting them batter it.

"Elena." His voice whipped through the phone, startling me out of my fearful fog. "You are my fighter, a gladiator. You do not cow in the face of adversity. Do not be afraid. I'm going to talk you through this. There is a dashcam in the car. Frankie is hacking into it now, and I'll be able to guide you, *capisci*? Chen just left, and Adriano's already in Brooklyn. They'll get there as soon as they can. Try to get over the Verrazano Bridge and they'll meet you on Belt Parkway."

I nodded even though he couldn't see, sucking in a deep breath to settle myself. This was just like facing the mafiosos in our little urine yellow house in Naples.

This was just bravery.

Coraggio.

I'd be fine because Dante wouldn't let them hurt me. Even an hour away, I knew he wouldn't let them get to me.

That unshakable faith, something like I'd felt as a girl for God, settled me deeply.

"*Va bene,*" I agreed as I put the car in reverse and gunned the engine. "Let's go."

The Ferrari shot backward so quickly, my torso jacked forward.

It had the desired effect.

The bike behind me swerved madly as it tried to get out of my path, forced to divert into the other lane on a barrage of shouting horns. I took the opportunity to peel across two lanes away from the exit they'd been trying to force me into. The lane opened up in front of me as the road changed to Drumgoole West.

"Take Richmond to Forest Hill and try to lose them in the park," Dante instructed over the roar of the Ferrari as I pushed the speedometer from 55 MPH to 60 then 65. "Don't worry about the cops, Lena. We can deal with them later if we have to. Just drive."

It was easier said than done. Weaving in and out of traffic in the bright daylight of a weekday morning in Staten Island was hardly inconspicuous. Horns and rough shouts followed me as I blew by other cars. I clipped the edge of a Volvo, felt the clang in my teeth, but didn't stop.

The motorbike was still behind me, weaving with ease through the traffic. The SUV struggled with a half-block lag.

I wasn't a professional driver. The only car I'd ever owned was the family's ancient Fiat back in Naples, and though I'd always loved cars and driving, even the occasional drag race with Sebastian, I hadn't done much of it since I'd moved to America. I wasn't equipped to deal with this, not really, but my body seemed to have found its own adrenaline-filled calm. My vision was razor-sharp, my eyes unblinking as I stared as if through a tunnel at the road ahead of me, my instincts quicksilver as I jerked in and out of lanes without indicating.

I'd always had a very well-honed sense of fight or flight cultivated over years of being faced with such situations over and over again, but this took it to another level.

I'd never actually had to flee for my life.

The tires squealed against the asphalt as I careened from Richmond onto Forest Hill, the left side of the road giving way to trees, and then, up ahead, the rolling green of a manicured golf course.

There was a sharp *crack*.

"What was that?" I cried right before another shot was fired.

The bullet lodged in the back of the vehicle with a dull *thwack*. I pressed harder on the gas. "*Dio mio*, they're shooting at me!"

The motorcyclist had a clear shot at me now on the road, and he was gaining ground, one hand raised with the unmistakable sight of a gun in his hand.

Hot metallic anxiety pooled on the back of my tongue as another shot was fired and broke through the back window, glass chattering like teeth as it broke into the car. I ducked slightly, panting.

"Take the golf course, Elena," Dante ordered, his voice a calm, steady weight pinning down my reeling thoughts. "Now!"

Without thinking too much, I wrenched the steering wheel to the right, taking the car off the road through a gap in the trees and onto the smooth grass of the fairway.

"Frankie is looking up the course, but you should be able to follow it across to Richmond Road," Dante told me as I traversed the green.

A curse tore from my mouth as the car fell from the edge of a small hill, soared over a bunker, and landed lopsidedly on the green once more.

"*Dio mio, Madonna santa,*" I chanted, forgetting my atheism and my Americanism in my all-consuming panic.

The motorbike had veered off the road behind me, but I could see in my rearview mirror that the SUV had continued on, probably looking to cut me off somewhere ahead.

"Dante, if they get me––" I started.

"*Stai zitto!*" he barked, ordering me to shut up. "Do not say such things. Focus, Elena. *Coraggio!*"

So, I focused.

A golfer dove out of my way as I zoomed past a tee box. A ball cracked the front windshield. I almost lost traction trying to slow down to maneuver through a small copse of trees, but finally, the clubhouse appeared in the distance and the parking lot beside it.

"*Benissimo*, Elena," Dante praised me as my hands cramped painfully around the wheel. "My fighter."

Distantly, I was aware of sirens building to a crescendo.

The car skittered over the grass at the end of the first hole and jumped the curb into the parking lot. I lost control for a split second. The body of the Ferrari spun out, and the passenger side slammed into a parked Bentley. My head hit the door with a painful crack I felt reverberate in every bone of my body.

"Elena?" Dante snapped. "Are you okay?"

I shook my head, gritting my teeth. Behind me, the motorbike went around a bunker and barreled toward me, gun raised once more. There were people on the green, around the clubhouse, in the parking lot.

A shot fired, and screams erupted around me.

"*Andiamo*," Dante shouted at me.

I put the car in reverse, cringing at the grind of metal on metal as I pulled away from the crumpled Bentley. My hands shook around the wheel, fingers aching as I gripped it too hard. But I ignored all of that and stomped hard on the gas pedal to peel out of the driveway just as the motorcycle jumped the curb.

As I raced out into the street, the GMC SUV nearly T-boned

me when it pulled up. I swerved in time to avoid the worst of it, getting clipped at the front right as I shot forward onto Richmond Avenue.

I watched with bated breath as the motorbike wasn't as lucky.

It flew into the side of the stalled car, the biker's helmet crashing through the passenger side window. When the man pulled back, not hurt so much as pinned between his bike and the other car, I caught a flash of longish black hair.

Another vehicle coming from the other direction caught the edge of the SUV, spun out, and crashed into the ditch on the other side of the road, blocking traffic.

Blocking my pursuers.

"They crashed," I croaked, my throat so dry the words hurt.

"Keep driving," he commanded.

I drove.

Dante coolly instructed me through the neighborhood streets to Staten Island Expressway, which took me over the Verrazzano Bridge into Brooklyn. A black sedan peeled in front of me from an onboard ramp at 92nd Street, and I instantly tensed, air hissing between my teeth.

"*Calmarsi*, Elena," Dante soothed. "It's just Adriano. You can follow him home, si?"

I nodded again.

"Talk to me," he ordered gently.

"*Bene*," I whispered, then cleared my throat. "Okay, I'm good."

"That's my girl," he told me, the warmth of relief and pride in

355

his tone washing over me through the speakers. "Adriano will see you home. I'll be waiting."

"Don't get off the phone," I hastened to say, too shaken to be embarrassed by my need. The shaking in my hands had traveled up my arms into my shoulders and chest. I vibrated like a second engine in the driver's seat. "Stay with me."

There was a silence that felt like a hand cupping my cheek, holding me still for one long, deep breath.

"*Bene, Elena, io sono con te.* I am with you."

I followed Adriano home on autopilot, my brain still under fire in the aftermath of the chase.

Logically, distantly, I recognized I was still in shock. There was a numb cold in my limbs in the wake of the fiery adrenaline, a kind of muffled quiet in my head as I slowly recognized that I was safe and alive.

It wasn't the first time a criminal lawyer had been caught in the crosshairs of their client's ordeals, but it was my first, and it had a profound effect on me.

Only, not the way I would have imagined.

As I clued into my body methodically, atom by atom, I realized that what I felt was not horror and weakness but exhilaration and victorious rage.

Those *stronzi* had come at me, trying to intimidate me perhaps or kidnap me at worse, using me as a pawn against Dante or to send a message to the Camorra in general.

But they hadn't succeeded.

For the first time in my entire life, I felt as if I had come out on the other side of the conflict with the mafia as the winner. I felt as if the entire organization could come at me the way they had come at my family in Naples, and I could take them head-on in that fight. I could show them what it meant to battle a Lombardi, what it meant to face a woman at the end of her rope.

What had happened was more than just a car chase.

It was a pivotal point in my life.

One where I could make the conscious decision to take ownership of my flaws––the anger, the violence, the ruthlessness––of my circumstances––Dante, the Camorra, this game of corruption–or I could succumb to them––return to what I had always been before, unable to stand the heat of this new existence compared to my prior deep freeze.

I could give up the idea of being a hero and rise up the villain beside a man I was beginning to understand was so much more than that.

He was the kind of man who called his seven-year-old niece the love of his life and watched episodes of some cheesy vampire show to give a lonely woman some comradery. He was the kind of man to rip someone apart with his bare hands for wronging him or his, but he was also the kind of man to take the fall for a woman's crime because she was the sister of his heart.

He was everything I'd feared and everything I'd never consciously known I longed for.

And all that, six-foot-five inches, two hundred thirty pounds of

British-Italian man, could be mine.

All I had to do was be brave enough to reach out and take it.

Coraggio.

By the time I pulled onto Dante's street in Manhattan, my breath was coming fast for an entirely different reason than it had been before. Almost blindly, I followed Adriano into Dante's private parking garage beneath the building.

Dante was there standing on the asphalt by the elevator dressed in his requisite black, his hair noticeably disheveled, his entire body tensed like a beautifully carved sculpture in the underground shadows.

As soon as I drove down the ramp into the space, he was powering across the concrete toward me.

As soon as I parked, I climbed from the car, not even bothering to close the butterfly door after me.

My feet hit the ground, and I was off like a shot, tearing across the space between us in my towering heels, each step as sure as if I was flat-footed.

I didn't stop. I didn't even slow down as I neared him.

I just hurtled myself into the marbled arms that opened instantly to catch me and haul me tight into his solid body. Instinctively, my legs locked around his waist, my arms around his neck. I burrowed my face in the junction of his strong neck and shoulder, my lips pressed to his pulse beneath his skin. Vaguely, I was aware of him squeezing me tight, of his orders to Adriano and whoever else was with us in the garage to *leave*.

Only vaguely, because my lips on his skin were not enough. So I used my tongue to lap at his jugular, and when that didn't satisfy the yawning abyss of desire cracking through my core like a crater, I sank my teeth into the muscle and sucked hard at the column. The bright and warm salt taste of him scoured through me, going straight to my head, fogging it with the heady idea that this skin was mine to touch and taste.

A groan vibrated through his throat onto my tongue, his hands spasming on my bottom as he held me tight to him.

Distantly, I knew people were still leaving, turning to face us as they entered the elevator before the doors closed.

I didn't care.

When Dante wrapped my hair slowly, firmly around his wide palm, I could only pant as he pulled my head back so I was forced to look at him. His dark features were carved out of stone, harsh with possession and stark desire. There was no question in that gaze, but he didn't need one.

There was only possession, the same feeling echoed in the drumbeat of my heart pounding between my ears.

A mad desire to beg and plead for his touch scorched through my blood, but before I could succumb to the flames, Dante was taking control, pinning my head in place with that hand in my hair so he could plunder my mouth.

The first hot swipe of his tongue parting my lips, thrusting into my mouth like it belonged there, sent everything I'd ever known about sex and desire tumbling from my head.

There was no history of abuse.

No nerves about how my newly recovered body might react to such passion.

There was only Dante Salvatore.

And me.

Not Elena Moore or Elena Lombardi. Not lawyer or sister, bitch or loner.

Just a man and woman tangled together in the most fervent kiss I ever could have imagined.

I couldn't be close enough, and I couldn't pretend I was okay with that. My hands pulled hard at the short strands of his inky hair, clutching him harder to my mouth, parting it wider for the hot expertise of his tongue. My legs flexed around him, hips shimmying as I rocked instinctively against the steel ridge behind his trousers.

We panted, his breath my breath as he ate it off my tongue the way he'd once promised to.

"I need," I tried to tell him as he captured my lower lip and dragged it sensuously through his teeth.

"Hush," he ordered me, hands flexing hard on my ass before one ran down the crease of my buttock and thigh to dive beneath the edge of my rucked-up skirt. The rough pads of his fingers caught on the thin silk of my stocking as they trailed up to the bare skin of my cheek. "I'll give you everything you need."

I didn't doubt him, but the desperation coursing through me was new and all-consuming. I couldn't seem to get a handle on the sheer extremity of it. My thoughts lost to its magnitude the second they tried to form.

Dante started to move, his mouth still fused to mine, back toward the car. I gasped as he lowered me slowly, the muscles in his chest flexing against me as my back hit the still-hot hood of the Ferrari. The second I was down, I pulled at the buttons of his shirt, needing to feel the strength of his quilted muscles under my hands, needing to reassure myself with his strength. When my fingers fumbled for the second time, Dante cursed savagely and reared back just long enough to rip the shirt open, buttons popping and scattering across the hood and the ground.

"Yes," I hissed, wet flooding my sex at his display of ferocity.

Leaving it open and hanging from his shoulders, he covered my body again. Impatiently, I claimed his mouth, loving the rough abrasion of stubble on my cheek, the contrasting plushness of his too-red lips.

"I've never wanted someone so badly it felt I would die if I couldn't take them," he growled as he pushed my blazer off my shoulders then rucked up my blouse over my breasts before pulling down the cups of my bra to attack my furled nipples with his teeth and tongue.

I hissed and gasped and moaned, making noises I'd always assumed only came from fake scenes in bad pornography. But I couldn't stop myself, didn't want to, and didn't care. Nothing mattered but taking this beast of a man inside me, feeling him fill me up. I wanted to know how the new connections in my body would react to such a punishing invasion.

"I need to feel you," I panted even as I gripped his head to my breasts, shocked at the sensation he created there, the way he made my nipples burn and pulse with twin beats.

"You will," he swore, lowering even farther to place a surprisingly chaste kiss to my belly before swirling his tongue in my naval. My thighs jerked with the sensation. "You'll feel every inch of my cock as I work it into this tight cunt."

I'd lifted my head to watch his progress to my inner thighs, the kisses he placed on the skin close to my core, but it thunked back against the hood as his words rattled through me.

I'd never enjoyed dirty talk.

It hadn't seemed necessary at best and shameful at worst.

But this, Dante's exotic voice growling over my skin as he spoke about taking me like some kind of conquering victor was almost too much to bear.

It validated the dark thoughts swirling in my heart and gave voice to the desire I had no hope to name myself.

I tugged too hard at his ears, pulling him up my body and squeezing him close with my thighs. "Now," I begged, undone by the sensations careening through me at dangerous speeds like the Ferrari through the Staten Island streets. "*Cazzo,* Dante, *now!*"

Unwilling to wait, my hands dived down to his belt, undoing it with a harsh clang before unzipping and diving beneath the fabric to search for his length. I gasped, eyes wide with shock and a little fear as my fingers wrapped one by one around the broad shaft.

Dante pressed his forehead to mine, his eyes all black. "You can take it. I'll make you."

A shudder rippled through me at his words, at the kick of his length in my hands as I pulled it through his boxer briefs and the gap in his trousers out into the cold garage air. Dante hooked a finger in the soaked satin placket of my panties, pulling it aside so I could notch the hot, broad head of his cock against my slick folds.

The feel of him against my most intimate place rocked through me so hard it ripped feelings out from my locked-down heart: longing so acute it burned, belonging like I'd always hoped for, acceptance so sweet it made my teeth ache.

"*Lottatrice mia,*" he groaned, rubbing our noses together the instant before he pushed into me, my walls clinging hard to his fat head in a way that made us both shiver.

"*Figa mia,*" he asserted, *my pussy.*

I gasped in affirmation, my head thrown back on the slick black hood, my eyes squeezed close as I fought through the pain-edged pleasure of taking that thick phallus to the root inside me. He worked himself in and out in short, hard strokes, taking more and more of me with each thrust.

Poised at my entrance, he threaded his hands through the hair over my ears and forced my chin down so I had to look into those soul-destroying black eyes.

"My Elena," he told me intractably, the way a monk spoke as if from God, with the kind of willful authority that made it seem impossible to doubt him.

Then he thrust straight to the hilt inside me, and sensation exploded through me like a grenade. Sharp pieces of pain and pleasure wheeled through my body; sexual shrapnel I had never known could feel so exquisitely excruciating.

My long nails scored into the skin of his back beneath his open shirt as I met him thrust for thrust, as I coaxed him and scratched him in a silent bid for more.

One hand moved to my throat, gently holding it with his thumb on my jugular to feel my breath and pulse, to remind me in the last possible way he could that he was the one fucking me.

The one owning my pleasure and building it beyond anything I'd ever known.

I started to panic as sensation swelled too high, threatening to overtake me. My breath fled my body like the ocean sucked back by the force of a tsunami.

"Dante, Dante," I chanted. "I can't, I can't."

"You can," he promised, sweat beading on his forehead, sliding down his cheek.

I reared up to lick it off, then sealed my mouth over his, needing the comfort of his tongue sucking at my own to deal with the barrage of pleasure hammering at me from every direction. My womb felt tight, my pussy wet and open, my breasts swollen as they brushed again and again against the short, crisp hair over Dante's hard chest. His silver cross lay on my belly between us, swaying with the force of his thrusts.

The sight of it tripped the last of my mental defenses.

Fucking on the hot hood of a car in a public parking garage with a beast of a man churning between my spread thighs, I cried out in fear and awe as an orgasm crawled through me, tensing every muscle until I vibrated. The need to burst apart, to unravel the tension almost terrified me, my breath caught on a choke in my throat.

"*Vieni per me,*" Dante gritted out between his teeth. "Come for me, Elena. Let me feel you come apart around me."

A scream burst from my compressed lungs like a gunshot tearing up through my gut, destruction following in its wake. I thrashed, pinned between Dante's unyielding body and the car, shouting and crying at the sheer force of sensation searing through me, tearing apart the tension in each muscle, electrifying my heart until it pumped madly, and I thought I might honestly die.

I was all body and blood as the first true orgasm of my life ravaged me and wrung me completely dry. My mind floated in a kind of peaceful cloud for a moment before I struggled to find the earth again.

When I did, tears were cooling on my cheeks and a burn scorched my throat from all the yelling. My body was loosely wrapped around Dante as he churned slower now inside my wet pussy, the sloppy noises of our union making my skin flush and my tired sex clench hard once more all around him.

Dante's neck was strained with the effort to hold on, the strong column corded, his Adam's apple bobbing harshly as he tried to swallow past his pleasure.

The pleasure I was giving him.

A different kind of satisfaction curled through me like smoke after the fire. I pulled him tight to me with rubbery limbs and sucked at the lobe of his ear before I whispered, "I've never orgasmed like that before." And it was true, though he didn't know how much. "Now, I want to see *you* come for *me*."

"*Cazzo*," he cursed, squeezing his eyes shut as he powered hard into my slightly aching, buzzing pussy. "You feel better than a dream."

"Show me how much you love it," I dared him, nipping at his lobe, then moving down his neck, sinking my teeth into that dense column to feel his strength as he fucked me harder and harder again. "I want to watch what I do to you."

With one last savage groan, Dante reared back, pulling his throbbing length from my clutching folds to wrap his own meaty fist around it. I watched, shocked and astoundingly aroused by the sight of him beating his cock so viciously over my prone body. He loomed over me, shirt open around the tight, quilted tapestry of his abdomen, face tight with the wildness of his passion. I had never seen or imagined a man sexier than Dante Salvatore.

And then he slammed his free hand against the car beside my hip, the swollen head of his dick shuttling fast between his fingers, and he cried out roughly as the first spurt of his seed shot onto my naked, quivering stomach. I was enthralled by the sight as rope after rope of cum splashed hotly against my skin, coating me in him.

It was base. So dirty it should have been *wrong*.

But God, it only felt right to have him mark me that way, possess me in such an elemental way with his seed.

Finished, panting as he braced himself above me, Dante released his still-hard length and lazily smeared his cum into my skin in wide, firm circles. A violent shiver tore its teeth into my spine, but I didn't stop his possessive act.

Emotion bubbled up in the wake of the passionate fire that had razed me so totally to the ground, new spring growth erupting from the fertilized soil of my soul.

I knew it should have been filthy and wicked, what we did, so publicly and rabidly like animals in heat.

But I'd just had the first truly erotic experience of my life at twenty-seven years old. Not just a flutter of pleasant sensation occasionally and the gentle intimacy of holding a man against me, but the teeth-chattering, bone-rattling euphoria I'd only ever read about in books or heard about from friends and family.

It was more than that, though. It satisfied a bone-deep longing I had for so long to be wanted fiercely, above all else. To the point, even, of insanity.

And that final act? Dante watching his hand massage his essence into my skin as if it would stay there like a tattoo, a brand, forever?

It settled some primal need to be owned fully by someone else.

To be wanted and accepted.

To belong.

Before I could tamp down the impulse, a sob fell wetly from between my lips. I hastened to cover my mouth, eyes wide over my hands as I stared at Dante who looked down at me in horrified shock.

"Did I hurt you, *cara?*" he demanded, quickly tucking himself back in his pants and righting my own clothes before reaching down to collect me gently into his arms.

It only made me sob harder, my chest a cold engine stuttering to life with furious emotion. I couldn't stop. Panicked, I clutched at him even as I tried to hide my face in his neck, the tears sliding hot and heavy down my cheeks into the open collar of his shirt.

"Hush, hush," he murmured as he stood, my body easy in his hold. "*Io sono con te.* I am with you."

I could do nothing but cry. The tears scalded my eyes as they pooled on my lower lids, flooding my face until it was hot and itchy with salt. I rubbed my cheeks back and forth over Dante's skin and shirt like a child unable to handle the amount of sorrow in their blood. I was inconsolable with emotions too big to be harnessed by words. Even when I tried to open my mouth as Dante took us into the elevator up to his apartment, only whimpers and sucking gasps left my throat.

Where did one learn the right vocabulary for such things?

How did I learn to thank a man for the simple yet profound act of loving me?

With his body.

As a friend.

Looking after me even though it was a wretched job I'd never be able to make easier.

Seeing me when I'd been secretly fearful for so long that I would die unseen and unknown.

I cried, and I cried until my chest burned and snot ran from my nose, hiccups the only way I could get air into my exhausted lungs.

Dante carried me into the apartment, through the living room where I knew some of his men were probably waiting for us. I wanted to ask him to take me to my bed, but he didn't. Instead, he went through the kitchen to the back hallway that led to his office.

And his bedroom.

A shiver of anticipation pinched between my shoulder blades as he knocked the ajar door open with his shoulder and ferried us inside. He didn't stop at the bed or the couch I glimpsed through my tear-damp hair near the windows. Instead, he powered us straight through to the black marble bathroom.

I tried to suck in some deep breaths while he perched me on his hip and a slightly raised thigh to lean into the massive walk-in shower and turn it on. Water fell from all three of the four sides. After adjusting the temperature, he moved us both inside the glass doors and backed up into the spray, lowering me to the ground only for long enough to take off my hastily righted clothes.

I shivered even though steam was beginning to billow in the glass and marble enclosure.

"*Vieni,*" Dante ordered softly as he tugged my naked body close. Come.

I was too tired and overwrought to be embarrassed by my naked flesh.

With a gusty sigh and another little sob, I let him press me like a flower between the pages of his heavy arms and strong torso. He kept me there, hugging me, as the water rained all around us. Minutes passed, my diminishing tears lost to the spray, my breath evening slowly. I focused on the feel of a strong man around me, shielding me from the outside world but also from myself. When I would have wanted to be alone for my rare and shameful breakdown, Dante had suffered no bashfulness and forced me to share it with him.

I thought about being embarrassed then, in the wake of the emotional storm that left me ravaged like the wreckage after a tropical hurricane, but I couldn't muster the energy even for that.

So, instead, I pressed my cheek harder to Dante's steely pec and wrapped my arms around his torso to hold him close right back.

When enough time passed that I was certain our skin had turned to prunes, he finally shifted back enough to look down at me, pinching my chin to lever my face up at his.

"Better?" he asked, eyes solemn.

I nodded, biting my lips then shrugging weakly. "That was probably the first time you had sex with a woman who went to pieces in your arms afterward."

He didn't laugh or brush it off the way I thought he would. His thumb swept over the corner of my mouth, reminding me of the fact my makeup was probably running down my cheeks, and he said, "It was the first time for a lot of things, Elena. None of them bad."

I'd never told him explicitly what my surgery had been for, but he'd spent the last four weeks watching me convalesce. Knowing Dante, he probably had a decent guess of the ailments I'd suffered from.

I forced myself to swallow the whimper that rose in my throat, done with weakness.

As if reading my mind, he bent his legs so he could drop closer to my face. "Sometimes there is more strength in tears than in austerity."

I laughed limply. "How do you always know what to say? Is there some kind of class for that?"

His lips twitched. "It's my natural-born charm. But it's also this. Whatever you and I are made of, it's the same. You don't have to be good with me, right or true in any sense, but especially the conventional. You can be your worst self with me, because Elena, it's the contradictory nature of your soul that intoxicates me."

Dio mio, how was any woman supposed to resist such stark and brilliantly cut honesty from a man? He offered his sincerity to me like a jewel, this priceless treasure I wanted to lock away inside me forever.

No matter what he said, we weren't a thing that was made to last. We were too opposite, too set in our different ways. This was nothing but animal attraction, something I was experiencing for the first time in my life, something I was no longer willing to resist.

But I could learn from the people I respected, and I'd come to understand I respected him. His candor and loyalty, his complete lack of fear around anything emotional or physical. He took on the chaos of life head-on and laughed while he did it.

I hoped that whatever happened, I'd be able to ingest a little of that before our time was done.

"Aren't you going to ask about my breakdown?" I asked, my own self-hatred peeking through again.

He scowled then sighed, turning me around with one hand as he reached for the shampoo with the other. "No. If you want to share, you can. But I think I have a few ideas. The adrenaline crash alone would justify it. I'm just happy to have shared it with you. Being able to be there for you is a privilege I have the feeling you don't afford to many people."

When his strong fingers began to knead my scalp, the citrus scent of him intensified by the product he worked into my hair, I groaned raggedly. "That feels so good."

"There are many things I can and *will* make you feel," he promised darkly. "Now that I've had you, I won't let you go until I've had my fill, and I have a feeling that will take a very long time."

I closed my eyes as he pulled me back against his body, the burgeoning swell of his shaft pressing against my butt cheeks. When he tipped my head back on his shoulder to let the water carry away the suds, and one of his calloused hands followed the path down the front of my naked body, I gave myself permission to surrender once again to sensation.

Because I knew, even if Dante didn't, that no fire ever burned eternally, and one as hot as the inferno between us would burn out before we knew it.

So I'd enjoy it--the pleasure, the bravery, the discovery-- while I could.

And hope that after everything, I wouldn't be bitter the way I was after Daniel left me. I'd be changed for the better from letting Dante storm past the walls I'd let no one behind before.

CHAPTER TWENTY-FOUR

elena

I'd almost assumed Dante would try to keep me from work the following morning because it was something Daniel might have done and even Seamus.

But he didn't.

When I'd woken up in my bed alone because I'd insisted on it after showering with Dante, needing the space to shore up the walls around my heart, I'd prepared to fight him about my need to work despite the chaos of the previous day. I was focused on it to the exclusion of all else as I showered again and readied myself for the day with my arsenal of Chanel cosmetics.

It was easier to concentrate on a possible confrontation than it was to acknowledge the monumental way our relationship had shifted last night.

The monumental way *I* had shifted.

I'd entered the living room dressed in my favorite classic black

Dolce & Gabbana high-waisted pencil skirt and slightly sheer white silk blouse, my hair pinned back in an artfully loose bun, my six-inch Valentino pumps at my feet. I wore my well-groomed professionalism the way knights had worn their suits of armor, ready to do battle with whatever might face me during the day.

And I was ready to fight Dante about my right to go to work.

"I'm going in to the office this morning," I'd stated strongly right off, holding my Prada purse in front of me like a shield.

Dante lounged at the patio table through the open French doors even though it was almost November and the wind was icy, wearing a black cashmere sweater over a white button-up. He looked quintessentially European, the Italian language newspaper in one hand and a cup of espresso in the other.

He'd looked over at me with slightly raised brows and inclined his head slowly, addressing me as if I was an infant. "Yes, okay. It is a weekday."

I blinked. "Well, yes. So, I have to work."

He blinked right back, head cocked as he narrowed his eyes at me, assessing me. "Yes, that is typically how it happens."

I nodded curtly, thrown off by his easy acceptance. "Okay, I'm leaving, then."

"*Buona giornata,*" he called mildly as he turned back to his newspaper.

I blinked at the back of his head, struggling with the feeling pushing up through the cage of my ribs.

It took me a moment to identify it as I made my way to the

elevator.

Disappointment.

I'd expected him to fight me about it so I could find him wanting, roast him for being misogynistic like so many Italian men could be, wanting to keep me in the home under his thumb and assuming I'd accept that just because we'd had intercourse.

But also, an even smaller voice in the depths of my lockdown soul whispered that I wanted him to fight me about it because it would show that he cared.

I struggled with the dueling sensations as I got in the elevator and rode down to the basement where Adriano usually waited to take me to work.

Seeing him in the black Beamer brought me mild satisfaction, and I smiled at him as I got into the backseat.

"Good morning, Addie."

"Hey," he grunted, completing our morning ritual. He wasn't exactly the most verbose man. Then, as he pulled out of the parking garage, he met my eye in the rearview mirror and added, "Glad you're good after yesterday."

Warmth moved through me like a summer's breeze. "Thank you, me too."

"Acted like a real *donna*," he told me with admiration clear in his gravelly voice. "Made us proud."

Donna like the queen in a chess set or the queen on a playing card.

Donna like a female boss.

Bruno had called me that a few times, and Frankie. I hadn't noticed until then what a compliment it was and how much it meant coming from men like these.

I leaned forward to pat his boulder shoulder. "You guys are rubbing off on me."

It could have been wishful thinking, but I thought I saw a faint blush stain his deep olive-brown cheeks.

When we arrived at my office building, I prepared to alight from the car at the curb, but Adriano didn't pull over the way he normally did. Instead, he idled beside orange cones and a sign that pronounced the cordoned-off area a construction zone.

He rolled down the window and yelled at a passing man. "Hey, do me a solid and make space in the cones, yeah?"

The twentysomething hipster he'd called to gaped at him, obviously disconcerted by the sight of the massive Italian man leaning out the window at him.

"Well?" Addie grunted, his thick brow pulled low over his eyes.

Instantly, the kid shot into motion and made space in the cones so Adriano could pull the car into the space and park. He even moved the cones back into place after we were settled.

Addie moved toward him on his lumbering gait, the kid visibly cowering, then offered a handshake with a bill folded discreetly against his palm.

"*Grazie*," he offered with a smile that was anything but friendly on his rough-featured face.

The kid accepted the handshake with a tremulous smile and

took off.

When Addie turned to face me, there was laughter in his eyes.

I shook my head at him. "You eat children's dreams for dinner, don't you?"

He cackled lowly as he escorted me to the door. I didn't say anything when he followed me into the lobby, but when he went to step through the security barricade with me I held up a hand.

"What are you doing?"

Reaching into an inner pocket in his leather jacket, he produced a security badge with the name Adrian Smith on it.

Despite myself, I laughed. "You couldn't think of anything more original than Smith?"

He shrugged.

"Okay, but why do you have that? I'm safe in the building," I insisted, crossing my arms to level him with my coolest stare.

"Boss's orders," he responded.

I was really coming to hate that phrase.

"What're you going to do? Sit outside my office all day?"

He shrugged again. "Not if I don't gotta. You're supposed to text if you need to go somewhere."

I rolled my eyes. "And if I don't check in like a toddler?"

"Your funeral," was the response.

We stared at each other, Addie's face totally blank, mine a mask of indignation.

"New boyfriend, Lombardi?" Bill, one of the associates on the Salvatore case with me, called as he passed through the check-in security beside us.

I shot him my middle finger.

Addie grinned. "Yeah, we really are rubbin' off on you."

A breath huffed between my lips as I tried to expel some of my exasperation. "Okay, I have no plans to leave the office until this afternoon. I'll text. But for God's sake, please do not escort me up to my office like a child. This is my *job*. I'd like to retain whatever professionalism I can still muster."

He blinked at me, and for a moment, I thought he was unmoved, but then he reached out and patted me--*hard*--on the shoulder in agreement. I watched him turn on his heel and walk back out of the building, where he leaned against the glass wall beside the doors and lit up a smoke.

I sighed, knowing that was as good as it was going to get.

But as I moved through security and into the elevator, a little smile crept over my face.

Because apparently, not only did Dante care about my safety but the guys did too.

And that felt better than it should have.

I was eating lunch in the conference room while I tried to figure out what to do about Dante's illegal gambling and racketeering charges when movement at the door caught my eye.

"Hi, Elena," Bambi said almost bashfully, a curtain of thick blond hair sweeping over her shoulder to partially hide her face. "I'm sorry for disturbing you at work, but I-I wanted to continue the rest of that conversation we never got to have."

"Of course," I offered immediately, shifting my papers and the plastic bowl of salad around on the table to make room for her to sit opposite me. "I thought I gave you my number?"

"You did, but I thought I should talk to you in person." She sat down with her back to the door and then peered over her shoulder through the glass at the lawyers walking through the hall and got up to shift to a chair on my side so she could see the hall without turning.

Huh.

My interest piqued, I crossed my legs and folded my hands in my lap. "I'm all yours."

She chewed her lip almost frantically as she looked down at her hands. "I'm not married, and I'm not a widow. Did you know that? That's why Dante takes care of Aurora and me. When I had her out of wedlock, my parents...they weren't happy."

No, I could imagine they wouldn't have been.

When I was briefly pregnant with Daniel's baby before I lost it to an ectopic episode, Mama had been kind about the fact we weren't married. I wondered if that was because I'd always assumed it was just a matter of time until I became Daniel's wife or if Mama was less rigidly traditional than I might have given her credit for.

I knew women in Napoli who had been cast out of their family homes for having sex before matrimony, let alone giving birth to a baby out of wedlock.

"I'm sorry," I said to Bambi even though the words felt trite.

It made me furious that women were held to such impossible standards, and I ached for the sweet blue-eyed woman who'd had to go through it all alone.

"*Grazie*," she said graciously. "Aurora was two when we met Dante. My own brother wasn't talking to me, but he let me clean his house for some extra money, and Dante was there one day. He saw Aurora first playing pretend with a feather duster, and he crouched down to play with her." There was a dreamy quality to her gaze, a soft smile pressed between her lips. I wondered if Bambi was in love with Dante and hoped very much, for reasons I didn't want to delve into, that she was not. "Later, he found me in the bathroom cleaning a toilet, and he was so big he barely fit in the doorframe. At first, I thought maybe he was going to yell at me for bringing Aurora to work, but he only asked me for my name and if I was available on Thursdays to clean his place."

She laughed, shaking her head. "I had no idea what to make of his mixed accent, of his authority and his charm. It was such an alien combination. But I agreed. He was a capo. What else was I going to do?"

I sympathized, having been put into a similar but much more intense situation by Dante before when he forced me to move in with him.

"One day of the week became two and then three, and then suddenly, he was employing me full time to take care of his home.

He found Aurora and me a better apartment close by and insisted I pay rent to him at a very obviously reduced price. It was a dream come true, really."

It sounded like it, the start of a fairy tale where the pauper fell in the love with the dark prince.

I was startled as I realized that in a sense, that was very much like my own story with the mafioso. I'd been born poor in the slums of Naples; Dante was a duke's son in the moors of England. Even though I had raised myself up independent of him, his case would still bring me the money and success I'd always wanted, and that was its own kind of happily ever after.

Wasn't it?

I didn't dare hope for anything more.

Though by the stain on Bambi's cheeks, it was obvious she did. "My brother even started talking to me again because of Dante. I owe him everything, really. Which is why I'm here." She fixed me with those enormous blue eyes filled with stern resolve. "I need a lawyer."

"Okay," I agreed easily, wanting to help her. "Why?"

"My...There's a man in my life, and lately, he's been scaring me." Her voice quavered. "Scaring Aurora."

Anger roared through me. "Has he hurt you?"

"Only once," she admitted, chewing her lip so hard it bled. "But I went to the hospital and everything, so they have it on record. He punched me in the gut, and I couldn't stand straight for two days."

"Is he... a member of the Family?" I asked lowly, wondering if that was why she had gone to such lengths to hide her plea for help.

I didn't care who it was hurting her and scaring Aurora. I'd do everything in my power to get them free of the bastard.

Her nod was slight, but it was the fear in her eyes that settled it for me.

"Can you tell me who it is?" I pressed softly, leaning forward to gently tap her knee with my fingers. "It could help me keep you safe."

Frantically she shook her head. "No. I don't want to tell you who it is. We don't have that attorney-client silence thing, right?"

"No," I admitted. "If it's a problem with one of Dante's men, it would be a conflict of interest for me. And it's a domestic case, so I'll have to refer you to someone who covers that area of the law."

"Okay, that's kinda what I figured," she admitted. "I don't know many law types, and you've always been so good to Aurora and me. I just knew you would help."

Her praise warmed me, and I felt horrible for my momentary bout of jealousy.

"Have you considered asking Dante for some time off so you can get away while we sort this out?" I suggested. "It might get ugly with this guy before we can file a restraining order."

"I could do that if it gets bad," she agreed. "But I hate to leave Dante in a lurch."

"He would understand," I promised because I knew he would.

The heartless capo I'd made him out to be at our first meeting was only a mirage. The real Dante might have had the flat black eyes of a criminal, but he had a heart of gold for those he cared about.

"Why do you think this man is acting this way toward you now?" I asked curiously.

She winced as if she had hoped I wouldn't ask that. "It's tough for me, you know? Even though he's doing some...bad stuff, I care about him."

Growing up, many of the girls I'd gone to school with had ended up married to Camorra foot soldiers, and many of those had gone on to be beaten, raped, or neglected by their husbands. I hated the thought of pretty, sweet Bambi under the hands of some thuggish creep.

She hadn't said it was her boyfriend, but it was easy enough to read between the lines. Only powerful love would keep her from turning him in even though she knew what he was doing was wrong.

The thought hit a little too close to home, so I smiled thinly and pressed on. "I understand but, Bambi, you and Aurora need to come first. I'm going to call my friend Tilda at another law firm and get her on your case. She practices family law, and she was one of the top in our class at NYU, so she will take good care of you."

"You're taking good care of me," she corrected, reaching out to squeeze my hand. "I can see why Dante admires you so much."

"I could say the same thing," I offered, pushing that pang of jealousy aside because Bambi was a good woman, and I wanted her to know she deserved more than this schmuck of a boyfriend.

Her answering smile was weary as she waited for me to go through my phone. I had just hit send on Tilda's number when Bambi chilled me to the bone by adding, "Oh, ask her if she knows how to draw up a will, okay?"

CHAPTER TWENTY-FIVE

DANTE

I loved New York the second I arrived in the city, and that appreciation had only deepened over the years. The place was teeming with humanity, not just the bodies in the streets but the countless thoughts and actions of men made into towering buildings and cultivated parks. It was such a mortal city, riddled with flaws like cramped alleyways filled with crime and sin, and glories like the sunsets that spilled through the cracks of the manmade cityscape, illuminating even those dank hovels in its golden light from time to time.

Much like the red-headed Italian woman who haunted my thoughts, she was a chaos of contradictions I wanted to spend my life untangling.

When something interested me, I threw myself into the pursuit of knowing it as deeply as I could. I was in the middle of one such endeavor now with Elena, but I'd already spent years delving into New York City's quirks and histories to better understand them.

To better *use* them.

I was standing in a place that was the fruit of that research currently, deep beneath the parking garage at the base of my Upper East Side apartment building. I hadn't picked the apartment for its character or the neighborhood for its good schools.

I'd chosen it because of its history, the thing that made it precious to me.

The defunct subway station Track 83 had been one of the first stations built in the early 1900s, and service was closed in 1954. There were many such old metro stops forgotten to history beneath the city, the Old City Hall and Track 61 beneath the Waldorf-Astoria being two of them that still allowed some degree of public access for spectators.

No one knew about Track 83 beneath the Smith Jameson Building except the previous owner of the building, who was now deceased, a man at the city planning record hall I had on payroll, and *me*.

It was my sanctuary, an outlet from the cage of my apartment so many floors above. It seemed fitting to own the penthouse, my own personal Mt. Olympus, and the subterranean tunnels that threaded through the entire network of New York City's underworld.

This was where I conducted the business the probation office didn't see, and Elena couldn't hear.

The curved high ceilings with their faded frescos were appropriately Italianate and created lovely acoustics for the sounds of a man's scream.

My fist thudded dully into the bones of Carter Andretti's face, the skin splitting open like overripe fruit at the force of the blow. His head went careening to the side, bloody spittle flying in a wide arch across his prone body and my black suit.

This was why I wore black. Not because it cut a dramatic image, but because blood was impossible to get out of anything else.

"You have thirty seconds to start talking again, *figlio di puttana*," I growled as I reared back to deliver another fierce jab to his other cheek, evening out the pain. "Or I'll string you up from the ceiling, put on my brass knuckles, and use you as a punching bag."

He groaned weakly as his head slumped between his shoulders, blood dripping down his torso.

"Even if he does talk, I'm not convinced."

The voice that spoke belonged to one of the most infamous sinners in the city, a man with a reputation so notorious it was said women just handed him their panties when he entered a room.

Caelian Accardi.

The son of Don Orazio Accardi.

Usually such a familial tie would guarantee him a place of prestige, but Caelian was the black sheep, his father's greatest disappointment. Caelian didn't care about learning the family business, but he did care about dabbling in the entertainment of it—the girls, the drugs, and the gambling.

No one in the Accardi borgata gave Caelian a second look.

But I had, and I did again as I turned to face one of the two men

giana darling

I'd brought down there that day.

He was young, late twenties, and the youth still in his face and the bright sheen of blond hair that hadn't gone burnished yet with age. Still, there was a certain quality about him, that athletic form held very still, those blue eyes too placid. It was the look of a man whose still waters ran very deep, very dark.

I was counting on that.

"You're an idiot if you doubt him," Santo Belcante scoffed from the opposite side of the room. "The di Carlos have always been greedy bastards."

Santo was no one's son. He had been taken in by Monte Belcante as a boy and had been groomed as his successor until Monte died of cancer last year. For reasons I didn't know, Nario, Monte's brother, had taken over the family instead of Santo.

I was counting on the very bitterness I heard in Santo's tone.

Frankie had discovered who had tried to run Elena off the road in Staten Island.

The motherfucking di Carlos.

Traffic cameras had captured Agostino di Carlo, Gideone's older brother and one of the two men contending for the throne, climbing into the GMC SUV at a restaurant the family owned in Brooklyn an hour before the chase.

The fuckers were coming for me and mine.

It wasn't just about the fact that Cosima had killed Giuseppe and that she was a known associate of Tore and me (though no one but the three of us knew to what extent).

It was about kicking a man when he was supposedly down.

They wanted control of my operation.

More, they wanted control of the entire city.

Carter Andretti had been only too happy to explain in the early hours of the morning that Agostino di Carlo had paid him to shoot out Ottavio's deli.

Not to get rid of Cosima.

But to get rid of his uncle.

He'd orchestrated the entire damn war between our two families so that he could use the opportunity to take power for himself. It was the kind of selfish, unthinking act that had led to pure chaos in the 80s and countless Made Men being put behind bars.

It was idiotic and foolish.

Especially because Carter Andretti had told me they wouldn't stop at the Salvatore borgata.

The motherfucker di Carlo brothers wanted it all.

Which was why I had brought the two looked-over members of the Accardi and Belcante outfits into my confidence. If I could convince them the di Carlos were a threat to their own organizations, that meant allies, and I knew well enough that the older generations were just as happy to see me dead as the Cosa Nostra.

Without warning, I reeled back and threw another punch at Andretti. His cheek crumpled under my heavy fist, the bones crumbling.

"*Fermo!*" he groaned, head lolling.

"I'll stop when you tell us what I want to hear," I offered reasonably as I wiped his blood off on his equally dirty shirt.

"It's true," he whimpered softly through his split lips. "They paid us to hit Otto's. Agostino and Gideone. It was the first step."

"And the second?" I pressed, flipping a knife out of my sleeve to scrape the blood out from under my nails.

His eyes darted madly between the knife and my face, then over to Accardi and Belcante. "They were gonna kill you and go for the others."

"How?" Santo demanded, stepping forward until he was at my side, looming over him. "You tell me how, or I'll use Salvatore's knife to skin you alive."

"They were gonna blow up your deal with The Fallen MC," he panted, bloody spittle drooling down his chin. "Apparently, they got an in with the New York chapter."

Santo cursed savagely.

"And the Accardi family?" Caelian drawled from behind us as he began to saunter forward, lighting a cigarette.

Carter went quiet.

Caelian sighed, took a drag of tobacco, and then leaned over to blow it out in Carter's face. "You have one chance to tell me."

The sharp, acrid scent of urine perfumed the space as Carter pissed his pants, the heavy steam dripping from the chair he was tied to.

Still, though, he didn't talk.

He was a decent foot soldier.

But no match for three furious capos.

Caelian shrugged almost casually, then reached forward to grasp Carter's face in one hand while he put the cigarette out with the other...straight on the inner corner of the di Carlo soldier's eye.

His scream echoed throughout the cavernous space.

"He was gonna take Ravenna," Carter shouted, neck straining as he fought his bonds. "Take her and rape her and marry her."

Anger rolled through Caelian, and for the first time since I'd known the bastard, he looked every inch the ruthless mafia don his father was.

"I've heard enough," he decided, looking over his shoulder at me. "What are you suggesting, Salvatore? I imagine you have a plan."

I grinned at them both. "I do."

After they'd left, I'd let my inner crew into the sanctum and given Adriano a crack at Carter to make sure there wasn't any information I might have missed. I was pleased. The shit show my life had become in the past year was slowly beginning to untangle itself.

I had a plan for the di Carlos.

A plan for the Irish fuckers.

And a plan for Elena, even if she didn't know it yet.

"How could you trust those *bastardi?*" Jacopo muttered from over my shoulder as I surveyed the trunks of weapons we kept stored in one corner of the abandoned station.

I straightened gradually before turning to stare down the few inches into my cousin's face. We weren't blood relations, but I'd always treated him like a brother, a close confidant. Sometimes, it meant he wasn't as respectful as he damn well should have been.

"I have my reasons," I said opaquely even though I knew it would frustrate him.

Life itself seemed to frustrate Jaco, which was why everyone called him Grouch. It irritated me that he was always the victim, whining about his lot in life when he'd been born with a silver fucking mafia spoon in his mouth. His father had loved him before he was killed by the Ventura Mexican cartel for attempting a side hustle outside of the family's schemes on their territory.

We hadn't gone to war with them over it.

Emiliano had made his bed when he went against the family interests, and he had to lie in it, six feet beneath the ground.

Jaco hadn't liked it, but then, I couldn't blame him.

If anyone hurt Tore, I'd rip him apart with my bare hands. But the difference was, Tore would never be so stupid as to act against the borgata.

So, I put up with Jaco's surliness and his need to badger me about every single fucking thing I did because his parent had been killed, and that was a wound that didn't heal.

I knew from experience.

"I wanna know them," he pressed, pushing his overlong black hair behind his ears. "Those are fucking rival capos, Dante. Maybe this house arrest has made you *pazzo*....maybe that woman has."

"That woman?" I asked quietly, my entire body coiled.

He didn't sense the threat I posed, as always, too riled up by his own antics. "*Si, quella donna.* You've been goin' crazy for her since the first. She's a goddamn lawyer, D. They're one step up from scumbag cops. You can't trust the bitch, and I've stayed quiet about it long enough. She's fucking living in your place? Where the magic happens? You're asking to be put away for life and then this stunt with Accardi's reject son and the *Santo barstardo?*"

He was shaking his head so he didn't notice me lash out at him, grabbing the thick column of his neck in the palm of my hand and squeezing as I lifted him to his toes. His eyes bugged out with shock, hands flying to scratch at my grip, mouth flapping like a dying fish.

None of the other men in the station made a single move to stop me.

I brought Jaco's face to mine so I could sneer softly, just for him. "You call Elena a bitch ever again, Jaco, I'll carve the word into your forehead with my blade, *capisci?*"

I dropped him unceremoniously, turning my back to finish my inventory of the guns.

Behind me, he choked and sucked in breath. "What the fuck, Dante? I'm your *cugino.* We're fucking *blood.* Yet you treat me like this for calling it like it is? You've gone mad."

"You've gone mad if you think you can talk to me like this," I informed him coldly as I replaced the lid on the trunk and turned to face him again. "You forget I am *capo dei capi* of this outfit. Not you. I'm open to hearing what you've got to say, Jaco, but only if you can say it like a man and not a whiny *troia*."

"*Vaffanlo*," he cursed, gesturing rudely with his hand as he told me to fuck myself. "I'm just trying to look out for you. For this family. It's all I got left, and I want to protect it."

I softened just slightly, stepping forward to clasp him a little too hard on the shoulder. "I get it, *cugino*. You just have to remember, all I do, I do for this family."

He deflated a fraction, but a petulant frown still dented his brow. "Not her."

"No," I agreed because that was true. "Elena is just for me."

"'S stupid, D," he argued again, but he knew he'd lost the fight.

"*Forse*," I allowed that maybe it was. "But our biggest successes have come from my most daring gambles. I'm willing to stake a lot on this one."

"You always said women ruin a man," he reminded me perniciously. "They make them weak."

I cocked my head, my hand squeezing his neck painfully. "Did I? I think you misunderstood. Maybe it was my accent, mm? What I said was that a man in love has one weakness, his woman. It's his Achilles' heel. But that same love makes the rest of him impenetrable, strong as a god." I clapped my free hand to the other side of his throat and strangled his neck for one brief moment so he could feel my strength. "What do you think, Jaco? Do I seem weak?"

His pale brown eyes swarmed like the surface of a swamp with mixed emotions, his pride tangling with his love and loyalty. Finally, he reached up and planted his own hands on my shoulders in a show of brotherhood and dipped his head slightly. I bent forward to kiss his head and let go of my hold on him.

"*Va bene,*" I told him, dismissing both our argument and his presence. "Go pick up my niece and Bambi. Give them my love."

He nodded almost to himself, then shot me a sheepish grin. "*Grazie, D.*"

I lifted my chin at him. "*Vattene.*"

He left.

I watched him go with my hands crossed over my chest, brain whirring. I wasn't surprised when Frankie stepped up beside me and adopted the same pose.

"You think we got a problem with him?"

I sighed, scrubbing my hand over the sharp stubble at my jaw. I wanted to be upstairs with Elena, preferably inside her, discovering more of the ways I could make her come for me. Instead, I was deep underground dealing in the shadows I'd lived in my entire life.

"I find it hard to believe he'd risk a business he stood to inherit if something happened to me. He's a man motivated by his family name and the success attached to that. We're doing well despite the RICO case. As long as we bring in money, Jaco should be loyal beyond the ties Tore gave him. But after Mason, I'm not sure about anyone. Wouldn't be sure of you if you didn't owe me your goddamn life."

Frankie nodded. "If I ever thought of leaving, Liliana would kill me."

I laughed because that was the truth. His wife was not to be trifled with even though she was just a slip of a thing.

"Elena's got it too," he continued as if picking up the thread from a conversation we'd been having before.

"What?"

"What it takes to be *donna*."

I blinked because even though Elena had been on my mind, in my fucking blood, for weeks, I hadn't thought hard about our future. Maybe because I knew logically we couldn't have one.

She was too proper, too upstanding and moral. Too disgusted with the details of work that made up my entire existence. There was no way we could ever have a...relationship beyond the walls of my apartment, beyond the scope of this case.

Yet the idea of giving her up made me mad. Crazed as a beast gone feral, foaming at the mouth.

I was the only man who had ever made her come.

The one to make her curse and make her beg.

The one she allowed to care for her even though she hated to seem weak.

How was it possible there could be a time when she didn't seem like *mine*?

But *donna.*

Boss.

The queen to my kingpin.

A partner not just in this case against me but in crime.

In my shadowed underworld.

It should have seemed ridiculous, but a part of me could picture her there under the faded frescos, checking guns and ordering *soldati* coolly, efficiently.

She would be fucking magnificent.

"Love's made you foolish," I finally told him, trying to shrug off the fantasy, let the idea of it roll off my back. "I live in the real world."

"You live in the world you create," he corrected. "That's why you're the boss."

A growl worked in my throat, part frustration, part something else.

Triumph maybe, at the thought of corrupting her so fully. At the thought of having a woman like her stand beside me.

"If this plan doesn't work out, we won't be here to worry about that," I reminded him.

Because I was capo.

I knew well enough that the best-laid plans often went to shit. So I had plans A through E. And not one of those included Elena Lombardi.

They couldn't.

CHAPTER TWENTY-SIX

DANTE

I heard it the moment the elevator doors parted.

The music.

The very quality of it had transformed my apartment from the familiar masculine oasis I'd spent the last three months of my life locked inside into something ethereal. I could picture the Italian countryside outside Tore's house as if I'd stepped through a looking glass. The olive trees bursting with tangy fruit, the sloping waves of hillside gone from green to gold under the summer's intense rays. I was reminded of the first time I'd visited as a boy, the wonder I'd felt at seeing grapes on the vine, the tart burst of an unripe merlot exploding like a sour grenade on my tongue. I'd always enjoyed music, but I'd never been to see a concert pianist, and now I wondered how I could have been so remiss.

Because the magic Elena pulled from that instrument was art I felt plucking at the strings of my own soul.

The last of the sunset spilled syrupy light like apricot juice through the windows, the glistening of it pooling directly under the grand piano no one ever played in the corner of my living room.

She sat on the bench, head bowed as if in prayer, eyes closed lightly, lids just touching as she moved with the power of the song that flowed through her fingers and into the keys. Her hair was longer than it had been when I first met her, tumbling down her shoulders, a shifting, shimmering mass of carmine silk. The bare skin of her arms was pebbled with goose bumps as if she was just as affected by the force of her song.

I moved closer.

Wild dogs and armed *Cosa Nostra soldati* couldn't have kept me from moving closer to witness Elena Lombardi like I had never seen her before.

It was different this time than the first when she had played such a sad tune in her brownstone that night I showed up to test her mettle. The notes she stroked softly out of the ivory and black keys weren't sad or lonely.

They were bright as the syrupy sun, as that burst of tart grape juice on my tongue.

This was the reason there was music; when words suffered from limitations, and the only way you could express those gargantuan nameless emotions was through song.

I wanted to know if she played it for me.

If the gold bright notes were about us.

With Elena, it was never as straightforward as simply asking

402

her for the answer. Like music from the keys, it had to be coaxed out with masterful hands.

So I didn't say a word as I crossed the room on silent, impatient strides. The sound swelled vividly all around us, so she didn't notice when I stopped just a hairsbreadth away from her, swaying back in its black nightgown.

I didn't want to disturb the sonata, but my hands burned, and the only thing that could put out the fire was the cool touch of her skin against mine. Gently, I whispered my fingertips up her slender biceps, over her shoulders, and gathered her wine-red hair in my hands.

She didn't falter.

In fact, my touch seemed only to spur her through the climax of the song, her fingers like water rushing over the keys, a river of sound.

I moved the heavy length of hair over one shoulder, baring the long white column of her neck.

I needed to know if the pulse that throbbed just there beneath the skin tapped out the same tattoo as the notes she played, so I bent to press my lips to her neck. The warm, floral scent of Chanel number 5 perfumed her satin skin. So lightly against skin so soft that I barely felt it as I feathered my mouth up and down that delicate throat.

"*Sei bellissima*," I murmured as I touched my tongue to that fluttering pulse point.

It was a habit I'd built around her, this need to feel her heart beat, to feel the woman who thought she was made of ice pulse with fire.

A little shiver worked between her shoulder blades, but her fingers didn't miss their cue.

"Do you play for me, *lottatrice*? Because this sounds like the sweetest song of surrender," I continued low against her ear, my teeth scraping down the side of her throat.

The soft hiccup of breath through her parted lips. They were free of red lipstick, a natural color like ripe plum I wanted to suck into my mouth.

Seducing Elena was mesmeric. I got tangled up in the same mechanisms I used to soothe her, transfixed by her subtle, storied responses to even the slightest touch, the most innocent of phrases.

There was such longing in her, a deep well of it that until now, until me, had gone untapped.

It was drugging to know I had access to all that dormant sensuality.

My fingers moved down both sides of her neck over the long jutting bones of her collar to the expanse of skin on her chest. She shivered against me, pulling music from the piano as I pulled pleasure from her, both of us in tandem set by some invisible metronome.

Tiny straps held the lace edged silk nightgown in place on her shoulders.

I broke one beneath my forefinger and thumb.

Snap.

Barely a whisper in the music.

The fabric slid down the slope of her breast into her lap, revealing a peaked nipple adorning the soft swell.

Snap.

The other gave way, baring her chest entirely.

Still, she played.

"Bene, Elena, suona mentre io suono te," I told her.

Good, Elena, you play while I play you.

My hands traced the underside of her breasts, testing the swell before I palmed them in my big hands. Those ruddy nipples caught between my knuckles, and gently, I pinched them.

Then, when she gasped, missing a note, I did it again.

Not so gently.

Air sucked between her teeth.

I dragged my nose behind her ear, inhaling the heady, feminine scent of her. Just that made my cock kick hard in protest within the confines of my trousers.

I'd never been so affected by a woman.

Because Elena wasn't just gorgeous. Every single aspect of her fascinated me. I felt like an explorer discovering new lands as I rolled her nipples in my fingers and scratched my short nails lightly over the twin swells of her breasts. Every sensation I eked out of her was a fucking wonder.

"I'm going to fuck you like this," I promised her darkly, my excitement surpassing the tempo of her song, ratcheting too high to continue like this.

I could still feel the impossibly snug squeeze of her walls around me as I wedged myself inside her. The way she'd shouted as she came, a coarse hallelujah of shock and awe. The way she'd rippled around me, clutched me to her as if any space between our bodies was unbearable.

I was wholly consumed by the need to be inside her again.

Impatient now, I left her swollen breasts, one hand arrowing up to her neck so I could hold that slender column in my palm, her femininity against my strength oddly compelling. The other slid, fingers and palms wide and claiming, over her quivering belly, under the pooled silk to the apex of her thighs.

She wasn't wearing anything beneath the nightgown.

"You wanted me to find you like this," I murmured against her neck, teeth plucking at her skin sharply so she hissed. "You played like the piper to beckon me here. Were you hoping I would touch you like this? Did you fantasize about this moment?"

The song shifted from one to the next, this composition warm and languid, honey spilling from the ivories.

"Because, Elena," I continued as my hand cupped her entire wet mound. *"Nemmeno immagini cosa ho intenzione di farti."*

You cannot even imagine what I am going to do to you.

I hunched over her slightly until the angle was right and curled two of my thick fingers inside her hot cunt. Her head fell back against my shoulder, eyes fluttering closed as I began to rub them against her front wall, the heel of my hand pressing firmly into the swollen bud of her clit.

406

"I'm going to make you come like this on my hand, and you are going to play for me all the way through your climax," I ordered. "Because I want to watch you fail. I want to see you lose control just for me."

She shivered, her nipples hard enough to cut glass, her hips rolling gently against my ministrations.

Still, she played, the notes sluggish, the song fading as if we'd walked away into another room.

It only made me play her harder. I plucked at those achy nipples until they throbbed while my other hand owned her pussy, pressing and stretching the tight walls to accommodate a third finger. I wanted her stuffed full of me. Following the impulse, I brought my free hand to her mouth and offered her my fingers to suck.

After a brief, humming hesitation, her mouth closed over my digits, her tongue sliding along the grooves.

"I can feel how much you want to orgasm for me," I purred into her ear because every time I spoke filthy words, her sweet cunt tightened and pulsed, and her skin flushed a deep red.

She was embarrassed by her reaction, but it only heightened her response.

"You're going to come all over my fingers for me, Elena." She panted, her fingers trembling on the keys, her legs shaking beneath the piano. "And then I'm going to bend you over this instrument and bury myself inside you while you are still coming."

"Dante," she gasped, that same edge of fear in her tone as from the night before.

This was new for her.

Not sex.

But the intimacy of taking pleasure from her lover, of wanting intercourse to satisfy her own longing.

Fuck, it was gorgeous.

"*Si, bella*," I encouraged her as she gave up trying to play, one hand slamming down over the keys discordantly. "Break apart. Come for me. And say the name of your capo when you do."

That did it.

Her neck arched as she threw her head back, eyes squeezed shut, legs stiff and straight, core tense before the explosion.

And then *bam*.

She broke.

Cries fell from her lax mouth as she trembled softly against me, hands sliding from the keys to grip the piano bench as she shuddered through her second orgasm.

She was such beautiful chaos, such a windstorm of contradictions that even she was helpless to understand their currents. Watching her break apart was as compelling as standing in the middle of a tempest as it surged through the streets of town, ripping apart buildings, tearing up trees. The sheer power of her splendor and intelligence was enough to raze even a man like me to the very ground.

Whatever softness I'd been able to retain shattered as I held her through her climax. A roar built in my gut, a possessive, almost jealous rage that I hadn't been seated inside her to the hilt while she came.

So I did as I promised her.

I dragged her to her feet, lifted one of her legs to place it on the keys with a cacophonous clang to get access to those gorgeous, dripping folds.

"Hold yourself open for me," I ordered as I unbuckled my belt, unzipped, and pulled my aching, leaking cock from my pants.

Her fingers shook as she reached back with one hand to hesitantly hold the cheek of her raised leg.

"That's it," I praised her warmly, running my hands all over every inch of her body I could reach, currying her like I would a nervous mare. She settled under my touch, arching into every passing stroke. "You are breathtaking like this. Not because you are naked, but because you are vulnerable and for a man like me? There is no bigger turn-on."

A little whimper escaped her mouth as she pressed her torso to the lacquered piano top and canted her hips just a little higher.

I took the invitation for what it was and stepped closer, guiding my cock to her slick, pink folds. The first touch of my head to her heat made me hiss. The first gliding inch of my shaft inside her little pussy made my head feel like it was going to pop off.

"I've got to fuck you hard," I gritted out, sweat beading on my brow from the effort of my restraint. "I've got to own this sweet cunt, Elena. Tell me you want it."

"I do." The words were almost sobbed as if she couldn't bear the truth of them any more than she could bear to keep them unsaid. "Please, Dante."

"You know I love to hear you say that," I ground out as I pulled back completely, just the tip of my cock at her entrance. "Say it again, and I'll show you what it's like to fuck a capo."

Her entire body shuddered violently as she clung to the piano, the knee propped on the keys jostling errant notes. "Please, please. *Per piacere. Per favore. Ti prego,*" she chanted please in every way she could think of, mindless with need.

My next thrust sent me straight to the root inside her.

Together, we cried out with the sheer beauty of it.

But it wasn't enough.

No matter how hard I fucked her, it couldn't satisfy the bestial craving inside me.

The piano shook and jangled with sound as I thrust her again and again into it, her hands and raised leg banging into the keys.

"I need more," she cried out, shaking her head. She arched her back as if she was trying to climb out of her skin.

"I'll give it to you," I promised, covering her back to clasp my teeth around her neck in a way that made me want to roar with pride.

I pinned her there with my teeth and my body, one hand diving around her hip to frame her swollen clit with my fingers, sliding back and forth in her wet until the friction built like flame.

"You're going to make me come," she wheezed in Italian as she braced for impact. "*Dio mio*, Dante, oh my God."

I took a risk and reared my hand back from her clit before slapping my palm lightly back down over it.

The single slap popped the top off her climax.

"Fuck," she cried out, scrambling against the keys as she thrashed and trembled and kicked out against the force of the pleasure ripping through her.

I held on tight, her slick limbs slipping against my own. Her pussy clenched me so tightly I couldn't thrust, only seat myself to the root and feel her break apart all around me.

It was enough to feel that. To know I had made Elena Lombardi fracture so beautifully. To know I was the only man who had ever brought her such pleasure.

I ground my hips even deeper and spilled myself inside her. My forehead pressed to her shoulder, and I came and came and came, filling her with my seed.

Vaguely, I was aware of her gasp as she felt me kick and spurt within her.

Not so vaguely, I was aware that she reached one hand back to press into my hip in order to hold me closer.

After, squeezed dry like a used tea towel, I sprawled against her, panting hard as I struggled to remember my own name.

"Well," Elena's soft voice sounded after a moment, muffled by her hair and the weight of me plastered on top of her. "I'm not sure I'll ever be able to play the piano again after that without becoming aroused."

I laughed, the sound deep in my belly, the feel of it almost as good as the climax she'd wrung from me. Giving in to my affectionate impulses, I rubbed my nose into the back of her hair before I stood to help peel her off the piano. When I turned her in my arms, she wasn't smiling, but there was a softness in her eyes, the gray velvet with contentment.

It just about took my breath away.

Soft, content Elena.

Somehow even better than the weapon of a woman she presented to the world.

This Lena was only for me.

I pressed another kiss to her forehead, needing to touch her again.

"Maybe we should do that on my desk," I suggested lasciviously. "It would make my accounting much more interesting."

She giggled—*giggled*—and I wondered if she was a little love drunk, climax high.

I didn't want her to close down just yet, insisting she had to sleep in her own fucking bed and leave me there in a room still echoing with her song, still perfumed with us. So, I tugged her over to one of the couches and then wrapped her in a bear hug before lifting her from the ground and flopping to my back on the cushions.

"You oaf," she protested without fire as she tried to get up.

I wrapped my legs around her too, pinning her against me. When she canted her head back to look into my eyes with a raised brow, I winked.

"What? Capos need cuddles too."

"Ridiculous," she muttered, but a smile haunted her lips. "How am I supposed to resist you when you act like this? The big bad capo and the boyish charmer with the big heart."

"Awe, she thinks I have a heart."

I winced when she pinched my side in retribution.

We were quiet for a moment, the kind of easy silence that doesn't need filling. I focused on recovering my equilibrium after my savage orgasm, already planning what I might do to her and with her next.

"Aren't you scared at all?" she asked softly, stroking her fingers through my chest hair as if she wasn't even aware she did it. "You're on trial for murder, Dante. That's serious."

"No," I said honestly. "No matter what happens, I'm not going to jail."

She blinked at me, and I knew she wanted to ask questions, real questions about my business. She had been so careful to avoid any topic that might be too intimate or too criminal until then. But she was curious, and it excited me to see that the truth didn't make her flinch anymore.

It made her think.

Still, she didn't ask. Instead, she put her cheek to my chest and cuddled just a little bit closer. "It won't be easy, but I promise I'll do whatever I can to get you free."

Fuck me, but this woman could be sweet under that brittle shell.

"I know," I told her because I did.

"I'm happy," she admitted after a minute, almost bashfully, adorably girlish. "For a long time, I've felt as if I didn't deserve that."

Her words nearly winded me. I squeezed her, wishing I could extract the poison of her self-loathing through sheer will. "Why wouldn't you deserve that?"

For a short pause, she seemed to drown in all the things she wanted to articulate but couldn't. "I'm not a very nice person sometimes. I-I lash out at people when I'm hurt and say horrible things. When I found out about Daniel and Giselle, I told them both they would never be a part of the family, that I would always hate them. I meant it at the time, and a part of me means it still, but…I ended up alienating my entire family because of it. Even though I was the victim, I ended up acting in a way that made me the villain of the whole situation." She shrugged soddenly. "It's been hard to live with that."

"Not everything is so black and white, Elena," I murmured as I slid a lock of her deep red hair between my fingers. "Between the hero and the villain, there is the anti-hero. A person who may do evil deeds and seem unscrupulous, but who, within their own set of morals, possesses a big heart and the willingness to protect that which they know to be good. I know you well enough now that whatever cruelty you gave those two stemmed from the fact that they didn't love you enough to treat you with kindness."

Her sigh was accompanied by a shudder. "You can't know that, for sure. But...I like that you give me the benefit of the doubt." She tipped her head to the ceiling as if to confess to God. "It's you that's made me happy today. A man I thought I'd hate is now one of the men I most admire. I just don't know what that means."

Her admiration felt like an anointment from God.

"It doesn't have to mean anything," I assured her. "Happiness is the point."

She pursed her lips around her knee-jerk reaction to argue with me, then sighed. "You make everything sound so simple when it's not."

She was right; it wasn't. But lying there naked and cooling after some of the most intense sex I'd ever had, I couldn't help but wonder if it could be.

If there was a way to ensure we could be happy together for longer.

Maybe even forever.

CHAPTER TWENTY-SEVEN

elena

It snowed the day we finally heard when Dante's case would go to trial.

April 17th.

That unlucky number.

The number of death.

I sat at the table staring blindly out the window after Yara passed on the news. I should have been working, filing some of the cases a senior partner had given me to work on, or putting my plan for the bookie who had rolled on Dante into action.

But I just sat there and stared out the glass as the first December snow fell on Manhattan and turned the calamitous, colorful city into a muffled world of white.

I officially had an end date for the risk I was taking that could make my career or destroy it.

An end date for my assignation with the capo.

So why did I feel so...out of sorts? Gloomier than I had in months, since well before I'd moved into Dante's vivacious home.

Maybe that was it. I would just miss his company. I would miss his crew and our routine. I would miss Rora's precocious chatter and inability to cook without making a mess. I'd miss Bambi's sweet laughter and gentle presence. I'd even miss Tore, in a way, though we never conversed very much. I'd miss him because I liked to see the way he made Dante smile.

I groaned, dropping my head to the conference room desk.

This was *not* good.

In the week since the car chase that had culminated in our tryst on his Ferrari, Dante and I had found time and reason to touch every day. He'd fucked me on the piano, in that colossal shower of his, and in his office pinned to the same bookshelf where he'd pressed that searing, significant little kiss to my neck weeks before. We came together explosively every single time.

I knew logically it was because Monica's procedure had worked. The painful, stunting cysts on my ovaries that had kept me from feeling anything more than lukewarm pleasure were gone. After nearly two years of intense therapy, I was finally in a good place with my body and my past.

It could have been any man after that to make me orgasm.

But it wasn't just any man.

It was Dante Salvatore, the black-eyed capo.

How could I have allowed this to happen?

I was in no way objective about him as a client anymore.

In fact, I was in danger of losing my blind respect for the law and completely compromising my previous hardline views of morality because the truth was, they were not always properly aligned.

Dante was one of the best men I knew, and I could admit that now.

But he was also, without any doubt, a criminal of the highest order.

The old Elena would have wanted him behind bars for life.

The new Elena couldn't imagine even a single day without him.

It was a complete mess.

Worse, I was worried about him.

Worried that April 17th would come and Yara, the legal team, and I would fail to defend him properly. That the most vital man I'd ever known would be forced to spend the rest of his life behind bars.

I simply couldn't fathom that, and I didn't want to.

So I found myself doing something incredibly stupid.

I collected my purse and coat and left the office just after noon. A cab took me deep into the Bronx, to a heavily Irish neighborhood with a local watering hole called Father Patrick's.

I'd overheard Dante's crew mention it in conjunction with Thomas Kelly, the Irish mobster.

The man my father was working with.

I told myself I was being stupid even as I paid for the cab and slipped into the cold air, the flurries falling densely now, so thick

I could barely see across the street to the bar. I ducked into a little convenient store, bought a cheap, watery coffee, and stood at the window while I drank it. Watching.

Seamus Moore was a drunk and a gambler.

As a child, I could remember walking up to him passed out on the kitchen table surrounded by bottles. I'd always ushered him to bed before the others woke up, but the scent of hard liquor was burned into the grain of the wood table.

If this was where his crew hung out, he'd be there, even at just after one in the afternoon.

I only waited for forty minutes when I caught sight of vivid red hair tucked into a black knit cap. He moved quickly, braced against the wind, pausing for a moment at the bar door before ducking inside.

I sucked in a deep breath and called the number I'd looked up on my phone.

"Father Patrick's," a gruff voice answered. "What?"

"I'm looking for Seamus."

A pause then a disgustingly phlegm-filled sniff. "Not my problem."

"No," I agreed. "But he might be interested. Tell him it's his daughter."

Another pause, then, "Wait."

I waited, picking at a hangnail on my thumb until it bled, red running down to the inside of my wrist, staining my cream coat.

"Cosima?" Seamus said, a little eager and breathless.

I fought the urge to roll my eyes. "I doubt your favorite daughter would bother with you after you sold her to repay your gambling debts."

"Elena," he said, this time on a sigh. "Of course, it would be you. The only one of my children with more balls than sense."

I didn't have a response for his inaccurate statement, so I just cut to the chase. "I want to make a trade."

"A trade?"

"Have you gone deaf in your old age?" I asked sweetly. "A trade. I have information on the Salvatore borgata I think you would find...interesting. In exchange, though, I want to know what kind of relationship you have with the di Carlos."

There was a little pause, and then he said suspiciously, "Don't jerk me around, Elena. I'm not some *il novellino*. I've been doing this since you were in diapers."

"Then you should recognize a good offer when you hear it," I countered calmly.

"Why are you doing this? You told me you hated me, never wanted to see me again. Now you're offering to help out your dear old da?"

"No, I still hate you," I assured him. "But I hate Dante Salvatore more. He's unscrupulous and evil."

The words felt bitter on my tongue, but Seamus wanted to believe me so badly that he took the bait even though it stunk.

"We should meet," he decided. "Phones are too sketchy. You could be recording me for all I know."

"Okay," I agreed. "Bethesda Terrace at six tonight. I expect you to bring evidence I can use."

"You want to use it to put the di Carlos away?" he guessed on a laugh. "That's my girl. Never happy with what you have, gotta go for more."

His words burned in me because before then, they'd always been true.

I'd never been content.

Not even at the height of my relationship with Daniel as a shiny new associate at Fields, Harding & Griffith.

It had taken losing everything to realize how empty I'd felt as I chased and chased for more. I'd never taken the time to appreciate those things I already had. I'd let my relationships with my siblings' waste away. I'd prioritized my career so much I'd never made many friends, and I'd let the only wonderful man I'd ever wanted slip through my fingers because I was always running from my fears.

This time, I didn't want more.

This time, I only wanted to keep what I had.

"I'll see you at six," I told Seamus, and then I hung up.

But I didn't leave the little Russian-owned convenience store.

I waited for another twenty minutes until the familiar redhead ducked back out of the bar and headed west down the street.

I followed him.

It was actually much easier than I would have thought. His overlong red hair and beard were an easy beacon, but the snow made visibility difficult, obscuring the faces of the people in the streets. It was a busy enough neighborhood that I wasn't the only one behind Seamus, heading away from the Bronx toward Madison Avenue Bridge.

Of course, I was never going to turn on Dante.

The thought of it made my stomach cramp.

But my dad, the same man who had sold his own goddamn daughter into sexual slavery, didn't understand the concept of loyalty, so he had believed me all too easily.

I had counted on that same lack of dependability to lead my father to betray me. So I wasn't surprised when he huddled under the awning of a gas station just beside the bridge and waited.

I did too, from across the street pretending to window shop at a discount furniture warehouse.

I assumed he was meeting the di Carlo brothers or Thomas Kelly.

But I was not prepared who did pull up to meet him.

A sleek gold Bentley pulled into the gas station and up to a pump. Moments later, a man got out of the car and rounded the hood to pump his own gas.

He wasn't tall or particularly striking, but I knew who it was even from across the street, traffic and snow obscuring my vision.

His brown hair was swept back in its usual side part, the long black trench mostly obscuring his signature blue suit. He had the look of someone in power, an officer in the military or a police captain, his face almost austere in its sternness.

Dennis O'Malley.

The United States Attorney for the Southern New York District.

I blinked and breathed, too shocked to function, as Seamus meandered over to the pump station and leaned against the other side, pulling out his phone as if to text someone. But I could see his mouth moving.

Dennis was meeting with Seamus Moore.

What. The. Fuck?

When we'd spoken about my dad, he seemed so unaware of his past, his criminal history, but here he was having some kind of cloak and dagger meeting with him after I'd called to say I was going to snitch on Dante?

Dennis started speaking, prompting me to remember why I was there in the first place. I tugged off my leather glove with my teeth and raised my phone to take a video, my thumb tapping the photo button as I recorded. It wasn't the best quality and, if I hadn't seen Dennis's face hundreds of times in the past few years, maybe I would have had a hard time identifying him. But there was no doubt in my mind who that man was.

Fury sparked in my gut and more than a little outrage.

I'd been indignant when Yara had turned out to be corrupted by the mafia, but it made sense. Fields, Harding & Griffith were among the top firms in the city, but they were all notorious for taking on unsavory clients. They were about money and the bottom line, not putting the right kind of bad guys away for life.

But Dennis...

Dennis represented an institution and an aspect of law I'd always admired. He was supposed to put criminals behind bars, not associate with them outside of the courts.

It was a shocking betrayal even though Dennis himself didn't mean anything to me.

It was the betrayal of my own ideals, this construct I'd created like a house of cards in my own mind. The good guys versus the bad guys.

I'd allowed myself to be teamed up with the bad ones because I'd been told I was bad all my life. First by Seamus, then Christopher, and when my own family shunned me for my treatment of Giselle after she and Daniel cheated on me.

I'd allowed that for myself because I felt I deserved it, but I'd secretly always wanted to be one of those good guys.

And now I was faced with the fact that it was all an illusion.

Dennis was just as motivated to win as we were. His greed and pride had corrupted him just as easily as the Irish mob had.

For one long moment, I was deeply disoriented. I didn't know how to evaluate anything or anyone anymore.

On the one hand was Dennis, a man who was renowned for putting criminals away, who was making a bid for the Senate on the basis of his superhero record.

And on the other was Dante.

The most infamous mafioso of the last twenty years, a man who was on trial for a murder I knew he hadn't committed just as I knew he had committed others.

I realized I had this idea of a hero as someone who was socially accepted, someone who was revered by the masses. But heroism didn't always arrive dressed in white and topped with a halo or on the back of some shining steed.

Heroism was about your willingness to right wrongs, to sacrifice your own comfort and safety to affect change when you crossed something that needed changing. It was assuming responsibility for people who didn't have the power to stand up for themselves.

It was about being brave enough to live life by your own rules and accepting who you were, flaws and all.

I stood on that snowy corner for a long time after Dennis and Seamus parted, letting my entire world view crumble at my feet, and when I felt my skin frozen but my blood on fire, I felt lighter than I had in years.

I gave the footage to Yara.

She didn't ask any questions. Instead, she'd raised a single dark brow and called for an emergency meeting with the prosecution before Judge Hartford.

I was giddy as we cabbed to the courthouse, my thigh bouncing with nerves the entire way.

Yara didn't seem to share in my excitement. If anything, she seemed oddly morose, her eyes, when they met mine, almost sorry.

I didn't understand until we were in the judge's chambers.

Martin Hartford was wearing a suit, sitting in one of two leather chairs drinking a glass of brown liquor when we were allowed entry to the room.

In the other chair sat Dennis O'Malley.

I frowned at him as he tipped his own glass to me.

"Scotch?" he offered with that handsome stock smile, wooden around the edges.

"What is this?" I asked even though it wasn't my place to do so.

"Martin and I were just catching up when you called," Dennis explained mildly. "We're old friends. What's it been now, Marty? Twenty-two years?"

"Twenty-three," he corrected.

"Twenty-three." Dennis pointed at one of the old photos on Judge Hartford's wall. "That's the two of us as lowly first years at the DA's office. We both worked on Reno Maglione's case."

Reno Maglione was one of the most prolific turncoats in American mafia history.

"We've been putting away the scum of the streets for a long time," he continued, raising his glass for the judge to click it against his own. "Here's to many more years, my friend."

Beside me, Yara sighed softly.

"You met with Seamus Moore today," I accused, shocked by the proceedings. "We're demanding a mistrial on the basis that you're directly involved with the Irish mob."

"He was an informant," he said with a shrug.

"That is not the proper way to meet an informant," I reminded him, feeling heat build under my skin. "We will call you to testify to that fact on the stand, and you will be forced to recuse yourself. A lawyer representing a case cannot be a witness in the same trial."

"Very good, Ms. Lombardi." He laughed. "A plus student indeed. Only, this isn't a mock trial. This is real life and real court. I'm certainly not going to recuse myself from this case. If we win this, I'm well on my way to being the next state senator."

I looked at Judge Hartford incredulously, but his face was entirely placid.

"Fitzgerald's term as mayor is almost up," Dennis told us slyly, leaning forward to clap the judge on the knee. "I think Marty would be a shoo-in."

Oh my God.

I couldn't believe this.

It was beyond comprehension.

This was the kind of thing that happened in Italy, not in America. Wasn't it?

From the look on Yara's face, it wasn't.

There was corruption everywhere, and it seemed I'd just been too willful and naïve to see it.

"If that's all?" Judge Hartford asked. "I'll see you all in court on April 17th."

I stood there mutely for a moment before Yara took my elbow and led me from the room. It was only when we were in the car on the way back to the office that I finally found my voice.

"You knew this would happen."

Her sigh was long, an unraveling of weariness. "You're still young, Elena. When you play with the big dogs, you learn they have very different rules."

"As in *none*," I intoned. "Dennis O'Malley met with a known associate of Thomas Kelly, a mobster with ties to the di Carlo family, and nothing happens? The trial just goes on as planned."

"Why do you think I feel so justified using our own unscrupulous means?" Yara demanded. "This is how it's done, Elena."

"Yeah, well, it's fucked," I proclaimed.

"You're worried about him."

I didn't bother denying it, but I didn't respond either, crossing my legs as I stared out the window at the snow.

"I wouldn't worry too much. You're just entering this world, but Dante has been king of his corner of it for years. He knows what he's doing."

I didn't respond because the truth was, I was reeling.

I was desolate because I felt I had let Dante down. I'd been so sure Seamus would lead me to something that could help him, but if anything, it had only made the entire situation worse.

I was scared that Dennis would do anything to get Dante convicted.

I was petrified he would win and Dante would spend the rest of his life in a federal penitentiary.

I was horrified that a man I was coming to care for more than I was ready to admit was going to leave me.

And I'd be alone again, somehow even more so than I was before.

CHAPTER TWENTY-EIGHT

elena

Later that evening, I was just packing up to leave work early because I hadn't been able to focus since our return from the courthouse when my phone rang.

I didn't recognize the number, and wondering if it was Gideone di Carlo again, I almost didn't answer it.

At the last minute, I swiped to accept the call and put the phone between my shoulder and ear as I continued to pack up.

"Hello?"

There was a pause that sent chills down my spine.

"Hello?" I repeated, my eyes scanning the bullpen for signs of anyone that shouldn't be there.

"I'm disappointed in you, *cara*," Seamus finally said in a soft voice.

My heart stopped. "How did you get my number?"

"I have more than that," he assured me. "I know where Mama is right now in Soho at her little restaurant. I know the address of

Giselle's apartment in Brooklyn...I'm looking at her right now, in fact. What a beautiful little girl Genevieve is."

My breath froze in my lungs. Could it be possible that Seamus was this evil?

"What are you doing?" I asked slowly. "Don't bother Giselle and her daughter."

"No?" He laughed. "Always trying to protect your family, even from your own dad. Even when Giselle stole your boyfriend. Poor little Elena. The family never did treat us right."

The ice melted into nausea as I thought about Seamus watching Giselle and Genevieve, both of them completely unaware.

"You don't want anything from them," I reminded him. "What do you want from me?"

"Clever girl," he praised. "I want you to know that your little stunt today cost me big time. Kelly is furious. We got a delicate balance going right now, and you nearly broke that."

"You want an apology?" I couldn't stop the incredulity from seeping into my tone. "There are a few I think you should get off your chest first."

"I didn't want to have to do this." His voice was sad, almost like a little boy filled with contriteness for doing something he shouldn't. "But you gave me no choice. Instead of standing beside your father, with your family like I raised you to do, you turned your back on me, and now I have *no choice.*"

"Just like you had no choice to sell Cosima," I snapped. "She made you gamble any money you ever made? She made you so in

432

debt to the Camorra that her beauty was the only chip you had left to play?"

"*Stai zitto* about Cosima," he roared through the phone.

There was a moment of silence as he collected himself.

"You're going to meet me downstairs in ten minutes," he told me, calm once more. "You're going to get in the black sedan idling at the curb, and you aren't going to disconnect this call until you do so."

"No," I said simply.

Another gusty, dramatic sigh. "Can you hear this, Elena?"

There was a change in sound as he put the phone on speaker, the greater noises of the world around him apparent to me too. Distantly, I heard female laughter.

"Giselle is enjoying showing her daughter snow for the first time," Seamus narrated.

There was a crunch of snow as he moved, the sound of that familiar voice growing louder.

"*Ma petite choux*," I could hear Giselle sing from somewhere too close to Seamus. "Look at you, loving the snow!"

My belly burned as if I'd swallowed lit coal.

"Don't do this, Dad," I asked him softly. "Please, just listen to yourself. That's your daughter and your first grandchild right there. Stop this. If you stop this, it's not too late. You can make amends to everyone. You can meet Genevieve properly, and we can have a relationship again."

He laughed, but the sound was broken and lopsided, ugly in

my ears. "No…no, I know it's too late for that. I've looked into the eyes of two of my daughters, and all I've seen is hate. You can't fool me again, Elena. You might be a fighter, but you got that from me." Then quietly, almost as if he didn't know he even spoke the words. "I'm just trying to fight to stay alive here."

"I can help you," I tried again, so desperate I could taste the metallic panic on my tongue. "Dante could help you."

I offered, and I knew in my heart he would. Even if they were enemies, Dante would help Seamus for Cosima.

He'd help Seamus for me.

"Five minutes now, Elena," he said again, his voice at full force, whatever moment of reflection he had succumbed to totally forgotten. "Don't be late. I'd rather not have to interrupt Giselle's day. Remember, don't hang up. I'll be listening."

He went quiet, but the connection didn't drop, and I knew he'd muted me.

I kept the phone pressed to my ear for a long moment as I fought not to cry.

Get it together, Lombardi, I ordered myself.

First, I sucked in a deep, stabilizing breath to clear some of the fearful fog from my mind, and then I stared at my phone. I could still text even with the line occupied.

There didn't seem to be any kind of quick fix for this situation.

If I didn't go, I couldn't put it past Seamus to abduct Giselle and Genevieve. He'd done worse before, and he was between a rock and a hard place. Animals had chewed off their own limbs for

434

less, and Seamus was just that— a cornered monster desperate to survive.

No matter what happened between us, there was no way in any world I could let someone hurt Giselle and her baby.

Absolutely no way.

Even though tears burned the backs of my eyes because I honestly didn't see how I would get out of this situation intact, I shouldered my purse, swung on my coat, and left the office.

Adriano wasn't waiting for me outside like he usually was even though I'd texted him fifteen minutes ago to tell him I was ready to leave. Worry twined with my panic and made me want to puke.

Before I left the security area, I did the one thing I could to ensure the best chance of this working out.

I texted Dante.

And then I strode across the lobby, pushed through the glass doors, and held my head high as I moved toward the black sedan idling at the curb.

Once, Dante had lectured me about sacrifice, but I didn't truly understand until I opened the door and slid into the interior of that car.

"Hello," Thomas Kelly said with a wide grin, and a moment later, he was on me.

CHAPTER TWENTY-NINE

DANTE

I was sitting at my desk listening to Roberto Brambilla detail his plan to use a local motorcycle gang to mule the drugs we brought in from the Basante family when a shudder seized my shoulders and wrenched at my spine painfully. My whole body seized with the sensation, then left in its wake a horrifying certainty.

Something monumentally wrong had happened.

My first thought was of Cosima and Alexander, so far away in England. My mind raced through theories, a bitter old member of the defunct Order of Dionysus who had escaped the judicial noose returning to kill them, an associate of Noel's bent on revenge, to the more innocuous, a fall from Cosima's Golden Akhal-Teke horse, Alexander in a motor accident.

Tore was at his house in upstate New York for the week, and even though I'd just gotten off the phone with him, I sent him a text coded to ask if anything was amiss.

I didn't think of Elena until I was already calming down, having convinced myself premonitions didn't exist, it was just a passing chill.

The moment her name sounded in my mind, I knew with bone-deep certainty, something had happened to her.

"Call Adriano," I barked out to Marco, who was in the room with Roberto and me. "I want to know where Elena Lombardi is right fucking now."

The claws eviscerating my gut, reducing my insides to ground meat, told me they wouldn't find her. I ignored the men in our meeting, opening the drawer in my desk to reach for my two cell phones.

I had a text from Elena on one of them.

Seamus was going to take Giselle and Genevieve, maybe Mama, too. I had to go with them. I know you'll find me, capo.

Xx,

E

Fury like I hadn't known in years boiled my blood, eviscerating everything else in its path until I was a pure flame locked in human flesh.

A moment later, Chen appeared in my office doorway, his skin whitewashed with panic and his mouth tight, that stretched leash on my control snapped, and I exploded.

"Where the fuck is she?" I roared as I swept everything off my desk--computer, lamp, paperweight, stacks of money--and fisted my hands on the surface to lean over it into the men who filed into my office with their fucking tails between their legs. "Were you not supposed to keep an eye on her, motherfuckers?"

"*Si, capo*," Chen said in flawless Italian, his jaw clenched so tight it was a wonder the words made it out of his mouth. "Adriano isn't answering his phone either."

"*Figlio di puttana*," I cursed savagely as I ripped my hands through my hair. "*Va bene, va bene*, we are going to fix this. Get every motherfucking capo on the phone, Frankie. Marco, Chen, hit up Father Patrick's. The *bastardi* Irishmen have taken Elena. Burn the fucking place to the ground if one of those assholes doesn't give you answers. Jaco, you hit the streets. I want you talking to every goddamn person we know."

Everyone nodded except Jaco, who worried his lip between his teeth as he lingered in the door.

"What're you gonna do, Boss?"

I pinned him with an impatient glare. "You volunteering to take my mind off it? I could use a punching bag."

His eyes widened slightly before he nodded and beat it out of my office.

Then, I did what I hadn't done in the history of my leadership of the Family.

I called the Commission.

"Accardi," I said when Orazio, the head of the Accardi family, answered the phone with a staccato grunt. "A woman's been taken.

439

I need to mobilize the families to find out any info they can get on who might have taken Elena Lombardi."

There was a long pause filled with heavy, choking silence.

"Dante," he finally said in his nasal voice, disrespecting me by addressing a Don by his first name. "You misplaced your hot *figa* of a lawyer, ugh?"

The case on my phone creaked and then cracked sharply in my hand as I squeezed it in my fury. "No, Accardi, she's been goddamn taken. She was snatched by the Irish. If they torture her, we're all in hot shit. So, mobilize your goddamn *soldati* and get me some information."

"This sounds like a personal problem, *bimbo*," Accardi drawled, having the balls to call me the Italian equivalent of kiddo. "Deal with your own shit like a real man."

And then, the *stronzo* hung up on me.

Within thirty minutes, every single one of the other Dons had done the same thing.

Frankie was in my office to report at the end of the last call with Maglione, and he watched dispassionately as I ripped a Picasso painting from the wall and broke the frame over my knee.

"Got a call back from Thumper Ricci," he said while I stood there panting, trying to control the fury rolling through me like the waves off Napoli in the stormy winter months. "Said one of his men saw Elena over in the Bronx by Madison Ave Bridge this afternoon. Said she was watching two men talk at a gas station."

"*Cazzo*, Francesco, I need information now," I barked.

"I know, boss," he said, completely unthreatened even though I felt one second from breaking someone's neck.

Elena was taken.

After I'd fucking promised her I'd keep her safe, after she'd finally given in to this simmering, fucking sensational pull between us, and I'd already betrayed her.

Just like the other *bastardi* in her life.

"D, I know you're angry enough to power a nuclear bomb right now, but you gotta get your shit tight. We need to use our brains here, not our brawn, and you are not doing that by trashing your office."

I glared at him for a long moment, blowing hot air through my mouth, irritated with both of us because he was right.

I had to channel Elena's interminable cool.

This wasn't the time to rip things to shreds. I could do that when I found the motherfucker Irishmen holding her.

Without saying a word to Frankie, I grabbed my cell and made two calls.

Caelian Accardi and then Santo Belcante.

They both agreed to help with limited soldiers. We didn't want to blow our long game before it had even begun. But I was grateful for their help, and it wasn't something I'd ever forget.

This was why I'd met with them.

Because the Old Guard was stuck in the past, antiquated and close enough to death to merit a little push in the right direction.

The Dons, all of them, would die for this one day.

"We've got everyone looking," Frankie told me. "Liliana and her crew even went out. We'll find her. I got an algorithm searching through traffic cam and security footage right now."

I raked a hand through my hair, almost pulling out the strands.

There was no way I could stay in this goddamn cage while Elena was out there waiting for me to get to her.

"It's time."

Frankie blinked at me. "No, I told you, I can disable the anklet, but I can't get it back online. You've got one shot at leaving here, D, and you won't be coming back."

"I know."

We stared at each other for a long minute where I imagined each tick of the clock.

"You doing this because of Cosima or because of the girl?" he finally asked.

I almost winced because not once had Cosima crossed my mind. "Elena, you fool."

He nodded curtly. "Fine, come into the living room. If you want to fuck all our plans to high hell for a woman, God knows I'm not in a position to stop you."

I got a call twenty minutes later.

"Boss," Marco said. "I found Addie. He's in rough shape, but he can talk a bit. Told me four of them jumped him when he was coming back from the john at lunch. He was in the Subway across the street from Elena's office. Around five fifteen."

"Get him to Dr. Crown," I ordered, and then I hung up. "Is it ready?"

"As soon as we know where we're going, I'll remove the SIM card," Frankie explained as his fingers flew over the keyboard. Beside him, a mesh wire cage the size of a microwave. "Put the tracking beacon in the Faraday Cage, and I'll spoof the network so it sends the GPS location from the apartment as if it was never removed."

"*Va bene*," I said even though I didn't know the finer intricacies of the plot. I trusted Frankie to know what the hell he was talking about. "I want our crew ready to go the second we get news."

"They're ready."

"And the plane?"

"Fueled and ready at Newark. Bobbie Florentino is already onboard getting things prepped."

"Good."

"We'll find her, D."

I didn't respond.

"Boss?" Chen said into the phone.

I was pacing, the anklet heavy around my left leg as I stalked around the apartment answering phone call after phone call that led nowhere.

"What?"

"We found Kelly's piece. She went into Father Patrick's and got talking to Marco, liked the look of him." He laughed coldly. "She took him to the back for a blowie, and I was waiting. Me, she didn't like so much."

"What did you get?" I growled impatiently.

"Nothing on where he lives, but apparently, he took her to a friend's once in Marine Park. Somewhere on East 34th."

"Start knocking."

I called Daniel Sinclair.

"Hello?" he answered, his voice as coolly polite as Elena's could be.

"This is Dante," I said brusquely. "I don't have time to talk, but I wanted you to know. I think it's a good idea you get home to your wife if you aren't already. You can't get there in good time, I'll send a guy."

A pause then the sounds of someone quickly gathering their things. "I'm on my way. She's safe for now?"

"Yeah." *Thanks to Elena*, but I wouldn't tell him that.

I went to hang up when a shout made me put my ear back to the phone.

"Is it Cosima or Elena?" he asked quietly, voice vibrating with intensity.

I didn't have time for this *stronzo*, but a part of me felt for him, so I grunted. "It's none of your concern anymore. I've got it under control."

Another brief hesitation and then, "Good luck. Thank you for calling."

Two hours after Elena sent me her text, I finally got the call I'd been waiting for.

"Think they're in a white clapboard house on the corner of East 34th and Filmore," Marco whispered. "You want us to go in?"

"No," I ordered darkly, snapping my fingers at Frankie, who immediately started doing his thing on the computer. "I'll be there."

"Boss," Jaco protested as he came in from the elevator. "What the fuck are you doing?"

"I'm going to get her."

He blinked at me in shock as Frankie bent to the anklet with thin tools and started to fuck with it.

I glared at my cousin over Frankie's dark head. "You got something to say, Jaco?"

"Why the hell are you doing this?" he asked with pure exasperation. "This is what they fucking *want*. She's goddamn bait."

"You think I don't know that?" I asked low, the words dredged taken and probably hurt because of me? Why the fuck do you think I'm doing this?"

"You'll go to jail," he told me what I already knew. "You'll go to jail when you didn't even kill Giuseppe."

I didn't bother to respond to him. The plastic tracking bracelet popped off with a *click*, and Frankie quickly produced the SIM card from a tiny compartment then put them in the Faraday Box.

"You're good," he said without looking away from the blue screen of his monitor. "Go get her, and I'll see you on the other side."

I picked up my Glock from the table, shoved it into my holster, and then threw on my leather jacket before starting for the elevator.

Jaco blocked me.

"Let one of the men go," he urged. "The cops or the probation office find out you know how to disable the tracking anklet, it'll ruin everything. Why risk it for this pussy?"

"I'm fucking going," I said with deadly calm. "You want to get in my way, Jaco, be my guest, but I'll paint you black and blue with my fists and leave you for dead if I have to."

"Just let her go," he tried to reason still, his eyes almost frantic. "Don't let her make you weak."

I used my shoulder to knock him out of the way. Only when I was in the elevator did I lock eyes with him and say, "I'm not afraid of a woman, Jaco. Why are you?"

CHAPTER THIRTY

elena

It wasn't a very good plan.

I mean, really, it was clear I didn't get my brains from my father.

They were set up in the basement of some old house, the ceiling dripping steadily, the concrete subfloor stained with mysterious dark splotches. I was tied to a support pillar with zip ties around my wrists and ankles that were closed too tight. The circulation was cut off, so I struggled to stay upright on my dead-weight feet and not put more pressure on my bleeding wrists.

They didn't beat me.

Kelly and Seamus fought about whether or not to slap me around a little to see if I'd give anything up, but in the end, Seamus won. He even shot me a victorious look as if he was proud to have gone to bat for me, and I should be grateful.

I spat at his feet.

"You won't get away with this," I told them calmly. "Someone is going to find me."

They laughed, Kelly and Seamus, the four other armed men that patrolled the house.

"We're counting on it," Kelly said, moving closer to the single overhead light so I could see his smile. "The di Carlos are willing to pay like you wouldn't believe for Dante Salvatore. You're just the bait. Why do you think we tried so hard to get you that day on Staten Island?"

I rolled my eyes. "You obviously think I mean more to Mr. Salvatore than I do. I'm just a lawyer on his legal team. Despite the obvious fact that he's on house arrest, he wouldn't come for me even if he could."

"Oh?" Kelly asked, eyebrows raised to his hairline. "I didn't realize…"

He moved away to a table in the corner and then returned, tilting a piece of paper into the light.

Only, it wasn't a piece of paper.

It was a photograph.

In it, Dante had me caged against the open French doors to his balcony, his face in my neck, my eyes closed as if in ecstasy.

Obviously, they'd been watching.

"Now she's quiet." Kelly laughed, and I got the feeling he found all of this--crime, danger, and violence--fun and exciting as if it was all one big game. "Seamus, your daughter is a capo's whore."

Behind him, my dad didn't move an inch. There was a tension in him, a kind of rending down the middle as if he was tearing himself in two from the inside out. When he looked at me, his eyes were unfocused, his mouth slack. I wondered what he saw in my face, if he realized how alike we were. Not just in appearance, but in having that same quality.

I'd been trying to rip myself in two for years.

The good Elena and the bad.

How impossible that seemed now, especially watching Seamus fight himself.

He was going to lose.

As if in answer to my thought, he shook his head to clear it and then moved to the coat he'd discarded over a box. Fishing in the pocket, he produced a flask, untwisted the top, and devoured the contents in one endless gulp.

"Dad," I called, just to make it harder for him. "Dad, are you really going to let them do this?"

"They aren't doing anything," he countered, wiping the alcohol from his mouth with the back of his hand. "You're safe."

"Safe?" I echoed. "I'm tied to a pole, and I'm bleeding. Your asshole friend drugged me to get me here."

Kelly shrugged almost manically, and I realized he was definitely not all there. The thought scared me. Seamus could be reasoned with, but there was a frenetic violence to Kelly that said he couldn't be reasoned with easily.

His phone rang, and he took it into another room, shooting Seamus a careful look before leaving us alone together.

"Dad," I tried again. *"Papa, per favore, aiutami."*

Papa, please, help me.

He hesitated, and I could see that his eyes were slightly glazed over in the dim light.

"You haven't seen me in years," I coaxed. "Come closer and let me look at you."

Outside, a dog barked, startling him. His eyes darted between the boarded-up window at the top of the ceiling beside him and then to me.

"I won't help you, Elena," he told me as he came closer, standing right under the overhead light so that it cast long, ghoulish shadows over his face. "I would have tried, maybe, if you didn't try to fuck me. You followed me? Huh? Thought you could get one over on dear old dad? Well, you can't, and I'm ashamed you would even try."

Then, in Italian, he added, "You were also so ungrateful. Do you have any idea how hard I worked for our family? I provided for you. I kept you clothed and put a roof over your head. Your mother turned you against me when she fell in love with that Italian scum." He was getting worked up the way he used to when he'd been drinking, his hands gesturing wildly as he bounced on his feet. "I did *everything* for you, and what did I get? My own daughter threatened me if I didn't leave you all. Now another daughter risks my life to better her career!"

"Better my career?" I bit out, struggling as the plastic ties dug deeper into the bloody mess of my wrists. "I was trying to help the man I love."

My own words rocked through me.

Love?

"Love?" he echoed my shocked thought, then laughed so hard he almost lost his balance. "My fighter? My cold fish? You never loved me, and you never loved your family. You wouldn't have betrayed me if you did."

"You betrayed me first," I cried out. Tugging at the bonds, I wanted to claw his eyes out. "You betrayed all of us by gambling and lying and putting us in jeopardy every day of our lives. Even now, you. Are. Still. Doing. It."

Pure malice overtook his features a second before his hand lashed out across my face. Pain exploded under my left eye, and my head cranked to the side so hard, my neck spasmed.

"*Puttanna ingrata*," he snarled into my face. "You don't know half of what I've suffered for you."

He was close enough.

I slammed my head down, my forehead connecting with his face perfectly. Stars wheeled over my vision at the impact, leaving me dazed, but I was aware of Seamus cursing, holding his bleeding nose.

"You bitch," he shouted through the blood.

Kelly opened the door from the other room and popped his head in to check on us. "Is everything--"

Pop.

Pop.

They both froze. Kelly's phone to his ear, and Seamus's hands to his nose.

Pop. Pop. Pop.

Even I recognized the gunfire.

It was close too, close enough that the neighborhood dog couldn't hear the muffled shots. They were already just outside the house.

A grin sliced open my face like a raw wound. "They're here."

Kelly cursed, shouting for his men as he tossed his phone and grabbed the gun from his belt before dashing up the stairs.

Seamus stayed with me.

Calmly, he moved to the table in the corner again. I thought he was grabbing a gun, but when he turned there was a roll of duct tape in one hand. He moved closer to me and smiled through the mess of blood on his face. "Your capo is going to die today, Elena, and I'm going to be the one to kill him. You deserve it for choosing him over your own father."

I opened my mouth to protest when he hit me again, this time a glancing blow to the same cheek. My jaw felt as if it came unhinged. Fire and tears flooded my eyes at the bright, brilliant pain. Before I knew what he was doing, he smacked duct tape on my mouth.

"Such a disappointment, *cara*," he said sadly as he cupped the same cheek he had just hit twice. His thumb rubbed over my split cheekbone, my blood staining his skin. "I'm sorry I failed you and Cosima. You could have been so much more if I'd been given the chance..." He trailed off with a little sigh, then backed away.

I cursed at him from behind the tape, struggling against my

bonds even though it hurt.

It was almost impossible to fathom the level of narcissism it took for Seamus to be able to spin his life story into a tragedy inflicted against him as the victim. My blood boiled as I watched him move to the table. He took a gun out of a drawer, checked to make sure it was loaded, and then put one finger to his lips as he slipped beneath the table into the shadows underneath.

Panic seized me in its electric hold as I realized his plan.

He'd known Dante would come for me.

He'd known he would get inside the house.

He'd counted on it.

He was going to hide in the shadows until Dante reached me and then kill him.

Pure, cold terror moved through me unlike anything I'd ever known before, not at the hands of Christopher or any of the mafiosos in Napoli.

I could only hope that Dante had stayed at his apartment, properly attached to his ankle monitor, waiting for his men to bring me back safely.

But a small voice in my gut told me differently.

This was the man who had taken murder charges instead of letting my sister go to prison.

He might not have loved me like Cosima, but we had a bond. He had promised to keep me safe.

He was the kind of man who would die before breaking his oath.

I knew in my bones he would come for me himself.

I listened over the harsh sound of the breath from my nose as the struggle continued upstairs. There was a crash of glass, *pop-pops*, and thuds overlaid by shouting in both English and Italian. It was impossible to tell who was beating who.

Then the door popped open at the top of the stairs only for a body to tumble backward, the man hitting each tread with a sickening *thunk*.

I craned my neck to see if I recognized the body and nearly cried when I didn't.

Kelly and another man were next, running down the stairs to sink into a crouch at the base of them, their guns trained at the top.

We waited.

Upstairs, the struggle went on, but no one seemed close to the stairs.

Then there was a long, low creak like wood peeling from plaster. Kelly and his man looked over to the wall with the one small boarded-up window.

"Fuck," Kelly yelled as the plywood was torn off and the glass shattered.

The man beside him fell to the ground, a bullet hole through his face.

A scream tore through me, muffled by the tape as I watched the life drain from him, blood pooling heavily along the floor toward where I stood.

Kelly fired off a round at the window, then cursed as more

gunfire came from the top of the stairs.

My father, the weasel, continued to hide quietly.

"I'll warn you once," a voice said from the top of the stairs. It was cold, low as fog rolling down the treads. "You touch another hair on her goddamn head, I'll rip you apart with my bare hands and then hand-feed the pieces of you to the neighborhood dogs."

A sob bubbled up my throat and caught there with nowhere to go.

Dante.

I closed my eyes, trying to breathe through the relief.

I needed to focus.

Seamus was still lying in wait, and Kelly was still vigilant.

"I'd like to see you try," the Irishman called on a breathless, yip-like laugh. "You're big, but I'm fast."

Someone fired through the window again, drawing Kelly's attention there. Dante took advantage by basically jumping down the short flight of stairs. His body angled through the air, hands extended.

Kelly tried to turn at the last moment to shoot him, but Dante was too close already.

They collided, the force throwing them both back into the wall.

There was a squeal of tires outside and then more yelling and shooting.

But my mind was fixed on the struggle.

Frankie came midway down the stairs, his guns trained on the tangled bodies, but he couldn't get a clean shot, and he couldn't get around them to me.

Finally, Dante went to one knee, one hand on Kelly's throat, the other reared back to hit him.

Thud.

Thud.

Thud.

The steady sound of a heavy fist pounding into human flesh filled the room as Dante methodically beat Kelly's face in. He stood when he was done, Kelly a moaning mess on the floor, but he didn't kill him.

Instead, he pointed at Frankie, then down at the prone Irishman.

And then he turned to me.

Tears flooded my eyes, pouring down my cheeks as he started toward me, his face a mask of relief and lingering rage.

Frantically, I shook my head and struggled against the zip ties, screaming at him from behind the tape.

His step faltered.

I looked at the table and then to him, calculating the angle.

Dante was still behind me slightly, out of range.

He peered at me, trying to read my face through the blood, tears, smeared makeup, and tape. "Elena, I won't hurt you."

NO! I wanted to scream. *Of course, you won't, you stupid, gorgeous man.*

He moved closer, reaching the side of me that was still protected from Seamus. Gently, he started to cut the cable ties with a utility knife from his belt. When my hands were free, I ripped the tape from my mouth and started to yell, "Seamus––"

Finally, his eyes flickered, and comprehension dawned on his face.

Unfortunately, it dawned on Seamus too.

He pushed out from the back wall under the table with his feet, sliding on his back, gun raised, and fired a shot off at Dante.

I screamed as Dante jerked, once, then twice as two bullets found their way into his big body.

"*Cazzo,*" Dante cursed as he dropped to one knee, favoring his right side as he tried to drag himself behind the pole. Seamus got off another shot, this one drilling into the middle of Dante's chest. I screamed as he fell to the ground, prone in the middle of the room, his gun skittering to rest just out of his reach.

His eyes weren't open, and I couldn't see his chest rising or falling through the veil of tears in my eyes.

Frankie fired at Seamus too, but he didn't have a good shot. I watched as my father got to his feet, using me for cover from Frankie, and slowly approached Dante, motionless on the ground.

"I'm sorry, *cara,*" he told me again, but his eyes were on his prey beyond me.

I couldn't move my feet, but my hands were free.

It wasn't a decision so much as an animal impulse.

A bear defending his mate.

I let my wobbly legs collapse, taking me to the floor. Seamus stopped, eyes flickering with worry as I fell, but I was already moving, rolling closer to Dante so I could grab the gun near his hand.

"Elena," Seamus snapped, gun raised still trained on Dante's body beside mine as I raised Dante's weapon at him. "You don't want to do that."

But he didn't understand.

He'd taught me exactly what he meant to.

Family was everything.

He just wasn't my family anymore.

I watched his eyes dart to Dante and the way his fingers flickered over the trigger.

And I did it.

I shot him.

Pop.

The bullet went wide, taking him through the upper right chest.

"Elena," he gasped, his mouth a mimicry of his bleeding wound. "What--"

Pop. Pop.

I fired again, close enough that even though I had no idea what I was doing, the bullets found their way into Seamus's chest. The gun kicked fiercely in my hands with each shot, bruising my hands, but I didn't feel it.

I only felt bone-deep relief as Seamus crumpled to the floor, the gun falling from his hand.

I sobbed as I tried to get closer to Dante but couldn't because of my tied feet.

"Hey, settle, *amica*," Frankie soothed, suddenly at my side.

He touched my shoulder as he moved on to check Seamus, collecting his gun before he returned to hand me another knife. Hands shaking, I sawed through the zip ties around my bloody ankles and then scrambled over the bloody ground to Dante.

His eyes were closed, breath feathering faintly through his mouth. I looked up at Frankie frantically, but he ignored me as he cut open Dante's black sweater and revealed the Teflon beneath.

Two bullets were grouped in the center of his chest, flat as disks.

Frankie removed the Velcro straps and lifted the vest from his chest.

A second later, Dante sucked in a deep breath and opened his eyes.

"Oh my God." I didn't think I'd ever cried so much in my life. "Dante, you idiot. What are you doing here saving me?"

Dante blinked up at me, then looked at Frankie for a second before laughing, wincing at the pain in his ribs as he did. "Only you would be mad at me for saving you, my fighter," he teased, the nickname my father had used somehow poetry from Dante's lips.

And then his hand fisted in my hair, and he pulled me down to kiss me.

Hauling me halfway over his body even though it had to hurt, he kissed me like he hadn't taken a breath since the last time he saw me, and he was dying for fresh air.

I kissed him right back, pouring every single inch of me into that embrace. There were no words for the relief and gratitude and love flowing through me, so I fed them to him with my lips.

"We gotta go," Frankie grunted from beside us. "You can do that in the car."

I pulled away and reached out to squeeze his arm. "Thank you, Frankie."

His smile was tight but genuine. "Jaco said the police scanner picked up the disturbance. They'll be here in minutes."

Dante nodded, grimacing again as he got to his feet, reaching for me the second he did. He untangled me from his side and took his gun from Frankie before stalking over to Seamus. I didn't know if he was dead. Honestly, I hadn't cared.

The only thing I needed was for Dante to be okay.

Still, I gasped as Dante stared down at my father and shot off three rounds into his skull. When he looked at me, his eyes glistened like an oil slick.

I didn't ask him if Seamus had already been dead or if he'd killed him.

I understand that was part of the reason he'd done that.

To show him I understood, I extended my hand to him and watched as relief moved over his face. He stepped away from the body and tucked me under his chin as he ordered Frankie, "Clean up and burn it down. Leave the bodies."

"You're bleeding," I whispered as he tugged me into his body, and I caught sight of the bubbling wound to his left shoulder, just beneath his collarbone.

"I'm fine," he assured, punctuating the words with another savage kiss I felt in my numb toes. *"Andiamo, lottatrice mia.* It seems I have to thank *you* for saving my life."

"I think it was a team effort," I said on a giddy, mindless laugh as my adrenaline started to fade.

Dante held me to his side as we climbed the stairs, walking over the odd dead Irishman as we left the house. Frankie stayed behind downstairs, and I caught sight of Marco with a canister of gas in the living room on the main level.

By the time we made it to the car at the curb, flames were already flickering from inside the house.

There were no neighbors in the streets. It wasn't the kind of neighborhood with park committees and neighborhood watch.

Chen was in the driver's seat when we got in the black SUV, and he tipped his chin up at me in the rearview. "Sorry it took a minute."

Another reckless laugh galloped from me. "That's okay. I knew you'd come."

A minute later, after two figures ran from the house into another waiting car, we took off, and I finally took a breath.

And then another.

Each inhale bringing more panic than it had before.

Dante held me against him, turning despite the pain in his shoulder so that he could face me head-on and cup my face in his hands.

"You're okay," he said in that British-Italian accent I'd once hated. "*Io sono con te*. I am with you now, *si?* You are safe, Elena."

I blinked at him, falling into those night-dark eyes, finding solace in them when I used to find immorality. My hands moved over him, touching whatever I could just to reassure myself that things hadn't ended differently in there. That he was alive and Seamus hadn't succeeded in taking yet another thing from my life.

And I knew it then.

What it was to truly be in love with someone, body and soul, everything else be damned.

Because I'd known as I picked up the gun, heavier and hotter than I would have imagined, that I'd raze every single one of my morals and mandates to the ground if it meant keeping Dante alive and at my side.

I'd happily follow him to Hell if it meant being with him forever.

I opened my mouth to tell him as much when he pressed his forehead to mine and admitted, "I have to go."

My heart stopped.

"I'm sorry, Elena, but we disabled the ankle monitor to get to you. They'll notice within twenty-four hours."

"You can't go to jail," I said instantly, fear pulling the words from me.

I'd just got him, just realized I even wanted to have him.

"No," he agreed slowly, his thumbs rubbing the length of my cheekbones, gently over the abrasion my father had left on one. "I'm running."

I blinked.

"I have a private jet out of Newark. It leaves in…" He checked his watch. "Just over an hour. I have to go. You know I didn't kill Giuseppe di Carlo, and I had a plan for that too, but…" He shrugged. "This was more important."

You were more important.

I didn't know what to say or do. My entire world had turned on its axis in the past twenty-four hours, and I couldn't see straight anymore. All my life, I'd run from the dark, only now I seemed unable and unwilling to escape Dante's shadowy embrace.

"I don't want you to leave," I said pathetically.

His sigh fanned over my mouth. "I know, *cara*. I don't want to leave you, but I must. Where I am going, it is not safe for you to follow. And even if it was, I would never ask you to leave your entire life behind. I'm afraid it wouldn't be waiting here for you when you returned."

There was nothing I could say to that.

It was true.

I couldn't run away with Dante into the night like some criminal fairy tale. Where would we go? What would I do?

I was a lawyer with a career, a home, and a life here.

But how much of a life was it? a little voice whispered. How much had I been living before I'd met the black-eyed capo who had just risked everything for me?

"We're dropping you off at your house," Dante continued as he touched me, long strokes of my arms, into my sweaty hair, over my dirty clothes. Like he couldn't stand the thought of not touching me again in a few hours, and he was shoring up his memories.

A sob lodged in my throat, and I choked on it.

"Bambi will see that you get all your things returned to you. Marco called Beau, and he's going to be waiting for you there. I don't want you to be alone after all this," he continued, in full-fledged capo mode, organizing my life as if it wasn't coming apart at the seams.

I said nothing.

My voice was lost in the depths of my tossing, storming gut.

So, I just pressed my entire body into his good side, turned my nose into his neck and breathed in his sun-warmed citrus and pepper scent.

We arrived at Gramercy Park too soon.

"Will you... can you call or contact me?" I asked as Chen pulled up outside the building.

I didn't want to go in.

For the first time in my life, the sight of my brownstone made me want to burn it down.

Maybe if I did, Dante would have to take me with him.

"I shouldn't," he said, his face creased with pain and exhaustion, but those beautiful eyes so clear as they looked at me, so full of tenderness. "But I will."

We stared at each other, caught up in the vortex that existed between us and always had since the moment I shoved him into a hospital wall and threatened his life if he hurt my sister.

He was right, what he'd said about us being made of the same stuff. We weren't opposites, not even close. He was a chaos of contradictions, and I was a contradictory chaos, but that was why we worked. In all my life, the only person who had ever understood me despite my best efforts to stop them was Dante.

And now I was losing him.

I curled my hand into his blood-soaked black tee and yanked him so I could kiss him. Because I didn't have words, I only had the fire he'd started inside my soul, and the only way I could share it was by sliding it like a present under his tongue.

He took it with a moan, eating at me, devouring me.

I never wanted it to end, and I whimpered when he pulled away.

But still, I didn't have the words.

"*Sono con te, lottatrice mia,*" he said, "*anche quando non lo sono.*"

I am with you, my fighter, even when I am not.

My vision blurred as tears fell silently down my cheeks. I stamped a bruising kiss on his lips, wishing I could brand it there, and then I pulled away, already moving to the door.

"I'll see you again," I whispered thickly, the words more breath than sound.

He nodded curtly. "You will."

I echoed his nod, then turned quickly and got out of the car.

A sob blossomed in my throat, so big I couldn't swallow it down so I held my breath as I rounded the car to the curb and climbed up the stairs to my slightly unfamiliar front stoop.

I didn't look back.

I knew if I did, I would run back to that car, throw myself on the hood, and never look back at my house, New York, and the life I'd painstakingly built for five years.

I'd just follow Dante blindly into the night.

The door to my house swung open, and Beau stood there, backlit by a halo of warm light.

"Elena," he said, so much in the one word I made a note to ask him how he did that so I could try to learn.

And then I collapsed into his open arms and gave up trying to stand.

Behind me, the car pulled away soundlessly and disappeared down the street.

EPILOGUE

elena

Beau made me shower.

Which was fair.

I was covered in the blood of my father and my lover.

I should have been disgusted by it, but I was only numb as I stood under the hot spray and let it sluice over me, pink water swirling around the drain.

Beau was waiting when I got out, holding the towel out for me like a child. I didn't say a word. He hugged me in the fabric as I stepped into it, rocking me back and forth for a moment.

"I don't know what to say," he admitted into my ear as he held me close. "I want to give you advice, but how can I? A stranger named Marco calls to tell me to be at your place 'stat' and not to be alarmed that you're covered in blood."

He sighed raggedly as he turned me in his arms to face him. "Lena, I was gone for six weeks, and I come back to find you shacked up with a mafioso?"

"He's more than that," I whispered impulsively. "I-I can't explain how much."

Beau's blue eyes widened as they searched my face. He pushed a wet lock of hair back from my forehead and then pulled me in for another hug. "Okay, Lena."

I sighed into the hug, trying to take comfort from the short, slender arms of my friend when I ached for the all-encompassing embrace of another man.

"Why don't you get dressed, and I'll make some tea, okay?" he suggested as he pulled away.

He kept looking at me like maybe I would turn to dust if he did something wrong. I tried to reassure him with a little smile, but it felt like cracked plastic between my teeth.

"Sure."

He left with one last look over his shoulder.

My wrists and ankles were aching, cut open into smooth circles by the zip lines. I pulled out the antibiotic ointment and hissed as I tended to the wounds before getting dressed in a comfortable cashmere set. I brushed my hair and teeth, then moisturized my face and body all on autopilot.

If I didn't think, I wouldn't think of him.

Or the fact that I'd probably killed my father.

Patricide.

That was what it was called.

A class-C felony for manslaughter.

Maximum fifteen years in prison if convicted.

"Elena," Beau called from down the stairs. "Come on."

He was in the kitchen assembling a tray when I appeared. My favorite Japanese teapot and little cups arranged with some dried flowers I recognized from my entryway.

He ushered us into the living room, put the tray on the coffee table and reached for me, wrapping his arms to pull me down on the couch at his side. He arranged us together the way he did models on set, deliberately fiddling with our limbs until we were twined together, forehead to forehead.

Before Dante, Beau and Cosima were the only people I ever let get close.

My eyes burned as I blinked at him.

"Talk to me," he pleaded, stroking my damp hair. "What happened?"

"So much," I whispered, my throat too swollen with sorrow to make any sound. "So much, I don't even know how to think about it, let alone talk about it."

"Try," Beau coaxed. "Start with the most important things."

"I love him." Tears formed and broke free of my eyes like diamonds rolling down my cheeks. "I do. I love him. I don't know how it happened...He just...he wouldn't leave me alone."

I laughed wetly, and Beau did too a little.

"He's not anything I ever would have allowed myself to like or know. He's my client. Being with him risks my career. Being with him risks my life," I tried to explain, but the words just kept coming more and more panicked. "It makes no sense, Beau, but we are compatible. He's a criminal, a hedonist, a sinner. But everyone likes him. You should see it. It's impossible to dislike him because he has this smile and this charm…"

"He sounds like a complicated man," Beau said gently. "Fitting for a complicated woman."

I nodded, rolling my teeth under my lips to keep from sobbing. "He tells me to be brave."

"And do you feel that way with him?"

Another nod, my lips wobbling.

"Then what happened? Why can't you be with him?"

"He's leaving," I murmured. "He has to leave now because of me. He's going, and I don't know where or for how long, but I probably won't ever see him again. And *I love him.*"

The tears were burning up as my skin heated with something like anger, something with bite. Suddenly, I was furious at the world for doing this to me, for giving me this beautiful man in this wretched situation and then for making it impossible for me to be with him.

"I can't explain what's happened inside me," I cried, clutching at my heart through my chest like I could pry it from between my ribs and show him how it had been altered. "But I'm not the same anymore. I used to think I knew who I was, but I never felt like this before."

"Like what?"

"So alive I burn."

Beau blinked at me as I leaned over him, panting with the force of the turmoil coursing through me. "Elena, why can't you go with him?" he finally said.

"Because, because I just told you! I have no idea where he is going or for how long or with who. I have a job here and a life, and I can't just leave that for...for a giant question mark."

"You're not leaving it for a giant question mark," he reminded me gently. "You're leaving it for him."

"He didn't ask me to go with him." It burned in me, but it was the truth. He'd never asked. He'd only told me I couldn't. That I had to stay.

"Are you so sure he didn't ask because he didn't want to ask you to give up your entire life for him?"

"No," I admitted. "That's basically what he said."

"Then you have a choice, Elena, and I don't envy it," Beau said. "But I think you should consider it hard. I've never seen you like this."

"A mess?" I said with a snotty laugh.

"So alive you burn," he repeated my words back to me softly. "I'll be right back, okay?"

I barely noticed him leaving. I just flipped to my back and stared at the ceiling.

I'd shot my dad.

Together, Dante and I had killed him.

I knew it wasn't something I was going to get over anytime soon. I knew I'd need endless rounds of therapy to even begin to make sense of the tangle of relief, justification, anger, and despair I felt about the act.

But I didn't regret it for one second.

He'd threatened Mama, Giselle, and Genevieve.

He'd destroyed our lives in Naples and sold Cosima into sexual slavery.

He'd nearly killed Dante.

And even if none of the other things had happened, I knew in my heart that would have been enough reason for me to kill him.

I couldn't bear the thought of knowing I existed in a world where Dante didn't.

And he had done the same for me.

I'd always known Dante was a killer.

You only had to look at those massive hands quilted with muscle, ribboned with tendons and veins that popped beneath his deeply tan skin to know that there was sheer murderous power there.

But this was different.

Knowing that Dante had killed for me, that he had risked his freedom to search for me and helped end the life of a man who had made me suffer the entire length of mine, resonated somewhere deep inside.

It was the same place that burned when he touched me, when he taught me what to do with his body and what to do with mine. It was the same place that stirred whenever my family had been threatened in Naples and I'd stood up to protect them.

472

Because they were mine to protect.

Just as it seemed, now I was Dante's to protect.

It was a place of instinct, a primal impulse in my gut that transcended thought and even feeling.

Dante was mine.

How could I just let him go?

I jumped to my feet and froze in my living room, gazing at the furniture and art I'd collected from another life with another man. It seemed ridiculous to me now that I'd held on to it for so long.

I'd stopped grieving Daniel a long time ago. The truth was, I never loved him the way I should have, and obviously, he'd felt the same way about me. What I'd mourned from that loss for years wasn't the man, but the woman I'd thought I had been with him. No, more than that, I lamented those last shreds of hope I'd retained then lost when he left me for Giselle.

I missed my capacity to love, my propensity to have faith in people and mostly, in myself.

Dante had taught me how to love myself again.

He'd taught me how to let someone in again.

How could I possibly give that up?

"Beau!" I screamed as I started to run from the room down the hall back up to my bedroom. I took the stairs two at a time. "Beau, I have to go!"

When I careened to a stop in my bedroom door, Beau was already beside my bed, calmly folding clothes into an open Louis Vuitton suitcase.

"I know," he said, smiling sadly at me. "Of course, you do."

I stood there and beamed at him like a lunatic until his smile cracked and spread wide too. And then we were laughing, laughing so hard our bellies ached. I ran to his side and threw my arms around him.

"I love you," I said. "I'm sorry I don't say it much."

"Doesn't mean I don't know it," he responded, hugging me tight. "Now, hurry up. You don't want to miss his flight."

"It's Newark," I said, panicking, throwing the rest of what Beau had on the bed into the case and zipping it up. "I can buy new clothes there. We have to go now."

DANTE

"Ready, Boss?" Chen asked me from the front seat as we waited on the tarmac at Newark Airport for the plane to get clearance for a runway.

"*Si, Chen, grazie,*" I told him. "Are you sure you don't want to come?"

He laughed. "As if I don't get enough shit Stateside about being a non-Italian Made Man. I'll save us both the hassle and hold down the fort here. God knows Marco and Jacopo can't do shit by themselves."

I chuckled, but it echoed vacantly in my chest.

"Right, well, *in bocca al lupo, fratello,*" I told him, leaning forward with my good arm to clap him on the shoulder. "I will see you soon."

"Right, Boss," he agreed, then hesitated. "I'm sorry, you know. She was something else."

I nodded curtly, not ready to examine the wound to my chest. Not the insignificant bullet hole I'd have Frankie stitch up on the plane, but the gaping hole in my rib cage where Elena Lombardi ripped out my heart to keep it for her own.

I didn't mind. I wanted her to have it.

But the pain was fucking excruciating.

I stepped from the car and made my way to the jet that would take Frankie and me back to the place that had started it all. It was an escape from jail, but it felt horribly like replacing one prison for another.

New York was a tepid fish pond compared to the shark-infested waters of Italia.

"Blood's not your color," Frankie told me as he met me at the base of the stairs with a few bags.

The rest of our shit was already on the plane. Bambi had packed it and had Bruno drive it over while we were en route from Brooklyn.

"If you're going to crack bad jokes the entire flight, please, just shoot me in the head now and put me out of my misery," I said dryly as we ascended.

"If you're going to be grumpy the whole trip because you didn't have the balls to make Elena come with us--"

"*Stai zitto,*" I snapped at him to shut up.

"Too soon?" he asked with faux innocence.

I was about to growl at him when a screech of car tires exploded in the silent night. Immediately, Frankie and I both pulled our guns.

A moment later, Chen rounded the plane again.

"What the hell is...?" I trailed off as he pulled to a stop at the base of the stairs and a familiar redhead appeared out the back door.

I blinked, wondering if the bullets had given me a concussion somehow.

"I see her too," Frankie whispered.

"Dante," Elena called as Chen and Beau both emerged from the vehicle and went to the trunk. "I'm coming with you."

My chest was so tight I couldn't fucking breathe.

"I didn't ask you," I told her.

Because this wasn't a joke.

We weren't going on vacation to Bora fucking Bora.

We were going on the *run.*

As in I was jumping bail and facing serious prison time for skipping the country, and I'd have to be careful about every single move I made from here on in.

"I don't care," she yelled back. "I'm coming."

I stared down at her, thinking that even with wet hair and no makeup, Elena Lombardi took exquisite to a new level. *Cazzato,* but I wanted her. I needed her. The idea of leaving her behind tore me up from the inside out.

But I couldn't be that selfish.

How could I take her from every single thing she had ever known and throw her straight into the deep end of my criminal life?

She turned on her heel to collect her bag from Chen, giving him a kiss on the cheek, before she enfolded Beau in a big, long hug.

She was saying her goodbyes.

She wasn't going anywhere, and she was saying her goddamn goodbyes.

But I didn't do anything to stop her.

Not when she pulled away from them and began to walk across the tarmac or when she started up the stairs toward me.

Instead, I found myself walking down to meet her.

The smile that spread across her face dazzled me as we moved toward each other, faster and faster.

Then she was right in front of me.

Elena Lombardi.

And all I could think was *mine*.

I opened my arms, and she stepped right into them, dropping her bag to wrap her hands gently around my neck so she didn't jostle my shoulder.

"I won't go back to my life before this," she murmured into my chest as she hugged me. "Don't leave me here in this purgatory where nothing makes sense anymore except you."

"I have too much of you in my heart to say no," I admitted

gruffly, pulling her head back by the hair so I could see her face.

Her eyes were that soft gray velvet, warm and glowing. Looking into them, knowing she wanted to risk her entire life for me the way I just had for her, I had never felt more powerful.

"*Ti amo,*" she told me as if the words couldn't bear to go unspoken. "I love you, and I'm going with you."

I laughed. I laughed because we were both crazy and mad and hopelessly lost in this new and wild thing between us, and I didn't give a damn about the consequences.

"*Sono pazzo di te,*" I told her before I claimed her lips for a bruising kiss. "I'm crazy about you, Elena. But this new life," I warned her one last time, "costs a pretty penny. It'll cost you the full price of your old one."

She laughed too, her head tipped back to laugh with the stars.

"Okay," she said simply when she finished, smiling at me, more serene than I'd ever seen her. "They're all afraid of you, and they all hate me. What a pair we make. Two villains in love. I'm not afraid of anything that will come at us, Dante. I just don't want to be without you."

"Then you won't," I promised.

And I kissed her.

I wasn't sure if there was such a thing as happily ever after for people like us, but I'd fight tooth and fucking nail to make sure I gave Elena Lombardi the world. It wouldn't be the world she thought she wanted, but I'd make her regina of my dark kingdom and in the end, I'd ensure every single one of my *soldati* would die for her just as they would die for me.

The End.

For now.

When Villains Rise (Anti-Heroes in Love, #2) releases June 18th!

giana darling

THANKS ETC.

I've been waiting to write Elena's story since I first conceived of The Evolution of Sin Trilogy when I was sixteen years old. Interesting fun fact, though Elena's personality was apparent to me from the beginning, her career went through many iterations. First, she was a photographer then a journalist before finally becoming a lawyer. It was the perfect job for a woman who was scarred from a young age by villainy and who was driven by her insecurities to be revered by many.

Dante came later, exploding on the scene randomly while I was writing about Cosima's mysterious past. He appeared in The Secret as a black-eyed mafioso with a bullet wound and untold swagger. He was hotly passionate, dangerously charming, and hellacious when crossed.

The perfect foil for my ice queen, Elena.

I couldn't wait to write their story and I hope you love them as much as I do. I hesitate to call this an opposites-attract love story, because at the end of the day, Elena and Dante are very similar. They are both whip smart, ruthless when crossed, and in possession of incredibly tender hearts they protect at all costs. Simply, they were made for each other, the other's perfect foil and other half.

Writing this story was so much fun. I did incredible amounts of research so almost everything that happens in the story is based loosely around a real mafia story or act in the past. Dennis O'Malley is loosely based on Rudy Guiliani, the heroic mafia prosecutor who went on to be a powerful and successful politician only to have his credibility questioned in later years because of his protentional connection to the mob and other shady characters. Dante's court case is a compilation of hundreds of similar mafia trials that have taken place since the 80s, with millions of government dollars spent trying to take down an organization that is structured like a hydra, one head cut off never destroys the whole beast. I could talk for hours about how fascinating the mafia is in all its iterations and why I made the decision in this book that I did, but at the end, all that matters is whether or not you loved their action packed story, and I very much hope you did.

Now, on to the people who make everything possible for me.

Annette, if Elena had a presence like yours in her life, she would never doubt herself again. You are my sunlight and my anchor, the positive voice in my ear whenever I doubt myself at work or need love in my personal life. You mean so much to me, I refuse to ever imagine my life without you.

Allaa, I love you endlessly. There has never been anyone I feel comfortable discussing my ideas with before I met you so many years ago and I'm so grateful for the way you let me use you as a sounding board and also give me positive feedback.

Michelle, what can I say that I haven't said before? There are few people in this world with a heart as big as yours and I'm honoured to have a place in it.

Ella, my ride or die, my hilarious and steadfast best friend. Just hearing your voice brings me joy. Thank you for punctuating my days with your loveliness.

Candi, thank you for being not only an amazing PR boss lady, but for also being a steadfast, fun, and loving friend.

Jenny, I will always and forever be grateful for you putting up with my messy manuscripts and short turnaround times. Thank you for turning my dirty words into gold.

Sarah Plocher, thank you for being such a sweet friend and support while also being incredibly proficient and professional when proofreading for me. I value you so much.

My girl Ramzi who swooped in to make the paperback absolutely extraordinarily beautiful! Love you and so happy to have a friend like you.

Giana's Poppies Street Team! Ladies, what can I say, but that I love you endlessly for the support and love you give me constantly. Thank you for being the best hype women an author could ever dream of.

My ARC team, I am honored you love my words enough to read them no matter the subject matter. Your confidence in my storytelling buoys me when I doubt myself.

Giana's Darlings, my gorgeous corner of the internet with nearly 8k of you (*gasp*). Thank you for being excited about my books, spreading the word about them, and always being down for new content.

Najla Qamber, you are the queen of graphiclandia and I am

so blessed to have found you at the very beginning of my author journey. You bring my visions for book covers and aesthetics to life so brilliantly, I am in awe of your talent.

Thank Veronica for providing invaluable perspective on Italian language and culture. I would have been lost without your expertise!

Thank you to Jennifer Severino for being my legal expert and answering my myriad of questions. Your guidance was crucial to the success of this story.

There are, as always, countless bloggers, Tiktokers, and Instagrammers to thank for their support of this release, but I can't possibly name them all so please know, I am grateful for every post and share about my work. In addition, a special thanks goes out to Tish from @booktheif28, Mary from @makeupandmary, Jess from @peacelovebooksxo, Weroinca @littlesteamyreads for her love and graphics, Pang @shereads_pang for her support and gorgeous edits, and last but never least, Emilie from @fansofgianadarling who is CEO of my fandom and one of the sweetest souls ever.

Fiona and Lauren, you are the most loyal and generous best friends a girl could ever dream of having. No matter what is going on in my life, good or bad, you are always there for me and it means more than words can ever say.

Armie, my love, without you I really don't think I would have pushed so hard to make writing my viable career so I am endlessly indebted to you for putting up with the tapping of my keyboard while you slept and drove us around the United Kingdom for three months. Because of your support, I was able to make my dreams come true.

Albie, you've been my best friend since middle school and since then, we've seen a lot together. You always enrich my life and make me feel loved.

To my fur babies, Romeo and Persephone. For those who don't know, the week before release, both of them were suffering. Persephone has congestive heart failure and we discovered she won't be with us much longer. Romeo was attacked by another dog. Loving a creature is a special kind of bond because it is utterly unconditional love, they never betray you or lie to you or treat you poorly. They love you with their whole souls and only want the same in return. I am so grateful for the supreme light and job they bring to my life and I only hope they will be with me for as long as possible.

Last as usual, but never in a million years least, the love of my life, H. Like Dante with Elena, you taught me everything I know about the enormous capacity for love to change and better our lives and ourselves. I am endlessly grateful to the universe for throwing us together at eleven years old with your blond mullet and my brace filled mouth and proud of us for evolving together from fifteen-year-old kids in love with no idea about life to grown adults with a healthy and extremely happy relationship. You are the dream that feels too good to be true every single day.

giana darling

OTHER BOOKS BY GIANA DARLING

The Evolution of Sin Trilogy

Giselle Moore is running away from her past in France for a new life in America, but before she moves to New York City, she takes a holiday on the beaches of Mexico and meets a sinful, enigmatic French businessman, Sinclair, who awakens submissive desires and changes her life forever.

The Affair
The Secret
The Consequence
The Evolution Of Sin Trilogy Boxset

The Fallen Men Series

The Fallen Men are a series of interconnected, standalone, erotic MC romances that each feature age gap love stories between dirty-talking, Alpha males and the strong, sassy women who win their hearts.

Lessons in Corruption
Welcome to the Dark Side
Good Gone Bad
After the Fall
Inked in Lies

giana darling

WHEN HEROES FALL

Dead Man Walking

A Fallen Men Companion Book of Poetry:
King of Iron Hearts

The Enslaved Duet

The Enslaved Duet is a dark romance duology about an eighteen-year old Italian fashion model, Cosima Lombardi, who is sold by her indebted father to a British Earl who's nefarious plans for her include more than just sexual slavery... Their epic tale spans across Italy, England, Scotland, and the USA across a five-year period that sees them endure murder, separation, and a web of infinite lies.

Enthralled (The Enslaved Duet #1)
Enamoured (The Enslaved Duet, #2)

The Elite Seven Series
Sloth (The Elite Seven Series, #7)

Coming Soon
Fallen King (A Fallen Men Short Story)
When Villains Rise (Anti-Heroes in Love, #2)

giana darling

ABOUT GIANA DARLING

Giana Darling is a USA Today, Wall Street Journal, Top 40 Best Selling Canadian romance writer who specializes in the taboo and angsty side of love and romance. She currently lives in beautiful British Columbia where she spends time riding on the back of her man's bike, baking pies, and reading snuggled up with her cat, Persephone, and dog, Romeo.

giana darling

Made in the USA
Las Vegas, NV
14 July 2023

74717637R00278